CONTENTS

ROSEMARY CLEMENT-MOORE

TWO NOVELS
Prom Dates from Hell AND *Hell Week*

EMBER

Prom Dates from Hell copyright © 2007 by Rosemary Clement-Moore
Hell Week copyright © 2008 by Rosemary Clement-Moore
Cover art copyright © 2012 by Kim Camilleri (girl) and Shutterstock (fire)

All rights reserved. Published in the United States by Ember, an imprint of Random House Children's Books, a division of Random House, Inc., New York. This omnibus edition comprises *Prom Dates from Hell* and *Hell Week,* originally published separately in hardcover in the United States by Delacorte Press, an imprint of Random House Children's Books, New York, in 2007 and 2008, respectively.

Ember and the E colophon are registered trademarks of Random House, Inc.

Visit us on the Web! randomhouse.com/teens

Educators and librarians, for a variety of teaching tools, visit us at RHTeachersLibrarians.com

Library of Congress Cataloging-in-Publication Data is available upon request.
ISBN 978-0-385-74245-0 (trade pbk.)
ISBN 978-0-307-97521-8 (ebook)

RL: 7.0

Printed in the United States of America

10 9 8 7 6 5 4 3 2 1

First Omnibus Edition 2012

Random House Children's Books supports the First Amendment and celebrates the right to read.

Prom Dates from Hell

To my dad, Robert Wallace Clement,
who never forgot how to tell a story

1

as an interactive horror experience, with beasts from Hell, mayhem, gore, and dismemberment, it was an impressive event. As a high school prom, however, the evening was marginally less successful.

I should start at the beginning, but I'm not entirely certain when that is, so I'll start with the day I realized that despite my most determined efforts, I was not going to be able to ignore the prom entirely.

The end of April, and a rabid satin and tulle frenzy had attached to every double X chromosome in the senior class. All available wall space—hallway, cafeteria, even the bathrooms—sprouted signage in the most obnoxious colors possible. I was assaulted by flyers in the courtyard, and harassed by thrice-daily announcements. Had I gotten my tickets yet? Had I voted for the class song? Had I voted for the King and Queen? No, no, and Hell no, because voting for royalty was not just moronic, it was oxymoronic.

No one was safe from the Prom Plague. When dog-eared copies of *Seventeen* magazine started circulating through AP English, I knew I'd soon have to fall back to the band hall and call the CDC from there.

Then one day my neutrality was over. My indifference punctured. Stanley Dozer asked me to be his date.

Stanley Dozer was even lower on the high school food chain than I was, and I was in the journalism club. Sometimes I think God must have a kind of divine craps table; every once in a while He shoots snake eyes and the next baby born is screwed from the jump. I mean, "Stanley Dozer," for starters. Maybe he could have aesthetically overcome this name, but the guy was about six foot five, pale and bony as a corpse, with hair the color of spiderwebs. His ankles and wrists shot out of his too short jeans and the sleeves of his plaid button-down shirt. I sympathized with the sizing problems, but I had to wonder at the complete inattention to fashion. And by fashion I mean "camouflage."

Back on the middle school Serengeti I learned that, lacking a certain killer instinct, my best bet was to avoid standing out from the herd and making myself a target for the apex social predators, at least until I'd built up a tough skin. Now I'm sort of like the spiny anteater. Small and prickly, trundling along, a threat to no one. Except ants, I guess, which is where the metaphor runs out.

Back to Stanley's ambush. On the second-story breezeway that overlooked the courtyard below, the Spanish Club was selling candy to raise money for their Guatemalan sponsor child and I was taking their picture. Privately I thought little Juanita would benefit a lot faster if they sold tequila shots instead. Not that I advocate underage alcohol, but I bet there were a few teachers who could use a drink this time of year.

"Hi, Maggie!" Stanley's voice startled me.

I spun around, narrowly missing hitting him in his bony chest with my camera. I'm used to looking up, but with Stanley I had to crane my neck and squint. "Oh. Hi, Stanley."

Behind me, the Spanish Club giggled. What was Español for "Bite me"?

"How are you?" he asked, hefting his book bag onto his shoulder. The canvas bag bore the logo of the natural history museum. High on the geek quotient, but worlds better than the briefcase he'd carried freshman year.

"I'm taking some pictures for the yearbook." I hinted broadly that I was busy. After all, the next box of Chiclets might be the one that sent little Juanita to college.

"I saw you up here, and I thought . . . Well, you know how the prom is coming up?"

"Is it really?" I mumbled, messing with the settings on my camera. "I had no idea."

Sarcasm sailed over his head, which was a trick considering his height. He shuffled from foot to foot, giving the unfortunate appearance of a dancing skeleton. "Well, I was thinking you could go with me. We could, you know, go together."

The words entered my ears, but my brain rejected them.

Stanley Dozer was *not* asking me to the prom. Words failed me, and that's just not something that happens. Ever. I'd known Stanley since his paste-eating days, and had always tried to be nice to him. I was the spoilsport who pulled the KICK ME sign off his back, or helped him pick up his books after he'd been tripped—either by his own overlong legs or someone else's. I guess if I were a better person I'd have befriended him more thoroughly. I felt bad about that, but not that bad.

"Wow. The prom." I stalled as the rest of the school continued normal operations, electric bells calling students to class, kids buffeting us as they passed on the breezeway, calling to the people below. "I really wasn't planning to go," I said honestly. "I might have to take pictures, but I'd kind of be working."

"Yeah, but if you have to go anyway . . ."

"Oh, you wouldn't have fun that way." I flipped through my mental student files, clinging to the notion that there is somebody for everyone. "What about Karen Foley? Weren't you guys in Mathletes together?"

"Until she blew our answer in the district semifinal round," Stanley sneered. "She's not nearly as smart as everyone thinks she is."

"Oh-kay. That was a little harsh."

"Yeah, well, Karen Foley is a dork."

And *that* was unkind and rather nasty. Also, Mr. Glass House didn't have any business throwing stones. But before I could react, someone grabbed Stanley from behind. Amid laughter and alarmed squeals, the breezeway cleared of traffic as Biff the Jock bent poor Stanley over for a noogie.

Biff wasn't his name, but he reminded me of the bully in *Back to the Future,* so that was the name my brain supplied. Though Stanley had half a foot of height on him, the football player was muscular, so watching Biff rough up the poor dweeb was like watching an English mastiff pin an Afghan hound.

"Hey, Bulldozer! Trying to get a date?" I willed Stanley to fight back; he should have leverage to his advantage if nothing else. But his spindly arms and legs just flailed around as the pack of jocks and cheerleaders jeered.

"Leave him alone," I said, not much more effectively.

"Awww." Biff wrapped a meaty arm around Stanley's neck and baby-talked, "Does oo haff a widdle girlfriend, Dozer?" His friends roared at this example of their leader's wit. Stanley's face was turning purple with what I hoped was rage and not asphyxiation.

"I said, leave him alone. Go find another Mack truck to pick on."

Biff's girlfriend—whose name, like half of the cheer squad, was Jessica—got up in my face. "That's so cute! I think she likes him back."

"How sweet." Biff and his friend pushed poor Stanley to the edge of the breezeway, pretending they were going to launch him over the brick barrier onto the courtyard below. "You going to *fall* for her, Bulldozer?"

Stanley didn't answer; he looked paralyzed by terror. The jocks might have been pretending, but the horror on Stanley's face was very real. I raised the best weapon at my disposal and clicked off a rapid-fire series of pictures on my camera. It got Cheerleader Barbie's attention.

"What are you doing!" Yell-leading had definitely developed her lungs. Her shriek made my right eye twitch, but I replied calmly.

"I'm documenting the event. Maybe for the principal. Maybe just for the school paper. Maybe for an insert, right next to the ballot for prom queen."

"You can't do that!" My eardrum gave a seismic shudder. "I've worked for four years. My mom already bought my dress. It's *all planned*, you hag." My camera clicked in her livid, bug-eyed face. It is probably all that saved me from her claws. Instead she turned to her boyfriend. "Let him go, Brandon! You and your stupid sense of humor."

Brandon. That was his real name. He and his buddies let poor Stanley go, and the geek collapsed onto the concrete in a jumble of bony elbows and knees as Brandon turned on me. "You are nothing but a snitch and a tattletale, Quinn."

"It's called investigative journalism, asshole. The next time I even hear about you attacking someone, I'll e-mail these pictures to the principal, the local paper, and the admissions board of every school with a Division One football team."

Brandon took a threatening step toward me, but restrained himself when I raised the camera. He gestured to his knuckle-cracking goon squad and they lumbered off, followed by Jessica, Jessica, and Jessica, who each gave me the death eye before they flipped their hair and flounced after them. I wondered if they worked on that synchronized hair flip during cheer practice.

When they'd gone, the Spanish Club and their customers emerged from behind the table where they'd been

6

hunkered, and began to applaud. I pshawed and, with a sense of whimsy, dropped a deep curtsy that probably looked silly in my jeans and Doc Martens.

"You bitch." The depth of venom in the word prickled the skin on the back of my neck. The faces of the Spanish Club changed as well, like villagers in a werewolf movie, when their kindly town grocer suddenly turns into a slavering beast.

I whirled, but saw only Stanley. He was a mess; his colorless hair stood up in limp spikes, and his clothes were askew, so that even his skin didn't seem to fit quite right. The sight should have been comically pathetic. But his eyes blazed at me from his thin face, so poisonous that I took an instinctive step back. "I don't need your help handling those asswipes. I don't need anyone's help!"

"Of course you don't." I made my voice soothing, the way they talk to crazy people on TV. I wanted to tell him to get over himself, but the malice in him stopped my tongue. I was fighting the urge to cross myself, like Granny Quinn did when she talked about the evil eye, or bad news, or my mother's cooking.

"You don't believe me." He brushed by, bumping me aside, stomping past the Mexican candy table. We all watched him, maybe afraid to look away, in case he sprouted another head or something. It didn't seem impossible. "You'll see. I don't need anyone's protection. You'll all be sorry."

Still muttering, he flung open the glass door and went in. I heard the Spanish Club exhale their pent-up breath, and someone laughed nervously. I didn't blame her. Talk about your B-movie dialogue. It was ridiculous to feel anything but sorry for the guy.

That's what I told myself as I rubbed my arm where Stanley's bony elbow had hit me, hard enough to leave a bruise.

2

avalon High was the older of the town's two public second-
ary schools. The oldest building on our campus had been
around since World War II, and I was pretty sure my civics
teacher had been on the faculty then.

Mr. Wells lectured straight from a series of overhead
transparencies that dated back to the Reagan administration. I wasn't sure if the material was that outdated, or if
the government process was that stagnant, but it meant
that as long as you copied down the information from the
overhead (or got the transcription later), you could pretty
much do whatever you wanted and the slightly deaf Wells

would keep droning on, like the little bald-headed engine that could.

This, and the fact that I had D&D Lisa to share my misery, kept me from skipping too much, despite it being the last class of the day.

Lisa had been D&D Lisa since the seventh grade. When she'd moved into the district midterm, there was already a Lisa in our class. Asked to "stand up and tell the students something about yourself," the new Lisa said shamelessly, "I like to play Dungeons and Dragons."

We laughed, of course, but she repeated this introduction in each new class period, with the same result. Finally I asked her, "Why do you say that, when you know everyone's going to laugh?" She told me it was the quickest way to separate friend from foe: one laughs *with* her, the other laughs *at* her. "And when I take over the world," she had said, with a very straight face, "I will know who to embrace into the fold, and who to feed to my undead zombie minions."

That was Lisa. She said outrageous things, and you could never tell if she was being sarcastic or not. Geeky pretty, like that Goth girl on the TV show *NCIS*, and wicked smart, she didn't even need fashion camouflage. She had the armadillo plating of unflappable self-confidence, and nothing she said, no matter how droll, seemed impossible.

Since I had no desire to be Zombie Chow, I resolved to stay on her good side. Eventually, I got over my intimidation and we became good friends, despite our obvious differences. Though she gave up the spikes and black nail polish in tenth grade, Lisa still had a way of throwing together vintage-store finds—things that should never go together—

and somehow making it work. When I do that, I just look like I dressed in the dark.

Maybe it helped that she had a tall and naturally slender physique, with chestnut hair that fell in a smooth curtain around her face. I'm short, but otherwise average, which means that I wish my butt were smaller, but I don't wish it enough to actually exercise. My dark hair is cut in a bob, which is supposed to look like Velma Kelly in the movie *Chicago*. Only it never works out that way. My hair has a mind of its own, so with my round face and pointed chin, I mostly look like that crazy girl in *Fight Club*, only without the chain smoking and the, you know, crazy part.

Maybe I'm just saving the chain smoking, binge drinking, and crazy wild sex until I go off to college. But at the moment, my major vice is sarcasm, with a side of caffeine addiction.

Anyway, Lisa had the Geek Chic thing working for her, was the front-runner for valedictorian, and though she was in no way popular, she knew people in every subgroup in the school and had her finger on the pulse of the student body in a way that even I—plucky girl reporter—could only envy.

"I heard you took on the Jocks and Jessicas this morning," she said as we sat in civics class that afternoon. The hum of the overhead projector covered our conversation easily. "When I am an evil overlord, you may be my minister of disinformation."

"Thanks. I'll need a job after you dissolve the free press."

"Of course you will."

Mr. Wells changed the transparency and we copied

down the overview of the judicial system. Test questions came word for word from the notes, making rote memorization the path of least effort. "I heard Stanley Dozer totally wigged out."

I made bored curlicues out of the bottoms of my *g*'s, *p*'s, and *y*'s. "Who could blame him after the meatheads roughed him up?"

"Did he really call you a bitch?" I nodded and she made an annoyed sound. "That's gratitude for you."

"The fragile male ego makes no exceptions for nerds, I guess." Finished copying the page, I slumped back down until the next installment, and rubbed the bruise on my arm. "You think he might climb the clock tower with an assault weapon one day?"

"Dozer? He's in the Chess Club, for crying out loud." She chewed the end of her pen. "Besides, we don't have a clock tower."

"You know what I mean." No one really talked about Columbine High School anymore, but when I was in middle school we had three drills: fire, tornado, and one that involved locking the doors and huddling together as far away from the windows as possible. They told us this was an "extreme-weather drill," for when there wasn't time to move to safety. But it didn't take a genius to figure out that nobody locked a door against a tornado.

"I'll make you a deal," Lisa mumbled around the pen in her mouth. "If Dozer comes to school in a black trench coat, we'll ditch the rest of the day."

"We can take my Jeep."

Wells changed the transparency again, and we had to

shut up because the plastic was yellowed to the point where deciphering the print took all our concentration.

✳ ✳ ✳

"There's no coffee." At five-thirty the next morning I stood in our kitchen in my pajamas and ratty old bathrobe and stared at the coffeemaker stupidly. "Why is there no coffee?"

My father continued to eat his cereal, showing not nearly enough concern for this crisis. "Write it on the grocery list." He gestured with his spoon to the scrap of paper that was stuck to the fridge with a Disneyland magnet. "Your mom is going to the store this afternoon."

"I don't need coffee in the afternoon. I need it now." I was whining, but I didn't care. I needed caffeine.

"Have some tea."

Grumbling, I opened the fridge. There was no Coke, either. This day was shot to Hell already. I scuffed my bunny slippers to the breakfast table and sat, head in hands, moaning piteously until he noticed my misery.

"What's the matter, Magpie? You're up early."

"I had a nightmare." I laid my cheek on the table. "I couldn't go back to sleep, so I figured I'd get up."

"You're not nervous about your exams, are you?"

"No." True, I was a little swamped at the moment. But the nightmare that rattled me wasn't a brain dream, where my anxieties ran around in my skull like ADD gerbils. It was what, when I was little, I used to call "gut dreams," after the "gut instincts" I still sometimes get. Those flashes were easier to filter than the dreams they sparked, because my defenses were down while I slept.

This nightmare was little more than disjointed images, but I'd awoken in a sweat, certain that something was very wrong somewhere. I had stumbled downstairs to try and chase the shadows away, but without my usual morning stimulant, the unease simply would not fade.

"Is Mom all right?" I asked.

Dad set down his spoon; his bowl was empty except for three Cheerios clinging together like tiny lifesavers in an ocean of milk. "She's delicately snoring away." He paused, then gave me a verbal nudge. "Did you dream about your mom?"

"No. It was really vague." I frowned, doubting myself. "Probably just random stuff."

"Tell me. Maybe you'll feel better."

Eyes fixed on those three little oat rings, I let my thoughts drift back to the dream, which always worked better than trying to purposefully remember details.

"I was somewhere really hot," I began haltingly. "As hot as that blast of air when you open the oven door. There was fire, and really foul-smelling smoke." My brows knotted. "Or maybe I only thought there were flames, because of the heat and the smoke. It was more the *impression* of fire, of trying to leash a force of nature."

He nodded. I saw the motion in the corner of my eye as I let my mind float with the Cheerios. "And smoke?"

"All around me, burning my eyes and my throat. The smell was horrible, like a Dumpster on a hot day. Rotten eggs, spoiled meat, and something like gunpowder." The images played before my unfocused eyes and I went on describing them in a droning voice. "In the center, the smoke thickened. Not solid, but with substance. Viscous, maybe."

I wasn't sure that was the right word. I remembered the toy slime I'd had as a kid, and the way the goo would slide through your hands, and squish through your fingers. The stuff also made a comical farting noise when you pushed it into the jar, but there was nothing funny about the formed yet formless darkness in my dream.

"What else happened?" Dad leaned on his elbows, eyes alive with an academic interest.

"A voice was calling out a list of names. Gibberish or another language, but definitely a roll call of some kind. I knew they were names of people. And I knew which name was mine."

The images slipped away now, faster and faster the more I tried to grasp them. Then Dad bumped the bowl; the Cheerio rings broke apart, and with them my concentration. I breathed deep, and scrubbed my hands over my face.

"That's all I remember." My fingers speared through my thick mop of hair, worsening a raging case of bedhead. Dad watched me carefully, and I dredged up a sheepish sort of smile. "The whole thing doesn't sound that scary when I say it aloud."

He rose, gathering his breakfast dishes, and gave my shoulder an encouraging squeeze. "Isn't that the point?"

"I guess." I rubbed a little crust of sleep from my eye and asked, as casually as I could, "What do you suppose the dream means?"

"I don't know, Magpie. What do you think?"

"I think it means I'm going to Hell."

His dishes clattered in the sink. "What in God's name makes you say that?"

"Come on, Dad. Fire? Brimstone? And that roll call, like

Gabriel, only on the crispy end of things." I did feel better voicing the fear. Things lose a lot of power once you name them. "I'm probably going to Hell for telling Stanley I wouldn't go to the prom with him."

"Professor Dozer's son?" Dad taught history in the same department where Stanley's mom taught anthropology.

"Yeah. He asked me yesterday."

"Heh."

That was the support I got from my loving parent. "Heh." I also noticed that he didn't deny I might be Hellbound. I was *so* glad we'd had this little heart-to-heart.

I got up and shuffled toward the hall. "I'm going upstairs to get dressed. I'll grab some coffee on the way to school."

"You need to eat some breakfast."

"Yes, *Mom*."

"Maggie?" I turned at the door, my hand resting on the jamb. "If you want, you can talk to your granny about the dream." Despite the length of the kitchen between us, he spoke softly, in case Mom was awake. There are certain things that make Mom give this *sigh*, a sort of forced exhalation of see-what-I-have-to-put-up-with martyrdom. Granny Quinn's "superstitions" rank somewhere between not eating breakfast and Dad's insistence, every year, that there is nothing wrong with leaving the Christmas lights on the roof until Valentine's Day, as long as you don't turn them on.

"Thanks, Dad. But it's no big deal. Probably just graduation anxiety. I mean, we've got eight bazillion seniors. That ceremony is bound to be hellishly long if nothing else."

He smiled, I smiled, and then I turned to go. With all

that smiling, you'd think at least one of us would be reassured.

✻ ✻ ✻

I climbed the stairs without my usual caffeinated zip. A few years ago Mom had been hinting about a new house, but Dad didn't want to move. He has tenure at the university, and he can walk from home if he wants. All the shiny new subdivisions are all the way on the outskirts of town, near the state highway that leads to the big city. Plus they have no trees.

To compromise, my parents remodeled our raised ranch-style house so that it looked less like the Brady Bunch lived here. Among other things, they'd moved me upstairs into what used to be the game room, and my old room became Mom's home office. I think the plan was to encourage me to stay home and go to school here. It isn't that I don't like Avalon. It's a college town, with an idealized retro feel. We didn't even have a Starbucks until a year ago. People love it or hate it here. I love it, but it's not really on my road to the Pulitzer Prize.

In the meantime, I had a pretty nice setup: the whole loft for myself, with bedroom stuff on one side of the room, a study area on the other. The decorating scheme, though, was Early American Disaster Zone. I had to wade through the clothes on the floor. My computer equipment took up the entire desk and had started to spill onto the adjoining table. Every surface was covered with books, paper, binders, disks, and CDs.

But who had time to clean? Besides the Dance-That-Shall-Not-Be-Named, there were pep rallies and games, the

Big Spring Musical and end-of-the-year band concerts, field trips, service projects—not to mention term papers and final exams. School spirit is not my thing, but I was on both the school paper and the yearbook staff. The night before I'd taken pictures at the basketball game, then written an essay on *Julius Caesar* before going to bed to be tied in knots by my subconscious.

I was down to my last clean pair of underwear, but a search unearthed some jeans that didn't yet stand up by themselves. At the back of the closet was a shirt from Aunt Joyce that I'd never worn because it was a little too Woodstock: kind of gauzy, with a tiny floral print, belled sleeves, and a square neck trimmed with thinly crocheted lace.

Any port in a storm, I groused. Then I felt guilty because of little Juanita in Guatemala; they could clothe her village with what lay unwashed on my floor.

Stress and guilt. The longer I was awake, the easier it was to believe that the nightmare was just that. I kept trying to put a rational face on things, even when my instincts said otherwise.

When I was little, I loved Granny Quinn's tales of the fair folk, will-o'-the-wisps, and *bain sidhe*. My dreams seemed part of that at first, more fairy stories and make-believe. Nobody took them seriously, until one morning at breakfast I asked how long until Aunt Joyce had her baby. Mom told me not to be ridiculous. That afternoon, her sister called and said she was pregnant.

After that, Mom started getting a pinched expression when I talked about my dreams, even as Gran and Dad took them as a matter of course. Then one night—was it eight years ago already?—I woke up screaming, babbling about glass and metal and blood, hysterical with fear. Mom was still quieting my tears when the phone rang.

No good news ever comes in the middle of the night. While Mom listened on the phone, I stood beside her in my Little Mermaid pajamas, and slipped my small hand into her icy one. Her face was a mask, but her eyes were snapshots of grief. Dad, awakened by the phone, stumbled out of their bedroom and froze at the sight of us.

"There was a terrible crash," I told him, trying to be strong for Mom, trying to be grown up. "Nana and Pop are dead."

He held her hand while she listened to the police officer on the line. She made the appropriate responses as tears coursed down her face. Then she hung up, and drew me in tight. Tight between them, like she was afraid I'd be lost to her, too. She clutched at us both and we held her up while she wept for her parents, gone in the swift, bloody instant that I'd seen in my dream.

✳   ✳   ✳

I blinked, coming out of the dark room of memory into the morning light. I had been thoroughly immersed in the past. I guess that was what made last night's dream so hard to dismiss. The rather vague nightmare had somehow stirred the pot of my psyche, and old, hibernating parts of me now creaked awake.

I looked around the room; my hands had been busy while my mind had been wandering, sorting laundry into reasonably contained heaps. Likewise, the flurry of paper that had blanketed the carpet of the study area now sat in neat stacks on the desk. The books were either back on the shelves or waiting tidily by the computer. The lair that time forgot hadn't been this neat since middle school.

Something glinted at me from the carpet, and I picked up the thin gold chain that held the crucifix Gran had given me at my first communion. I wondered why it wasn't where I'd left it, but since I couldn't remember where that was, I didn't linger on the thought, or on why it seemed natural to drop it on top of the pile of clothes I was going to wear that day.

What a weird morning. My brain hurt from thinking so much while in a state of caffeine deprivation. I was headed toward the shower when my cell phone rang. I fished it out of my schoolbag, not entirely surprised to see Granny Quinn's number on the caller ID.

"Hey, Gran. I was just thinking about you."

"I know you were, dear." Her voice was brighter than anyone's had a right to be while the sun still moved upward. I could hear the background whirr of her treadmill, which explained her slight breathlessness. "That's why I called."

Why couldn't I have inherited the chipper genes instead of the spooky ones?

3

You wouldn't think that a day could go downhill after dreaming you were on the roll call for Hell. But it did.

"Have you voted for the class song yet?" A student council drone shoved a half-sheet of paper in my face. Astrobright Orange is painful at any time of day, but at seven-thirty a.m. it was vomit inducing. Also, the only thing perky I want in front of me at that hour is a coffeemaker. Since the drive-thru line at Take-Your-Bucks had stretched to Canada, I was still severely caffeine deprived.

I voiced my preference in the life-and-death matter of Gwen versus Ashley by wadding up the ballot and throwing it over my shoulder on the way to the Coke machine. "You don't have to *litter!*" yelled Student Council Sally. "The recycle bin is right *over there*."

My response to that was equally nonverbal.

"Maggie Quinn!"

I knew that tone. Mr. Halloran, the assistant principal, must have looked up the word *stentorian* in the dictionary on his first day at work, and practiced in the shower until he got the voice just right.

Busted, a scant twenty feet from the Coke machine. So close, and yet so far.

"Yes, Mr. Halloran?" I Goody Two-shoed. "May I help you?"

The administrator stood by the doors leading from the courtyard to the front hall. He was fairly tall, with a full head of suspiciously thick brown hair. He was the type of stocky that comes when gravity turns linebacker shoulders into a desk-job gut. I would lay down money that he'd been a Biff in high school. "I'd like to see you in my office."

"Ooooooooo," said the kids in the courtyard—either a taunt or the buzzing of their hive mind.

I followed the assistant principal inside, not quite meekly. Student Council Sally smirked as I went by.

I waved at the secretaries managing attendance and they waved back through the chaos. Halloran waited at his office door like a prison warden. I entered and stood until he closed the door and gestured for me to sit. The office windows made sure we were properly chaperoned by all the staff. Everything was correct and polite and did nothing to explain why my hair wanted to crawl off my head.

"So, Miss Quinn. I hear you were involved in a hazing incident yesterday."

"Nobody hazed me yesterday, Mr. Halloran."

"Don't get smart with me, Quinn."

This seemed like an odd thing for a school administrator to say, but since he was glaring down at me, hands on his hips, I kept my opinion to myself.

"I have a reliable report," he continued, "that you were witness to some students bullying a classmate."

By "reliable report," I assumed he meant "rumor." I still hadn't had any caffeine, my head was feeling funny, and baiting the assistant principal could hold my interest only so long. "Then I don't see why I'm here. If there was a witness to my alleged witnessing, then you don't need me to tell you what happened."

He settled on the corner of the desk in an aren't-we-buddies way. "I understand you took some photos."

Irritation jabbed me; I couldn't imagine who had gone tattling to Halloran. Stanley? The Spanish Club? I guess I'd been overestimating the intelligence of the general populace. Blackmail has power only as long as it remains secret.

I considered Stanley, and his desire for revenge. But he'd been adamant that he didn't need my help, so I didn't think he would tell Halloran that I had pictures of his humiliation.

"I don't know what photos you are talking about," I lied. I was already on the list for Hell—what did one falsehood matter?

"The photos of the hazing incident," he said, getting a little red in the face.

"I don't have any photos of a hazing incident." This was less of a lie. "Hazing" was making freshmen wear stupid hats. Pretending you were going to drop someone off a balcony was not "hazing." It was "terrorizing."

"Then you won't mind if I look at your camera."

I had to clamp my teeth on some choice words that would get me expelled. I was offended for the entire fourth estate. As a journalist, I wanted to tell him to get some sort of court order and then we'd talk. As a high school student still five weeks and three days from graduation, I knew there was nothing I could do to stop him.

Furiously mute, I dug into the backpack at my feet and handed over the camera. Halloran turned it over, his big thumbs pressing tiny buttons as he reviewed the pictures on the memory card. Pictures of the Spanish Club's fundraising table, with its rows of gum and candy, and last night's basketball game, including a stellar shot of Eric Munoz nailing an NBA-worthy jump shot.

But no Biff, a.k.a. Brandon. No bug-eyed Jessica. No terror-stricken Stanley.

Halloran grunted with frustration, started to say something, then thrust the camera at me. "Get out of here, Quinn. And don't be late for first period, because I'm not giving you a pass."

I didn't have to be told twice. Despite the big windows, the office felt claustrophobic. Maybe it was Halloran and his power trip. Maybe it was the wall behind his desk, filled with pictures of past sports triumphs—not the school's, his own. The thought that this was what bullies grew into, minor tyrants who took jobs where they could relive their glory days by continuing to terrorize students, made my head ache.

I felt immediately better when I left the office, as if the air were somehow cleaner. My granny might say something about the Quinn ability to sense things unseen, but more likely it was the evil power of Halloran's aftershave.

The warning bell clanged directly over my head. I had five minutes to find a caffeine infusion before English, which was on the other side of the building from the nearest Coke machine. (I had them all plotted on a sort of mental MapQuest.) I could make it if I ran. But pairing my graceless jog with a hurriedly gulped-down soft drink seemed like a recipe for disaster.

So I went to class, sans soda.

✳ ✳ ✳

In English, we turned in our homework assignments, and were given the rest of the time to work on our term papers, due in a week. My theme concerned Jonathan Swift and the use of sarcasm in social commentary, and Lisa was flipping through my notes.

"I could get behind a guy who proposed that eating Irish children would solve both the famine and the population problem. I'm going to remember that when my despotic plans come to fruition."

"He was being satirical, Lisa."

"Maybe I am, too. Maybe not." She wiggled her eyebrows maniacally. Lisa had finished her paper a week ago. Her subject? Machiavelli. Sometimes I thought my friend was one of the drollest people I knew. Other times I thought she was one of the scariest.

"What did Halloran want?" she asked.

"Are there *no* secrets in this school?"

"My spies are everywhere."

"Girls!" We jumped guiltily as Ms. Vincent called from her desk. Well, *I* jumped. Lisa merely turned complacently. "Are you working on your papers, or are you gossiping?"

My compatriot replied with a composed lie, "I'm helping Maggie, Ms. Vincent. She needs advice on solidifying her argument."

The teacher accepted this with insulting ease. "Why can't *I* be helping *you*?" I hissed at Lisa as we pretended to get back to work. "I'm the future Pulitzer Prize winner. You're just the future Lord High Poobah of the World."

"You can be helping me next time." She brushed a glossy lock of hair over her shoulder and asked again, "What did Halloran want?"

"The pictures I took of yesterday's bully-o-rama."

Her brows lifted. "You got actual dirt on Brandon Rogers?"

"Yeah. Snapped a really unflattering picture of the prom queen front-runner, too."

"You didn't hand them over, did you?"

"No. I deleted them from the camera last night after I downloaded them onto my computer."

"Smart thinking. The camera is school property, like the lockers, with no expectation of privacy. Well done, my Padawan apprentice."

I tucked my hair behind my ears and tried to get back to work. I wasn't very successful, because I was now thinking about Halloran and bullies instead of Swift and Lilliputians.

"Why do you suppose Halloran wanted the pictures?" I mused aloud. "He likes good ol' Biff. Why would he want incriminating evidence on him?"

"To take it away from you, of course, and make sure it never sees the light."

"But I have copies."

"You ought to put them in an envelope marked 'Open in the event of my mysterious death or disappearance.'"

"Gee thanks, Lisa. I would never have thought of that. How handy to have a criminal mastermind as a friend."

"I prefer Evil Genius. And you're welcome." The class began gathering their books. There was no visible signal, just the action of the collective unconscious. Lisa and I rode the wave.

"See you in civics," she said as the bell rang.

I had journalism next. The class was supposed to be separate from the lab where we worked on the school's weekly newspaper, but by this time of year the structure was pretty fluid. I turned in my article on the Spanish Club and gave Mr. Allison the pictures of the basketball game. He whistled when he saw the jump shot. "Great photo, Maggie! You really caught the motion."

"Thanks." Sports and action photography took a knack and a bit of luck. I think I'd been more lucky than anything else, but I was still proud. "May I have a pass?"

"Where are you going?" he asked, reaching for his pen.

I didn't think "To the Coke machine" was going to cut it, so I said, "To the auditorium. Big Spring Musical is this weekend, and I thought I'd interview the cast."

"Good idea. Phillip was saying we could use something to round out the edition. Think you can have it ready tomorrow?"

"Just a fluff piece? Sure." Phillip was the student editor and he had a gift for knowing exactly how many inches of story the edition lacked at any given moment. Mr. Allison tore the pass off the pad, I took it with a cheery "Thanks!" then grabbed my backpack and headed to C Hall where lay the Band Hall, Choir Room, auditorium, and, not coincidentally, several vending machines.

Finally! Sweet liquid ambrosia of caramel-colored, high-fructose, caffeinated bliss. With the carbonated burn coursing down my throat and the sugar rushing through my veins, interviewing the Drama Club seemed a small price to pay.

✳ ✳ ✳

Mr. Thomas, the drama teacher, was a harried-looking guy who didn't seem long out of high school himself. "All those things need to be organized on the prop tables, stage right and left. How are we coming on costumes? People! We *open* in less than three days!"

He might have been addressing the air for all I knew; there was no discernible change in the chaos in the auditorium, where there seemed to be an awful lot going on, but very little getting done. I coughed to get his attention and he turned his wild-eyed stare on me. "Hi. I'm Maggie Quinn, from the Avalon High paper. I was hoping I might interview a few of the cast members."

"Excellent! I'll introduce you to our star." He called toward the stage at a volume that made me jump. "Jessica! Have you got a minute?"

Boy, this day just kept getting better and better.

The model thin blonde who turned at her name was not, thankfully, the Queen Jessica—the Jessica Prime—though I did recognize her from the Jessica chorus in the Incident with Stanley on the Breezeway.

She joined me at the edge of the stage with a distinct air of noblesse oblige but no sign she knew who I was, other than paparazzi, and therefore a necessary inconvenience. That suited me fine. I flipped open my notebook and donned the armor of professionalism.

"Why don't you start by telling me what made you interested in Drama Club."

"First of all"—she tossed her blond hair—"it's not the Drama Club. It's the *Thespian Society.*" She mistook my blank expression for a sign that said *Yes, thank you, I would love a generous helping of condescension.* "Named for the Greek god Thespis?"

I hated when people did that, went up at the end of a statement when the only question they were asking was "Don't you realize I'm smarter than you?" Especially when they didn't even know that Thespis was not a god, but just some ancient Greek whose life must have sucked so bad that he had to write a bunch of plays about it and call it "tragedy." Sort of like a preteen with a blog, only with less Avril Lavigne lyrics.

"O-kay." Professionalism, Maggie. "Why don't you tell me what made you interested in the *Thespian Society*?"

"Actually, I've been performing for a long time. Ever

29

since I won the Little Miss Princess Pageant when I was six years old. And maybe you've seen my television work? The commercial for Calaway's Quality Used Cars?"

"Oh really?" My response wasn't strictly necessary. Thespica was used to an audience that didn't talk back.

"Honestly, I really didn't have time for the musical this year. After all, there's cheerleading tryouts—I'm an officer, so it's a *big* responsibility, choosing the next squad—and the Prom Queen Nominating Committee. But when Mr. Thomas *begged* me to audition, I knew I had an obligation."

"Your dedication is truly awe-inspiring." Maybe I would invent a society named after the Greek goddess Sarcastica. "Talent can be such a burden."

She sighed, completely without irony. "I know. You'd be surprised how many people never realize that."

I had to leave then, or bust a gut laughing.

Back in C Hall, I breathed deep of the unpretentious air outside the auditorium. I didn't feel like walking all the way back to class for the five remaining minutes, so I ducked into the nearest restroom. It wasn't entirely unjustified. I had, after all, gulped down that soda.

I took care of business and was straightening myself back out when a whiff of something half-remembered made me pause. Obviously, there are plenty of odors in the school bathrooms, none of which I wanted to investigate too closely. But the sickly sweet smell tickled the back of my throat, and brought back a not-quite-clear memory of smoke, flame, and . . .

Pot. Someone had lit up a joint in the boys' room, and the smoke was seeping through the vent.

The door to the bathroom opened, and I heard familiar voices. It was the unholy triad of the ruling class, Jessica Prime and her two most senior handmaidens—Jess Minor, and my new friend Thespica, who was briefing the others on our meeting.

"I cannot believe that Quinn actually *asked* for an interview with you." Jess Minor was the queen's permanent shadow, copying everything she did, but not quite as well. The result was a tweaked stunt-double resemblance and a slightly desperate air of tries-too-hard. "What a loser."

"It's pathetic." Jessica Prime's voice, when not shrieking like a banshee, was sugar sweet and slightly husky from years of yell practice. "Does she really think that sucking up to you is going to do anything for her social credibility?"

"Maybe she thinks I'll be her friend. You should have heard her fawning all over me."

From my hiding place, I rolled my eyes. It was wishful thinking that they would conveniently go into the other stalls and allow me to escape. I guess girls as perfect as the Jessicas never had to pee.

Instead, they planted themselves in front of the sinks, applying powder, lip gloss, and venom. They went on about me for a while, talking about what a loser I was, then numbering me among all the other people they considered geeky, poor, fat, unfashionable, or otherwise beneath contempt, and how they'd rather die than be any of the above.

As fascinating as this insight into the bitch psyche was,

the smoke was getting stronger and making me slightly nauseated. Granted, I didn't have a lot of basis for comparison, but this had to be the worst smelling weed ever.

"What is *that*?" Prime's voice held such horror, I figured she smelled it, too. "Jess, is that . . ." She seemed to be having trouble even saying it. Not the smell, then. I edged forward, peering through the gap in the stall to see Jessica Prime staring at Minor's purse as if something slimy were crawling out of it. "Is that a . . . knockoff!"

Lip gloss wand suspended in midair, the lesser Jessica looked baffled. "No. My mom bought it for me at Saks when I was staying with her on spring break."

Prime laughed, making me think about D&D Lisa, and the important distinction between laughing *with* and laughing *at*. "You didn't get that at Saks."

"I did!"

"Jess!" She grabbed the bag and pointed to the metal insignia on the front. "It says *Conch*. You didn't buy a purse, you bought a type of fritter."

Thespica peered at the name. "It does say Conch, Jess. I'm afraid you've been had."

"Did you buy it off the back of a truck or something? Maybe your mother did."

"No! She took me to the store!"

"It's okay, Jess." Prime patted her shoulder in a consoling, condescending way. "Everyone gets taken sometime."

Jess had dropped the lip gloss in the sink and grabbed her purse with both hands, reading the metal tag. "It says 'Coach.'" She sounded like a lost little girl. "You two are making fun of me."

I never thought I'd feel sorry for a Jessica; her confused hurt almost made me forget she was one of them. That was one of the most loathsome things about the breed. The pack could turn on its weakest member just as quickly as on an outsider.

Queen Jessica finished applying her makeup, pressed her lips together, then studied the effect of her pout. "Don't worry, Jess. As long as you hide that thing in your locker, we'll still let you eat lunch with us." While Jess Minor continued to examine her bag with a bewildered expression, Prime stepped back and studied her own reflection with the slightest frown. "Does this skirt make me look fat?"

"Of course not," said Thespica, completing her own toilette. "I wish I had your figure."

As far as I could tell, she did. I was so sick of their nonsense that I was ready to burst out of the stall and take my lumps. Whatever had possessed me to stay hidden in the first place? At this rate I'd be well prepared for a job with the *National Enquirer*.

Finally, they left. I barely stopped to wash my hands before I vacated the place myself. There was an intolerable stink in that bathroom, but it had nothing to do with the toilet.

4

My phone buzzed in my pocket only a moment after the bell rang. My father, according to Gran, is not eligible to have The Sight because he is a man, but Dad's timing often makes me wonder.

"Are you free for lunch?" he asked when I said hello.

"Where are you?"

"Parked out front. Come eat with us."

I didn't know who "us" was, but I wasn't going to turn down an excuse to get out of the building. We have an open campus, so I zipped out the door with the other parolees. Dad waved from beside his Saturn and I galloped down the stairs to meet him.

My steps slowed as a complete stranger unfolded himself from the shotgun seat and held the front door for me. Dad had brought a friend. A young and handsome friend, with a tall, lean build and a lopsided, Han Solo sort of smile. He wore an oxford shirt and khakis and his dark hair was cut conservatively short.

"Maggie," said my dad, "this is Justin MacCallum. He's a student in the history department. You don't mind if he comes with us, do you?"

"No problem." I was suddenly rather glad that Aunt Joyce's shirt had been the only thing clean.

I got a bit of a Boy Scout vibe from the guy, which was confirmed when he held the door for me. Dad put the car in gear and asked, "Where do you want to eat?"

"I don't care." My stomach was pretty excited about the idea of food, though, and growled loudly. I tried not to blush. "Not too heavy, though; I have P.E. right after this."

"Are you still swimming?" Dad laughed when I groaned an affirmative. "Maggie doesn't like the water," he told Justin.

"Dad!" Bad enough I was treating us to a gastric symphony. I didn't need all my idiosyncrasies trotted out for the *Embarrass Maggie Show*.

Justin looked amused in a "laughing *with* you" way, only I wasn't laughing. "Not even to drink?"

"I don't like to get *in* the water," I explained, shooting daggers at my father.

"She does take showers," said my oblivious parent, "as you can tell by the fact we don't have to roll down the windows."

"*Dad!*"

"That's interesting." Justin leaned his elbows on our bucket seats. "Most people love the water. It's natural, ingrained. Reminds us of the womb."

"I must have been a really seasick fetus."

That got a chuckle. Score for me.

"What's the criteria, Mags?" asked Dad. "Has to be shallow?"

"I have to be able to see the bottom."

"That's right." He glanced at Justin, who was still hanging between us. "I remember when Laura, her mother, tried to put her in a bubble bath one time. She screamed bloody murder until the bubbles went away."

There ought to be a law against naked baby stories in front of strangers. I changed the subject. "You have class with my dad, Justin?"

"Yes. I'm doing some research on folklore, actually, and Professor Quinn was nice enough to introduce me to your grandmother. I wanted to hear some of her stories from the old country."

I glanced sideways at my father. "The fairy stories?"

Dad kept his eyes on the road. "And some family history."

My eyes narrowed. "What family history?"

"You should go see your gran after school" was Dad's random answer. "If your day doesn't improve."

"Martians could invade and it would be an improvement on my day. What does that have to do with anything?" Justin and Dad exchanged glances in the rearview mirror and my suspicions flared. "All right. Cut to the chase. Why were you there? And for that matter, why are you *here*?"

Justin cleared his throat. "Your grandmother says that you—your family, that is—share a gift. She sensed that you were having a rough morning, in fact."

I stared at my father, disbelieving and betrayed. "You *told* him? You told a perfect stranger?"

He took a placating tone. "It came up in the conversation. Your grandmother is not shy with a receptive audience."

I scowled at Justin. "What, exactly, are you studying?"

"Well, my major is history, but I'm doing an independent study on the history of the occult in different cultures, from folk tales to high magic. . . ."

"Stop the car."

"Oh, Maggie," said Dad. "Don't be ridiculous."

"Stop. The. Car."

He slammed on the brakes. It was a good thing we were only going twenty-five miles an hour and everyone was wearing their seat belt.

I turned to them both. "I am not some kind of freak. I don't see things. I don't *know* things. And even if I did have . . . whatever . . . I sure don't want to be someone's research project." I opened the door and climbed out, hauling my backpack with me, which made my wrathful dignity a little harder to maintain.

Dad leaned across the gearshift. "What are you doing?"

"I'm walking back to school. It's not that far." I slammed the door. Dad argued with me through the open window for a while but I took a shortcut between two houses and left them behind.

✳   ✳   ✳

By the time I got back to school I was still hot under the collar, but mostly from lugging my gargantuan book bag for five blocks. The angry churning in my stomach had time to die down, too, until I remembered it was time for P.E., and the pool.

It wasn't that I couldn't swim. I could keep my head above the water and move from place to place with all the grace of a Labrador retriever. I'd made it through the past five weeks by stubbornly moving down my lane in a sort of combination dog paddle/breaststroke so I could keep my eyes on the bottom of the pool, and anything that might be sneaking up on me from below.

The other problem with swimming in P.E., which had nothing to do with my fear of the water, was the difficulty of embarking on this exercise without, at some point, being completely naked in the locker room. Most of us changed in the shower stalls. But even so, to stand there in the buff, for even a transitory moment, while your classmates lurk on the other side of a very flimsy curtain was fifty kinds of vulnerable.

I had done extensive experiments in changing in stages: Remove pants. Slip suit on while shirt hides important bits. Wiggle arms out of sleeves while keeping shirt down around other bits, then contort out of bra and into remainder of suit.

Having worked up quite a sweat this way, I bundled up my clothes and bent to pick up my shoes. Gran's cross swung lightly against my collarbone as I straightened. I'd forgotten about it until then. I debated for a moment, then unclasped the chain and stuffed it into my shoe.

We made our way out of the locker room and into the cavernous aquatics gym. The administration was always telling us how lucky we were to have a pool. Only they called it a "natatorium," which is an old-fashioned term for "really expensive indoor swimming pool." I hate that word. It's too much like "crematorium" and I have enough liquid issues as it is.

Some sadist at the health department had decreed we had to shower before getting in the pool, so we trudged through the spigots then stood dripping in our swimsuits while we received instruction from the girls P.E. teacher. Coach Milner had the whipcord-lean frame of a long-distance runner. She'd competed in the Boston Marathon for ten consecutive years. Her age was difficult to determine, because her fitness regime clearly did not include the vigorous application of sunscreen.

The deal with Coach Milner was that she didn't just run marathons, she lived them. "Quitters never win," she had yelled at me as I wheezed around the track. "Never say die," she hollered up at me as I dangled from a rope trying to climb more than four feet off the mat. "Mind over matter," she cajoled as I threw up my lunch after taking a basketball to the gut. Fitness was her religion, and she preached these things like the Gospel according to Nike.

The class lined up like a multicolored, omnisize, Bizarro-world Miss America contest. Coach Milner strode in front of us, our judge, jury, and executioner.

"Congratulations, ladies. Today we move on to the diving portion of our aquatics unit. We'll be in the deep pool now, so grab your towels and—" My hand shot into the air. "What is it, Quinn?"

"I just ate," I lied. "Aren't we supposed to wait an hour before going in the water?"

"Winners never make excuses. That's an old wives' tale. Twenty minutes is sufficient." She grasped the whistle hanging around her neck and blew a rousing note, like Gideon on his trumpet. "Come on, ladies! This way."

Coach marched us from our spot beside the lap pool (good-bye, safe haven of only moderate distaste) to the diving area (hello, bottomless pit of liquid doom).

"Are you all right?" A blur of fingers broke my gaze and I dragged my eyes from the depths and focused on the concerned little moon of Karen Foley's face.

"Huh?" That was all I could manage. Behold the wordsmith.

"You look really pale." Karen was one of the nicest girls I knew, which was why, though I pitied Stanley, after his spiteful words about her, I didn't feel much sympathy for him.

I tried to rally. The champion who faced down Biff et al. should show a little gumption. "I'm always pale."

"Yeah, but I think the undertone of green is new." She touched my arm. "And you're all clammy."

A chorus of giggles made us turn. Jessica Prime and her henchbitches clustered together in a lump of malice. I usually gave the witless triplets a wide berth, but yesterday's debacle had incurred the wrath of the Jessicas. As much as I wanted to ignore them, I was now firmly on their radar.

"You're not scared of a little kiddy pool, are you, Maggie?" Prime taunted, with a toss of her blond head and a smile of parade-float insincerity.

I gave an exaggerated sigh. "Not everyone has installed personal flotation devices, Jessica."

A scarlet flush darkened her perfect tan. I knew that expression; I had a close-up of it on disk. "You'd better watch it, Quinn. No one likes a smartass."

"That must make the world a more comfortable place for you, then."

"I'm warning you! Someone is going to serve you up a big plate of comeback one of these days. And it's going to taste a lot like my foot up your butt."

"I think you mean a 'big plate of comeuppance.'"

"What?"

"Comeuppance. A 'comeback' is what John Travolta kept having in the nineties."

Jessica showed me her palm. "Whatever. You are such a loser. I should have known you'd watch disco movies."

"Let's keep the line moving, ladies!"

Holy Cheez-Its. I'd been having so much fun baiting the Barbies that I'd almost forgotten about my imminent demise.

"Steady there." Karen grabbed my elbow when my knees threatened to fail me.

It was Jessica Prime's turn. She climbed onto the board, waggled her manicured fingers at me, then with a leap as graceful as a gazelle, made a perfect arc into the water. The board applauded with the "wocka wocka wocka" of its spring.

If I didn't hate her before, I sure did now.

Jess Minor took her place with a snotty glance my way. Her dive was true to form: a knockoff of Prime's perfection.

Thespica came after, and I guess there wasn't a diving portion of the Little Miss Perfection Pageant. But her lackluster effort was still better than anything I could do.

Finally, there was no one in front of me. Just Coach Milner, her whistle, and the diving board. "You're up, Quinn."

"Uh . . ."

"Come on. You're holding up the line."

"Er . . ."

"Let's go, Quinn. Fear is the mind-killer. Get up there and just do it."

"Geez, Maggie," said Jessica Prime, fluffing her dripping hair back into shape, "it's the low board for crying out loud. It's, like, three feet above the water."

High board, low board, made no difference. It was the indigo invisibility of the water below that kept my bare feet rooted to the tile.

Coach Milner shook her head sadly, jotting a note on her clipboard. "This is going to affect your grade, Quinn. Quitters never prosper."

If she was going to humiliate me, she ought to at least get her clichés right.

"I'll go first." Karen took my place in line with a bracing smile. "After I belly flop anything you do will look like a swan dive."

My ears began to burn. Nothing that Milner said shamed me more than Karen the Mathlete climbing confidently up the two steps to the diving board, unconcerned about the water below, or the jiggle of her thighs, or the snickers of the Jessicas.

"A hippo would look like a swan after her." One's hiss was indistinguishable from the others.

"If she belly flops, there won't be any water left in the pool."

I spun around and whispered in tight, soft fury. "I swear to God, Jessica, one more word, and that picture goes up on the school Web page."

Prime's eyes flashed, but a movement over the pool caught my eye and I turned back to watch Karen, standing at the back end of the board, taking a deep breath.

The class broke out of line to watch. I drew a breath with her, and held it as she stepped out. Her stride, her placement at the end of the board, looked perfect. She gathered herself as the springboard dipped down, and then released that energy upward.

Again my eye snagged on some dark movement—her shadow on the water? I barely had time to wonder, a half-fired neuron of warning, then everything went wrong.

Karen's foot shot out from under her and her arms flung out, catching nothing but empty air as she tumbled backward toward the board. The impact echoed through the natatorium as her head smacked the fiberglass. Her limp body hit the water with a splash, and sank slowly into the stygian depths.

5

Coach Milner dove into the pool, slipping into the fathomless water after Karen. I couldn't see how she would be able to manage the girl's limp weight without help. I edged toward the pool, not sure what I could do. Below the surface I could see them, distorted by ripples and depth. Surely some help was better than none, if I could just make myself take that step off the ledge.

"I got it." A guy's voice, someone from the boy's P.E. class that had taken our place in the lap pool. He dove in while the rest of us were still reeling.

His action shattered the horrified spell that held us in

stasis. I grabbed the girl to my right. "Get the boys' coach." The concrete-and-tile vault of the gym was so loud, it might take a while for the news to spread. Meanwhile, I ran to the wall where the life preservers hung, returning just as three heads broke the surface: Milner and the boy, with Karen hanging between them, blood trickling from under her hair.

I tossed out the life preserver. Milner caught it and draped Karen's arms over the ring, balancing her. Amanda and Sarah took up the rope and we pulled the three of them to the side of the pool.

"Watch her head." The boys' coach had arrived, with the class following behind, like curious rubberneckers on the freeway. I supported Karen's head while they lifted her out. As her stomach hit the side of the pool, water trickled out of her mouth, and she began to cough. A relieved sigh rippled outward from the ring of students.

She coughed until she retched. Coach and I turned her on her side until all the water came up and out, and with it a strange smell. You'd expect puked up pool water to smell funny. But the chlorine odor was mixed with rotten eggs and burnt toast, and my hands began to shake.

We rolled her back when she started to breathe more easily, in hoarse pants instead of asthmatic wheezes. Someone handed me a towel to put under her head, as Milner ran to call 911. I pressed a second cloth to the gash on Karen's head. Blood mixed with the water on the tile deck, so that we were awash with it, real horror movie stuff.

"I'm so sorry, Karen," I whispered, not really knowing what I was apologizing for.

Her brow squinched up and her eyes opened slightly. "For what? Did something happen?"

"Yeah, you could say that."

"My head hurts."

"I'm sorry," I repeated. I'd been trying not to press too hard on the cut because of the enormous lump that was under it. It looked like a gory Mount St. Helens.

"Get out of the way, Quinn." Coach Milner brushed me aside. "How many fingers am I holding up, Foley?"

My knees had stiffened while I knelt on the deck and I had to struggle to my feet as the paramedics arrived and took over. The tension drained quickly after that. Assistant Principal Halloran showed up to take care of anything official; I bet there was going to be some paperwork on this one. Our classes were dismissed to go change but I hung back, watching silently as the EMTs put a brace on Karen's neck before they lifted her.

As the paramedics strapped her down for the ride, I sidled up to where one of them stood writing on a big metal clipboard. "Is she going to be all right?"

"I can't really say." He glanced up from his chart and saw my face. Maybe I looked as tightly wound as I felt, because he added, "She'll definitely be needing tests and observation for a concussion, but it could be worse."

In other words, it was a lot better to have a big bump going out than a big dent going in. The EMTs gathered their stuff quickly, and after a last signature from the assistant principal, they whisked Karen away.

The air seemed eerily quiet once they were gone. The gym was pretty much empty, and the lap of the water echoed strangely on the concrete and tile.

I found myself at the edge of the pool, looking for . . . I don't know what. Another glimpse of black shadow, a whiff of something other than chlorine. I'm not sure what it would mean if I *did* smell something. That I was crazy? Or I wasn't.

My hand touched my throat. It took me a moment to realize I was unconsciously reaching for Granny's necklace.

Was it possible that my dream had somehow been a warning?

I rejected the idea almost immediately. I was too old to believe in fairies and soothsaying dreams. What I had was very good intuition, and sometimes things I picked up subconsciously play out in my dreams. That was the only logical, adult explanation.

And I never saw the future. I couldn't have warned Karen any more than I could have warned my grandparents that night. There was nothing I could have done.

"Of course there wasn't."

My heart slammed against my ribs. I jumped, too, arms windmilling to keep myself from somehow defying physics and falling into the water three feet away.

"Whoa! Careful." Big, tanned hands caught my waist. Well, where my waist would be if I wasn't wearing the World's Most Unflattering Swimsuit.

As soon as I was steady, I backed away, my heart still pounding. Mostly I was startled. But it may have had a little to do with the blue plate special of hot, athletic goodness standing in front of me.

Finally, I had a good look at Bobby Baywatch. The lifeguard patch on his well-worn swim trunks explained his quick action earlier, as well as his bronze tan, washboard stomach, and muscular shoulders. He had a great face, too—good bones, blue eyes, and a mouth that looked like it smiled more than not.

It was also a familiar face, and my brows pinched together as I made the unwelcome connection.

"Oh Hell," I said. "You're a Jock."

With a capital *J*. As in, one of the Jocks and Jessicas, a lord of the watering hole.

He didn't pretend he didn't know what I meant. "Maggie, right?" I nodded. "Look, Maggie, I'm sorry about what happened yesterday. Brandon went too far, and . . ." He faltered and finished weakly. "I'm just really sorry."

I could see plainly that he was repentant, embarrassed, and a little ashamed of himself. But that wasn't my problem. "I don't need an apology. You didn't do anything to me."

"I know. I'll apologize to Stanley, too. But I just don't want you to think I'm like those other guys."

I had to tilt my head back to look him in the eye. I'd had a craptastic day, and there was enough weird stuff going on in my life to fill an episode of the *Twilight Zone*. I didn't have the patience to coddle his guilty conscience.

"I don't know why it matters to you, but here's the deal. You may not have helped, but you stood there and did nothing while the people you call your friends demeaned and physically assaulted someone weaker than them."

He flushed guiltily and looked away. "I just didn't know what to do that wouldn't make things worse."

His whipped puppy expression made me feel guilty, too, for lecturing. "Yes, well, I don't want to be late to class, so . . ." I gestured for him to move out of my way. If he thought it was strange that I didn't go around him on the pool side he didn't say so, but just backed up to open more ground. I hadn't gone far, though, when he called, "Hey, Quinn!"

I turned back, lifting my brows in inquiry.

"It's not the same thing," he said.

"What's not?"

"Yesterday and today." He closed the gap between us, looking down at me with spectacularly blue eyes. Not that it changed my opinion of him, of course. "I heard you talking to yourself. It's true, there was nothing you could have done. If you had jumped in, we'd have had two people to pull out instead of one."

"I can swim." If your definition of swimming was broad enough.

"Swimming and rescuing are two different things." He smiled, a little ruefully. "I thought it was cool that you thought about it, though. I guess that's why I wanted to . . . make an excuse, I guess."

I understood that I'd been paid a compliment of a sort. By a Jock. The Weirdness just went on and on.

I didn't know what to say so I settled on, "Thanks. I think."

With all that had happened that day, I had much more important things to think about than how my rear end looked in my bathing suit as I walked to the locker room. But I worried about it anyway.

∗ ∗ ∗

I had less than five minutes to change and get to my next class, on the other side of the planet from the pool. I unlocked my stuff and hauled it all into one of the shower stalls. I had no time for Victorian hang-ups about nudity, or wrestling matches with my clothing. I shucked off my suit, pulled on my panties and had just fastened my bra when the curtain flew open. Jessica Prime, head bitch of the universe, snapped my picture with her camera phone.

That's right, ladies and gentlemen, in one short day—eight short hours, actually—I'd gone from worrying that the demonic forces of the universe might be appearing in my dreams, to wondering whether, by six o'clock tonight, most of the student body would have received an e-mail attachment of me, looking like a deer in the headlights, wearing my washday underwear.

6

She text messaged me between classes: NOW I'VE GOT A PIC-
TURE, TOO. Hello Queen of the Obvious. But I understood the
implied threat. If I went public with her impression of a
screaming baboon, she'd broadcast me and my Hello Kitty
underwear to her entire friends list.

Chemistry lab demanded my attention, and I was glad
for it. Given the choice between (1) angsting over whether
Jessica Prime was petty enough to distribute the picture for
the heck of it, or (2) blowing myself up in my distraction,
the decision was fairly easy.

"Your experiment is set before you." Professor

Blackthorne walked through the lab benches, hands clasped behind his back. "You are to follow the instructions—to the letter, Mr. Anderson—adding Powder A to Liquid B and heating the resulting Solution C as indicated, and based on the resulting reaction, identify Product D. Understood?"

We chorused a trained "yes, sir" so hearty that you would have thought we lived to identify Product D from the reaction of Liquid B and Powder A. Truthfully, our experiments were usually interesting if not pyrotechnic. Professor Blackthorne loved a good exothermic reaction.

I should point out that on Halloween, my chemistry teacher dressed up like Professor Snape from the Harry Potter books, and he sometimes referred to his course as "Potions Class" even when it wasn't October. He had a last name out of a Brontë novel and he looked like the mad scientist from *Back to the Future*. I love Professor Blackthorne.

"Right then. Goggles on . . . Is something funny, Mr. Hobson?"

I tensed with dread as the football player tucked something under his desk. "Er, no, Professor Blackthorne."

"That's not a cell phone, is it?"

"Oh no, Professor Blackthorne." Except that it totally was.

"Good. Cell phones should always be turned off during lab experiments. Should they ring, even in silent mode, the arriving signal could cause a static charge that would ignite any volatile fumes in the air, and the user would certainly go up in a fiery ball of agonizing death." He stared down his nose at the wide receiver. "And we wouldn't want that to happen, would we, Mr. Hobson?"

I want to marry Professor Blackthorne.

"Now! Goggles on . . . and begin."

∗ ∗ ∗

The instant the bell rang, I headed toward civics. It was pointless to dwell on what a malicious bitch Jessica Prime was and the senseless cruelties she inflicted on girls every day. But I did anyway, jumping at every chirruping cell phone, convinced my picture would be all over the school by seventh period.

It wasn't that I had some enormous popularity at stake. I occupied neutral territory—a sort of social Switzerland— nowhere near the "in crowd" but not so far out that I had to sit by myself in the cafeteria. No, the only thing at risk was my total humiliation. And the more I thought about it, the larger it loomed, until I was convinced that every laugh in the crowded hallway was aimed at me, and the Cingular air- waves were burning up with the traffic of my downfall.

New plan: Duck into the nearest bathroom and hide in a stall. I was getting good at that. It would be handy in my career as a tabloid reporter, which was the only job I would be able to get once that picture was posted on the Internet, available to anyone who Googled me.

My phone buzzed against my hip. I pulled it out and looked warily at the caller ID, then flipped it open.

"Where *are* you?" Lisa's voice blared in my ear.

"Hiding in the bathroom."

"Which one?"

"B Hall. By the computer lab."

"I'm there."

I heard her enter only a few moments later. "Get out,"

she told the freshmen primping in the mirror. I saw their little feet scurrying toward the exit, then my stall door flew open.

"Are you all right? Why are you hiding?" she demanded, one hand braced on top of the swinging door, the other on her hip, a warlike, gray-eyed Athena in vintage Gap.

"I'm having a terrible day." My voice cracked pathetically.

"I know, Mags. I heard it was awful. But you're all right?"

"*Awful?*" So she'd sent it. And even my best friend thought I looked awful with my fish-belly-white thighs and bug-eyed expression. My eyes began to sting, despite my best efforts not to cry. "Was it really that bad?"

"Well, you were there."

"I know. But I didn't think she'd really do it."

Lisa frowned, her arched brows drawing together. "You didn't think she'd really jump?"

"No. I didn't think she'd send my picture to the whole school."

She dropped the other hand to her hip. "What are you talking about?"

I stared up at her, realizing we were talking about two different things. "The picture Jessica Prime took of me mostly naked in the locker room. What are *you* talking about?"

"Karen Foley's accident." She pressed her palms to her forehead, paced away from the stall, and came back. "You mean I've been worried sick about you, about Karen, and you're in here crying about a *Jessica*?"

Jumping up, I defended myself. "I was not crying. And I think I'm entitled to five minutes of self-pity."

"Are you in the hospital? No. Are you the first person those bitches have humiliated? No."

I shoved past her, out of the stall. "You know what? You could give me a little perspective without being such a witch about it. You're supposed to be my friend."

"My friends don't hide in toilets from a little humiliation."

"Kiss off, Lisa."

"That's the spirit." She handed me my backpack. "Let's go to civics."

I grabbed the bag from her, squared my shoulders, and set my chin, daring her to give me any more grief.

"Good girl." She smoothed my hair, fluffed the sleeves of my blouse, and straightened the neck. "I'm glad you're all right."

"Afraid I'd turn into Self-Pity Girl permanently?" I asked, still sulking.

"No. I heard about the accident and worried."

My anger abated. I can never keep it up very long, especially when I'm sort of at fault, too. "I'm fine. Karen was the one hurt, not me."

"But it could have been. She took your place in line, didn't she?"

I hadn't thought about it that way, and the idea was like a punch to the gut. Was it possible I had dodged some kind of bullet of Fate?

After school, Gran was waiting with tea and sympathy. Literally.

I hadn't told her I was coming over, but by the time my Jeep Wrangler pulled into her driveway, the tea was hot in the pot and the cookies were warm on the plate. I'd resolved to be done feeling sorry for myself, but there's something about a grandmother's couch. Before I knew it, I had told her all about Jessica Prime and the picture, Halloran's ambush, Karen's accident, and even the dream that kicked it all off.

"I knew there was something going on." Gran withdrew her arm from my shoulders. "I knew this morning that you weren't being straight with me."

Self-pity time had expired, I guess. I sighed and poured myself a cup of tea. The brew was Darjeeling, but the pot and cups were Japanese, which summed Gran up pretty well. She had an icon of the Virgin and Child on one wall, and a set of Buddist temple bells hanging near the door. She looked like a red-headed Debbie Reynolds, dressed in a lavender tracksuit, completely American except for her lingering Irish lilt.

"It was just a nightmare, Gran."

"You keep telling yourself that and you may miss an important clue."

"To what? All I dreamed about was fire and smoke. That's not a lot to go on."

She lifted her steaming cup. "That's your own fault. If you had honed your ability instead of ignoring and repressing it . . ."

Surging to my feet, I paced across the small living room,

56

endangering a bamboo tree in my frustration. "I don't have an ability!"

"Then why are you here?"

I didn't answer her, just folded my arms with a sullen expression. Stubborn? Who, me?

"You are here because something about your dream will not allow you to ignore it." Gran set down her cup and clasped her hands together. "I can sense there are forces at work around you, Magdalena. You sense it, too, or you would not be wearing that." She pointed to the delicate gold cross around my neck.

I reached up to trace the shape. "I just found it while I was cleaning up my room, and since I hadn't worn it in a while . . ."

"Nonsense. Your subconscious recognizes the threat, the need for spiritual protection. Why don't you?" For a woman of her years, she had relatively few wrinkles, but every one of them was drawn deep with annoyance.

Pacing again, I tried to answer. "Because it's just—" Scary? Ridiculous? "—impossible."

"There are things in the world that cannot be dismissed simply because they cannot be quantified. You have a gift—"

I started to protest. "Gran, I don't—"

"Honestly, Maggie." She interrupted me, clearly at the end of her patience. "If nothing else, you have a *brain* and the obligation to use it to take a stand against Evil."

"Evil?" She had pronounced it with a capital letter.

"Yes, Evil. It doesn't take much for Evil to flourish in the world. People invite it in much more readily than they do Good. Evil is easy, effortless. Good requires action."

I flopped onto the sofa, thinking about my words to Lifeguard Jock. There was a quote from Edmund Burke that I'd spared him, but spoke now to myself. "'The only thing necessary for the triumph of evil is for good men to do nothing.'"

"Exactly." She leaned forward, catching my gaze. We have the same green eyes, and I could see my pale face reflected in hers. "It worries me that your denial may blind you, Maggie. Promise me that while you're applying your formidable brain you won't ignore your intuition."

It sounded so reasonable when she put it that way. But wasn't that why I'd come here, to be bullied into admitting what I couldn't deny any longer?

"Okay." My admission made her relief a palpable thing, as her tension uncoiled from her compact frame. "So how does this thing work?"

Her brows screwed up at the question. "It isn't that simple. It's different for everyone."

"That's not a lot of help, Gran."

"What did you expect? There isn't a magic spell. It's a skill like anything else, and it has to be practiced."

I sighed. Loudly. "That doesn't do me any good right now, though, does it?"

She refreshed her cup of tea with an astounding lack of concern. "You could stop being so stubborn, for one thing. Just let go once in awhile. Trust your instincts."

"Yes, Obi-Wan Kenobi." Gran reached over and tweaked my earlobe, hard. "Ow!"

"Don't be flippant with your elders."

I rubbed my ear. She looked so modern, I sometimes

forgot that my grandmother was old school when it came to getting an erring child's attention.

"While I'm being disrespectful, what's the big idea telling a complete stranger about me?"

"Justin MacCallum? He was so polite and curious about my stories. And so handsome, didn't you think?"

I did, but that was beside the point. "Can't you think of a better way to play matchmaker than telling him I'm a freak?"

Gran gave me an odd look, as if she couldn't believe I was so dense. "Honestly, Maggie. He's a young man who spent his morning recording an old lady's fairy tales and believed without question that The Sight runs in our blood. What makes you think *he's* entirely normal?"

7

In Gran's world, you didn't go to a sickbed empty-handed. I arrived at the hospital bearing a batch of chocolate chip cookies for Karen and for her mother, two paperbacks, a travel toothbrush, a variety of tea bags, and a bottle of aspirin.

Mrs. Foley, who probably had her daughter's friendly smile when her mouth wasn't framed by deep lines of worry, held up the pain reliever in wonder. "How did you know?"

"The Force is strong with my family," I answered. "Do you want to take a break, go down and get a drink or something? I can bore Karen until you get back."

The offer tempted her, but she glanced at her daughter

in the hospital bed. "Go," Karen said. "I'm fine, and Maggie will be here."

She wavered another moment, then said, "I'll just be a few minutes." She picked up her purse and the aspirin.

"No hurry." I turned to Karen. "You look better than the last time I saw you." It was true. Her color had returned and she wasn't covered in blood. She looked pretty good except for the goose-egg on her head. They'd had to shave some of her hair to put in stitches. Maybe she could manage a tasteful comb-over.

"Thanks." She gestured to a chair. "You want to sit down?"

I sat, mostly so she wouldn't have to strain to look up at me. "I'll bet your mom was pretty freaked."

"God. I thought she was going to come apart. But Coach kept telling her: 'Don't give up the ship, Carol. Winners stay focused. Eye on the prize.'" We laughed at her Milner impersonation, and Karen winced, holding her head.

"How about you?" I asked. "How are you feeling?"

"Well, it hurts when I laugh."

"You really scared the crap out of me. Out of all of us." I studied the Technicolor lump on her head. "Have they said when you can go home?"

"They did some X-rays and an MRI. They want to make sure no swelling develops, but it looks pretty good."

"Not on the outside, it doesn't."

"Gee, thanks." A smile told me she hadn't taken offense. "I hope I can get back to school soon. I can't let my grades slip."

I rolled my eyes. "Because a concussion wouldn't be an excuse or anything."

"I'm trailing D and D Lisa for valedictorian. I know she's your friend, but I can't let her off easy."

"No argument here. You should definitely make her work for it." I paused, trying to frame my question without influencing her. "At the pool, you couldn't remember what happened. Has any of it come back to you?"

"Let's see." She gazed at the ceiling, trying to recall. "I remember you turning chicken . . ."

"I did not!" There was a disbelieving pause. "Okay, I totally did. Please continue."

"I climbed on the low board, and heard the hags cackling. And then I started to jump, and that's all I remember."

"So you don't know what went wrong?"

Her forehead knotted, not with pain, but confusion, maybe.

"Coach Milner said I must have placed my foot wrong, not had it all the way on the board."

"Well, she would say that, wouldn't she? I mean, if you slipped, it could have been the equipment, and then the school would be in trouble."

Her brows knit more tightly. "Did I slip?"

"I couldn't really tell what happened." I tried to reassure her. She seemed upset by the hole in her memory, and who could blame her? "It doesn't really matter, does it? I'm just glad you're okay."

"I just had the strangest feeling . . ."

I waited a polite nanosecond, then prompted, "Did you remember something?"

She gave her head a very careful shake. "I don't know. I have this memory of jumping into the air and seeing my shadow underneath me, but it was moving in the wrong direction. I wonder if it's some kind of distortion from banging my head."

"Optical illusion, maybe?" I kept my voice neutral. "That's not so strange."

"That's not the weird part. There was—or I imagined there was—a horrible smell. Like food gone bad. I thought, 'No wonder Maggie doesn't want to jump in there. It smells like a sewer.'" She worried at the memory a little longer, then let it slip away. "And that's the last thing I remember."

With a slightly determined smile, she changed the subject. "I didn't do anything to help you get over your phobia, though. What do they call that? Aquaphobia?"

"I-don't-wanna-die-ophobia."

"Ow! Don't make me laugh."

"Sorry."

We talked about random, unimportant things—gossip, school, homework, college—until her mother came back. Mrs. Foley looked better for the break, and I gave up her seat.

"Here's my cell phone number." I scribbled it on the pad by the phone. "Call me if you need anything or . . . well, anything." I didn't want to say "if anything weird happens," because I wasn't even sure what was normal anymore.

For instance. You could have blown me over when five minutes later I met Stanley Dozer in the hospital lobby. I actually said "Stanley?" though there was no mistaking his pale, gangly form for any other.

"Hi, Maggie." He didn't look very pleased to see me, which, considering he'd called me a bitch the last time we'd met, wasn't really a shock.

"What are you doing here?"

"Mr. Yanachek asked me to bring Karen her math homework." He held up a folder and didn't meet my eye.

"That's nice of you." Considering that you called *her* a dork, I added silently.

"Yeah, well. No one else wanted to do it."

"You really try and spread sunshine and light wherever you go, don't you, Stanley?" He looked at me blankly. I sighed. "I'll take it up for you, so you don't pain yourself."

"No. I have to explain the problems. You'll never understand it."

"There are lots of things I'll never understand," I said as I strode past him. Then I paused. "Hey, Stanley. What did you mean when you said that everyone who picked on you was going to be sorry?"

He gave me a long, unreadable stare, then shrugged. "You know what I mean. I'll join the space program, and they'll end up like their kind always do: fat, divorced, and managing a Safeway."

Yeah, well, *there* was a fate worse than death.

I watched him go, wondering if there was something different about him, or if it was his outburst yesterday that changed my viewpoint. I didn't spend too much time on it, though. I had bigger fish to fry. It was time for some old-fashioned sleuthing. I was going to have to unleash my inner Nancy Drew.

8

Maybe Nancy Drew isn't the coolest role model. There are a lot more kick-ass heroines nowadays, like Buffy and that chick from *Alias*. But I had a retro fondness for the girl detective. I didn't know what I'd find at the pool, but I knew I had to take a closer look. If Karen caught a whiff of icky weirdness, too, then it wasn't just my freaky intuition.

The school was far from deserted when I pulled into the parking lot. The baseball and basketball teams had practice. There was a meeting of the decorating committee for the You-Know-What. There would be people still in the newspaper and yearbook offices. And of course, rehearsals for the musical would go until late.

I was worried the aquatics gym might be locked, or full of swimmers, but my timing was good. As I wove through the locker room, a bunch of dripping, broad-shouldered girls passed on the way to the showers, chattering about split times and fly strokes. I acted like I was supposed to be there, nodding to them and walking purposefully to the pool entrance.

I hung back against the wall until I saw the boys and their coach pass, leaving the gym empty. My rubber-soled shoes squeaked on the tile as I ventured in. The high dive loomed at the end of the vaulted building, the low board squatting alongside like its own little henchman.

I forced myself to the lip of the diving pool and looked down. A wave of vertigo hit me, as if I were standing on the edge of a high building. If I fell, the water would swallow me, suck me under, as whatever lurked unseen in the depths captured me with fins and tentacles and dagger-like teeth.

Get a grip, Maggie. Sweat prickled under my arms. *What would Nancy do?*

She wouldn't let her imagination defeat her, that's for sure. Taking my camera from my bag, I inspected the safe end of the low board first, working up to the hard part. No greasy spots, no loose screws. When I could put it off no longer, I hung my camera around my neck and grabbed the handrail. Nothing left to do but walk the plank.

My palms left foggy prints on the metal as I edged toward the end of the railing and stopped. My next step would be over the water. I extended my foot . . .

And retreated.

My inner chicken was firmly in control.

"All right, Mags." My voice rang in the empty gym. "Don't be ridiculous. Suck it up and just do it."

God. I sounded like my mother, gene-spliced with Coach Milner. But it had become a point of honor now.

Fists white-knuckled on the railing, I lowered myself to straddle the board. Then I scooted out, my center of gravity glued to the fiberglass. A ridiculous method of locomotion, but it worked. My feet dangled over twenty-one fathoms of water.

I reached the end with a thrill of satisfaction that quickly turned to disappointment. I'd risked my continued enjoyment of oxygen for nothing. But then I ran my finger over the textured surface and left a swath of lighter-blue behind.

A strange grimy blackness outlined the whorls of my fingerprints. It wasn't slippery, like motor oil, though there *was* an oily sort of quality. But sooty, like the stuff that collects on the chimney glass of a hurricane lamp.

Could it have caused Karen to slip? I didn't think so. I could vouch for the nonskid treatment of the board; my jeans had rasped with every scoot. Plus, no one else had fallen and the scum coated the board in a thin, complete layer.

After photographing several angles, I sat for a moment, getting the courage to unclamp my legs and move again. I knew I should appease my grandmother by looking at this with my, I don't know, instinct, inner sight, third eye, whatever you want to call it. But I didn't know how to begin. I'd been slamming shut the door of my skepticism for so long, I had no idea how to open it.

I sighed and gave up trying to make it happen. As soon as I did, I got a flash, clear as a bell: I had to get out of there. The sudden certainty of it made my stomach jump and twist.

I hurried, but not even the *Amityville Horror* moment could make me anything less than overcautious. I scooted backward the same way I'd gone out, and as soon as I was over dry land I swung off the board, grabbed my backpack, and fled.

✳   ✳   ✳

The locker room was empty except for the drip of the showers and the musty smell of mildew and old sneakers, but the feeling didn't abate. I ducked out, and the door had just closed behind me when I saw Halloran headed down the hall, wearing a face like thunder.

"Margaret Quinn!"

First of all, my name is not Margaret. Second of all, no one could hold a candle to my mother when it came to the Invocation of the Full Name. The mere threat of Mom bellowing "Magdalena Lorraine Quinn!" had always guaranteed my unwavering obedience. All other attempts at given-name intimidation fell far short by comparison, especially when attempted by ex-Jock assistant principals who couldn't be bothered to get it right.

"What are you doing back here?" He might not know my name, but he did know that I didn't darken the door of the gym unless my graduation credits demanded it.

"I left my swimsuit in the locker room. But the door is locked, so I couldn't get it."

Eyeing me suspiciously, he tested the door. It didn't budge. No mojo there; I had heard it latch behind me. Unable to catch me out in a lie, he turned grumpy. "What are you doing at school so late?"

"I need to take some pictures of play practice." Boy, those thespians were darned handy.

"Well, I'm headed that way myself. I'll walk with you."

The auditorium was in the opposite direction from my car. But if Halloran suspected I'd been taking pictures of the diving board he'd confiscate my camera in a second, on the remotest possibility of a lawsuit.

So I let him escort me to C Hall. He watched me all the way up to the auditorium doors, where I slipped in without saying thanks.

Rehearsal was in full swing; compared to that morning, it was a marvel of organization. On the stage was a simple but artistic set and in front of it Thespica danced in a blue gingham dress, singing about chicks and ducks. Honesty forces me to admit she seemed quite good, for someone singing about farm animals.

The drama teacher saw me. I held up my camera, then pointed at the stage. He nodded and went back to scribbling notes on a legal pad. I found a good angle and took some shots of the star, then of her "Granny" as she came onstage in a frumpy outfit that *my* granny wouldn't be caught dead in. Though the same could be said of the farm, really.

When they stopped the action to work out a scene change, I slipped backstage, thinking I might grab a couple of pictures of the crew. Foolishly, I did not realize it would be pitch-dark there. The only lights were blue—either a blue bulb or a normal work light with some kind of blue plastic covering it.

"Hey," said a guy in a black T-shirt, looking officious. "You're not supposed to be back here."

"I wanted to get a look behind the scenes. At the unsung heroes, you know." Yes, shameless flattery is my friend.

"Well . . . all right. But try and stay out of the way."

"Thanks." I edged toward the wall, where a blue light illuminated a stand with a script on it. Backstage was not as big as I thought. Set pieces and actors and crew were stuffed tightly in the available space.

I think the black clothes were supposed to make the stage crew inconspicuous, but I noticed Stanley Dozer almost immediately, despite the crowded darkness. Man, that boy kept turning up like a six-foot, five-inch bad penny.

Still more interesting, he looked nothing like the sour dweeb I'd seen earlier. I watched him bend to listen to something a girl in costume said, then he gave a muted laugh.

Stanley Dozer, you fickle son of a gun. I couldn't judge if the girl returned his interest, but his infatuation was plain on his homely face.

"Dude."

It took a moment to realize that someone was talking to me. I'm not the girliest girl ever, but no one has ever mistaken me for a guy before.

"Dude." The guy at the prompting stand repeated it until I turned. "Your ass is glowing."

"What?" Definitely not something I expected to hear in the normal run of things.

"Your ass is glowing. Dude, what did you sit in?"

I craned around to look. Sure enough, in the deep violet lamplight, the seat of my jeans glowed fluorescent blue.

Great. A radioactive butt. What a topper for the wedding cake of disaster that had been my day.

9

finally, all those *CSI* reruns were going to pay off. As soon as I got out to my Jeep, I stripped off my jeans and tucked them into a plastic grocery sack, tying off the top to preserve the evidence. Of course, this meant I had to drive home in my underwear, but I had a ratty old wool picnic blanket in the back of the car. I wrapped it around my waist, and headed home.

Beltline was the most direct road, but it was the main drag through Avalon, and always clogged with traffic. The street led past the most important places in town: the red brick downtown area, the university, my school, the hospital, and if you kept going it would take you to the mall near the state highway bypass, the "new" high school (built only twenty years ago), and the treeless subdivisions where my dad refused to live. Going south you'd pass the Wal-Mart, the bars that catered to people who wanted to drink more than dance, and eventually the lumber mill and the paper plant, thankfully far enough away that it only stank when the wind was very strong from the southwest.

The upshot of this arrangement was that Beltline was the last road you'd want to take when you were bottomless in a topless Jeep.

The back way home wound through a residential area, between a park and the west side of the university campus. There was exactly one traffic light on the route. I was stopped there, mulling over the glow-in-the-dark spooge, when I heard my name.

"Maggie?" Justin MacCallum was loitering on the corner, wearing a sweat-soaked T-shirt and athletic shorts. His short hair stood up in damp spikes, which emphasized the clean, chiseled planes of his face. And the rest of him . . . Wow. Michelangelo could have sculpted those thighs.

He smiled as though I hadn't been in a total snit the last time he'd seen me. "I thought that was you."

"What are you doing here?" Not the most intelligent question, but at least I managed to drag my gaze up to his face.

"I was running in the park."

"Running from what?" The light turned green and the car behind me honked. With a gesture to Justin, I pulled through the intersection and into the tree-shaded parking lot.

I turned in the seat as he jogged over. "Actually, I have a question for you."

He looked surprised. But then, so was I. The words had sort of popped out of my mouth. My thoughts were going in a bizarre direction, and I would have rejected the idea completely, except maybe I still had my Nancy Drew thing going on, and good detectives don't eliminate things without examining them from all angles.

"Okay, shoot," he said, with a crooked sort of smile.

The afternoon was warm and humid, and the wool blanket was extremely itchy, but I tried not to scratch. "Is there really such a thing as ectoplasm?"

"Ectoplasm?" His eyebrows shot up in surprise.

"You know how in *Ghostbusters,* when the ghosts leave behind that slime when they touch something?"

"Why are you asking *me*?"

"Because you're the one getting a degree in weirdology."

He opened his mouth to argue, then shut it, mulled over a few responses, and finally settled on, "Do you think you've seen a ghost?"

"I don't know. Maybe." I'd begun thinking about phantoms when Karen told me about the shadow, even before I found the fluorescent soot. "I'm considering all possibilities."

Justin seemed intrigued; he leaned on the roll bar of the Jeep and I couldn't help thinking that he smelled awfully good for such a sweaty guy. "Okay. The way I understand it, ectoplasm is—supposedly—an ethereal substance that manifests when a spirit is present, like while a medium is channeling at a séance."

"So it's sort of like a psychic snail trail?"

His brows twitched in suppressed laughter. "I haven't heard it described in quite that way."

I thought about taking issue with his amusement, but stayed focused. "But does the stuff actually exist?"

"There was a lot of research done when that kind of spiritualism was popular at the turn of the twentieth century. But there are so many frauds, it's hard to say."

I pursed my lips, dissatisfied with the nonanswer. "What about you? Do *you* think it exists?"

"I keep an open mind." He smiled at my frustrated sound. "I have some books." A pause, while he seemed to mull something over. "That's my dorm there. Drive over and I'll get them for you."

"Sorry. I can't. I'm not wearing any pants." Now *there* was a phrase I never thought I'd say out loud.

"Oh." He glanced down, then quickly back to my face. "I just thought that was a very ugly skirt."

"Thanks." I grabbed my phone from the drink holder. "What's your number? In case I have more questions."

He rattled it off and I punched SAVE.

"What if I want to get in touch with you?" he asked.

"About my alleged psychic powers?"

"Maybe."

"Then think about me real hard, and I'll know to give you a call." I flashed a sunny smile, put the Jeep in gear, and drove away. For the first time that day, I felt as if I'd gotten the upper hand in a human interaction.

✳ ✳ ✳

I dreamed of blue fire that night, burning in a big, beaten metal bowl, with engravings scrolling around the edges.

There was liquid in the brazier, too. It didn't quench the fire, but made the clean blue flame hiss and spit and throw out thick black smoke. As the darkness rose, it didn't drift aimlessly, but pulled into the center and coalesced into a shapeless mass.

I watched, both repulsed and fascinated as the thing built itself from soot and shadow. It seethed above the flames with sentient awareness. Though it had no eyes, I knew the moment it looked back at me. Somehow, on some strange dream plane, it saw me. More than that, it *recognized* me.

A shock of fear and revulsion jolted me awake. My eyes opened but I lay frozen, afraid to move in case some *thing* was there, in the room with me. I heard nothing but the blood pounding in my ears, saw nothing in the stripes of moonlight that fell through the curtains. I forced myself to turn my head, to search the darkness, but I was alone.

Just a dream. I repeated it like a mantra.

Then I whispered it like a prayer.

✳ ✳ ✳

I woke in a lousy mood. I had washed underwear and shirts the night before, but my last marginally clean pair of jeans had been bagged and tagged. I found a casual skirt and put it on with a sunny yellow T-shirt and a pair of Converse. Mom's reaction when I reached the kitchen was predictable.

"Is that what you're wearing?"

I got my coffee cup out of the dishwasher as I answered. "No. I just put it on to annoy you."

"If you would go to bed at a decent hour, you wouldn't be so grumpy in the morning." She frowned at my extra-tall travel mug. "You wouldn't need to drink so much coffee, either."

"It's my drug of choice, Mom. Be grateful."

She sighed. "I know. I just thank God you turned out as well as you did."

I cast her a grumpy look on my way to the door. "It's nice to know you think I could have turned out worse."

Her voice followed me out. "You need to eat some breakfast!"

I scored an excellent parking spot at school, and was downing the last of my coffee when a shadow fell across me.

"Cheese and Crackers!" I screeched and mopped at the splashes on my skirt. "What is it with you and sneaking up on people?"

Bobby Baywatch smiled. "Sorry. I didn't mean to scare you."

"It's been a rough couple of days. I'm a little jumpy."

"I noticed." His hair had pale highlights from the sun, which might have looked girly on someone else. With his tan and his lifeguard physique, though, it worked.

"Can I help you carry anything?"

"Let me get out of the car, first."

I loved my Wrangler. My trusty steed was safari brown—mostly—and bore the scars of a long and useful life. But it was impossible to exit with any grace. It figured I would be wearing a skirt.

Once I'd lost my dignity but gained my feet, I handed him my books then grabbed my backpack and the plastic bag of jeans. He ignored my attempts to reclaim the heavy stack of texts, and started walking toward school. "Hey, Sir

Lancelot." I trotted after him. "Isn't there a Jessica looking for you somewhere?"

He shortened his stride; considerate of him not to make me run to keep up. "There might be, but that's her business. I'm friends with Brandon and Jeff. I don't . . . None of the girls is . . ."

"Your girlfriend?" I felt sorry for any girl who was, since he couldn't even say the word.

"Right."

"My mistake. Three guys, three girls. You always look paired off like tasty packs of snack cakes."

"Well, we're not."

We passed the tennis courts and the gym, and curiosity got the better of me. "So are you stalking me, or what?"

He stopped, and I did, too, since he had my books. "Listen, I'm sorry about what happened in the locker room yesterday."

The day had been so jam-packed with wackitude that it took me a moment to realize what he meant. As soon as I did, my heart twisted in dread. I could literally feel the blood drain from my face, like someone had pulled a plug. "The picture? She actually sent it out?"

"No." His quick reassurance didn't make me stop wishing for a bathroom to hide in. "She just showed it to the gang."

"Oh, just to the six people who hate me the most. Great. I hope you had a good laugh." The blood had rushed back to my head, making my ears burn.

"Well, *I* didn't laugh."

I groaned and covered my face with my hand. *Okay, get a*

grip, Maggie. What would D&D Lisa say? So they laughed at me. No novelty there. At least I could honestly say that nobody's opinion mattered less to me than the Jocks and Jessicas.

Bobby Baywatch was watching me like I might burst into tears. "I'm really sorry."

I glared up at him, not hysterical, just pissed. "Why do you keep apologizing for things that aren't your fault?"

His shoulders lifted in a shrug. "I guess because they're my friends, I feel responsible."

"Maybe you need to find new friends." I reached for my books, but he held them out of reach.

"Let me walk you inside. Maybe it will help."

His intention dawned on me, absurd as it was. "Are you offering me the protection of your reputation?" My sense of humor was returning along with my perspective, and I gave a short laugh at his chagrin. "Boy, you *do* feel guilty."

"I'm sure not offering because of your charming personality."

"Oh, ouch." I put out my hands. "At least let me carry my own books. This isn't *Our Town.*"

He handed them over and we walked the rest of the way into school, mostly in silence. Embarrassment aside, I didn't have a social standing to preserve, but it was a nice gesture. I didn't want to like him, but he was making it hard not to, just a little.

✳ ✳ ✳

With a half hour before the bell, I found Professor Blackthorne in his chemistry classroom, drawing molecules on the board. He heard my groan and turned.

"Not a fan of organic compounds, Miss Quinn?"

"I would say no, but I'm here to ask a favor."

"A chemistry favor?" He didn't *quite* rub his hands together in anticipation. "Have you brought me something interesting?"

"Maybe." I set the grocery sack on the lab bench and untied the handles. As the plastic bag opened, we both took a hasty step backward. A horrible odor escaped, like when you accidentally open something green and fuzzy from the very back of the fridge, only about fifty times worse.

"Good God, girl!" Blackthorne blinked his watering eyes. "Did something die wearing these trousers?"

"They didn't smell that bad last night. Maybe the fumes built up in the closed bag."

"Possible." The stench was dissipating slightly in the well-ventilated lab, but I felt sorry for the first-period class. Blackthorne put on a pair of gloves before he touched the denim. "Now, let's see what you've brought me."

"Do you have a blacklight?"

He pointed toward a cabinet where I found a handheld lamp. I turned off the overhead; even with the residual light from the windows, we could see the eerie phosphorescence under the ultraviolet glow. "I sat on something."

"Obviously." He scratched his chin. "I'm loathe to think in what sort of seedy places you've been spending your time."

"Okay, that's just . . . eiew."

"No Dumpster diving recently? Well, smells can be deceiving."

"There's a test to figure out what that stuff is, right?"

"Certainly. Gas chromatography."

"So can you work some *CSI* magic on those pants?"

"Not here. This is a high school chemistry lab. I have difficulty getting money to buy paper towels." Brow furrowed, he drummed his thumbs against the slate lab bench. "We could send it to Dr. Smyth at the university. She owes me a favor."

"Excellent!"

"They may have to take a sample from your trousers, though."

"You mean cut a hole in them?" I really liked those jeans; they made my butt look great. Honestly, the sacrifices a detective has to make. "When do you think she can do it?"

"I'll take them to her after school. She'll have to work it into her schedule, though." He bundled the jeans back up, then put the grocery sack inside a small trash bag and tied it closed. I didn't blame him for doubling up. I'd thought the stench was bad in my dream, but smelling it through my real, live nose was the difference between a cheap pair of headphones and a symphony orchestra of stink.

"Hey, Professor Blackthorne." I followed him to the chalkboard. "Is that what sulfur smells like?"

Hexagon chemical bonds had his attention again. "Hmm? No, sulfur doesn't have a smell."

"I thought it did. That whole 'stench of brimstone' thing."

"Burning sulfur gives off sulfur dioxide, which is probably what that phrase means. It's noxious and extremely irritating to the lungs." He added a few more notations to the diagram on the board. "Though you may be thinking about the thiols—the sulfhydryl group. They are quite odiferous. In fact, ethanethiol is added to natural gas so that leaks can be detected by the 'rotten egg' smell."

"So maybe that's what's on the jeans?"

"Do you want to open them back up and take a whiff, or wait for the chromatograph?"

"Um, no. I'll wait for the test."

"As you wish." I shouldered my backpack and started out. His voice stopped me at the door. "If you want my opinion, and not a scientific fact, I'd lay money that either putrescine or cadaverine will be in the mix." He went back to writing, talking more to himself than to me. "Yes. I think I'll make a bet with Dr. Smyth. See if the nose still knows."

Boy, I could have gone my whole life without knowing I'd gotten something named after a putrid cadaver on my butt. On the upside, though, I was no longer ambivalent about destroying those pants.

10

I knew that my personal humiliation had a limited comedic lifespan, but I didn't expect to have turned invisible before second period.

"What's up?" I asked Jennifer Fitzwilliam, catching up to her on the way to class. She was the most reliable source of gossip in the entire school. If someone bought someone else a Coke at lunch, five minutes later Jennifer would have the scoop on when they'd met, whether they were going out, and if they were, how many dates they'd had before going all the way.

"Jess Michaels"—translation: Jess Minor—"showed up

wearing a knockoff Donna Karan top, and Jessica Prentice"—a.k.a. Prime—"spilled the beans in front of everyone. Jess threw her Snapple in Jessica's face, and we were all set for a catfight, but Brian Kirkpatrick got between them and broke it up."

"Brian Kirkpatrick?"

"You know. Swim team, baseball team. The guy who carried your books into school today," she added with a coy look.

So that was his real name. He was Brian Baywatch, not Bobby. I had to admit, Bob would be a sad name for anyone in the lifeguard profession.

"Was it really a knockoff?" I asked.

"Seems to be. Ironic, isn't it?" We'd reached the journalism room, which was buzzing with a frantic kind of schizophrenia as students bounced from being reporters, to editors, to publishers, trying to get the paper laid out in time to send to the printer.

"What's ironic?" I dropped my backpack beside my desk.

"Well, Jess Michaels is something of a fashionista, isn't she?"

"True," I answered, but I was losing interest in the Jessicas and their drama, and I was glad when Jennifer continued to her own desk so I could get to work on more important things.

In addition to the little piece about the Big Spring Musical, I'd written a few inches about Karen and her fall. Besides being newsworthy, it gave me the excuse to look into the history of the "natatorium" to see if there was any kind of trend of suspicious accidents. The building wasn't very old, especially compared to the parts of the school that dated back to the 1940s. I found nothing in the paper's online archives, which only meant that I had to broaden my search.

"Quinn!" Phillip, the student editor, had watched too many movies with irascible newsmen bellowing for their errant reporters. All he lacked was the cigar and the beer belly. "Where's your copy!"

"On its way, Chief." I knew he'd miss the sarcasm in the title. Ghosthunting would have to wait until the paper was put to bed. I wonder if Brenda Starr ever had this problem?

✳ ✳ ✳

By lunchtime a rampant rumor was circulating that Jess Minor shopped at Wal-Mart. In P.E. the tension hung thick in the air. Jess and Jessica ignored each other with an acid deliberateness, and Thespica tried to act as though there were nothing wrong. A few hangers-on were quick to exploit this possible opening in the inner circle. When Jessica Prime snapped her fingers, one sycophant supplied a hairbrush. When she needed a nail file, another one appeared. And when she said, "I look so fat in this" (at least five times), all the toadies were quick to reassure her it wasn't so.

I ignored this, or tried to, while I searched for the Get Out of Diving Free note Dad had written. It turned out to be unnecessary. Coach Milner came in and announced:

"I want you all to know that I believe we should get right back on that horse and not give up the ship. But the administration has decided that we will finish up the aquatics unit by practicing our racing dives in the lap pool."

Oh fabulous day! No more diving board, and soon, no more swimming pool, either. Things were looking up.

✳ ✳ ✳

Despite organic compounds in chemistry and a film in civics that was so old, Chief Justice Rehnquist was alive and well and still had a full head of hair, my good mood carried me all the way to the parking lot that afternoon. There was a cherry limeade in my future, and research in the city newspaper archives, but first . . .

But first, furious Jocks. My steps slowed warily on the asphalt as I saw a familiar threesome, the Jessica's masculine counterparts—Biff/Brandon, Brian Baywatch, and Henchman Jeff—in a taut group, the air around them blue with curses. Jeff authored most of the profanity, aimed at the rassin', frassin', son of a gun who had scratched the beautiful, cherry red, vintage Mustang. I paraphrase, of course.

The entire school knew how Jeff Espinoza lavished love and attention on that car. And he was a big guy. I had to say, that was one brave rassin' frassin' son of a gun.

"What are you looking at, Quinn?" Jeff was eager to transfer his rage to a handy target.

"Yeah," Brandon echoed. "Where's your camera? You could take a picture. It would last longer."

"Thanks, Mr. Originality. But some people I'd rather forget."

He took a menacing step forward, but Brian grabbed his arm and redirected his attention to the car, and soon they were once more cursing the walking dead man who had damaged Jeff's manhood.

I left them to it and hurried to my own car. The phone rang just as the engine grumbled to life. "Hi, Gran."

"What is this about a ghost? Why do I have to hear from someone else? Have you lost my phone number? Do I have to draw you a map to my house?"

"I'm well, thank you for asking. How are you?"

"Madder than a wet hen."

"I guess Justin MacTattletale called."

"He's here now. I *knew* something otherworldly was at work near you. Come over this instant."

"I have to stop by and see my friend in the hospital."

"Are you coming over after that?"

"Yes, ma'am." This seemed to appease her. "Put the fink on the phone."

"Justin is a nice young man. You should be glad he told me what you were up to."

I plucked at my T-shirt; it was hot with the late April sun bearing down on the roofless Jeep. "Just put him on. I'll see you in an hour, tops."

She murmured dire predictions if I didn't make good on that, and a moment later I heard a baritone voice on the line. "Hello?"

"Go in the other room." I fished in the glove box for my headset so I could drive and chew him out at the same time.

"Why?"

"Because I'm going to yell at you and I don't want Gran to hear."

"If you had given me your number . . ."

"Oh, don't *even* go there. You could have just asked her for it."

"Yeah. I could have." But then he couldn't have needled me. He left that part unspoken, but I heard his amusement.

"So what do you want?"

"I brought you some books on . . ." I heard Gran banging around in the background. "On what you asked me about yesterday."

"You didn't have to do that."

"I didn't want you using *Ghostbusters* as a definitive source."

"Thanks." I pulled out of the parking lot and onto the drag. "I need to stop by to see my friend. You want to wait at Gran's, or what?"

"I'll wait. There are cookies."

"Those are *my* cookies. There had better be some left when I get there."

"No problem." His voice dropped in volume. "I think your grandmother cooks when she's worried."

"She's not worried, just irked I didn't tell her first. See you in an hour."

Was it weird that I was more pleased than pissed that he'd tracked me down through Gran? If he hadn't gotten her worked up, I wouldn't be upset at all that a college guy wanted to help me bust ghosts.

✳ ✳ ✳

Karen was alone when I tapped on the hospital door. "Boy, you must be bored if you're doing homework."

She looked up from a dog-eared copy of *Animal Farm* and grimaced. "Trying to stay caught up, remember."

"You are an inspiration."

"Not really. I can only read a little at a time before my head starts to hurt. I haven't even started the calculus homework that Stanley brought me."

"Speaking of Stanley—" Because it seemed like I was doing that a lot lately. "Has he seemed a little . . . gruff to you?"

She shrugged. "We're all ready to be done with school."

"Good point. Any word when you get to go home?"

"Maybe tomorrow. They sort of freak out when you lose consciousness, even for just a minute. And they're worried about pneumonia from inhaling pool water."

I touched her hand. "I'm so sorry, Karen."

"You keep saying that." Her smile was gently quizzical. "It's not your fault."

How weird that this morning I'd been on the other side of the exact same exchange with Brian. Maybe I was having the same kind of guilt that my inaction had somehow put Karen in harm's way. "It isn't logical. But you took my place in line and . . ." I took a deep breath. It seemed as good a time as any to ask to perform my little experiment. "And I keep thinking about your shadow. The one you mentioned yesterday."

Her eyes narrowed. "You mean the one you said was probably an optical illusion?"

"Uh, yeah. But, well, this is going to sound crazy, but . . ."

"But you don't think it was my shadow." I must have looked surprised that she said it so plainly and so calmly. She smiled ruefully. "I haven't had anything else to do but think about it, Maggie. I know my own shadow, and I know when something is . . ." She struggled for the right word. "Foreign."

I let out a pent-up breath. This was going to be easier than I'd thought. "Do you mind if I do a little experiment?"

"Nope. I'm relieved you don't think I'm off the deep end."

I dug into my backpack and took out the blacklight I'd borrowed from the chemistry lab. I did ask. I'm not sure that Blackthorne really heard me—he'd been happily explaining carbon bonds to a glassy-eyed student—but I *did* ask.

I had a distinct memory of the way Karen's leg had shot out from under her, as if it had been yanked. Flipping off the light, and feeling ridiculous, I shone the lamp on her ankle, and saw a familiar fluorescent glow.

"Oh my God." Karen stared at her own foot as if it belonged to someone else. "What is that? And why didn't it come off when I washed?"

"Honestly, I don't know." I didn't see a reason to mention putrescine or cadaverine. "I found it on the diving board, too."

"What do you think it is?" Her brown eyes searched mine, avidly curious. I still hesitated.

"It sounds kind of crazy."

"I promise I won't laugh." I gave her a narrow-eyed look and she raised her hand, as if taking an oath. "Scout's honor."

"Okay. Have you ever seen the movie *Ghostbusters*?"

11

I arrived at Gran's house with fifty-nine seconds to spare. Justin sat at the kitchen table, books spread around him. He was wearing jeans today, and another oxford shirt, untucked this time, and there was chocolate smeared at the corner of his mouth.

"How's your friend?" he asked as I came in.

"Pretty amazing, actually." I was stunned at how easily Karen had accepted the idea of the supernatural, and more to the point, how non-freaked-out she was at having been touched by it. I'd only *dreamed* about the shadow and I was kinda wigged.

"Have you ever known someone for years, and then

something happens, and all of a sudden you realize you've never really known them at all?"

"I think we've all done that." He didn't look particularly freaked out, either. Was I the only one who was dizzy from spinning back and forth between "this is real" and "this is crazy"?

I picked up one of the books: *Ghosts and Specters: An Empirical Study.* Another one was, *A History of Paranormal Experience.* And another: *The Literature of the Supernatural.*

"I thought you were a history major."

"I'm getting my bachelor's in history. I want to do graduate studies in the anthropology of myth and occult experience."

"That should open up a world of career choices for you." I set the book down. It was the size of a toaster but considerably heavier. "What made you choose an advanced degree in creepy?"

He shrugged. "I've always been interested in the theory of the supernatural. My upbringing wasn't exactly conventional."

"Do you have a nutty grandmother, too?"

Her voice came from the other room. "I hear you!"

"I love you, Gran!" I called back, then poured myself some tea and sat down near the plate of cookies. "Anything on ectoplasm?"

Justin folded his arms on the table. "Let's back up a bit. Tell me why you think you've encountered a ghost."

Gran bustled into the kitchen, carrying a load of laundry. "I want to hear this. Since it's the only way I'll know what my granddaughter is up to."

Sighing, I took a chocolate chip cookie for fortification.

While Gran folded towels and Justin made notes, I told him about my frustratingly vague dream, and the unease I couldn't shake. I described the strange awkwardness of Karen's fall, and the smell I might have just imagined. I related her glimpse of a shadow moving over the water. When I finished describing my impromptu detective work, they both stared at me.

"What?"

"I'm just stunned," said Justin. "Because yesterday you seemed very, um, resistant to the idea that you might have some extrasensory perception. And now you're tracking down a ghost."

"First of all, I don't have ESP. I don't bend spoons or see dead people, or any of that freaky stuff. I just have good intuition." From the corner of my eye I saw Gran roll hers, but she didn't say anything. "Second, I'm not tracking a ghost. I'm investigating the possibility it *might* be a ghost."

He gave me a look I was starting to recognize. It meant he thought I was funny but didn't want to piss me off by laughing. "Okay. Let's be logical about this, then. What makes you think it's a ghost?"

"Well, the shadow, I guess." The evidence seemed sparse, once I tried to lay it out. "And the spooge it leaves behind."

"Which we don't know is related." He wrote down "shadow" but not "spooge." "It could be nothing more than a strange sort of mold or mildew."

I snapped, irritated at his skepticism. "You're the Mulder here. *I'm* the Scully."

"I'm just helping you be objective." He tapped his pen on the pad. "What else?"

"The smell," I said. "There's that awful smell."

"Okay." He jotted it down. "That's good. What about a feeling of cold or dread?"

"No cold. And I was faced with a bottomless well of dark water, so I wouldn't have noticed any extra dread."

"A sense of another presence?"

"Lots of people were around when Karen fell." I thought a moment. "But I did have a weird feeling later, when I went back."

"You can't be more specific?"

I raised my hands in a shrug. "It's not like telling if the lights are on or off. It's ambiguous. I was nervous about getting caught."

Again the pen tapped, an aggravated rhythm. "Your perceptions aren't a lot of help."

"Sorry. Next time I'll bring my spectrometer."

Gran spoke up, preventing an argument. "What about history? Has there ever been another incident or accident in the pool, or even the gym?"

"I didn't find anything in the school newspaper about the pool, but the online records only go back five years. I'm going to check the city paper archives tonight, and the microfiche at the library tomorrow."

"Good plan." Justin closed his notebook and started gathering his books. "Strange that those other girls were able to dive without anything happening. Karen must have been the unlucky number."

I must have reacted to that, because he looked at me closely. "What is it?"

"Nothing." I shook my head. Gran had taken the plates to the kitchen a few feet away.

His expression said I hadn't fooled him, but he let it go. He said his polite good-byes to Gran and as she saw him to the door, I took our cups to the sink, rinsed them, and put them in the dishwasher. By the time I'd finished, Gran had returned. She put her arms around me and kissed my hair.

"I am so proud of you."

"What for?"

"For opening your mind to the possibility of things you cannot see with your eyes."

The praise embarrassed me, since I hadn't so much flung wide my mind as cracked open the door with the safety chain still firmly in place. "It's no big deal, Gran."

"It is a very big deal." She cupped my face in her hands. "You have so much potential to do good things in the world. But you be careful. Listen to that intuition and be smart."

"Yes, Gran." I hugged her back. "I will."

I told her I'd keep in touch, then grabbed my stuff and let myself out the front door. I wasn't surprised to see Justin MacCallum still outside, leaning against the fender of my car and looking serious.

"So, what happened?" he asked, in a tone that didn't allow any arguments.

"Karen switched places with me in line at the diving pool," I said, giving in without a fight. "I've been convincing myself it was just random luck."

He thought for a moment, then said, "That's probably all it was." Another considering pause. "But . . ."

I groaned. Was there any more ominous word in the English language?

"But," he continued, ignoring my drama, "you should keep your guard up. There's a theory in science that the very act of observation can influence a situation. Once you start looking closely at something, it might start looking back at you."

Last night's installment of the subconscious creepshow came slamming back into my brain so hard that I flinched. Justin didn't need any ESP to interpret it.

"Something looked back at you, didn't it." He didn't bother to make it a question. "When? At the pool?"

"Last night. I saw the fire again, but this time the smoke thing . . . It *looked* at me, just like you said." I shook my head. "It was a dream, but it feels like it really happened."

"We should assume it did."

I liked that "we." Justin had a steadiness that made me glad to have him on my side. "Maybe your vision was a warning, that the spirit has noticed you. Or maybe you met in some kind of dream plane. I don't know."

I rubbed a hand over my eyes. I'd had a sort of buzzing in the back of my brain all day and the thought of wearing a supernatural bull's-eye ratcheted it up to a head-splitting volume.

Justin's hand touched my shoulder. "You okay?" I shot him a what-do-you-think look, and he lifted his hands in surrender. "Stupid question. Sorry."

I sagged into the driver's seat, half in, half out of the car.

"Four days ago my life was simple. All I had to worry about was avoiding the prom and living through graduation."

He ignored my whining and cut to the heart of the matter. "What happened four days ago?"

"I had the nightmare." I ran my hand over the leather-wrapped steering wheel, the rough bumps and tears keeping me anchored, and away from the deep water of fear and supposition. "And something inside me . . . woke up."

"Woke up?"

"That's what it felt like. I hadn't had a dream in years. At least not one I couldn't ignore." I sighed. "They ought to come with an instruction manual."

He didn't give even a courtesy laugh. He was deep in thought. "Weird."

"That's the understatement of the century."

"No, I mean, I wonder which woke first, the spirit or your visions?"

✳ ✳ ✳

What kind of ghost-hunter has to put the spirit world on hold while she finishes her homework?

The outline for my English paper had been unfairly disapproved by my teacher. Jonathan Swift was over two hundred and fifty years dead, so unless Ms. Vincent had a direct pipeline to the afterlife, I couldn't see a reason for her to call my well-annotated suppositions bunk. Then again, if she did have the ability to communicate with the dead, maybe she could actually be of some use to my current situation, which would definitely be a novelty for Ms. Vincent.

An instant messenger window popped up while I was knee-deep in Lilliputians.

0v3rl0rdL15a: Where did you go after civics? You shot out of there before I could ask you about the English homework.

I clicked over to the IM window and typed back:

MightyQuinn: We have English homework?
0v3rl0rdL15a: Five paragraph essay question on the last Act of Julius C.
MightyQuinn: :P I didn't want to sleep tonight, anyway.

We kept the chat window open while we worked, which probably wasn't very efficient, but I felt less lonely in my room. The sound of my parents puttering around downstairs made the house seem normal and safe. Even the sheer mundane boredom of homework settled my nerves and made my fears seem a little foolish. When I finished my paragraphs on J.C., I was even able to pick up the book Justin had lent me and thumb through it with a certain detachment.

It seemed weird that I hadn't talked about all this with my closest friend. Despite the D&D thing, Lisa was a rock of unflappable logic. I'd never told her about the dreams I'd had as a kid, never talked about my intuition. I didn't want her to think I was a flake. Even though I was beginning to admit that I was, quite possibly, exactly that.

MightyQuinn: Hey Lisa . . . Hypothetical question.
Ov3rl0rdL15a: ?
MightyQuinn: Do you believe in ghosts?

There was a long pause. Maybe she was just analyzing Julius Caesar and not deleting my name from her address book or marking it: "Nutjob."

Ov3rl0rdL15a: You mean cold spots in a room, or poltergeists, or what?
MightyQuinn: I dunno. Either one.
Ov3rl0rdL15a: Why do you want to know?
MightyQuinn: I'm not going to publish it in the paper. It's just a hypothetical question.

Another long pause.

Ov3rl0rdL15a: Do you?

Put up or shut up time, I guess. I was surprised she hadn't simply fired back a flippant reply. If she was entertaining an honest answer, I should offer a little trust.

MightyQuinn: Yeah. I guess I do.

What was with the pauses? Was she polishing her toenails between responses?

0v3rl0rdL15a: Interesting.

MightyQuinn: Is that all? Just "Interesting"?

0v3rl0rdL15a: I'm just entering it into
my mental files.

MightyQuinn: Look. I'm reading about
ghosts, and how many people believe in
at least the possibility of a
spiritual imprint of some kind. Maybe
not stacking furniture or—

I was out of window space, but not out of steam.

0v3rl0rdL15a: Chill. I'm teasing. Why are
you reading a book about ghosts?

MightyQuinn: There's a guy.

That was honest, at least.

0v3rl0rdL15a: Not Brian Kirkpatrick.

MightyQuinn: No! O-O

0v3rl0rdL15a: Good.

MightyQuinn: B.K. is The Hotness, but
he's a Jock.

0v3rl0rdL15a: So why'd you let him carry
your books?

MightyQuinn: He's bigger than me, and I
wasn't getting them back without a fight.

0v3rl0rdL15a: lol. Okay.

I went back to work. My essay was proofread and my outline revised to Curriculum Conformity when a new window pinged open.

```
Ov3rl0rdL15a: I do believe in ghosts.
  Don't tell anyone. It would destroy my
  frightening reputation.
MightyQuinn: My lips are sealed.
```

Now what was so hard about that?

∗   ∗   ∗

I had figured out this much about my dreams: If I wake with a sense of clarity, it was just random neuron firings, or my subconscious working out my fears or something. But if I wake with the dream still clinging to me, like I'd walked through a spiderweb and my brain was covered by sticky threads of night memory, it was more than that.

I had been dreading sleep, but when I couldn't resist my bed any longer, all I'd dreamed of was talking horses. Nightmare free was a wonderful feeling. I turned on the radio while I showered and dressed. I may have even danced around a little. When the rising sun warmed the gaps between my curtains, I flung them open to welcome the day.

The filthiness of my bedroom window startled me. The morning light had to struggle through the murky glass. It was depressing and simply *wrong* somehow. True, I wasn't the neatest person in the world, but the grime coating the window was just gross.

I opened the study curtains, and had to squint against the light. Slowly I turned back to the bedroom and realized with a sinking feeling that one window was much dirtier than the other.

Not dirty. Sooty.

Leaden feet carried me to the window. With shaking hands I flipped open the latches and raised the sash, then ran my index finger through the greasy, powdery film that coated the outside glass, leaving a streak of sunshine in the grimy shadow.

I drew my hand in and closed the window. Locked it. Then I got the little blacklight out of my backpack, went into the bathroom and closed the door.

My fingertip glowed a bright, spectral blue.

12

I arrived at school early for the third morning in a row. I had searched the online city paper archives for any news from the high school. Except for budget cuts, there wasn't much of suspicious malevolence. But there were sixty yearbooks in the school library, and a couple of decades of school newspapers archived as well. After my visitor last night, I was extremely motivated to get to the bottom of this.

Was that why I hadn't dreamed last night? Had the smoke specter decided to get a look at me in person?

Balancing an armload of textbooks and a venti vanilla

latte, extra shot, extra foam, I climbed the front steps, wondering why Brian Baywatch was nowhere around when I could actually use a hand. Then, as if the thought itself had conjured him, I saw him standing just inside the glass doors.

He broke off from his friends and opened the door for me, an act of necessity rather than chivalry; my hands were completely full. The Jocks were not the only ones loitering around the foyer. There was a mixed bag of cheerleaders, band geeks, and drama nerds. "What's going on?"

"I don't know." Brian glanced toward his buddies, who were staring at him with a kind of astonished contempt. "Jessica called Brandon and told us to get over here."

The auditorium entrance was closed. I saw no sign of any of the Jessicas—I assumed Brian meant Prime—but I caught a glimpse of the prompter from backstage and beckoned him over. "Is something happening in there?"

"I don't know, man. I heard some dude over there say they may be canceling the play."

"Why would they do that?"

The guy shrugged his slumped shoulders. "I don't know. Sure would suck, though, after all that work." He slouched off with one last "Dude" and a shake of his shaggy head.

Visions of *Phantom of the Opera* filled my head as I left Brian and elbowed my way through the crowd. I had reached the front when the doors opened and the Three Original Jessicas emerged. Thespica was crying great inconsolable tears, supported by her friends, Jessicas Prime and Minor—

their feud apparently forgotten in the crisis. They bore her limp and sobbing form toward the office.

Brian caught my eye. I shrugged, as clueless as he was. Then his pack leader beckoned and they trailed after the girls. Brandon, the alpha dog, gave me one last, long stare. It was almost territorial, which, gladiatorial subtext aside, seemed to say he thought I was a threat to his pack.

With a Nancy Drew determination to satisfy my curiosity, I ignored the closed doors and went into the auditorium.

I expected scenic carnage. Maybe not a smashed chandelier, but the state of artistic chaos seemed the same as ever. The director's hair was standing on end, as if he'd been trying to pull it out, but I think that was status quo.

"Mr. Thomas?"

He stared blankly for a moment before recognition dawned. "How did you get in here?"

"Through the door. Look, everyone outside is saying you're going to cancel the show tonight. I just wanted to get the real story."

A huge sigh rattled his chest. "I hope we won't. The female lead, Jessica Jordan"—Thespica, obviously—"has come down with laryngitis. She can't make a sound."

My brows shot up. "Really."

"Yes. No amount of tea and honey is going to fix that by tonight."

"What are you going to do?" I didn't have to fake my concern. I'd been making fun of the drama nerds, but I knew how much work they'd put into the project, how important it was to them. Even if I wasn't sympathetic to Thespica (and I wasn't, really), I felt bad for the rest of them.

Then someone called from the stage. "She's here, Mr. Thomas." The choir teacher stood alongside a vaguely familiar, very nervous-looking, brown-haired girl.

Mr. Thomas excused himself. "That's the understudy. If she's up to it, then we'll open as planned."

He scurried down the aisle. I watched him talk earnestly to the girl, then gesture to the choir teacher, who went to the piano. Understudy Girl started to sing the chicks and ducks song, and though she lacked a fraction of Thespica's confidence (and by that I mean rampant egotism), she had a pretty voice with nice inflection. It sounded like the day was saved, and the show would go on.

All praise the Greek god Thespis.

✳ ✳ ✳

"It's just like *Phantom*, isn't it?" Emily Farber gushed, turned around in her desk to chatter at Lisa and me. It was English class and we were—big surprise—working on our papers.

The understudy's name was Suzie Miller. She was in the afternoon AP English class, as well as AP Calculus with Karen and Stanley. Her ascension to stardom was seen as a score for the smart kids, and a much more interesting topic than grammar and subtext.

"Where the phantom sabotages the prima donna so that Christine could have a chance at the limelight . . ." Emily sighed. "That is *so* romantic."

"I don't get that movie." Lisa slumped in her chair. "What's so hot about a homicidal psychopath?"

"Well, those eyes, that voice, that face—the part not all melty and gross, I mean." Emily looked prepared to go on at length.

"Those shoulders," I added.

"Girls!" snapped Ms. Vincent. She really ought to set up a subroutine for that. "You're supposed to be working on your themes. They are due in a week."

Lisa groaned and slithered lower in her seat. "Wake me up when the term is over."

She had a theory that term papers were a sort of "get out of teaching free" card. From the start of the assignment to its end, anytime the teacher wanted to dodge lecturing, she could give us class time to work on our papers and expect us to be grateful.

Personally, I was grateful for any day I didn't have to listen to Ms. Vincent regurgitate the textbook analysis of literature and expect us to parrot it back without alteration.

"Hey, Lisa." I doodled on my paper to make it look like I was working. "Have you ever heard of a student dying, maybe here on campus?"

She opened an eye and gave me a monocular glare. "You're not referring to that thing we were talking about last night that we are not going to talk about at school ever, are you?"

"No. Well, not really."

She sighed, then thought about it. "I think there was some kid who killed himself about twenty years ago."

"In the gym?"

"In the band hall."

That was not particularly helpful. Then I remembered that geography didn't seem to be a real issue here.

"Are you going to the play tonight?" I asked, changing the subject.

She laid her head on her folded arms. "I wasn't. But if there's a chance Gerard Butler might show up in a tux and a half-mask, I'm there."

"Dude. Me too."

✳ ✳ ✳

Naturally, since I'd lost the research time that morning, my second opportunity—journalism class—was taken up by a lecture. In lab I discovered that while our high school might have four decades of archived newspapers, the index only went back one and a half.

"Curses!" I half-slammed the drawer closed. "Foiled again."

"What's the problem?" asked Mr. Allison.

I blushed slightly, having been caught in a temper tantrum. "What happened to the index before the nineties?"

"It was lost when they moved the journalism lab up here. They started again with the current year, and no one has ever had the time to replace the old one. There's not that much call for old football scores and homecoming courts."

"I guess not." I drummed my fingers on the metal cabinet.

Mr. Allison came around his desk. "Something I can help you with?"

"Maybe. I'm looking for record of any student who may have died here on campus."

"That's grim."

"It's for a research paper." I was getting too good at lying. "Someone mentioned there was a kid who killed himself, maybe in the Band Hall?"

"Oh yes. That was a shame." He shook his head sadly. "I was in school here at the time." He opened a file drawer and came out with a microfiche spool marked 1981–85. "Look through the spring of 1984."

"Thanks." I went over to the projector. I wondered if someday, when all the archives in the world were stored on computer, microfilm projectors would be extinct. Even now, it's a dying art. Like calligraphy and Morse code, and about that efficient, too.

* * *

"Only one week until prom!" I'd barely set foot in the courtyard when a neon green paper fluttered before my face. "Have you voted for your Royal . . . Oh. It's you." My friend from Student Council snatched back the ballot. "I don't have enough of these for you to wad up and throw on the floor."

"We're outside," I said, very reasonably, considering the neon green was hammering spikes into my eyes, which were aching from an hour reading little bitty backlit type. "There is no floor."

"Whatever. You can't have a ballot." She tucked the stack protectively against her chest.

"Are you taking away my constitutional right to vote for a King and Queen?" I raised my voice in outrage.

"Well . . ." She wavered as people around us turned to stare.

"I demand the right to choose my own representation of all that is wrong with adolescent social hierarchy."

"Right on!" said a voice near me.

"You cannot deny me a voice in the senseless aggrandizement of those already entitled by wealth and privilege!" Encouraged by cheers and laughter, I leapt up on a bench and orated with a fervor worthy of Patrick Henry. "No! I tell you, popular is not enough! They must be royalty."

A roar went up from the crowd. I grabbed a painfully green ballot and raised it in my fist.

"For we hold these truths to be self-evident! That there is no greater embodiment of the American Way than the choosing of a leader based on their physical beauty and mediocre intelligence."

Cheers and whistles filled the courtyard. The Spanish Club shouted "¡Olé! Viva mediocridad!" from the breezeway. A Biff-like voice called out "Freak," and then, over it all, the stentorian shout of the assistant principal.

"Margaret Quinn! In my office, right now!"

And that was how I ended up in detention for inciting a riot. I hoped that Syracuse wouldn't revoke my acceptance without giving me a chance to explain.

✳   ✳   ✳

I didn't mind spending lunch in detention, but I wish Halloran had seen fit to extend it through P.E. I would much rather have been studying chemistry than enduring the last day of swimming.

But there I was, dragging on my swimsuit and stuffing my clothes into my locker. Jessica Prime passed behind me. "You are such a freak, Quinn."

"Thank you."

"It's not a compliment, dumb ass."

Jess Minor followed, adding "Yeah, freak" as she walked by. The Jessicas seemed to have buried the hatchet. The upshot was, as Prime turned this way and that in front of the mirror, Minor was there to lavish attention on her, and the wannabes were once again pushed to the fringes of the queen's court.

Busy squeezing my fifty-pound backpack into the undersized locker, I rolled my eyes. I didn't understand this constant need for reassurance. Jessica Prime had a beauty pageant figure. Her cleavage was suspiciously full, but she was not, in any way, shape, or form, fat.

Coach Milner called time and we rushed out to the pool, all except Prime, who must have broken a nail or something. I finished the preswim shower, then realized I'd forgotten my goggles.

"Hurry up," snapped the coach. "And tell Prentice to get a move on, too."

I dashed to the locker room as fast as was prudent on the wet tile. My goggles lay on a bench, but I saw no sign of Jessica. Then I heard someone retching in one of the stalls. I thought about calling out or going for help, but before I could do either, the toilet flushed, and Jessica Prime came out.

She was startled to see me, but almost instantly had her sneer in place. "What are you looking at, freak?"

The queen didn't look any more interested in sympathy than I was, so I pretended I hadn't heard anything. "Nothing. I just came for my goggles."

With a dismissive snort she brushed past me, and my nose twitched at an all too familiar smell. Sudden fear cramped my stomach as my eyes followed her perfect, blond form. She passed the mirror, but my gaze hung there as a black shadow slipped across the surface of the glass, like oily smoke.

13

i had called Justin as soon as school was out and asked him to meet me at Froth and Java, the coffee bar by the university. He listened to me blather about Jessica Prime and the shadow, and calmly tried to restore my logic processes. "Back up a minute. Is this the first time you've seen the shadow around her? Did you smell the odor?"

I wrapped my hands around a tall mug of tea with extra sugar and nodded. "The air was thick with it in the stall where she'd been."

His fingers drummed on his own cup of coffee. "Have you ever gotten the sense that she was . . ." Trailing off, he looked embarrassed to complete the sentence. I wasn't.

"Evil? Most every day since I met her."

"Does she have a reason to hurt Karen?"

"Evil doesn't need a reason. She didn't need a reason to show my picture to the whole world, either." Okay, it was just her friends. But what was a little exaggeration when there was a point to be made.

Justin pulled his notebook closer and read what he had written. "But what about this other girl? The one in the play. I thought they were friends."

I was disgruntled at this flaw in my theory. "Jess Minor is her friend, too, but she's been telling everyone Jess's designer clothes are cheap knockoffs."

"True." The pen tapped. "It's also possible she's not doing anything intentionally. Poltergeists are said to attach themselves to adolescents and cause mischief around them."

"Putting someone in the hospital is more than mischief."

"Don't split hairs. I'm talking about the unintentional part. And . . ." He paused delicately. "You can't have missed the signs that your nemesis may be in trouble herself."

My expression solidified into a mask of I don't give a damn. "Yeah, I noticed."

He shrugged. "I'm just saying."

"So you said it. Move along."

Justin gave me a studying look, a real frog under the microscope stare, but with disapproval. I sipped my tea and looked around the room, anywhere but at him.

Froth and Java was furnished with cast-off chairs and comfy couches, usually packed with college students who came to study or just hang out. I pretended I was enormously interested in the group to our left—and absolutely refused to show any sympathy for Jessica Prime, no matter how long Justin stared at me.

Finally he sighed in defeat. "Did you ask your chemistry teacher about the test on your jeans?"

"He gave them to someone named Dr. Smyth at the university. She'll get to it when she can."

"What about the suicide you mentioned?"

I sighed, quoting the article I'd found. "A disenfranchised student, driven to a desperate act because he felt outcast. Hanged himself in the Band Hall."

"Tragic." The true sorrow in his voice made me finally look at him again. We exchanged a glance, feeling for that poor bastard, and all the others who couldn't see any other escape from their pain.

"Yeah." I dropped my gaze and shrugged. "I guess that's why I went a little bit nuts at lunch."

Justin tilted his head curiously. "What happened at lunch?"

"I led an insurrection." After that, I had to tell him the whole story. By the time I finished, he was holding his sides laughing as people at neighboring tables stared. I was laughing pretty hard, too, and God, it felt really good.

"That's great. The First Mediocrity Rebellion." He tried to catch his breath. "I'm sorry you got detention."

I shrugged. "It'll be forgotten by Monday. *Viva la revolución.*"

"Will you get in trouble with your parents?"

"Oh, Dad will laugh. Mom will be furious. Kinda the status quo around my house." I smiled sheepishly, and he grinned back. My cheeks grew warm for no good reason, except that he was handsome and smart and I'd never had a college guy smile at me that way before. Let's face it. Stanley Dozer was the best date prospect I've had . . . maybe ever.

"So what should I do now?" I asked. The question covered a lot of ground.

Justin closed his notebook. "To be on the safe side, don't make Jessica Prime angry. We can keep checking out the ghost angle, but—"

"I don't think it's a ghost."

He shook his head. "Neither do I. I'll do some research into other kinds of spirits. Luckily I have some resources."

I wished I had something else to say to keep him there. Right then, we could be any two students, studying something as normal as sociology or statistics. He handled this strangeness so academically, so reasonably, that it made me feel as if this wasn't all so strange and things were going to be just fine. "Justin?"

"Yeah?" He paused in collecting his stuff.

"Do you think this thing is like a vampire? Not with the blood sucking, but the part where it can't come into your house unless you invite it."

He gave the question his full consideration. "The boundaries of property figure strongly in a lot of traditions. Thresholds and holy ground and running water all mark territorial borders. It may not even be able to leave the school."

"I think it can." I squirmed as he gave me that patient,

no-arguments look, waiting for me to explain. "You know that residue I found on the diving board? The supernatural snail trail? It was all over my window this morning."

Justin sat back in surprise. "On your window?"

"Yeah."

He seemed to be thinking very hard, weighing options one against the other, discarding them as quickly as they came to him. "I think you should stay with your grandmother tonight."

"And leave my parents there if it comes back? Or worse, draw it over to Gran's house? No way."

"Yes, but . . ."

Hands flat on the table, I leaned forward. "See, this is why I didn't want to tell you. I knew you'd flip out."

"I'm not flipping out. I'm just worried for you."

"What you said about boundaries *feels* right. The spooge was all on the outside of the glass. I think it might be able to visit, but it can't enter."

"Maggie." Justin covered my hands with his. "You are a clairvoyant. A seer, to use your granny's word." I tried to pull my hands away, but he held fast. "I know you want to deny it, but hear me out. We don't know what this thing is, but I'll bet anything it wouldn't have to physically reach you to do harm."

I yanked my hands hard from his grasp. "Look. If I admit that I have this"—I gritted my teeth and finally said it aloud—"*Sight*. I can't just walk away because things aren't all fluffy bunnies and unicorns. Now that I See, I cannot just *do nothing*. It doesn't work that way."

Justin clenched his fists for a moment, then deliberately

relaxed. "All right." He took a deep breath. "You're right. But at least let's set up some kind of protection."

"You mean like horseshoes and holy water?"

"Something like that."

"Okay." I hid my relief. My brave words would go a lot farther if I had an Early Phantom Warning System. "Come over at six. I'll work you in between getting yelled at by my parents and going to the Big Spring Musical. It'll be loads of fun."

✳ ✳ ✳

I had seriously underestimated my mother. Not her anger at my getting detention, but her verbosity on the subject. We had gotten through "What were you thinking?" and "Better sense than that," and moved on to "Follow you for the rest of your life." She was just bringing Dad into it with "She's *your* daughter" when the doorbell rang.

Saved by the . . . well, you know. I jumped off the sofa like I had springs on my butt. "I'll get it!"

"Sit!" barked Mom.

I sat. Dad went to answer the door, but he raised a fist in solidarity as he passed behind Mom. She snapped without turning around, "I saw that, Michael Quinn!"

Boy, for someone who disavowed belief in the supernatural, Mom could be darned spooky.

With the interruption, she jumped to the closer. "I am seriously disappointed in you, young lady."

"Yes, ma'am."

"It is ridiculous for you to be making waves this late in the school year. You graduate in a month."

"I know."

"So if you could save mocking the establishment for a

time when your class standing will not be affected, I would deeply appreciate that."

"Yes, ma'am."

My complacency took the wind out of her sails. She floundered for a moment, then said in a calm voice, "All right, then. You're only grounded for the weekend."

"Grounded! You can't!" How was I supposed to fight the forces of evil if I was grounded?

"I can. You live under this roof, and you don't turn eighteen for two months—"

"Fifty-two days, Mom!"

"And you're still in school."

Dad cleared his throat in the hallway. "Maggie, Justin is here."

I saw him behind Dad, staring at the ceiling and pretending he was deaf. Mom looked questioningly at me.

"We're working on a project together. For school." I figured I wasn't really lying—keeping the campus safe from ghostly things counted.

"On a Friday night?"

"Mom!" I stretched the word to three syllables and jerked my head to where Justin lurked in Dad's shadow. She looked the young man up and down—nice frame, broad shoulders, trustworthy face.

"Oh." It would have been funny under other circumstances. She wanted to be the strict disciplinarian, but she was clearly pleased—and surprised—that I had handsome company on a Friday night. Finally, she gave in. "As long as you don't go anywhere."

I jumped up. "We'll be up in my study." She looked as if

she might protest, but I didn't give her a chance, gesturing Justin into the room and introducing him to Mom.

"Good evening, Mrs. Quinn." He extended his hand and she put hers out automatically, looking pleased at the formality. "You have a lovely home."

She smiled, finally relaxing. His air of good-natured steadiness had that effect on people. "Thank you, Justin. Maggie, you have enough sodas?"

"We're good, Mom. Thanks." I motioned for my guest to follow me up the stairs.

"Your mom seems nice," said Justin as we reached the landing and my study area.

"She is. A little tightly wound sometimes, but Dad balances her out." That summed them up pretty well, actually. Mom was conventional and rational. Dad was more like Gran—intuitive and spiritual. And there I was, smack in the middle.

Justin carried a heavy backpack with him; he set it on the hand-me-down loveseat as he looked around the loft. "This is twice the size of my dorm room."

"Yeah. I've got a pretty good thing going." I casually dropped last night's Coke cans in the trash. The desk had reverted to its wilderness state pretty quickly, but the rest still looked vaguely civilized.

"Which window was it?" he asked, getting down to business.

I led him to the bedroom half of the room and pulled back the curtain. There was enough daylight to see the dark, greasy film on the center of the three windows that covered the east wall. My skin prickled as he opened the window and ran his finger through the soot. Rubbing forefinger and thumb together, he gave a tentative sniff.

"It doesn't smell much when it's in the open," I said.

"No. But there's a whiff of something." He made a face. "It smells like death."

"Okay. I definitely don't want to think about death on my bedroom window."

"You want me to wash it off?"

"You do windows?"

My mom kept cleaning supplies under the sink in my bathroom, a blatant hint that I usually ignored. Justin and I discovered that soap and water only smeared the soot around, and even Pine-Sol didn't cut it. I ran downstairs and got some vinegar (and some strange looks from the parents) but that didn't improve matters, either. The glass was now a mass of black smears and streaks. Adding water was making the smell stronger, too, and the stink of pine-scented rotting garbage turned my stomach.

"Just close the window," I said. "We're only making it worse."

"Hold on." Justin hung out of the casement, trying to talk while holding his breath. Not an easy thing to do. "I want to try one more thing. Bring my backpack and some fresh water."

His satchel weighed almost as much as mine did. I brought it over, then dumped the old water and refilled the bucket in the tub.

When I returned with the pail, Justin threw a handful of salt into the water, soaked a clean rag in the solution, then wiped it over the grimy mess on the glass. In a few passes, the pane shone like a Windex commercial.

"Wow." I stared, amazed. It had worked like, well, magic. "We should market that. For all your home exorcism needs."

"Something like that." He swung his legs out; the roof jutted below. By balancing carefully Justin was able to clean the whole window, and give the other two a rinse for good measure.

"What else have you got in here?" I poked through his bag. No wonder it weighed a ton. In addition to the pound of salt, he had a package of nails, a couple of books, and half a forest of leaves and twigs. "What *is* all this stuff?"

He leaned in the window, setting the bucket carefully on the floor. I thought the water would stink to high heaven, but there was no odor at all. "Since we don't know what tradition the . . . whatever . . . comes from, I'm using a scattershot approach. Give me the nails."

I knew that one. Iron kept away fairies and bad luck in Celtic traditions, and like a lot of things had been adapted into Western/Christian superstition: nails equals crucifixion equals Christ's protection.

"What're these twigs?" They were covered with bright red berries. Kind of pretty, really.

"Rowan." His voice drifted in while he scattered the nails on the ledge above the window.

"Where did you get rowan twigs? Witch Depot?"

"There's a New Age herb shop near campus. Would you believe the hardest thing to find was the iron nails? They're all nickel alloy now."

"How inconvenient." I got out of the way as he climbed back in the window. He was filthy from all the window washing. We spread a thin line of salt and placed a rowan twig on every sill, then closed those curtains and went to give the study window a similar treatment.

The whole operation didn't seem nearly as silly as it should have. Maybe it was the way the saltwater had cleared the window and nothing else had. Maybe my idea of what was "normal" had taken a radical left turn.

I had just closed the window when I heard footsteps on the stairs. We exchanged panicked looks, but didn't have time to do anything other than hide the nails (Justin) and the salt (me) before Dad's head appeared at the landing.

"What the blazes are you two doing?" he demanded.

"It's a . . . chemistry experiment," I said, not guiltily at all. "Justin is helping me with a chemistry experiment."

Dad continued up, giving us the Paternal Eye. Justin actually squirmed. I think if we'd actually been doing anything illicit he might have thrown himself at my father's feet, begging his forgiveness.

As it was, when Dad held out his hand, Justin meekly gave over the package of iron nails. With resigned chagrin, I took the canister of salt from behind my back.

"Something I should know about?"

I glanced at my partner in crime. He gave a little shrug of his eyebrow as if to say it was up to me. Gran would believe us. Heck, Gran would help. Mom would wig out on so many levels, but Dad was a wild card.

"Actually," I began, choosing my truths carefully. "It's Justin's experiment with different protection superstitions, and since I'm, you know, sensitive, we're going to see if I feel more, um, protected."

The Paternal Eye pinned me with suspicion. "You know your mother would freak out if she knew about this."

Parents should not say "freak out." But I'd just been thinking that exact thing, so I simply answered, "Yes, sir."

Dad handed the nails back to Justin. "Don't worry about the doors downstairs. My mother did them when we moved in, and checks them every year." See. I was right about Gran, too. I had no trouble picturing her going around with a ladder, sprinkling iron nails over all the door frames.

"I'm taking your mom out to dinner." Dad smoothed his tie. "I convinced her that Justin is trustworthy, but she's not so sure about you."

"We're just about done, Dr. Quinn." Justin started gathering up his things.

"Right. Good to see you, Justin. We'll be home in a couple of hours, Mags."

"Don't hurry on my account."

Just as he disappeared, my phone rang. Justin gestured for me to go ahead and answer. As soon as I flipped it open, I heard Lisa's unhappy voice. "Are you coming to this thing or not?"

"The play?" I reordered my thoughts. I had not forgotten about it; I just hadn't figured out how I was going to get there, being as I was grounded and all.

"Yes, the play. I thought you were coming. I bought you a ticket. I'm out sixteen bucks here."

"I got kind of held up." Justin looked at me curiously. I made a face, not sure what it was supposed to convey beyond a general helplessness.

"Well, the damned thing is about to start. If you're not coming, then I'm not about to endure a lot of singing about chicks and ducks. Not to mention the drama triplets trying to steal Suzie Miller's limelight."

"The Jessicas are there?"

"And their Jock counterparts. The full unholy bunch. The Voiceless One is wearing sackcloth and ashes and the others are all telling her how selfless she is to be here to support the rest of the cast. I may hurl."

"Hang on, Lisa." I put the phone against my shirt while I asked Justin, "Can you drive me to the school?"

"Uh . . . I thought you were, um . . . you know."

"Yes. But I have a bad feeling."

My unease must have been obvious. I couldn't put into words the tight knot in my gut and my certainty that something was going to happen. I was more sure than ever that this was tied to Jessica Prime, maybe all the Jessicas together. If I sat in my room with this dread clawing around my insides, if I could do something and didn't, then all my fears about Nana and Pop, about Karen's accident would be real.

Justin hesitated a moment more, then nodded. "All right."

I told Lisa, "Leave the ticket for me in the front. If they won't let me in after the show starts, I'll see you at intermission."

"You'd better," she answered. "Do *not* make me suffer this alone, Magdalena Quinn."

"I'm on my way."

I grabbed some clean clothes from the closet and went

into the bathroom to change. I came out brushing my hair, thrust my feet into a pair of ballet flats, and searched for a purse.

When I found it, Justin gave me a handful of stuff. There were a few sprigs of the rowan, a couple of nails, and a Ziploc baggie full of salt. "This won't help against your mother," he warned me, "so I hope you know what you're doing."

I tucked them in my handbag, smoothed my skirt, and nodded. "It'll be all right," I said, with a certainty I didn't quite feel.

14

Murphy's Law for Ghostbusting must go like this: If you risk parental wrath by breaking your grounding and several speed limits to get to somewhere you are certain will be a hotbed of supernatural activity, then suffer through two hours of songs about ducks, not to mention a choreographed hoedown, assuredly *nothing will happen*.

"I can't believe it." I stood on the school's front steps where the "after-theatre" crowd milled peacefully, laughing and congratulating the cast.

"I know. I thought it would suck even worse." Lisa stood beside me, deeply inhaling the late April air, cooler now that the sun had gone down. "Though I think some of the laughs were unintentional. Like when Joe Cowboy dropped his partner. Or Stanley Dozer, looking like a seven-foot-tall mutant deer in the headlights when that scenery fell over." She grinned at the memory.

"No falling chandelier," I mused. "No plummeting sandbags. Nothing burst into flames."

"Yeah. I'm disappointed, too." We paused to watch Thespica swan over to Suzie Miller and graciously give her whispered congratulations. Suzie surprised us by throwing her arms around Thespica in an ingenuous hug. The Prima Donna's expression of horror and outrage sent Lisa and I into whoops of laughter.

"Hey."

I turned at the familiar monosyllable, still grinning at the Drama Queen's expense. "Hey, Brian."

Brian returned my instinctive smile with a broad one of his own. "Wow!" He put his hand over his heart, reeling back. "She actually smiles. I never thought I'd see it."

"Stranger things have happened lately." I could feel Lisa beside me, practically vibrating with displeasure. Had I always noticed those things, and never thought about it before? "Brian, this is my friend Lisa. Lisa, this is . . ."

"I know who he is."

Her tone could cut glass. "Geez, Lisa," I murmured.

Brian pretended not to notice. Maybe that was his conditioned response to unpleasantness. It explained why he did nothing when his friends acted like assholes, but then apologized for them later. Brian did not Make Waves.

"Good luck with the valedictorian thing," he told Lisa sincerely. "I saw you're the front-runner."

"By a hundredth of a point. Thanks for reminding me."

She turned to me, arms crossed tightly. "I'm going to talk to Emily. Come see me if you still need a ride."

She stalked off before I could say anything, which was probably just as well. Lisa took a certain pride in being a bitch and wouldn't appreciate me calling her on it.

"You look different tonight." Brian studied me in an exaggerated way. "I know what it is! No camera."

"It wouldn't fit in here." I patted my vintage beaded purse, hanging from its thin satin strap.

He shoved his hands in the pockets of his khakis. He looked nice, too. A lot of the kids were in jeans, but some had at least pretended it was a real theatrical experience, falling scenery aside.

"Listen. I was wondering if you might like to go out some time."

Maybe I'm not psychic after all, because I totally did not see that coming. "What, you mean on a date?"

He'd been looking at the tops of his shoes, but now he peered up at me with a wry smile that made his eyes seem incredibly blue. No, it didn't make sense.

"Yeah. On a date."

God, I was speechless. A Jock—a HenchBiff, no less—had just asked me out. I was stunned, outraged, appalled, and, on some level, illogically delighted because, well, I mentioned the hotness, right?

"That's . . . wow . . . um."

He ducked his head to search my face, his smile adorably uncertain. "Is that a yes or a no?"

"That's an 'I can't believe my ears.'"

A shrill voice shattered the Kodak moment. There was nothing wrong with Jess Minor's vocal cords, even if she was no match for her leader's cheer-honed stridency. "Brian! What's taking so long?"

Translation: What are you doing talking to that lower life form?

I folded my arms, my posture going defensive before I could check the movement.

"I'll be over in a minute, Jess." Brian was a lot nicer than I would have been, were I called to heel that way.

"Go on," I said. "You don't want to rock the boat."

"*Bri-an.*" Minor ramped up to a major fit of pique. "We're all about to leave. We're going to the Underground. Right *now.*"

"Ride with Jeff. I'll meet you guys there." He turned back to me with a sheepish smile. "I don't suppose you want to go to the Underground."

"I'd rather poke a sharp stick in my eye." The Underground was an eighteen-and-over club that catered mostly to the college crowd. I'd love to go, someday, but not with the Maleficent Six.

"What about next week? Come to my baseball game, and we'll go somewhere after."

"Sports give me hives."

"Then don't come to the game, and we'll go somewhere after."

I was playing with my cross and made myself stop, tucking my hair behind my ear instead, trading one fidget for another. "Look, Brian . . ."

"What are you doing, Kirkpatrick?" Brandon stood at the bottom of the steps, but still managed to loom somehow. "We're ready to go."

"I told Jess to go on ahead."

The alpha dog raked his eyes over me, then addressed his pack mate. "Jess will be real disappointed if you don't come with us."

"She'll live."

"Yeah, but I'll have to listen to her whine. So stop wasting time and let's go."

I looked Brian in the eye. "Go on with your friends. I'll see you around." I walked away, and he didn't stop me. I didn't really expect him to.

"Geez, Kirkpatrick." Biff didn't bother to lower his voice as Brian went down the steps to join him. "What are you doing? Some kind of science experiment?"

When I reached Lisa she glanced at me without sympathy. But she didn't say "I told you so," either. I guess that's why she's my friend. She just wrapped an arm around my shoulders. "Ready to go, kiddo?"

"Yeah." I figured my mom would have killed me by Monday anyway.

We said good-bye to Emily, congratulations to Suzie, and headed for the parking lot.

"What's with Dozer stalking Suzie Miller?" I asked Lisa. With black-clad Stanley hovering around after the show, I recognized her as the girl I'd seen him with backstage.

"Even dweebs can have crushes," she said.

I didn't see a need to mention how quickly his affections had shifted after he'd asked me to the prom. "I wonder if she'll give him the time of day now that she's a superstar."

Lisa snorted. "Suzie is a real-life ingenue. If she liked him before, she won't cut him off. And I say 'if' because . . . well, Stanley Dozer."

The butt numbing boredom of the play and the silliness

of Thespica's drama afterward had lulled me into complacency, but my Spidey Sense clawed the chalkboard of my nerves the moment we reached Lisa's compact Honda. Directly across from it, sharing the same island of halogen, were the Jocks and Jessicas. Biff opened the door of his Blazer for Jessica Prime, but rather than climb in she stopped to watch me with eyes full of venom.

Plenty of Evil there, but that wasn't what had fired the warning shot. Next to the Blazer was Jeff Espinoza's vintage Mustang, parked on the edge of the lamplight, not quite pristine, but lavishly loved.

There was a shadow within the shadow of the car. It squatted, waiting with an inanimate patience until I looked at it, and then it stirred, like smoke in darkness.

"Ow!" Lisa yelped. I'd grabbed her arm hard enough to bruise. "What's your problem?"

Brandon and all three Jessicas were climbing into his SUV. Jeff and Brian stood by the Mustang, discussing whether to stop and get something to eat before going to the club. I didn't realize I had changed direction until I heard my own voice.

"Brian!"

His head came up. Beneath the car, the darkness curled in on itself as if gathering to strike. My stride faltered as I felt its attention on me. Just like in my dream, I knew it *saw* me, even though it had no eyes. I couldn't make myself go any nearer, and stopped in the middle of the driveway.

Brian started toward me, his expression curious, but pleased. "What's up?"

"Don't . . ." My throat closed on the warning, choked by

self-preservation. I couldn't explain my knowledge, my Sight. If I warned him, everyone would know I was a freak.

Lisa called my name from beside her own car. "Maggie! What is *wrong* with you?"

"Don't get in the car," I whispered, reaching for his arm as if I could hold him back from danger.

"What?" He leaned closer. "I didn't hear you."

"Don't ride in the Mustang. Ride with Brandon."

Nails raked my wrist as someone snatched my hand from Brian's sleeve. I swallowed my heart when I realized it was only Jess Minor. Her face twisted with jealous fury, but it was nothing compared to what agglomerated in the dark.

"Don't you ever give up?" Her voice was reedy and thin, bamboo under the fingernails, and her complexion was flushed and blotchy in the streetlamp. "On what planet would one of *us* want anything to do with someone like *you*?"

Brian had stared at me with blank confusion. Now his gaze turned to Jess as if she were a space creature. Before he could say anything, though, Lisa was in Minor's face.

"Don't talk to her like that."

"Back off, egghead. Take your tramp friend and get out of here."

"Tramp!" I squawked in outrage.

Lisa pushed Jess's pointing finger aside. "Put that away before I break it, Michaels."

"Calm down, Jess—" Brian went unheeded as Brandon came up, Jeff lumbering behind.

"Hey! A catfight!"

"It's not a fight." I grabbed Lisa's arm and dragged her

away. I was shaking too much for the two of us to be any match for the six of them—five, if Brian abstained. "We've got better places to be."

"Good," Minor shouted after us. "Go poach someone else's boyfriends."

"Not hardly," Lisa threw over her shoulder. "We're going to Wal-Mart to see if we can find that outfit."

I should have just let Lisa handle her. They were both bigger than me. But when Minor launched herself at my friend's back, I acted without thinking, stepping between them and taking her weight full on. I stumbled backward, the hellcat's fists tearing at my hair, and banged hard into the fender of Lisa's Honda. Jess crashed into me and smacked my head against the trunk.

I swear to God, the thing under the Mustang laughed.

Brandon and Jeff hooted as Jessica Prime cheered and Thespica clapped and honked. With her friends egging her on, Minor put a knee in my gut and tried to twist my head off. She might not be the alpha bitch, but she was scrappy and mean the way the bottom of the pack had to be.

But I'm not the scion of Irish pub brawlers for nothing. I kicked her standing leg out from under her and followed her down, pinning her to the asphalt and dodging sideways when her French-tipped nails went for my face. She caught me in the neck and I felt the sting of drawn blood.

The shadow roiled, like a pot on the boil. The smell of rotting eggs and putrid meat grew stronger.

Off-balance, I couldn't stop her from flipping me like a tortoise, slamming me down with more force than I'd ever imagined a piece of fluff like her could manage. Her nails flashed at my face again. I flung up my arm to shield my eyes; when she scratched me again, the acrid stink surged into my throat, stealing my breath.

Or maybe that was her hands on my throat. "Meddling tramp!" She rattled my head against the pavement. "Stay out of my business."

I made a fist and punched. I felt the shock all the way to my shoulder. Jess reeled slightly, breaking her grip, then someone was pulling her away, lifting her bodily. Lisa's worried face filled my vision. I couldn't speak past the gagging, but I grabbed her hand, held her so she wouldn't go after Minor in retaliation. I could feel the shadow's hungry miasma of excitement, and knew the fight had to stop.

"Witch!" Minor shrieked at me as Brian held her, both arms wrapped around her waist. "You ought to be burned at the stake!"

"Jesus, Jess!" He struggled to restrain her, despite his size and strength. Even the Jessicas looked shocked, and Brandon and Jeff had stopped laughing.

"Freak of nature!" She screeched. The phantom stench was rolling off of her. Why couldn't they smell it?

I tried to crawl away, vomit rising in my throat. My hand touched the torn strap of my purse and, still gagging, tears running down my face, I pulled it to me and slid my hand inside.

"Calm down, Jess," I heard Prime say. "Jesus, what is wrong with you?"

"She's gone nuts. I told you not to play hard to get, Brian."

"Shut up, Jeff, and help me."

My lungs were on fire. I thought about what Professor Blackthorne had said about sulfur dioxide, about volcanoes, about brimstone. I was burning up, from the alveoli out.

"Just let her go. What's one less dweeb in the world?"

"Shut up, Brandon." Lisa crouched over me protectively, snarling up at Biff.

"Make me, Lisa."

I'd gotten my hand in the baggie of salt. On a whim, a hunch, a prayer, I gathered a handful and flung it out, covering the parking lot under Jess and Brian's feet with a smattering of white crystals.

The effect was immediate. Jess went limp in Brian's grasp and the shadow recoiled into the tailpipe of the Mustang.

And I took a deep, unfettered breath.

"Here." Brian said, as he shoved the flaccid Jess into Brandon's arms. "Take her."

I heard him crouch beside me, and his hand shook as it settled on my shoulder. "Get away from her," said Lisa, slapping him away.

"I'm just trying to help."

"Take your friends and get the hell out of here." Her slim arms wrapped around me, and helped me sit up.

I wiped my streaming eyes and looked at Brian, seeing the forces tearing at him. In that moment, I don't think he had any loyalty to the pack, but he didn't want to make things worse by breaking with them now. For the first time, he was right not to rock the boat. "Go." I sounded as hoarse as Thespica. "But not in the Mustang."

Still uncertain, he followed Brandon and helped lift Jess into the backseat of the truck, then climbed in himself. Thespica jumped in after, but Jessica Prime paused to cast a glance back at me, unreadable as an animal.

With the assistance of the fender of the Honda, I managed to stand up. Sort of. Lisa was helping me into the car when I heard Jeff arguing with Brian about riding in the Blazer.

"No way am I leaving the 'stang in the parking lot. What if those crazy bitches come back and do something to it."

"In case you haven't noticed, Jeff, we seem to have a lock on crazy bitches tonight."

"Screw it. I'm taking my car."

I tried to rise from my seat to stop him. But I didn't know how. Maybe I could puke on him. That seemed to be all I was good for just then. Lisa forced me to sit back down. "Leave them."

"But . . ."

"It's not your problem."

"You don't understand!"

"There is nothing you can do! I don't know what's got into you, but . . ."

The Mustang peeled out of the parking lot, ending the argument.

15

I expected it to be like that fifties song: The cryin' tires, the bustin' glass. But . . . Nothing. The Blazer pulled around so that Brandon could flip us off, then followed the sports car onto the street. The basso rumble of the truck's engine quickly caught up with the gravel-throated Mustang, and both faded quickly into the distance.

Lisa grabbed an empty soda can from her floorboard and flung it after the taillights. It bounced on the asphalt with an anticlimactic "tink."

"I hate those sons of bitches. Every last one of them. I hope they burn in a fiery conflagration that is only a prelude to the inferno of their everlasting exile in Hell."

Boy, Lisa could curse. I wished I could appreciate it, instead of flinching at shadows. "Please don't. You don't know what might hear you."

She covered her face with her hands, and when they dropped, she was in control again. We didn't have time to waste. I could see curious students, parents, and teachers approaching quickly. If Halloran was among them, he'd suspend me in a heartbeat, even if I'd only been fighting to defend myself.

"I'm not even supposed to be out of the house." The words scraped my raw throat. "Can we get out of here?"

"You bet." She jumped in the car. Just as we'd backed out of the space, Emily from English reached us and Lisa rolled down the window to answer her concerned question. "Spread the word that Jess Michaels went ape-shit when I made a crack about her wearing the softer side of Sears. They took off, and everything's cool now."

Emily leaned in the window. "Geez, Maggie. Are you all right? Your poor throat. And your blouse!"

I hadn't realized my shirt was torn. "Darn it! First my jeans, now this."

"She's fine, except for sounding like a frog." Lisa glanced in the rearview mirror at the gathering crowd, then caught Emily's gaze. "Just cover for us, okay?"

"Sure."

We zipped away, driving in silence until the school was out of sight. Then Lisa asked, "You want to tell me what's going on with you, Mags?"

"No," I croaked. "You wouldn't believe me."

"I don't know what to believe right now. What the hell

was that with Brian? When did you become so chummy? And the thing with the car? What do you think is going to happen?"

"I don't know why Brian suddenly finds me irresistible. I haven't exactly encouraged him. And I don't know how I know something's wrong with the car. Sometimes I just know things." I didn't mention the shadow creature. I didn't even know what to call it; how could I possibly explain?

She drove in silence for a moment. "What do you mean, you know things. Like the future?"

"No. Only the present. But sometimes that gives me clues that something might happen. Like if I know a teacher is planning a pop quiz, it's not the same thing as foreseeing a test. She could still change her mind."

We were cruising the main strip, the most direct way to my house. "Why didn't you ever tell me?"

"It hasn't happened in awhile."

"But now?"

I leaned my head against the window. I had a lump coming up, and it hurt to rest back against the seat. "Something is going on, but I don't know what."

She tightened her jaw, but didn't say anything else. My throat hurt, so I didn't encourage more conversation. Not until I put up my hand, and said, "Stop!"

"What?" Her foot tapped the brake. The speed limit wasn't very high along this curving stretch of Beltline, but everybody sped down it, in a hurry to get where they were going. "Another premonition?"

"No. There are flashing lights ahead. Oh God."

We slowed, along with the rest of the traffic, which was

being directed to the other side of the street by a uniformed cop. I glimpsed bright red, and my heart squeezed in my chest. Jeff's pristine Mustang was a misshapen heap of torn metal, wrapped like a fortune cookie around the front end of an SUV the size of a tank.

I rolled down my window, and I could hear the police officer talking to Jeff through the driver's door, telling him to stay still until the ambulance arrived. He was alive, at least for now. But the passenger side had taken the impact. Anyone riding with him would never have survived.

✳   ✳   ✳

The front porch was dark when Lisa dropped me off, which usually meant the parents had retreated into their room for the evening. I slid my key into the lock and turned it as quietly as I could. Slipping in the door, I closed it softly, then took off my shoes and crept to the stairs.

I'd left a note on my bed when I left. It's a strange dysfunction: Disobeying the parents was one thing, but it didn't seem right to worry them out of their minds. I wasn't surprised to turn my note over and read: "You'd better have a very good explanation for this. There will be consequences. —Dad."

Well, I expected that. I'm a novice rule breaker, but I suppose it was the price of being a crusader for justice.

I set my ruined bag on the dresser and pulled out my phone. I'd turned the sound off during the play, and now I saw that I had one text message from Justin (Call when you get home) and five missed calls from Gran (no message). Nice to know *her* Spidey Sense was operational. I went to the computer and left her an "I'm all right" e-mail.

Next, I phoned Justin, as ordered. I was quickly running out of steam, but I didn't want him to worry, either. He picked up the phone on the third ring, and for a moment all I could hear was music and laughter. "Hello?"

"Maggie! Are you all right?"

"Yeah. Are you at a bar?" Not that it would be my business if he was, of course.

"Hang on, let me go outside." More noise, then the slam of a door and silence. "My roommate. This is probably his last semester, so he's having a last hurrah."

"He's graduating?"

"He's flunking out."

"Boy, you attract the hard-luck cases." I pressed gingerly at the bump on the back of my head.

"So what happened? Anything?"

I was so tired, and the bed stretched out in front of me like a big, unmade ocean of temptation. "Yes. I'll tell you about it tomorrow."

"Why not now?"

"I'm too sleepy now."

"I have to study for finals tomorrow, or I'll be joining my roommate working at McWendy's."

Somehow I doubted that. Justin had an unshakable aura of studious industry. If he'd lived in the Middle Ages, he would live in an abbey and do nothing but transcribe ancient texts and preserve knowledge for the future.

"Okay. Short version? When I tried to stop the Jocks from driving their ghost-infected car, Jess Minor kicked my ass, and then Jeff wrapped the cursed Mustang around the front of a Hummer."

"Jessica *Minor* beat you up?" I had given him a rundown of the major players in this drama. Suffice to say, my opinion of Minor was rather dismissive, hence his stinging incredulity.

"Yeah, thanks for reminding me of my humiliation. It wasn't even the alpha bitch, just the wannabe."

"And what's this with the car? Is the guy all right?"

I shuddered at the memory of Jeff's blood-covered, pain-contorted face—the only part I could see, thank God. "They were taking him to the hospital. He was pretty messed up. No one else was hurt."

As Lisa had driven by—she had refused to stop—I'd seen the others clustered around the Blazer, and Jess Minor had been on her feet and clinging to Brian, so I guessed she'd had little lasting affect from her brush with the shadow.

"Look, if you want more than that, it's gotta wait for tomorrow. I'm gorked out." My sore head rested on my nice fluffy pillow, and it was getting hard to keep my eyes open.

"Okay." He paused, and I pictured his serious face pinched with worry. "But you're all right? You sound awful."

"I'm just tired."

"Did you escape detection?"

"Of course not." I yawned, and didn't bother to cover my mouth. "I can deal with my dad. He can ground me till kingdom come once this thing is . . . whatever."

"Vanquished?"

I rolled on my side and curled into a ball. "Or done."

"Done what?"

"With whatever it's trying to do." My eyelids had lead sinkers on them. Even the phone seemed to weigh a ton.

"How do you know it's trying to do something?"

"I dunno. I just do."

A pause. Or maybe I dozed off for a moment. Then I heard, "Hang up and go to sleep, Maggie."

"Okay." My thumb found the right button, even with my eyes closed. "'Night, Justin. Thanks for helping me tonight."

"You're welcome."

Almost immediately, I dreamed.

✳   ✳   ✳

Sand and wind scoured the ground, and the sun blistered the sky. Before my squinting eyes, dunes stretched to the horizon, a molten sea of white gold.

I turned in a slow circle, getting my bearings. I stood on a rocky outcropping that jutted between the desert sands and a large oasis where I saw palm trees and some kind of cultivated garden, as well as small adobe huts and large tents. As I watched, a young girl shepherded a herd of goats toward a well, where a woman was drawing water. Dream or not, I was suddenly parched, the hot, dry air torturous on my raw throat.

Stumbling down the slanted rock, I hurried toward the oasis. The sand slid into my shoes, scorching my feet, and the sun, which hadn't bothered me at first, drove me like a living force. By the time I reached the blessed shade, I could barely put one foot in front of the other.

I could smell the water, like a perfume. The woman at the well looked at me with no surprise, as if modern-dressed girls stumbled into their oasis on a daily basis. Up close, I could see the detail of her clothes, from the loose and gauzy texture of her head covering, to the crosshatched weave of her robe. A leather girdle circled her waist; her skin was dark and her eyes kind.

The detail was stunning, from the color of her clothes to the smell of the goats. I didn't know what to call any of these things, but they couldn't be any more real if I had gone back in time. *Dad would be so jealous.*

I unstuck my tongue from the roof of my mouth. "May I have some water?" As politely as I could, I gestured to the full water skin she had drawn, because even in my dream, the only foreign language I knew was bad Spanish.

The woman took a dipper, filled it, and offered it to me with a smile. I drank thirstily, and then gave it back to her, bowing my thanks. I was trying to think of a way to ask where I was supposed to be, when I heard a shout from the edge of the oasis, joined by more voices, raising an alarm.

The woman ran toward the sound and I followed. A group of men clustered together, two of them carrying the torn body of a lanky young man between them. The woman from the well gave a heart-rending cry and threw herself forward, touching his wounds with her hands, as if she couldn't trust her eyes. One of the men tried to comfort her; she shoved him away and fell to her knees, her scream of angry denial becoming a wail of anguish as she tore at her hair with bloody fists.

I was afraid to go closer, terrified to look at the dead man's face. Was I seeing an event from the past, or a metaphorical picture of the present? Would it be Jeff staring up at the bleached sky, dead from wounds inflicted in the car crash?

The grieving woman fell over the body, and saved me from having to look. I listened to the men, not understanding their language, but interpreting the gestures of the guys who had brought the man back to his wife. They'd found him outside of the oasis.

I went the way they'd indicated, covering ground in a quick fold of dreamtime, and found myself in a spot where human feet and animal claws had disturbed the sand in a ten-foot circle, the fetid air thick over the scraps of cloth and hair. The odor of rot had become an indelible association, the way hospitals smell like disinfectant, and locker rooms smell like mildew. If the man had been attacked by carnivores, why the hellish smell? Was the pack more than it seemed?

A wind came up, blowing my hair around my face and obscuring my vision. I turned into it, brushing the strands from my eyes, and in the seamless way that dreams have, it was now full night, and the desert air was cold on my skin. The moon painted the sand silver, except for a circle of flickering blue firelight.

"This again?" I huffed in frustration.

The first time I dreamed, there had only been impressions of fire and smoke and danger. The second time, I'd seen the brazier and the blue flames. Now I had a setting, though it didn't make much sense to my present problem. Another metaphor? Or was I seeing the origins of something I still didn't completely understand?

The same brazier rested in the sand; no stand, just a beaten metal basin about the size of a large dinner plate, with designs of some kind engraved around the rim. The smell of the fire burning in the shallow bronze container brought to mind fireworks and made my throat ache. Underneath it, though, was the same rotten odor.

I gathered detail with some excitement, studying the symbols. Maybe I was getting better at this vision stuff. A rolled-up piece of parchment lay on the raised edge of the brazier, and the fire crawled slowly up the scroll.

With a courage I might not have possessed in real life, I snatched the small cylinder from the flames. It was a new element in the dream, and might be important.

I blew on it like a match, but the fire wouldn't go out. With the same odd lack of fear, I handled the parchment by the safe side, and unrolled it. The letters were ornate and completely foreign to me, but they made a list of some kind. I thought of my first dream, and the roll call of names. A hex maybe? A curse? That would make sense, except for the feeling of sentience that I got from the black shadow.

The blue flames traveled more quickly across the parchment. I wondered if that was the origin of the acrid smell. Wasn't parchment once made out of sheepskin?

The fire singed my skin, and I dropped the list to the sand. The flames, however, stayed dancing on my fingertips. I held my hand before my face, horrified as the flesh began to blacken and blister. The choking, burning odor was coming from my hand.

Terror shook me in its teeth. I tried to scream, but couldn't force any sound past my throat. I could only watch the flames lick down my wrist, as the skin of my hand began to crack and peel from my bones.

What had Justin said? That I was vulnerable in my

dreams. Could I die? Could I go mad? That seemed a very real possibility, as pain and fear chased each other around in my brain, making it impossible to think, filling my head with the shriek of blind, unreasoning panic.

My unblemished left hand went to my neck, grasped the cross that still hung there, even in my dream. Wake up. I ordered myself. Wake up, now. Wake up wake up wake . . .

*　*　*

"*Up!*" I screamed, propelled out of the dream and straight up in bed.

My chest heaved like I'd run a marathon, and my clothes and hair were clammy with sweat. My left hand still clutched Gran's necklace—*my* necklace—and the tangle of bedsheets hid my right. It didn't hurt, but I'd heard that third-degree burns didn't, because all the nerve endings were dead.

Trembling, I made myself let go of the cross, then reached over to flip aside the sheet. My breath whooshed out when I saw my pale skin, unblemished by anything but a smattering of freckles.

"Maggie?" Mom's worried voice called from below. "Are you all right?"

"Yes," I croaked, but the word didn't carry. I heard her footsteps on the stairs.

I was still wearing my clothes from the play. Even if Dad had told Mom I'd been out, I didn't want to wave the red flag of my disobedience in her face. Scrambling under the covers, I pulled them up to my chin just as she reached the landing. "I'm all right, Mom."

Her sleep-tousled head appeared around the bifold door to the bedroom. "I thought I heard you shout."

I pushed myself up onto my elbows. "I had a nightmare."

"Are you feeling all right? You sound hoarse." Concerned, she came into the room, then hurried to the bed when she saw me. "Oh, Maggie! You're drenched." She laid the back of her hand against my forehead—do all mothers have a thermometer there? "And you're burning up. Are you sure you're not sick?"

"No," I rasped, lying back and tugging up the sheet. "Just a nightmare. A bad one."

"Oh." She sat on the edge of the bed, her thoughts marching visibly across her face. I wondered if she was recalling, like I was, the last time we'd done this, the night her parents died. She must have been, because she seemed to waver in her curiosity, wanting to ask, not wanting to know.

"Was it a . . . What did you used to call them? A gut dream?" She didn't look at me, but at her knotted fingers.

I hesitated, my instinct still to avoid this ground with Mom. "Kind of. Yes."

"Oh." Her fingers unlaced, shifted, and knit again. "Do you want to tell me about it?"

"No." It came out harsher than I intended. I didn't mean to reject her, exactly. My mom fell into the very reasonable, rational part of my life, and I liked it that way. Whenever I needed to think of something logically, it was my mother's voice in my head saying, "Oh, don't be ridiculous."

I tempered that rejection a little. "Nothing I want you to worry about, Mom. Just school stuff."

"Is the stress getting to you, sweetheart?" Her hand brushed my cheek, cool against my flushed skin.

"Not exactly." Mom loved to hear what was going on in my life. It was a shame that her only child was so boring, and sadder still that once my life got interesting, I couldn't tell her about it. Whether she believed me or not, she would, as Dad put it, freak out, and take action to inhibit my girl detective responsibilities.

"There are these girls," I said, choosing my truths carefully. "Cheerleaders. You know the type. Beautiful. Popular. Wearing their air of entitlement like designer perfume."

"Oh yes." That agreement carried a world of understanding.

"Well, they're making me miserable." At least that was honest. "I'm trying to just stay above it all, but that's harder than it should be." Especially with a ghostly shadow forcing my involvement.

"I know." Mom patted my knee. "But you just have to ignore them. Remember those girls are just jealous."

The conviction in that cliché made me laugh. Motherless Nancy Drew might have more freedom in her investigations, but I'd trade a lot of fretting for moments like this. "I love you, Mom."

"I love you, too, Magpie." She leaned over and kissed my forehead, as though I were eight instead of (almost) eighteen. With one last frown, she tucked the covers closer around me. "But maybe you should take it easy the rest of the weekend. You don't want to get sick this close to the prom."

"Oh, Mom," I groaned. She suffered from the delusion that I might yet decide to go to the dance, and kept asking if we should go shopping for a dress, "Just in case."

"Oh, Maggie," she echoed. "I don't want you to have any regrets. It wouldn't kill you to behave like a normal teenager once in a while."

Wouldn't it? Look what happened the first time I ever snuck out of the house.

"I'll think about it."

It took so little to make her happy. She patted my knee as she rose, "That's all I ask. Sleep tight, Magpie."

"'Night, Mom."

I waited until she'd had time to get to her bedroom, then threw back the covers. My clothes were strangling me. I stripped them off, pulled on my pjs, then went over to the desk. I was not eager to go back to sleep, even though, by the usual rules, I would be done dreaming for the night.

Picking up a pencil, I began to sketch as much as I could remember of the symbols on the brazier. I found that, just like my extra sense, I couldn't *make* it happen, but if I let my mind and hand drift, I could see the engravings and trace them on the page. Soon I was yawning, but I had six symbols I was reasonably sure of. They looked both familiar and strange, kind of a cross between Hebrew letters and the graffiti ciphers I saw spray-painted on buildings.

I dropped my pencil in defeat. Great. I had probably been influenced by the *Prince of Egypt* portion of the dream, and the last time I drove downtown. I hated not knowing what I knew.

At least the nightmare's power had faded with the detective work. I belatedly brushed my teeth, then switched off all but one small lamp in the corner.

I don't know what made me pause at the window. Maybe

I just wanted to see that the line of salt was still there, or comfort myself with those cheery red rowan berries. Brushing back the curtain, my eye immediately went to the moonlit street, and the amalgamation of shadows gathering under the neighbor's big pecan tree.

The inky darkness of the Shadow stood defined against the lesser gloom. It now had a distinct form, man-shaped, but not quite. There was a central mass, like a torso, and limblike outgrowths, and something head-shaped at the top. A breeze stirred the leaves of the pecan, and the Shadow's form shifted like a phantom, but with a core of material solidity.

It stepped out of the shelter of the tree, palpably obscure in the moonlight, a substance that cast no shadow of its own. The wind blew eddies of dirt and grass clippings around its half-formed feet.

How did I know it was trying to do something, Justin had asked me. The parchment, the list of names—maybe it was a curse, or maybe it was a means to an end. But I knew in that moment where this was headed.

Like some kind of nightmare Velveteen Rabbit, the specter was becoming *real*.

16

I woke feeling like I'd gone ten rounds with Mike Tyson instead of a skinny WASP Princess. It didn't help that I had slept on the ancient loveseat, as far away from the front windows as I could get. I hadn't planned to sleep at all, but as the small hours of the night crept larger and nothing happened, unconsciousness won out over fear.

I Frankenstein-walked to the bathroom, shedding clothes as I went. A hot shower eased my muscles but stung the scratches on my neck and arm. The joints in my right hand were stiff and I ached up to the elbow, but when I saw the bruises on my knuckles I realized this wasn't some weird transference from the dream. I'd gotten at least one good punch on Jessica Minor.

That happy thought gave me courage to consider my shadowy friend. The good news was the protections seemed to work at least a little, since the thing was on the street and not at the window. The question was, why was it here at all? Because I'd poked my nose into its business? From the acid words that Jess spewed while under the influence, the Shadow seemed to have a serious mad-on for me.

Which pretty much evaporated any improvement in my mood.

I pulled on jeans and a T-shirt and let my hair do its own thing. I was just thinking I should call Karen and see how she was doing, when my cell phone rang.

"Hi, Karen."

"Wow. Are you psychic or something?"

"Caller ID." I took the phone into the bathroom and reconsidered putting some powder on the bruise on my cheek. "How are you feeling? When do you go home from the hospital?"

"Maybe this afternoon. It depends." Something evasive lay under that, but she continued before I could ask. "Was that Jeff Espinoza's Mustang on the news this morning? They said that the driver was taken to the hospital."

"Yeah."

"Wow." She paused. "Is this anything like my accident?"

I'd given up on the mirror and gone back to the study, finding myself looking at the symbols I'd sketched during the night. I worried my lip, wondering how much to tell her. "Maybe."

"Huh. Well, okay." I stopped her before she could hang up.

"Karen, are you all right? Did you really call just to ask about the accident?"

There was another pause, a long, heavy one. "No. I don't know. Something weird is going on."

I sat down. "What is it?"

She made several attempts to start, as if getting up her courage. "I was trying to get caught up on my homework yesterday, and when I started my calculus the equations just . . . didn't make any sense. It was like trying to read Chinese."

"You've forgotten how to do calculus?"

"I can't make sense of any numbers at all." Her voice caught, a tiny, heartbreaking sound. "They think I may have swelling in a very localized part of the brain."

"Oh, Karen, that's so . . ." *Weird.* ". . . awful. I know how much you love math."

"I do, it's my best subject."

"I'm so sorry. But maybe if the swelling goes down . . . ?" I trailed off hopefully.

"If it does, the doctor hopes the ability will come back." She gave a laugh, half brave and half ironic. "You know, ever since I blew the answer in the State Mathlete Finals, I've had this fear that one day I would just lose it."

"You're not losing it," I reassured her. "It'll come back when the swelling goes down."

"I hope so. I didn't mean to whine about that. I mostly called because of the news. The whole school knows how much Jeff loves that car."

"Yeah." Something about that was important, but my brain needed time to work on it.

"Jessica Prentice was on the news. She looked haggard." Karen sounded only a little pleased with this report on Prime's appearance. "Is she sick?"

"Only in the head."

"Gotta go. Doctor's here."

Our time was up. I wished her good luck and closed the phone slowly, my mind spinning.

Karen loved math. Henchman Jeff loved his Mustang. Thespica loved the limelight. They had to be the first few turns of a pattern. Not enough to see what the completed shape would be, but definitely interlinked.

I went downstairs, still wearing a distracted frown.

"Everything all right, Maggie?" Mom and Dad had a Saturday-morning routine: sofa, bathrobes and slippers, newspaper, coffee, box of doughnuts. I grabbed one of the latter.

"Yeah. Karen's been out of school for a few days, so I was catching her up on the gossip."

Mom held up the local section of the *Avalon Sentinel*. "Is this boy one of your classmates?" Mouth full of doughnut, I nodded, and she tsked. "That section of Beltline is awful. They need more traffic lights."

The doorbell rang. "I'll get it." I snagged another dough-nut on the way to the door.

Brian Kirkpatrick stood on our front stoop, looking like he hadn't slept all night. He skipped right past the pleasantries and demanded, "How did you know about the crash?"

It was dumb luck I didn't choke to death on my doughnut.

"Who is it?" Dad called from the living room.

"Jehovah's Witness!" I yelled back as I stepped out and shut the door behind me. "What are you doing here? How did you find out where I live?"

"There aren't that many Quinns in the phone book. How did you know what was going to happen?"

I shushed him, as if my parents could somehow still eavesdrop. "I didn't. You haven't told anyone what I said, have you?"

"No. The others didn't hear you. Jess just thinks you were coming on to me."

Lovely. "Is she okay?"

"Yeah. And what the hell was *that* all about?"

"I couldn't tell you," I said in perfect honesty. "What about Jeff?"

"Compound open fracture of his leg is the worst of it."

"That's pretty bad."

Brian shook his head, looking grim. "He's lucky. And so am I. If I'd been in the passenger seat, I would have been crushed like a bug on the grill of that Hummer."

I glanced away, knowing it was true and unable to look at him with the mangled sports car superimposed on my memory. "Would you believe I just had a bad feeling about it?"

He stared at me for a long moment, evaluating my sincere expression, and the impossibility of any other explanation. Then he shoved his fingers through his short mop of blond hair. "Okay. I'll buy that."

I slanted a nervous glance up at him. "You won't tell anyone, will you?"

He seemed surprised at the idea. "No."

"Good. Because the last thing I need right now is the head cheerleader screaming, 'I saw Goody Quinn dancing with the devil in the moonlight.'"

A slow, reluctant smile turned up the corners of his mouth. "Yeah. Those girls in *The Crucible*. They were totally Jessicas."

We were laughing over that when Justin pulled up behind my Jeep in the driveway. Naturally. He climbed out of the car, pausing uncertainly when he saw me entertaining a gentleman caller on the front stoop.

I waved him over, trying to sober toward dignity. "Hi! I thought you had to study."

"I do, eventually." He started up the walk. "I tried to call you, but your phone kept sending me to voice mail."

"I must have been talking to Karen."

Justin glanced curiously at Brian. Brian slanted a look at Justin. And then they both looked at me.

Awkward.

"Justin, this is Brian Kirkpatrick, from school. Brian, this is Justin MacCallum, my, um, friend."

Brian offered a handshake instead of his usual "Hey." His forearm flexed handsomely during that hearty clasp, and Justin's knuckles went slightly white. Their expressions, however, were genially inscrutable.

See, this was when psychic mojo would come in handy. But my inner eye gave me no clue. My inner nose, on the other hand, detected the strong odor of testosterone.

The door behind me opened. "Phone for you, Mags. It's—" Dad stopped, looking at the two guys on our front walk. It was probably a sign of the apocalypse. "What is this? Grand Central Station?"

Brian took it as a cue to leave. "I'd better run. See you on Monday, Maggie?"

"Sure," I answered blithely, then remembered that he had asked me on a *date* for Monday. What had I just agreed to? From Brian's ear-to-ear grin, more than I'd intended. Consciously, anyway.

He nodded courteously to my dad, then to Justin, and took off toward the sporty car parked beside mine in the driveway. Dad glanced at me, one brow raised. "School stuff," I said evasively. "Can Justin come in?"

"Sure."

Justin followed us into the house, and I went straight to the phone extension in the living room. "Hello? This is Maggie Quinn."

"Hello, Miss Quinn. This is Dr. Smyth at the university's Chemistry Department. I hope you don't mind. I looked up your father's number in the faculty directory."

"Not at all! Thank you for calling."

"I've finished the gas chromotography on the sample that Silas Blackthorne gave me, and have the results for you."

Silas Blackthorne? Why was he teaching high school chemistry instead of penning lurid gothic novels?

"That's great news, Dr. Smyth. I've been anxious to hear from you."

"I imagine you have. You say you *sat* in something?"

Justin and Dad watched me curiously. "Uh, yeah. It's a little complicated to explain. Can you give me the information over the phone?"

"I could, but the results are as complex as your

explanation would undoubtedly be. I'll be in the lab for the rest of the morning. Are you busy?"

"No. I'd be happy to meet you." She gave me the building and room number. Justin peered shamelessly over my shoulder. "I'll be there in half an hour or so."

"No hurry."

I hung up and faced my audience. "I need to go to the Masterson Building. What street is that on?"

"I know where it is," said Justin, eager curiosity lighting his face.

"Let me put on some shoes."

Dad blocked my way to the stairs. He gave me a laser beam look, virtually identical to the ones I got from Gran. "Magdalena Quinn. What are you up to? I don't buy that you had to take pictures for the yearbook last night." He transferred a little of the intensity of that glare to Justin. "And I still have questions about what you two were doing on the roof."

"I explained that, Dad."

"You gave me a load of codswallop."

Codswallop? I knew it wasn't going to help my case to laugh so I forced my face into a concerned frown.

"Does this have to do with the nightmare you had last night?" he asked.

I didn't have to fake a scowl. "Dad."

"Your mother is worried about you. And your grandmother says to just let you be, which makes *me* worried." We could have stayed at an impasse all day, because I definitely get my stubbornness from his side of the family. "Just tell me this," he asked, "are you in danger?"

I paused to consider a lot of evasions. But meeting his

eye, I took the chance that he was as much like Gran as I was like him. "I don't think so, but others are. This is something I have to do, Dad."

This much I knew: I was in a race to learn as much as I could about the phantom before it grew any stronger.

He studied me for another long moment, then shook his head in defeat and stepped back. "All right. Go see Dr. Smyth. We'll talk more later."

"Thanks, Dad." As I ran upstairs, I heard him ask Justin, "Don't you have an anthropology paper that's due next week?"

"I'm on top of it, sir." Dad said something else, something that I couldn't hear despite straining my ears. Justin answered him, "I'll do my best."

He could have been talking about class work, but something told me not.

✳ ✳ ✳

Justin and I argued briefly over who should drive; I liked being in the driver's seat—big surprise—but in the end it came down to efficiency. His car was parked behind mine.

"What were you and Dad talking about while I went upstairs?" I didn't waste time once we were on the road. "You weren't making some macho, keep-the-little-woman-safe pact, were you?"

He flicked me a glance but otherwise kept his eyes on the road, Mr. Conscientious behind the wheel. "I can't imagine that any man who knows you would make that mistake."

A dogleg of an answer if ever I heard one. I spiked a volley in another direction. "You're not going to flunk out or anything because I dragged you into this mess, are you? I'm not sure I can afford the karma hit if you do."

His mouth turned up in a crooked smile. "I'm not going to flunk out. And you didn't hold me at gunpoint." I acknowledged that was true. "Anyway, I wouldn't be able to concentrate wondering what you'd left out of last night's drama."

"Did I leave anything out?" Sleep had been dragging me down when I'd talked to him on the phone. "I can't remember."

"Just start from the beginning. The long version."

I didn't have time for the long version; Avalon isn't that big of a town. I had just gotten to Jess Minor going postal, and the Shadow's malicious delight, when we pulled into one of the university's big parking lots, virtually empty on Saturday morning. Justin turned in his seat to face me, his square jaw set, one hand still grasping the steering wheel tightly.

"I wondered about the scratches." He reached out as if to touch my face, then redirected the movement, pointing to his own cheek instead. "You've got a bruise, too."

"Yeah." I held up my hand, knuckles out. "But look! I got in a punch, at least."

"Good for you." I couldn't interpret his tension, but I thought it might be that he was trying hard to restrain old-fashioned protectiveness. He confirmed my hunch when he asked, as if he couldn't help himself, "But you're all right? Your voice still sounds awful. I can't believe you didn't mention the almost dying part last night."

"I didn't almost die." I refused to believe anything different. "Do you think she was really possessed? I mean, her head didn't spin around or anything, but it was freaky."

"Possession is a term with a lot of baggage. Let's say, 'Overshadowed.'"

I shivered. I'd started thinking about the whatever-it-was as the Shadow, with a capital S. The word fit. "I'm cool with less implied *Exorcist* in my life."

Justin tapped his fingers thoughtfully on the steering wheel. "I wonder why the Minor one and not the leader? Or one of the boys, who might have easily done real damage to you?"

I shrugged and reached for the door handle. "Weak-minded but mean. She was the perfect hostess."

17

the Earth Science Building was limestone and granite, surrounded by a green lawn, spreading oaks, and tall pines. Bedivere University nestled just north of the center of town, an old, relatively small private school. A strong emphasis on arts and humanities doubtless accounted for the low enrollment. A shiny new science building was in the planning stages, but I would miss the cozy anachronism of the present one.

The chemistry lab lay on the second floor, up the stone steps and through a rabbit warren of plaster and paneled hallways. We found the room and peered in. It wasn't much different from the high school—rows of slate-topped lab benches, each with a sink and a gas spigot. (I'll bet the college kids were allowed to use theirs, though.) It was bigger, and had more equipment along one wall, as well as a computer workstation where a woman typed diligently.

"Dr. Smyth?"

She looked up. "Miss Quinn?"

"Maggie," I confirmed. "This is my friend, Justin MacCallum."

The professor was about my mom's age, with some of the same no-nonsense demeanor. Dr. Smyth had flaming red hair and a wildly curving figure not really hidden by her lab coat. She picked up a piece of paper and gestured us over, her expression serious. "Before we begin, I have to ask. Did Professor Blackthorne put you up to this?"

I blinked in surprise. "No ma'am. I asked him for help."

Dr. Smyth subjected me to an exaggerated scrutiny, then clicked her tongue and nodded. "All right then." She laid the paper on a meticulously neat lab bench. "What you have here, Miss Quinn, is a rather fragrant potpourri of organic compounds, amino acids, and a few minerals."

I scanned the list, as indecipherable as the foreign symbols in my dream. A couple of the suffixes rang a bell, though. "Ethanethiol and methanethiol? Those wouldn't be, ah, putrescine and cadaverine, would they?"

"No. Those are from the sulfhydryl group." Dr. Smyth sounded a little pissed, so I tried to prove I wasn't an idiot wasting her time.

"Dr. Blackthorne mentioned the thiols. Rotten egg smell."

"Yes. And swamp gas and cabbage. Skunk odor, too. Down here—" She pointed to two lines on the printout I wasn't even going to try to read, let alone pronounce. "Those are the two smelly little buggers that cost me a steak dinner."

"You bet a steak dinner on putrescine and cadaverine?"

"What would you have bet?" she asked curiously.

"That I might never eat meat again."

Justin had been reading over my shoulder. "I'm guessing those names are fairly descriptive?"

"Oh yes." Dr. Smyth explained with relish. "Both are released by the breakdown of amino acids during the putrefaction of animal tissue. In small amounts, they are present in living flesh as well, but we only notice them when things die and start to rot."

"Nice," I said, ready to move along. "Sulfur, sulfuric acid . . ."

Justin took the sheet from my hands. "That's green vitriol. It was a standard ingredient in alchemy formulas."

"Exactly," said the professor. "You see why I thought Silas might be pulling my leg. Especially with this one." She pointed to the list. "*Artemisia arborescens L.* Tree wormwood."

"Wormwood?" I asked. "Where have I heard of that before?"

"You may have heard of absinthe."

"There's a biblical reference, too," Justin added. "And C. S. Lewis used it as a name for a junior demon in *The Screwtape Letters*."

That all sounded familiar. "Isn't it a poison?"

Dr. Smyth shook her head. "Not this variety. It comes from the Middle East, and was brewed into a medicinal tea."

Justin spoke thoughtfully. "In Russian folklore, the literal translation for the plant is 'bitter truth' and it's associated with a spell to open the eyes of deluded people."

Dr. Smyth gave him an odd look and I explained, "His thesis." She nodded like this clarified everything. Maybe to another academic, it did.

I took the list back. "What's *Cinchona officinalis*?"

"That's where your fluorescence comes from. Quinine."

"Quinine?" Boy, which one of these was not like the others. "Like, for preventing malaria?"

"Yes. It's another organic compound. It binds to the blood cells so tightly that the malarial parasite cannot."

My mind was spinning, drawing a strange sort of picture. I flipped over the printout and sketched a flat, vaguely bowl-like shape. "Let's say I'm an alchemist."

"Okay," said Dr. Smyth, in a humoring-the-nutcase sort of voice. "Why are we saying that?"

What could I say that wouldn't get us tossed out of her lab so fast we bounced? She already suspected that Professor Blackthorne had set her up. I glanced at Justin, but he was no help. My next accomplice was going to be a much better liar.

"I'm working on a project." Dr. Smyth continued to gaze at me, bemused. "A creative writing project," I said with sudden inspiration.

The corner of her mouth lifted. I still got the feeling she was humoring me, but she said, "Okay, I'll bite." She leaned her elbows on the lab bench and looked at my drawing. "Is that your cauldron, then?"

"It's more of a brazier. For a fire, you know?"

"What is it made out of?"

"Does it matter?"

"Certain metals may be reactive with your potion." She seemed intrigued now. My dad was the same way, a sucker for an intellectual discussion, no matter how off the wall. "I assume that's where this exercise is headed."

I took up the gauntlet. "Say I start a fire, then add sulfur, which burns blue, right?"

"Yes." Dr. Smyth gave me a quizzical look. "But what purpose does it serve? It can't be just for aesthetics."

I considered the question. Professor Blackthorne is my favorite teacher, but chemistry is not my strongest subject. "Fire supplies the energy for the chemical reaction, right? What if the sulfur—or brimstone, since we're thinking like alchemists—is meant to evoke the energy of the earth?"

"Or of Hell," Justin added. I frowned at him, but he didn't back down.

Dr. Smyth nodded. "Right." She wrote "Fire and Brimstone" on the sketch and then, "Energy source." "If we allow for supernatural in your plot, then we allow for Hell."

"Can't we leave that out of the equation for the moment?" I could rationalize alchemy. It was, in its way, a science. "'Hell' sounds so melodramatic."

"Let's say the power of the underworld for now," said Dr. Smyth, writing it in parenthesis. "That covers the physical and spiritual possibilities. Now, what are we trying to accomplish with our spell?"

Their eyes went to me expectantly. I had been chewing on the idea for a while, but it was a struggle to voice. Talk about melodrama. "A curse. We're trying to curse someone."

Justin held my gaze for a silent moment. It was the first time I had acknowledged out loud that this wasn't a random spirit or undirected supernatural event. The thought that someone could have meant to kill or injure Karen or Jeff was an uncomfortable one.

"Excellent!" The professor continued with a brisk enthusiasm that drew me back to humor. We bent over the table to watch her scribble notes. "Wormwood—the bitter truth. We want to teach the cursee a lesson. The quinine . . ."

"It binds to the blood," I said. "Binds the curse to the victim." A thought distracted me: Or binds the servant spirit to the summoner.

Dr. Smyth continued. "Right. Putrescine and cadaverine. Well, those are harder."

"Not really," said Justin. "Eye of newt, toe of frog. Or whatever else is handy."

Dr. Smyth looked at him. "But why? Literary tradition? If the character goes to the trouble of putting this formula together, everything must have a purpose."

"A burnt offering," he suggested.

"Toe of frog?" she scoffed. "Not much of a sacrifice."

I straightened. "Decay is a kind of breaking down. Maybe we're trying to break down our victim, reduce him."

Dr. Smyth tapped the pen. "Seems a bit of a stretch metaphorically."

"So is 'bitter truth,'" I protested.

"That has a folklore precedent. But then, so does eye of newt and toe of frog." She jotted down "newt & frog." "But of course, it's your story, so you can write it any way you want."

Didn't I wish.

She and Justin squabbled amiably over what icky rotting things could be added, for what metaphorical or alchemical purpose. To Dr. Smyth it was an academic exercise, an amusement, and for a little while, listening to them, I let myself think of it that way, too.

But I realized what she didn't. The organic compounds, the nasty ones, didn't have to be part of the formula. They could be intrinsic to the thing that the spell had called.

✳ ✳ ✳

I thanked Dr. Smyth again as we left. "I appreciate all your help." We stood at the door of her office and I had the printout, with all our notes on it, folded in my hand.

"Not at all," she said. "I enjoy an esoteric puzzle, now and again. Good luck with the project." It took me a blank moment to realize she meant my very fictional fiction assignment. She pushed her hands into the pockets of her lab coat and continued. "The main thing to remember is that the supernatural has rules, just like the natural world. You simply have to figure out what they are."

"Right. Well. Thanks again."

We turned to go, but her voice called me back before we'd gone more than a few steps. "Maggie?"

"Yes, Professor?"

"I'm still curious. This substance that seems to have inspired your story. You never said where you came across it."

"The school gym," I said, because I was out of lies.

"Hmm." Her expression was doubtful, but she let it go. "Well, that would definitely convince me to wear flip-flops in the shower."

18

"You're quiet," Justin said once we were in the car.

"I'm trying to banish the mental image of Drs. Smyth and Blackthorne playing McGonagal and Snape in their off-duty hours."

He chuckled. "I'd like to meet Professor Blackthorne someday."

"He's a trip. I wish he taught English."

"It probably wouldn't be the same."

"It would have to be better than what I've got. Ms. Vincent has no sense of humor."

"I'll bet that's hard on you."

"What's that supposed to mean?"

"Only that you sort of live and die by the wisecrack."

I wondered if that was a good or bad thing in his eyes, and how much it mattered to me. "I like to keep my tongue honed to a sharp edge. I never know when I'll need it in a fight."

He navigated the left turn onto Beltline before he spoke again. "Want to get some lunch?"

"Don't you have to study?"

"I have to eat, too." Taking my silence for assent, he pulled into one of the restaurants on the strip. The Cadillac Grill had been a diner in the fifties. Back when *Grease* and *American Graffiti* were hot, someone had refurbished the building to all its *Rock Around the Clock* glory. Kitschy, but the food was good. We got one of the last tables without a wait.

I ordered a Coke, a cheeseburger, and fries without looking at the menu. Justin had iced tea and the chicken finger basket.

"Did they have chicken fingers back in the fifties?" I asked. "And what kind of name is that for food? Chickens don't have fingers and if they did, I wouldn't want to eat them."

His brows screwed up in the center. "I'm not really supposed to answer when you do that, am I?"

"No. I'm just showing you how clever I am."

"By mocking my food? Not very."

The waitress brought our drinks; I took a deep gulp of mine, and settled back in the vinyl seat. "So. What's your deal? You know practically everything about me, and I know almost nothing about you."

He clearly couldn't decide whether to be amused or not. "What do you want to know?"

I started with, "How long have you been at Bedivere?"

After a sip of his iced tea, he answered, "I transferred here last fall. I'm finishing my bachelor's and taking some grad-level courses."

"Are you in a big hurry to tackle that ivory tower?"

He smiled sheepishly. "There's a graduate internship I want to do this summer, and I had to have some preliminary courses to apply."

"Why Anthropology of the Bizarre? I mean, that wasn't something they really talked up at *our* Career Day."

An odd reserve entered his expression. "It's a long story."

I leaned forward, elbows on the table. "I hear the service here is slow."

He seemed to be considering things on some deep level, and I realized this was not something I could tease him about. But before he could tell me—or not—I heard my name.

"Maggie?" Instinctively, I turned.

"Oh hi, Jennifer." Great. The town crier, here at my table. "What are you doing here?" Besides spying on people.

"Eating, same as you." She addressed me, but her avidly curious gaze was on my tablemate. "Having a nice time?"

"Yes." I gave in to the inevitable. "Jennifer, this is Justin. Jennifer and I work on the school paper together."

"Nice to meet you." He smiled amiably.

"Same here." She beamed back, her shining brown curls falling over her shoulder as she turned her head. I couldn't decide if she had assumed he was my date, or assumed he wasn't, or which notion annoyed me more.

I shoved an unruly chunk of my own hair behind my ear. "So what's up?" I intended only distraction. I didn't expect her to pull up a chair and make herself comfortable, but that's what she did.

"I had to come tell you what I just heard, since we were talking about her the other day."

"Who?" A lot had happened in the last twenty-four hours.

"Jess Michaels. She was arrested for shoplifting a D&B bag."

Justin glanced at me curiously, and I mouthed "Minor" to clarify. I couldn't help him out with "D and B" though. I assumed it was a designer, and expensive. "But I thought she had money."

"*Everyone* thought so. As it turns out, her mother has the moolah, and she buys Jess stuff on her custody visits. But her dad can't afford the newest Prada, I guess, so she took a five-finger discount."

My mind circled back to the day I'd played tabloid reporter in the bathroom. "With Jessica Prime telling everyone her clothes were fakes, maybe she felt she had to have something new to save face."

"I know. But here's the thing." Jennifer leaned in close, as if revealing a secret. "I saw her wearing that blue Ralph Lauren sweater in September, and I swear it was the real label. But when I saw her yesterday, it was such an obvious copy I couldn't believe I'd ever been fooled."

"How strange." I spoke noncommittally, disinterested.

"Maybe Jess had to sell her good clothes," she mused, "and bought cheap replacements so no one would know."

"That's one explanation." A perfectly *un*natural alternative occurred to me, but why would a phantom care about fashion? "But that's just speculation, Jennifer," I cautioned. "I wouldn't spread it around."

She pantomimed locking her lips, but I didn't feel reassured. "I'll get back to my friends. Just had to say hi! Nice to meet you, Justin."

She fluttered off while the server put our lunch on the table. I sagged back in the booth, smacking the lump on my head on the wall behind me. "Ow. What just happened?"

"You were hypothesizing." Justin kept his voice neutral. "In unwise company."

"Just say it." I sat up and began to take the lettuce, tomato, and onion off my burger. "I was gossiping."

"I didn't know you were interested in fashion." He tested a poultry digit and found it too hot to handle.

"I'm not." I picked at my burger a moment longer. "It occurred to me this morning that all these people are losing what's most important to them. Image is extremely important to Jess Minor. She's always trying to keep up with the others. Losing status is the worst thing that could happen to her. Maybe there's some kind of illusion on her stuff."

He chewed a french fry thoughtfully. "That's why you suggested the chemistry experiment might be a curse."

I nodded. "I think that's why the Shadow leaves behind that stuff. If the—recipe, spell, whatever—creates it . . ."

"Or summons it," he said, ignoring his food now.

I didn't much like where that thought was headed, but a good journalist stays open-minded. "Or summons it," I allowed.

"So the question remains, what *is* the Shadow."

"Some kind of agent," I hypothesized, "fulfilling the curse. Like a messenger spirit."

Justin caught my gaze. "Like a demon, you mean."

"Well, I was trying to avoid that word." Especially in a crowded restaurant.

"Why can you say 'ghost' or 'spirit' without flinching, but not 'demon'?"

Good question. I tucked my hair behind my ears. "I don't know. Too many of those melodramatic connotations. Horns and pitchforks and things."

Leaning his elbows on the table, he gave me a long look. "That's a relatively modern, Western caricature, and not what I'm talking about at all."

"I know." I shook my head. "But I have to wrap my brain around this in stages."

The one thing I knew was this: If I was right, and someone had summoned some *thing* to bring down the Jocks and Jessicas, then regardless of the source, of the justness of the targets, the intent was Evil. With a capital E.

Justin looked like he might press the issue, but after a moment he let out his breath and reached for a chicken finger. "All right. Let's get back to Jessica Minor's shoplifting arrest. Do you think she might still be overshadowed?"

"No. I think that, robbed of what she valued, she'd do anything to try and recapture it." I picked up my burger. "Besides, I broke the connection, remember."

"You didn't finish telling me. How'd you do that?" he asked the instant my mouth was crammed with food. I tried to chew with undignified haste, then just picked up the saltshaker and mimed throwing it on him. He fell back against the bench, staring at me in surprised joy. "You mean it actually worked?"

My eyes bugged out of my head. I swallowed the much-too-big mouthful of burger and choked out, "What do you mean 'it actually worked'? You didn't *know* it was going to work?"

"Well, on paper, sure. But . . ." My outrage popped his bubble of satisfaction. "What? Everything I'd read said it should work as well as anything I could have given you."

"Everything you've *read*?" The sorority girls at the next table turned to see what I was squawking about. I lowered my voice, leaning against the table. "You mean you've never actually dealt with anything like this before?"

"Not personally, no."

"I trusted you!" My throat squeezed out the words, trying to be quiet. "I thought you knew what you were doing."

He threw the chicken finger into the basket. "It isn't as if I made this stuff up. It may be secondhand knowledge, but at least I'm not basing it on Bill Murray movies."

"That was just a starting place!" Indignant, I forgot about whispering. "I have been as logical and methodical as I can, under some pretty extraordinary circumstances."

He waved a hand in frustration. "You're trying to force this thing to fit in a real-world box, but you won't even fully admit it exists."

The truth didn't make it any easier to swallow. "At least I admit I don't know what I'm dealing with."

His eyes hardened to chips of stone. "At least I'm willing to commit to my hypothesis without closing my mind to the more unpleasant possibilities."

That stung. "Closed" and "minded" were fighting words for me, and I struck back below the belt. "Yeah, but you tested your hypothesis on me. Some paladin you are."

The angry color ran out of his face. I felt a prick of guilt for smacking him right in the self-image, for knowing how to hurt him and using it. But I was still too mad to take it back, even if I knew how. So I dropped my gaze and climbed out of the booth, digging into my pocket to pay for my burger. "I told you when we met, I didn't want to be your research project."

"Maggie, sit down."

"No. I'm too angry to eat."

"Then put your money away." He leaned on one hip to pull out his wallet. The waitress appeared as if conjured, like a pert blond genie from the lamp.

"Is there a problem?"

"We're going to need some to-go boxes." He handed her a twenty and she vanished before I could give her the wadded up bills for my half of the meal. Furious at being treated like an invisible child, I shoved them in Justin's direction. "Here. This should cover me."

"Stop being such a brat, and sit down."

That was the final straw. My face flamed with hurt anger, and rather than prove him right by bursting into a tantrum, or tears, or both, I turned and left.

"Have a nice day!" said the poodle-skirted hostess as I made a beeline for the door. I knew they made her say that, so I didn't tell her *exactly* what kind of day I was having.

Justin caught up with me in the parking lot. He didn't have the to-go boxes. "Don't even think about walking home."

How had I ever thought he was Mr. Nice Guy? "It's not that far."

"With everything that's happened around you? Across the street is too far."

"That's not your problem." I waved him off. "I absolve you of responsibility."

He clenched his jaw and ground out between his teeth, "I'll see you back safely." End of discussion. I ached to tell him he wasn't the boss of me, but didn't want to be called a brat again.

I stomped to the car instead, fumed while he unlocked the door, then huffed into the bucket seat. Justin went to his side, but paused for several calming breaths before he climbed behind the wheel.

He drove with tense deliberation while I sulked. The urge to scream or explode had evaporated; that only left the threat of tears. "Why don't you just say it?"

He kept his eyes on the road. "Say what?"

"Whatever is making that muscle in your jaw twitch."

"Because I'm focusing my anger on getting to your house in one piece so I can dump your ungrateful"—He struggled a moment, then settled on—"backside, and be done."

I folded my arms. "Oh, just say 'ass.' The world won't end if you're rude. My universe would have imploded a long time ago if rudeness were fatal."

He turned off of Beltline and onto a smaller, safer street. "Really? I thought you were making an exception for me."

I twisted to face him. "I thought you had experience with this stuff. I trusted you."

"I never said that, Maggie. Sure I have a broader base of knowledge than you—though that's not saying much. I've done research and interviews and studies. But it's not like there's some kind of paranormal lab practical."

Unreasonably I clung to the idea that it *was* his fault for projecting such confidence that, desperate to believe someone was equipped to deal with the supernatural, I'd given him more credit than he claimed.

He turned onto the residential road that led to my house. "Why are we even arguing about this? It worked, didn't it?"

"It might not have." Now I was just being stubborn.

"But it did!" Finally he was raising his voice.

"But you should have *told* me it might not work."

Another turn, onto my street. "Half of the power of a talisman is the belief that it will work."

"Like Dumbo and his stupid magic feather?"

"Yeah." He pulled into the driveway and stopped so abruptly that my seatbelt jerked me backward. "Exactly like Dumbo."

He unbuckled and got out of the car. I scrambled out after him. What kind of guy walks a girl to the door even in the middle of an argument? "What does *that* mean?"

"That for a smart girl you're acting pretty dumb, fighting over technicalities." He faced me, arms folded across his chest. "You need me. Who else is going to believe you, let alone help you?"

My posture mirrored his. "Apparently I can simply read a book."

"Great idea. Because a book will definitely give a damn

what happens to you when you get in over your head. *Further* over your head."

He seemed to be waiting for me to say something else, but reeling from the fact that (a) he'd cursed and (b) he gave a damn what happened to me, I hesitated too long.

"Fine." He dropped his arms and turned away. "You know where to find me."

I needed to respond. I wanted to say *something*. But I didn't know what would fix the mess I'd made of things. Except "I'm sorry" and even that wouldn't come out past the stubborn stranglehold of emotions in my throat.

So I just let him leave.

19

the real world marched along, for the moment at least. Regardless of what went on in the supernatural realm, I had an English paper due in a couple of days. As I plugged away at it without enthusiasm, my dad came halfway up the stairs and peered through the banister rail. "Mom and I are thinking about Chinese food for dinner. Are you in?"

"Yeah." My stomach growled at the thought. Those three bites of cheeseburger hadn't gone far. "I want egg foo young and an order of spring rolls."

But instead of going back down the stairs, he came up to the study. "Did you and Justin have a fight?"

"What makes you say that?"

"The shouting on the lawn was a clue."

I groaned and slithered down until my butt was nearly hanging off the chair. "I was such a brat."

"Probably."

"You're not supposed to agree with me."

"Why is that?"

"Because you're my father."

He bent over and kissed the top of my head. "That only guarantees that I'll love you when you're a brat, not that I'll never think you are one."

I sighed, deeply. "That's fair, I guess."

His curious glance fell on my desk. "What's this?"

I spun the chair with my foot. "My theory that the microcosm of the American high school is represented in the lands that Gulliver encounters in his travels."

"Interesting theory, but I was talking about this." He held up the sketch I'd made that morning, of the symbols engraved on the brazier.

"Oh." How much to tell him? If I spilled it all, he might believe me. And then he'd lock me in my room and call for a priest. That would put an end to my Nancy Drew—ing.

So I parceled out a little of the truth. "I dreamed about an oasis, with tents, and a woman at the well. There was a campfire, and those symbols were carved in the brazier that held the coals."

Dad raised his brows. "Interesting. They look Assyrian, or maybe Babylonian. That's not really my area."

"I thought they looked Hebrew."

He considered them again. "Perhaps the same family. I

can ask Dr. Dozer if you like. She's done a lot of work in the Middle and Near East. Went on some expeditions there, before the first Gulf War."

I stopped listening after the name "Dozer." Stanley. How could I not have seen it before?

Dad had stopped talking, expecting an answer. I backtracked to his question. Thank God for mental TiVo. "No, thanks. Let me do a little more research, okay? It could be just nonsense."

He laid the paper back on the desk. "Okay. You know I'll help you however I can."

I smiled up at him. "I know."

He headed for the stairs. "Egg foo young and spring rolls," he confirmed before he left.

I rooted through piles of paper and books until I found the flash drive where I'd stored those pictures from the week before. I plugged it in and clicked on the folder marked "in_case_of_death."

The first photo popped open, showing Stanley's face frozen in terror, his long legs hooked over the brick wall of the elevated walkway, while Brandon and Jeff, laughing like maniacs, held him suspended over the two-story drop. Brian stood back, looking torn and miserable, and the Three Original Jessicas pointed and twittered like the birdbrains they were.

Of the seven people in the snapshot, four had something strange happen to them. Only Karen wasn't in the picture. Did she not fit the pattern, or was I not seeing the whole thing?

I clicked "print" and picked up the phone to call Justin.

Then I stopped. I wasn't angry with him anymore, but my pride still stung. We'd both thrown a lot of darts, and maybe his were more just than mine. It was all very complicated, even more so because I was unsure if this was a friends and colleagues argument, or a guy/girl thing.

I had guy/girl thoughts about Justin, but I had no idea if he thought about me that way. When he met Brian today, his careful neutrality could have meant anything from "Me, Tarzan. You in my tree," to "Maggie's like a sister to me."

Brian, on the other hand, hadn't quite thumped his chest, but when I accidentally agreed to Monday's date, he was pretty clearly thinking "guy wins girl." If only I didn't have this picture of him, standing by and doing nothing while his friends terrified Stanley.

I stared at the photo, studying the faces, frozen in that pivotal moment. Stanley Dozer. "You'll all be sorry," he'd said. Had he found some otherworldly alternative to a black trench coat and an AK-47?

✳ ✳ ✳

I tossed restlessly in bed. Time had dilated somehow, and my paper was due tomorrow. Besides the Swift theme, I needed to write an article about Jeff Espinoza's accident, finish two chemistry lab reports, and compose a one-page essay for civics. No wonder my brain felt feverish and overheated.

I didn't remember getting up, but abruptly found myself at my computer, facing a blank document on the screen, my paper not even begun. I wondered briefly how I could have forgotten to start the darned thing; some deep, muted voice in my head said that wasn't right. Something was off about this whole scenario. But the immediate panic of the looming deadline drowned out all logic. I had to get cracking.

Let's see. Jonathan Swift. Irishman. Satirist and misanthrope.

I typed the title: *Satire for Social Change*. So far so good. Too bad I'd waited until the morning it was due, not to mention the seven chemistry reports and a six-page essay on the judicial branch of government.

Thesis sentence: *Jonathan Swift was a real good writer. When he rote stuff for the Irish noospaper, it pissed off the government and they said, we can tacks you all we want, because we're English, and we have a big army and a cool flag.*

Class started in fifteen minutes, and at this rate, I wasn't even going to be able to start those ten lab reports. I scrolled up and looked at what I'd done so far.

What the Hell?

Who wrote this crap? An illiterate twelve-year-old?

I deleted and tried again: *Jonithen Swift rote about stuff that was bad and made fun of it, and it was real funny, and made people think . . .*

I shoved back from the computer, rejecting the words there. They were moronic. Infantile.

"How did you get in this class?" asked Ms. Vincent, appearing at my desk. I wanted to ask what she was doing in my room, but I saw we were actually in her classroom, complete with the cartoon pencils and erasers dancing over the chalkboard.

"You should never have been allowed in AP English," said Vincent. "You'll have to finish the year in that class, over there." I turned to where she pointed; a door led to another classroom—this one filled with three football players (in uniform), a couple of Drill Team Barbies (doing their nails), a few stoners (stoned), and a pimple-faced, greasy-haired boy wearing a Wal-Mart smock, who pointed to a desk beside him and said, "You can sit by me, Maggie."

I turned to Ms. Vincent to protest, but all that came out of my mouth was gibberish. She looked at me pityingly and I ran from the room, into B Hall.

Halloran was there and I tried to tell him there was a terrible mistake with my schedule, but only nonsense words spilled from my lips. "Very funny," he said. "That's what you get for pretending you're so much smarter than everyone else."

This wasn't true, and I told him so, but still I could only speak Martian.

"Stop horsing around, Quinn," he barked, "or I'll put you in detention until the end of the year."

I ran the B Hall gauntlet of mocking laughter, sick heat spreading through me at the jeers and taunts. I found Karen, stitches on her head, and I tried to tell her what was happening. She looked at me in sweet-natured confusion. "I don't understand, Maggie. Is this a joke?"

"It's the thing I value most . . ." But of course my words made no sense to either of us.

At the end of the hall, Stanley and Lisa stood side by side. "You did this," I yelled at Stanley. "It's not funny!"

"Sorry, Maggie," Stanley sneered from his towering height. "I can't understand you. I don't speak loser."

I grabbed him by the plaid western shirt and pulled him down to my level. I wanted to hit him, to hurt him. To punish somebody for the panicked terror seizing my mind. "Take this curse off me!"

"You're dreaming, Maggie." Lisa's sensible voice. Just as it had while I was wigging out about the locker room photo, her droll practicality cut through my rioting emotions to the rational person inside. "Wake up now. Everything will be fine."

I turned my head to look at her, a bubble of hope rising in my chest. "Bewop?" I said.

"Yeah, really."

And with an abruptness that was almost anticlimactic, I woke up.

* * *

The room was dark, except for the nightlight casting shadows on the wall. I snaked a hand out from the covers, irrationally afraid something waited to grab it. The bedside lamp was more effective, and I sat up to cast my eyes suspiciously around the room. I didn't see or smell anything, but I could feel the sweat of panic drenching my nightshirt, and the dampness of tears on my face.

So, what had I learned from the dream? That I prized my communication skills above all else. And I was probably more proud of my brains than I ought to be. Sobering thought. Perhaps it wasn't so much a question of what they—okay, what *we*—valued most, but where our vanity lay.

I forced myself out of bed and to the computer; a jiggle of the mouse brought it to life. I let out a breath as I saw my nearly completed English paper on the screen. Then I sat down, opened a new document, and poised my hands over the keyboard.

I typed: "To be, or not to be. That is the question. Whether 'tis nobler in the mind to suffer the slings and arrows of outrageous fortune, or by opposing, end them."

I got up. Paced the room. Sat down. Read the words on the screen. They looked exactly as they should.

Then I entered: "The core dilemma for Hamlet is the question we all face: Do we endure the crap that life dishes out, or do we fight against it, even if it would be easier to just lie down and let fortune have its way?"

Not the most eloquent, but when I looked back at what I'd written, it didn't say: "Trouble, bad. Sleep, good."

I got up from the desk and rubbed my hands over my tired face. *To sleep, perchance to dream.* Screw that.

Walking to the window, I paused a moment, then brushed back the edge of the curtain. I saw no shadows other than those cast by the pecan tree, rustling lightly in the breeze.

I'd always thought *Hamlet* was a dumb play about a guy who can't make up his mind. I mean, I face the same drama in the lunch line. But at that moment I understood: When it comes to the big stuff, it *is* hard to decide whether to let things just happen, especially when its to other people, or to take a stand and cause yourself a world of trouble.

The dream could have just been the egg foo young, or the pot of my fears stirred by the events of the day. But no. I hadn't seen fire or smoke in the dream, but I'd felt the threat. I'd been warned, told to let slings and arrows have their way.

Like that was going to happen. Old Smokey had no idea who he was messing with.

20

monday morning I took up arms against a sea of troubles. I marched into the school office, asked to see the nurse, and learned we only have one on Tuesdays and Thursdays.

"What if someone gets sick on a Monday, Wednesday, or Friday?"

The secretary looked at me without humor. "Then you get to go home."

"I'm just learning this now? All those civics classes I suffered through, for nothing."

She sighed. "What do you want, Maggie? You know we're super busy before school."

I chewed my lip, deciding how to proceed. "What if I'm worried about the health of a student? Who would I talk to?"

The secretary tilted her ash-blond head. I could see her flick through the mental card catalog of possibilities—drugs, pregnancy, depression. "You could talk to one of the assistant principals."

"Is Mrs. Cardenas available?"

"No. Just Mr. Halloran. Would you like me to see if he has time to see you?" Her drolly bland expression said she knew the answer to that question.

"Uh, maybe later. First I have to make an appointment for that root canal I've been putting off."

"Right. See you, Maggie."

"See you, Ms. Jones."

I grumped out of the office, irritated to be sidelined so quickly. Bad enough I had to rescue Jessica Prime at all. I wanted to get it over with.

"Maggie!" Brian found me in the busy courtyard, a smile on his handsome face. He made a token effort to sober up. "I heard you and your friend had a fight at Cadillac Grill. I'm sorry."

"No, you're not."

"If he's just your friend, then I am. If he's more than that, maybe not." He flashed an unrepentant grin and I had to give him points for honesty. He handed me a ticket. "That will get you into the game this afternoon. When it's over, I thought we could get something to eat."

I had a lot to do that afternoon. Besides homework, newspaper, and yearbook, there was saving the world as well. Where was I going to fit in a date?

But none of these excuses actually made it to my lips and

Brian took my silence as assent. He dashed off before I could tell him to be extra careful.

I turned to go to my own class, but stopped when I saw Jessica Prime staring at me from near the picnic tables. There was malice in her eyes, but that didn't shock me. It was the sunken hollows in her cheeks and the collarbones jutting out like knives. She looked like a walking toothpick with a pair of grapes stuck on the front. Her fake boobs were the only things with any life. The rest of her was deflated down to the bones.

How had this happened so quickly? Was the change so fast, or was I looking with new eyes? Either way, it was clear I wasn't going to be able to wait for the nurse to return tomorrow. I had to take action immediately.

✳ ✳ ✳

I arrived in the locker room early, which should have given Coach Milner's marathon-conditioned heart an attack. She glanced up from her desk as I tapped on her office door. "Got a minute, Coach?"

"Certainly, Quinn. Have a seat. If you're worried about your grade for the swimming portion of the six weeks—"

She broke off with a raised eyebrow as I closed the door and sat down purposefully. "It's not my grade. Though I will point out that lots of people have phobias about the water. But this is about Jessica Prime—I mean, Prentice."

"Prentice? What about her?"

"Last Friday, when I went back to get my goggles, I heard her throwing up. In secret."

The coach's eyes narrowed. "You shouldn't jump to conclusions, Quinn. Maybe lunch wasn't agreeing with her."

"I don't think *any* food is agreeing with her."

"Look, Quinn. Not everyone with a trim figure is anorexic or bulimic. As a cheerleader, Prentice must be rigid about diet and exercise. You shouldn't let jealousy color your perceptions."

I sat back in the molded plastic chair. "Jealousy?"

"Yes. You struggle in every physical activity, when you bother to try at all. For your height, you could stand to lose at least five pounds. I've been teaching P.E. for a long time, and I can tell you, a healthy body comes with hard work."

"Yeah, well, I don't think that includes sticking a finger down my throat." Furious, I surged to my feet. "I thought you'd be an advocate for a healthy person, not just a thin body. My five extra pounds means an extra book read, or another banana split I shared with my dad. I'm happy like I am, and I am certainly not jealous of Jessica Cheers-for-Brains Prentice."

"That's detention, Quinn." Milner's face went red beneath her sun-bronzed tan. She shoved a D Hall slip at me. "Take it and go."

"Fine." I grabbed the pass from her. "But open your eyes and take a look at her *today*, not how you remember her looking last week. Just help her. Please."

I stormed out, leaving the door open behind me. I ran into a crowd of girls in various stages of dress, their changing interrupted as they gathered to stare in confusion at Jessica Prentice. It was impossible to call her "Prime" while she gazed at herself in the mirror and wept in unfeigned anguish.

"How did this happen?" she wailed, unable to tear her

eyes from her reflection. "I haven't eaten anything. I've exercised two, three hours every day."

I could sense the funeral pyre stench at the back of my throat. I was attuned to the smell by this time; it seemed faint. Days old.

Thespica stood to one side of the mirror, her face twisted with anxiety. "You don't look fat, Jessica." She wrung her fingers into a fearful knot. "Maybe, if you're worried, you should see a doctor."

The crowd parted for Coach Milner. If the scene weren't so pathetic, I would have relished her shocked expression.

"What's going on, Prentice?" Milner asked when she had recovered herself. She pitched her tone somewhere near its usual go-get-'em bluster.

"Look at me, Coach." Jessica could not tear her gaze from the mirror. "I'm so . . . fat."

"You're not fat, Prentice." She moved slowly, reaching to take the girl's arm. "You're going to be fine. Why don't we go in my office and talk?"

"No!" She pulled away. "I know you think I must be eating like a pig, but I'm not. I'm not eating at all." Tears slipped down her gaunt cheeks.

"I know you're not. Let's just go in my office. . . ."

Milner turned her gently away from her reflection. Jessica saw me, and started to shriek. That was always such a pleasure.

"It's her, isn't it? Did she tell you I'm crazy? She hates me, you know."

"Let's leave Quinn out of this."

"She's just jealous!" The girl began to sob. "Or she *was*. Now look at me! I'm disgusting."

I looked. Not at her, but in the mirror. When Jessica opened her eyes and gazed at her image, I saw her tooth-pick-and-grape figure burble and warp. In its place was a girl I had never seen before. It wasn't merely that she was fat. She was certainly overweight—rolls of flesh strained against her too-small clothes—but a wardrobe change would do wonders.

No, this girl in the mirror, wearing Jessica Prime's clothes, her hair, her boobs, was ugly. She had piggish eyes and a bulbous nose and as I watched, her face erupted in a minefield of gaping black pores and pus-filled pimples.

Jessica screamed. The sound echoed off the metal lockers and the tile floors. Some of the girls put their hands over their ears. Some were too appalled to move. They couldn't see what Jessica saw in her reflection. To their eyes, her perfection was marred only by her emaciation and slipping sanity.

She reached her hands to her face and began to claw at it, to tear the skin. I jumped forward to stop her, dizzy from the dual vision of the girl, nearly perfect and utterly grotesque. As she raked her nails over her cheeks, in the mirror the pimples popped and ran, and I gagged on the putrid smell. It was as if, in the vision-Jessica, all the rot inside her oozed out of her face.

I squeezed my eyes shut and dragged her hands down as Coach Milner came to help. Jessica fought us like a wild thing, flailing and kicking, shrieking at the top of her lungs. Milner got her in a restraining hold, wrapping whipcord arms around her from behind, and gently but inexorably lowering the struggling girl to the floor.

"Call nine-one-one," she said as Jessica went limp. In her weakened state, she was no match for the coach. She subsided, sobbing, a wretched heap of sticks on the cold tile floor.

21

I met Lisa after school at Froth and Java, desperate for a caffeine boost and some debriefing. "On the other hand," I told her at the end of my tale, "I did avoid landing in detention for the second day in a row."

Battlefield humor. We sat outside and the balmy afternoon with its endless blue sky stood in glaring contrast to my gnawing worry.

Lisa leaned back in her chair, arms folded. "How do you keep ending up in the thick of these things?"

I sipped my vanilla latte. "Believe me, it's not by choice."

"What do you care if Queen Jessica wastes away to

nothing? She took that humiliating picture so she and her friends could cackle at you."

"Thanks for reminding me."

Lisa plopped her elbows on the table. "I'm serious. If you were a different kind of girl, you might have slit your wrists."

"But I didn't. I never even thought of it." In fact, I was shocked at the idea.

"That's because you're reasonably together, and you have me for a friend. But you *were* hiding in the toilet."

My cheeks heated up. "That was temporary."

"And yet you know how it felt." She stabbed her finger on the glass table, nailing home her point. "How many girls commit suicide because of witches like Jessica? If not all at once, then slowly, by starving or eating themselves to death. Or by sleeping around to try and find some self-esteem."

"So that makes it right that Jessica Prime got hauled away to the funny farm?" Her screams still echoed in my head.

Lisa scowled and traced a figure in the condensation that dripped from her soda. "It seems fitting, if a little extreme. But you can't expect a Jessica to do anything without going over the top." She took a drink and set the cup back down.

I could see her point. The bane of so many girls' lives, flipping out in the locker room and having to be taken away in restraints? There *was* a kind of cosmic justice to it. But the cosmos, or Fate, or deity of your choice hadn't set this in motion. Someone earthly had meted a malicious and disturbing vengeance.

Lisa changed the subject and I was happy to let her. "Who is this guy you were arguing with at Cadillac Grill?"

"Justin. A friend of mine."

"Uh-huh. So why don't I know this 'friend'?" she asked.

I twisted the insulating sleeve on my cardboard cup. "Because he's . . . new."

"I heard he was cute."

"Very."

She gave me a squinty, what-is-your-damage sort of look. "Then why in heaven's name are you going out with Brian Kirkpatrick tonight?"

"I sort of agreed to it by accident." And since he was one of the six in the picture, I figured it might be a good idea to stick around him.

As if reading my mind—and I wouldn't quite put it past her—Lisa said, "I don't know what I think about your having this ESP, or whatever it is, if it's going to keep you hanging around the Jocks and Jessicas."

"Well, they're dwindling fast, aren't they? There aren't any Jessicas left."

"Oh, Minor will be back." Lisa paused with a devilish smile. "When she makes bail."

Now *that* I could laugh at.

* * *

Avalon High's home games were held on the university's baseball diamond. I arrived during the third inning; I could see the scoreboard from the parking lot. This was my compromise, to avoid seeming too eager for this to be a *date*.

It was a perfect baseball evening, with the kind of temperate weather that makes me love spring in Avalon. Under a very slight breeze, the sun bowed out gradually, lending a warm light but not too much glare: the magic hour, in photography terms.

I brought my camera with me and took pictures of the spectators with the light of the setting sun on their faces, bags of popcorn in their hands. Of the left-field guy, hands on knees in an anticipatory crouch, dirt-streaked uniform against the vibrant green grass. Idyllic, boys-of-summer stuff.

Eventually I found a seat behind the home-team's dugout. Brian got on base the first time I saw him go to bat. He was tagged out at second on what the guy beside me called "a really nice squeeze play." He was of a parental age, and wore a blue-and-gold Avalon T-shirt. This was either very cute or very sad.

When Brian jogged back to the dugout, he seemed unsteady on his feet. He waved his coach's concern away. Mine was less easily put aside.

"You all right?" I asked when he came over to say hi.

He pulled off his hat and rested his elbows on the fence. Even hat hair looked good on him. "I'm fine. Just a little hot. Are you having a good time?" he asked.

"Sure. Too bad about that squeeze play." I hope that impressed him, because it was the only baseball I spoke.

He shrugged. "That's how the game is played."

If you say so. What did I know?

The coach called out to him, "Hey, Kirkpatrick. Stop flirting and get on the field."

"See you on the next side out," I said.

Brian laughed and put his hat back on. "Funny. See you

next inning. Bye, Dad!" He waved at Mr. Squeeze Play, and then grabbed his glove from the bench and ran onto the field.

I reevaluated the parental unit. "You're Brian's dad?"

"You must be Maggie." He grinned and offered his hand. Yep. They were definitely related. "Glad to meet you."

"Likewise." Heck. How did an accidental date turn into a meeting with a parent? "Enjoying the game?"

"I'd enjoy it more if we were ahead. But it's only the fifth inning."

"Right." I returned to my seat. "I don't know much about baseball, I'm afraid."

"I'll explain it if you want, but I know my wife finds it equally satisfying to just enjoy the weather and cheer when I do."

"Sounds about my speed."

The opposing team's batter came up to the plate, and went back to the dugout. The next player hit two foul balls, then another one that managed to stay in the lines. He was out at first base, though, thanks to Brian. I cheered for that, too.

"Brian's a pretty good player, isn't he?" I watched as he took off his hat again, and wiped his face with his arm.

"Well, I think so. But the scouts from the University of Texas must agree. They offered him a full scholarship."

"That's great!" I tried to smile naturally while a chill spread through me. Anyone who has ever seen a movie—ever—knows that nothing dooms a character quicker than a bright future: pregnant wife, farm in Montana, baseball scholarship. . . . All the same to cinematic irony.

My eyes searched the grounds for Old Smokey. Though

the shadows around the field were lengthening, they weren't deep or dark enough to hold the phantom as I'd last seen it, and I didn't smell anything but peanuts and popcorn.

Out on first base, though, Brian swayed on his feet. He put his hands on his knees, but it wasn't the usual wait-for-the-pitch stance. Even from the stands he looked green.

"He doesn't look well," I said, stating the obvious.

Grimly, his dad shook his head. "He's been feeling bad all weekend. At first we thought it was because of his friend. You know, Jeff."

The coach called for a time out. He walked to first base and talked to Brian, as if telling him not to be a macho idiot. Or maybe that was what I would tell him, if I were out there. Finally, the coach signaled another player in from the dugout.

Halfway off the diamond, Brian's legs folded up under him. Mr. Kirkpatrick yelled in alarm and ran to the fence. "This way," I said, and led him to the gate behind the home-team's bench. We ran out onto the field, ignoring umpires, players, and the confused and concerned murmur from the stands.

Mr. Kirkpatrick dropped beside his son, putting a hand to his face, then placing his fingers against the pulse in his neck. I crouched by them. "Is he all right?"

Brian opened his eyes, blinking at the worried circle of faces that gazed down at him. "What happened?"

"You fainted," I said. Pained embarrassment crossed his face, and I remembered that his teammates were clustered around us. "I mean, passed out. Uh . . . took a header." What was the macho term for "swooned like a girl"?

"Did you lose consciousness?" his father asked, looking

into his eyes. I wondered if he was actually a doctor, or had just watched a lot of *ER*. "How many fingers am I holding up?"

"Three." It was the wrong answer.

"Can you squeeze my hand?" Apparently the answer to that wasn't good, either. "Raise your head? Move your legs?" He could, but with trembling effort, as if someone had tied sandbags to his limbs.

"Do we need to call an ambulance?" the coach asked.

Brian protested. "No, Dad. Let the guys help me up."

Dr. Kirkpatrick—I felt pretty sure about the profession—sat back on his heels, and his son's frightened gaze followed him. "You need to get checked out. Now. And I'm not taking any excuses."

"I promise. We can go straight to the emergency room, if you want. Just let the guys help me off the field."

Men.

I stood back as his teammates hoisted him up, his arms over their shoulders, and half-carried him off the field while the spectators clapped their encouragement.

Dr. Kirkpatrick went to move his car closer. On the field, play resumed, as Brian sat on the bench to wait, leaning wearily back against the surrounding fence. His hand caught mine and weakly pulled downward. I obliged the silent request and sat beside him.

"What's going on, Maggie?"

"Your dad is taking you to the emergency room, I think." The school should get a discount rate.

"No." He shook his head, then swayed woozily, grasping my hand to steady himself. "I mean, first Jeff, then Jessica, and the other Jessica. What's going on?"

His voice was so weak, I didn't think his teammates

202

could hear. Still, I leaned closer, clasping his hand between my own. "I don't know, Brian. Something bad."

"You have to figure it out, Maggie." He met my worried gaze, his eyes vivid blue in his pale face. "It's all of us from that day, isn't it? From the day with Stanley."

He'd figured it out more quickly than I had. "Yeah. Except Karen."

"Why didn't you give the pictures to Halloran?"

It took me a moment to realize what that meant. "*You* told Halloran about the pictures? Why?"

"Crisis of conscience, I guess. Too afraid to stand up to them alone, but didn't want them—us—to get away scot-free." He rubbed his hand over his eyes. "I guess we're not."

"Don't give up." I squeezed his hand. "I'm working on it."

He smiled. "I feel better already." His expression seemed almost shy. Or maybe that was his weakness. "Can I call you to ask how it's going?"

"Sure."

When his dad reappeared, Brian had regained enough strength in his legs that it only took one teammate to help him to the car. I followed behind, distant enough to ask Dr. Kirkpatrick if he had any idea what was wrong.

He shook his head, not quite in denial, but in disbelief. "I know what it *looks* like, but it's impossible for it to progress this fast."

Impossible had become a relative thing in my life. "What does it look like, then?"

"Well, it *looks* like MS. But he's never had any symptoms before. This is like a year of deterioration in a matter of days."

Multiple sclerosis? Didn't people with MS end up in wheelchairs?

I watched them drive off, then stood in the parking lot, unsure what to do next. I had failed to save anybody. Events had been escalating from mildly amusing to life-altering. As a ghost hunter, I was a total failure. I wasn't much of a detective, either, since I still didn't know exactly what the Shadow was or how to stop it. I'd even managed to lose my best ally. So far it was Powers of Darkness six, Maggie Quinn zero.

Time to face facts. I sucked at being a superhero.

22

by the time I'd finished two cups of tea and a piece of chocolate cake, I'd also caught Gran up on my extraordinary lack of success.

"I thought Karen was going to be okay. And the first two Jessicas, what happened to them was kind of funny. But then there was the car accident and Karen might have brain damage, Jessica Prime might be on psychotropic drugs for the rest of her life, and poor Brian may end up in a wheelchair."

"That's not certain, dear." Gran refilled my cup and pushed the sugar bowl my way. She had just come home from her retiree's dinner group at church, and was dressed in a fashionable skirt and top, her short red hair styled with a casual flair, much too mod to be pouring tea.

"I've screwed everything up. I haven't made any progress, and things are getting worse instead of better."

"Things always get worse before they get better. And I think you've made a great deal of progress. I think it was very clever of you to have that . . . what did you call that ghost goo?"

"Ectoplasm?" I sighed. "I watch too much TV."

"And I would never have thought of a curse potion."

"It's just a theory." I sulked into my tea. "And to top it off, I argued with Justin, so I've lost my best ally."

Gran set her cup in her saucer with a clatter. "Now that *is* stupid."

"Thanks for your support."

"What did you argue about?"

"Something that seemed important at the time."

"Well, it can hardly be more important than your overall mission." She gestured to the phone on the kitchen counter. "Call him up."

"Oh, Gran." I slumped back in my chair. "He said he doesn't want to help me anymore."

She rose and got the handset herself. "Of course he said that. Men have to save face. What's his number? Never mind. It's on the caller ID." She beep-beep-beeped through the recent calls while I made weak protests. Truthfully, I wanted to talk to him, but if he hung up, or told me to get lost, it would hurt. A lot.

"Hello? Is this Justin MacCallum?" Gran's accent always deepened on the phone. "I hear that you've had a bit of a row with my idiot granddaughter."

"Gran!"

She waved me silent. "Right. No, I wouldn't expect you to tell me what it was about. But she'd like to apologize." I held out my hand for the receiver. Gran ignored me. "Where would you like her to meet you? Well, where are you studying? At the library? She'll be there in twenty minutes."

Gran put the handset back into the cradle and turned to me expectantly. "Maybe you should freshen up a bit before you go."

"I could have just talked to him on the phone." Rejection would be a lot easier with AT&T as a buffer.

"Making up after an argument is better done face to face." She hauled me out of my chair. "Go powder your nose and comb your hair."

I bowed to fate. Easier to simply suffer the slings and arrows of my outrageous grandmother.

✳ ✳ ✳

The sun had gone down, but streetlights kept the campus well lit. So close to finals, there were a lot of people coming and going from the library, and probably would be for hours yet.

The west half of the building was built early in the last century; the other part dated back only to the eighties. Justin waited for me in the east lobby, on the far side of the theft prevention gates. The fluorescent lighting made his unsmiling face look forbidding, sculpted the lines of his cheeks and jaw too harshly.

A trick of the light. I hoped. I lifted a hand in tentative greeting. "Hi."

He cut right to the chase. "I don't want you to apologize just because your grandmother made you."

My eyes narrowed. "I don't do anything just because someone tells me to."

He raised his eyebrows. "True enough." Unfolding his arms, he jerked his head toward the stacks. "Let's get out of the lobby."

I followed him up some steps and through the rabbit warren of the humanities section. The tables and carrels were filled with students, heads diligently bent over their work. I'd used this library for school research, but I hadn't been to the enclosed meeting rooms before. Justin had one to himself; he'd spread his books out over the football field of a table, clearly not inviting company.

"Did you get your paper finished?" I warmed up with some banal small talk.

"Almost." He didn't invite chitchat, either.

"I won't take up too much time then." My nerves were balled up in my stomach, like a wad of Christmas tree lights when you get them out of the box in November. His resolutely blank demeanor gave me no clues how I'd be received. I took a deep breath and plunged into the frigid waters of apology.

"I'm sorry we argued," I said sincerely. "I don't know why I blew things so out of proportion, but once I got going I didn't know how to back up."

His shoulders relaxed; the air in the room seemed to palpably warm. He paused long enough to acknowledge the dodge in my phrasing. "I'm sorry we argued, too."

I took a relieved step forward, my heart lightening. "Thank goodness. I do need you, Justin. Your help, I mean."

A corner of his mouth turned up. That was progress. "I know what you mean."

"I shouldn't blame you because I wanted so desperately to think that someone knew what was going on." I laughed a little too loudly. "I know it's not me."

He shoved his hands in the pockets of his jeans and shook his head. "Your instincts are good, when you listen to them. You knew to throw the salt on the Jessica-shadow."

Sighing, I sank into one of the heavy wooden chairs. "Half of my brain still rejects this as impossible. You were right about that, too."

"No wonder you got so angry." I slanted a suspicious look up at his too-bland tone. He smiled crookedly and sat beside me. "To defeat this thing, you are going to have to commit your left brain, too, Maggie."

I rubbed my hands over my face. "I'm failing, Justin. Two more of the Jocks and Jessicas have fallen."

His hand brushed my shoulder, briefly comforting but not coddling. "Tell me."

"You need to work on your paper."

"It'll wait. Tell me what's happened."

I told him about the picture I took, about Stanley's humiliation, and the clique of six. I described Jessica Prime's breakdown, and Brian's collapse.

"Brian, the guy I met at your house?"

"Yeah." I couldn't help fishing a little. "Why?"

"No reason."

I also told him my theory, which I didn't get to explain on Saturday, that the spirit became more developed, more *real*, with every victim. I saw the telltale tightening of his jaw when I described the thing lurking in my yard.

He rubbed an irritated hand through his hair. "Why do you wait so long to tell me these things?"

That was a complicated question, and probably rhetorical anyway, so I went on. "Do you think it could become solid?"

"I don't know. Maybe it's just a sign of its growing power." He shifted through the papers on the table. "I was doing some work yesterday, and I found something. Does this look familiar?"

He set a Xeroxed photo in front of me. Color pictures never copy well, but I could still make out the wide, flat bowl with etchings along the rim. "That's the thingy from my dream! Where did you find it?"

"In the catalog of the university's archives. The brazier was found on an expedition to Mesopotamia back in the sixties."

I picked up the paper to study the symbols more closely. I had to squint. "Where is Mesopotamia, exactly?"

"It *was* between the Tigris and Euphrates rivers."

Those were names I'd heard on the news. "Where Iraq is now?"

He nodded. "My adviser, Dr. Dozer, did some expeditions there, before the last regime made that impossible."

"So on the edges here— Is that writing between the hatch mark things?"

"Yes, but the hatch mark things are letters, too. Cuneiform, one of the most ancient forms of writing. The squiggly looking bits are the language that replaced it. Kind of a proto-Hebrew."

I scrunched my brows in memory. "In the dream where I saw this, there was a big, biblical-looking village in an oasis. Some wild animal had killed a young man." I traced the picture with my finger. "But maybe he was the victim of the same curse. Someone cast it then, like someone is casting it now."

"Well, quinine hadn't been discovered yet. But everything else had." He pulled forward another book, flipped to a page he'd marked. "Most cultures have some notion of an evil spirit, something to blame for the random tragedies of life. The ancient Babylonians had a demon for everything—bad crops, bad weather, bad health."

He showed me a picture of a very ancient worn statue or fetish. "Is that one of them?" Just barely man-shaped, the thing reminded me of the quasi-human form the Shadow had taken.

"Possibly. This statue represents a personal god. They were supposed to serve an individual's interests, so I guess benevolence and malevolence could be relative." He reached over and tapped the photocopy. "What if this artifact actually invokes someone's demigod or demon?"

I rubbed my hands over my arms, my T-shirt completely inadequate for the air-conditioning. "Can you read the letters? Or do you know someone who can?"

"Not from that photo."

"What about from the actual artifact?"

Justin gave an ominous sigh. "I got permission to go to the archives, but the brazier wasn't there. Just a 'removed for cleaning' card."

My fingers fiddled with the copied page. "I wrote down what I remembered from my dream. Not the cuneiform—I thought that was just decorative. But I think I got the others right."

"I can find someone to translate them," he said with more excitement than I felt.

"Not Dr. Dozer."

Justin sat back in his chair. "You can't honestly think she might be cursing her son's classmates."

"No." I framed my suspicion obliquely. "But I know how much I pick up from my dad, just living in the same house."

"You didn't even know where Mesopotamia was."

"I knew it was in the Middle East somewhere, smarty-pants." I pushed out of the chair and started pacing. "It's too much of a coincidence that Stanley is connected to all the victims *and* the brazier."

"Well, you can't just march up to him and accuse him of cursing his classmates."

I paused to imagine the scenario and admitted, "Okay, I guess I can't. Not with only circumstantial evidence, anyway." How could I find out if he'd bought wormwood or quinine? You could get just about anything off the Internet, but unless I had either his computer or a Dozer-family credit card number, I was at an investigative dead end.

Justin watched me, reading the thoughts on my face; I'm not exactly Ms. Impassive. "Maggie." His eyes were sober, his tone cautious. "If it *is* Stanley, you should be careful not to let him know you suspect him. It would be easy for him to set the demon on you."

My hand crept up to clasp my necklace. "I'm not in the picture. I'm not part of the pattern."

"But you are. You're behind the camera." I blinked in shock. I hadn't thought of that. Were we back to Karen taking my place on the diving board?

He seemed to regret pointing out the connection I was too close to see. "I'm sorry. But I want you to be careful."

I tucked my hair behind my ear in a determined motion.

"I'm not trying to antagonize it. But it's hard to try and *stop* a thing without making it, you know, a little pissed."

"I realize that." He rose and took my fidgeting hand. "I'm not trying to be overprotective. But it's hard to know you're in danger and not be able to do something about it."

How strange, that a little thing like a hand could be the center of so much feeling. The nerves on the back of it where his fingertips brushed, in the palm securely wrapped in his, fired like sparklers. The sensation rushed up my arm and alighted, fizzling, in the middle of my chest.

"You put all those charms on my room," I said. "You put that salt in my purse. I'm not sure I'd be here if you hadn't. The fumes . . ." I broke off. I didn't like to think about that.

He shook his head. "But I'm just shooting in the dark. That's why I got so angry on Saturday. I wish I knew exactly what would protect you. But I can only make my best guess."

I glanced at the books and papers taking up eighteen square feet of table. "I think your best guess is better than a lot of people's certainties."

His smile warmed me from the inside out—crooked, rueful, and unwittingly charming. "Yeah, but it's not the same thing as riding in on a white charger."

I laughed, precisely because I could picture him doing just that. Justin was a throwback to another age. A scholar knight.

"I'm not much of a damsel in distress, though. Too mouthy."

"Too stubborn," he nodded.

He didn't have to agree quite so quickly. Not that I wanted to be a damsel in distress, of course. "So what do we do now?"

He looked at the books on the table and sighed. "I have to finish my paper tonight. Send me the letters you wrote down. Your dad can give it to me in class tomorrow. Meanwhile, note down everything in your dreams. And watch out for Stanley. And keep an eye on the last guy. What's his name?"

"Brandon." I frowned. "I wonder why nothing has happened to him yet."

"If I were a guy who'd been beaten up and humiliated by someone for years, I'd definitely save the big kahuna for last."

"Good point." Justin seemed to have accepted my theory of Stanley-as-puppetmaster.

He wrote "Still in use" on a piece of notebook paper and stuck it on top of his pile of books. "I'll walk you out to your car."

"You don't have to do that. You need to get back to work."

"Look, I know you don't need a white knight, but at least let me be a gentleman."

I gave a sheepish grimace, and agreed.

We left the library, winding back through the maze, past the dedicated students with their laptops clicking and pens scratching. On the short walk to the parking lot, Justin and I talked about college, and the pleasant night, and anything other than demons and curses and gangly, vengeful nerds. We reached the Jeep too quickly, and he saw me buckled in and on my way before returning to his work. It was just a few minutes of peace in the turmoil of the week before, and it would have been perfect, if only he'd taken my hand again.

I went to bed with both determination and dread, certain I'd meet Old Smokey in my dreams. I woke the next morning to the brain-melting beep of the alarm clock, tired and grumpy, but without any recollection of a vision or nightmare. Grumbling all the way, I schlepped into a hot shower, and stood under the spray until the cobwebs began to clear from my head and the bathroom was thick with steam.

Turning off the water, I reached for my towel, wrapping it around myself while I grabbed another one to wipe away the fog from the mirror.

The sweep of the cloth revealed nothing but roiling black mist and a pair of sulfurous yellow eyes, blazing out at me from the glass.

23

I screamed. Shrieked like the most girly, helpless damsel on the planet. I fell against the bathroom door, fumbling with the knob, whimpering and struggling like a rabbit in a snare. Steam hung in the air, stroked my skin. The demon didn't have to touch me; I was going to give *myself* a heart attack. My heart beat against my ribs like a caged bird—just like I beat against the bathroom door.

Footsteps thundered up the stairs, then the door flew open. I tumbled out, catching my towel close around me, staggering to stay on my feet.

"Close the door! Close the door!" I yelled.

Dad slammed the door closed. "What the Hell?"

"Yes. Exactly. Oh my God, it was in the mirror." I jabbered like a madwoman. "It has eyes now, and it was in the mirror."

"What are you talking about, Maggie? What has eyes?"

"The thing! The smoke thing from my dream!" My pulse still pounded. I could feel it in my brain, in my vital organs. "Get away from the door!"

He moved away, but only to get the afghan from my bed. Until he wrapped it around my shoulders, I hadn't known how icy cold my skin was. "It sounds like you were still dreaming," he said worriedly.

"I didn't dream last night." I could not drag my eyes away from the painted wood panels of the bathroom door.

"Mike?" Mom's worried voice floated up the stairs. "What's going on? Is she all right?"

Dad gave me a look and called back in answer. "She's okay. She says a mouse ran across her foot."

"That's absurd. We don't have mice."

"So I'm telling her."

Indignation helped chase away panic. "I'm not afraid of mice."

"Do you want me to tell your mother you think you saw a smoke monster in the bathroom?"

I pictured that scene and answered, "No, I guess not."

He rubbed a reassuring hand over my back. "Maybe you did dream, and got in the shower still half asleep."

"Yeah." That actually made some sense. More sense than Old Smokey getting past all my defenses and into the bathroom. I wrapped the afghan more tightly and shuddered, but the blind, flailing terror had abated. "Now I feel a little silly. It must have been just a dream. Sorry, Dad."

"Don't worry about it, Magpie." He hugged me in tight reassurance. "Do you want me to open the door before I go?"

If we saw nothing, I would feel even more foolish. If something was there, I didn't want it to see my dad. "No. I'm good."

"Actually," he looked a little sheepish, "it will make *me* feel better."

He smiled, but I saw him surreptitiously wipe sweaty palms on his trousers.

"Okay. But wait a second." I grabbed the canister of salt that still sat on the nightstand. Pouring a handful into my palm, I indicated with a jerk of my head that he should open the door while I stood ready to fire at whatever lurked inside.

Dad and I had seen the same action movies, so he got into place, all very *Lethal Weapon*. I mouthed, "One, two, three!" and he yanked open the door so hard it banged into the wall, showering plaster onto the carpet. The crash startled me, and I flung my barrage of salt into the bathroom with a stifled squeak.

Nothing waited inside. Only the humid blanket of air left over from my shower. The last of the condensation cleared from the mirror with the rush of air. There was no black smoke, no burning eyes. Not even a whiff of brimstone, just the clean, herbal scent of my shampoo. Well, plus the mess of salt on the floor.

"I'm getting too old for this shit," said Dad, making me laugh, mostly with relief. He examined the big hole the doorknob had made in the wall. "Your mom is going to kill us."

"I'll move the bookshelf over until we can fix it."

He didn't say anything about the empty bathroom. "I'll have the coffee ready when you get down." He went downstairs, and I heard Mom at the bottom ask him, "What in heaven's name are you two doing up there?" and Dad answer placidly, "Looking for the mouse."

For the record, I was never afraid of mice. I was, however, worried I'd slipped a mental gear.

✳ ✳ ✳

When I got to English, Lisa ambushed me, dragging me back out into the hall where the noise of students hurrying to their first-period classes covered our voices.

"What is going on with you?" Hands on her hips, she glared down at me. She wore a black-and-red blouse I hadn't seen since her Goth days, and though she'd paired it with faded blue jeans, the severe color still made her look very pale. "I tried to call you until eleven, and you didn't answer."

"I was in the college library. The reception is bad there." I shifted my heavy backpack. She hadn't even let me put my stuff down. "Why didn't you leave voice mail?"

A sophomore glanced at us curiously as she got her books out of her locker. Lisa grabbed me by the arm and pulled me a few doors down. "I heard about Brian. Why are you always around when these things happen? You have got to . . . I don't know." She pressed her fingers over her eyes. "You can't do that anymore."

"There *aren't* any more," I said. "Only Brandon. He's the last one."

She dropped her hands and stared at me. "The last what?"

"The last— Man, this sounds so crazy when I say it out loud." I whispered back, keeping our heads close together. "Remember I told you yesterday, I thought all these freaky things were connected? Well, Brandon is the last link in the chain."

Lisa shook her head in denial. "You have lost it. They may call me D and D Lisa, but at least I know the difference between fantasy and reality."

Ouch. I didn't quite flinch. "I know it sounds wild."

"It sounds certifiably insane!" She didn't bother to lower her voice now. "Paranoid and delusional."

I snapped back. "Maybe you could use the intercom. I don't think the whole school heard." She clamped her jaw in annoyance, but at least she stopped yelling.

"Look," I said as reasonably as I could, "it sounds crazy because you don't know the whole story. I haven't told you what's been going on, because, well, I know it's unbelievable."

She fell back against the lockers, folding her arms across her slim body. "You couldn't have left me happily in the dark?"

"Not with you getting up in my grill the second I walked in the door!" The hall was clearing; I didn't have much time to cajole her onto my team. "I'm telling you now. The fact is, I could really use your devious brain."

She stared at me for a hard moment. Then the bell rang, and she was forced into a decision. "After school?"

"Yeah. My house."

"There'd better be snacks."

I had to go out to the Jeep at lunchtime and find my chemistry lab book. Used to be, if you came to Professor Blackthorne's class unprepared, you had to wear the Molecule Hat, an absurd thing made out of Nerf balls and Tinkertoys. But a parent had complained that this was damaging to the students' self-esteem, so rather than be liable for a lot of expensive psychiatric therapy, the administration nixed the hat. Now unprepared students had to copy out the periodic table.

I didn't have the patience for charting elements, which is why I was in a mostly empty parking lot when Brandon cornered me between my Wrangler and an Explorer the size of Nebraska.

"Heya, Quinn." He filled the gap between the cars. To my rear, someone had parked their Mazda across two spaces, blocking any graceful exit. Bravado it was, then.

"Hi, Biff. No backup today?"

"Like I would need backup to talk to you." He leaned his mammoth shoulders against the SUV. "But now that you mention it, I *have* noticed that my friends aren't doing too well, lately."

"Oh really?" I decided to play dumb, which was an ironic reversal for any conversation with Brandon. "What could that possibly have to do with me?"

"You tell me." He walked forward, tall and muscular, a lot bigger than me. But even more unnerving was his confidence, his certainty that he could get away with things that ordinary people couldn't.

"You interviewed Jessica for the paper," he said, "and then

she lost her voice right before the play. You fought with Jess on Friday, and Saturday she got caught shoplifting. You were around before Jeff crashed the Mustang and you were there when Jessica got taken to the nuthouse. And now Brian."

"That's a fascinating recap, Brandon." The book retrieved, I swung my heavy backpack onto my shoulder with a whump. "You could write for *Paranoia Digest*, if there was such a thing and it wouldn't require some literacy." I stepped toward the exit, willing him to get out of my way. "There's no way I could be responsible for those things happening to your friends."

"Well, I was thinking about what Jess said that night of the play." He didn't budge, just folded his arms, making his broad chest look even more impassable. "Maybe you *are* a witch."

Laughing was probably not my smartest move. It really pissed him off. Go figure.

He moved fast, pushing me up against the SUV, his arms trapping me on either side, blocking escape.

I stopped laughing, and got pissed, too. "Get off me, asshole."

"Make me, Quinn."

"If I am a witch, what's to stop me from shriveling your testicles into raisins with my evil eye?"

His beefy forearms braced against my shoulders. I could smell his deodorant, see the flecks in his irises as he leaned down to look me in the eye. A dominance ploy. If I squirmed, he would win.

"I don't believe any of that magical bullshit," he said.

"But there's nut jobs that'll buy any rumor that goes around. It doesn't have to be true to royally screw up your life."

My stomach knotted. Witch hunts scared me. Not for the obvious reasons, but because they were so irrational that there was no defense against them. But I couldn't actually be hanged for a witch. Could I? I wouldn't put anything past the Republicans.

"What do you want, Brandon?" I bit the words out.

"I want those pictures to disappear. The ones you took of me and Dozer."

"Is that all?" A smart guy would have demanded to know what was happening to his friends, or worried he might be next. But you don't have to be smart to be a bully. "Sure. Whatever."

"And if they show up in anyone's e-mail—"

"It's a stalemate. I get it." He still had me cornered against the Explorer, and didn't look ready to move. "Are we done?"

His eyes narrowed, summing me up, and I realized we weren't done, because what he really wanted wasn't for those pictures to vanish, but for me to be scared of him.

"Well," he began, leaning in closer, "I'd like to know why Brian has been panting after you all of a sudden." Elbows against the car, he pinned me with his weight. "You got some hidden talent, Quinn?"

I dropped my fifty-pound backpack on his foot. When he bent over, cursing, I slammed my knee up into his gut. He was lucky, because I was aiming for the place where he kept his brain.

"You bitch!" he wheezed, the wind knocked out of him.

"Oh, *I'm* the dog?" I yelled, because I *was* scared of him, and I was furious with him for making me feel that way. "I thought you were just a bully, Brandon, not an oversexed sociopath."

"What's going on here?" That ringing voice could only mean Halloran. Oh, yeah. The screwing continues.

"Nothing, Mr. Halloran," said Brandon, trying to stand up straight.

"Nothing except sexual harassment," I said, still livid. "Maybe even assault."

"Now, Margaret. I'm sure there's just been a misunderstanding." The assistant principal made a placating gesture. "These mix-ups can happen between young men and women."

I stood trapped between him and Biff, and I didn't like the symbolism any more than the fact. "I don't think so, Mr. Halloran."

"And now you've gone and overreacted." He oozed soothing condescension. Brandon didn't even bother to fake innocence; he just smirked. Sure, I'd hit him, but not before he'd seen my fear.

"I'm going to overreact all the way to the school board if you don't get out of my way."

"There's no need for that," said Halloran, still trying to convince me we were all good friends.

I slung my bag over my shoulder and marched forward. He moved aside, proving he was at least a fraction of a point smarter than Brandon.

24

I pulled a steaming bag of popcorn out of the microwave just as Lisa called to say she couldn't come over. She had an appointment she couldn't change. "Just don't do anything stupid until we talk," she said, with traffic noise in the background. "Other people have noticed that you're always around when stuff happens. So stay away from Brandon, and don't talk crazy to anyone."

"Yes, my liege. Right now I'd rather take a chum bath in a shark tank than go near Brandon Rogers."

"I have to shut up and drive now. See you tomorrow."

Mom came in as I hung up. "Company coming?" she

asked, probably because I'd put the popcorn in a bowl instead of eating it out of the bag.

"Lisa was supposed to, but something came up."

"That's too bad." She took it as permission to raid from the snack bowl.

"Do you want a Coke?" I asked.

"A diet. Thanks." Mom sat on one of the barstools. She eats popcorn one piece at a time, but I prefer it by the handful. "Lisa is an interesting girl," she said.

"That's one way to describe her."

"Well, I didn't know what to think when you started hanging around with her back in junior high, when she wore nothing but black and had all that spiky jewelry."

I popped the top on my soda. "She grew out of that phase."

"Well, not completely. She was still wearing striped socks the last time I saw her."

"Yes, but they weren't *black*. And neither is her hair."

Mom waved that aside. "Anyway. I just mean that I think it's neat that she's going to be valedictorian. And has a full scholarship to Georgetown. That must make her dad so proud. He worked hard to raise her on his own."

My hand froze over the popcorn bowl. By mentioning the scholarship, had Mom just jinxed Lisa, too? She wasn't in the bully picture, but she had AP calculus with Stanley and Karen. In my last dream, they'd been standing next to each other. Did that mean anything?

That user's manual would come in real handy right now.

"Is Lisa going to the prom?"

I shelved my worries for the moment. "I don't know,

Mom. We don't talk about the You-Know-What. We made a pact."

"You could go together, if you didn't want to mess with dates and things."

"I don't want to mess with the prom at all, Mom."

She ignored me, placidly eating popcorn, piece by piece. "Some girls in my high school class did that and had a wonderful time. They weren't lesbians or anything. Not that it would matter if they were."

"That's nice, Mom. I'm glad you're so open-minded." I grabbed my Coke can and the popcorn bowl and headed for the stairs, because I could go my whole life without ever hearing my mother talk about lesbians again.

"Maybe you could take Justin to the prom," she called after me, laughter in her voice. "He is such a hottie."

Shoot me now.

* * *

I was doing the last edit of my English paper when I heard footsteps on the stairs. "Come on up." Saving the document, I turned to greet Justin. "I didn't hear the doorbell."

He climbed the last steps, looking exhausted. I wondered if he'd stayed up all night working. "Your mom was heading out. She said I could come in."

"Did you get your paper done?"

"Yeah." He fell onto the battered sofa. A burgundy slipcover hid a multitude of sins, including burnt-orange-and-brown-striped upholstery that was older than me. "Done, turned in. Now I'm free until finals."

"Cool."

He opened his own backpack and pulled out a folded

sheet of paper. "I e-mailed a friend and asked him to translate the letters you drew."

I scooted the desk chair closer to look. "That was fast."

"He's got a degree in biblical history, so he knew right where to look in the library."

"Not the public library, I assume."

"No, Henry's in seminary, studying to be a priest."

My eyebrows climbed. "Really?"

"Yeah. We went to high school together."

"Catholic school?"

"Yes," he said. My bemusement must have shown, because he asked, "Why is that surprising?"

"It isn't. Your love of khaki trousers and oxford shirts should have been my first clue."

He gestured to the paper, where he'd jotted down normal letters under the strange ones I'd sketched. "You want to see what I found out?"

I did, but I wasn't done with this line of inquiry just yet. "Do you still go to Mass?"

"Sometimes." He answered matter-of-factly, then pointed to my crucifix. "What about you?"

"Not in a long time." I chewed my lip, uncertainly. "Do you think it matters? I believe in God. I'm just not sure about the outward trappings, you know?"

"I do know." He contemplated my question. "I think that faith—in something bigger that yourself, no matter what form it takes—gives you a certain spiritual or psychic protection. If, say, the room caught on fire, it might not keep you from burning . . ."

"It did for Shadrach, Meshach, and the other guy."

"I said it *might* not. Can I make my point here?"

228

"Sure."

He seemed to reorganize his thoughts. "Bible stories aside, faith can't keep you from burning, but it might give you calm to, say, think of a way to put the fire out or escape. If you were under spiritual attack, however . . ."

"Like if a demon made me think I was on fire?"

That earned me a suspicious look, justified, since that was one of those things I'd neglected to mention. "Exactly like that. You might be able to see through the illusion, and overcome it. So I guess it depends. Is your evil a spiritual or physical construct? Personally, I do believe in miracles. But physics is physics so I always wear my seat belt."

I touched the small, gold cross that had become a talisman to me. Not of a religion, but of my strengthening conviction that if there was Evil with a capital E then there must be Good with a capital G, and I wanted to be on its side.

"Can we get back to work?" Justin asked.

"Sure." I took the paper from him and frowned at the letters. M A E L A Z. "I think it made more sense in Mesopotamian."

Justin pulled out the copied catalog page. "The problem is, the symbols go in a circle, and you can't tell exactly where to start reading."

"Let's see what happens when we Google it." I rolled over to the desk and opened the browser. On the search engine's main page I typed in: "maelaz." Google helpfully asked if I meant "Maalox."

"I guess that's a no." Next I typed: "Aelazm." The Internet netted nothing.

Justin leaned on the back of my chair, peering over my

shoulder. I was distracted for a moment by the warmth of his arm brushing mine. "Keep the first three letters together," he suggested. "Move them all to the back."

I typed in: "Azmael." The search engine churned for a moment and finally displayed a page of links to archaeology and anthropology sites. "Look!" I said, because I'm a dork when detective work pays off. "A site about ancient Babylon. That's in Mesopotamia."

"Yeah." He didn't look nearly as happy.

"How did you know to put the 'ael' at the end?"

"El was the top dog god to a lot of people in the region. The 'ael' would mean 'of El.'"

I clicked on the link. The hard drive spun and clicked as the page tried to load. "It must have a lot of graphics. My computer hates bells and whistles."

The whirring intensified, but the browser window remained dark. I felt Justin tense behind me. "Close the window, Maggie."

I clicked the mouse, but nothing happened. "It's locked up."

"Force quit the program."

The Internet had taken my computer hostage. "It's not quitting." I smelled ozone and burning plastic and my voice cracked in panic. "It's not doing *anything*."

Smoke poured out of the CD slot on the front of the tower and I jerked back, thinking phantom. But no. Just plain old burn-your-house-down fire.

"Get down." Justin pulled me out of the chair as the monitor exploded in a shower of glass. He reached under the desk and yanked the surge protector from the wall, then scrambled back as the CPU began to melt, flames licking out of the case.

The smoke detector went off, piercing my ears. I half-crawled into the bathroom and grabbed the little fire extinguisher from under the counter. I'd never used it before, so I struggled to read the instructions with the fire alarm turning my brain to Jell-O. Justin grabbed the extinguisher from me. He turned something, pointed the nozzle, pressed something else; frosty mist and foam shot out at the flames.

He emptied the entire canister, continuing to spray even after the last flicker disappeared. Finally I climbed onto the chair and turned off the screaming alarm.

My ears rang in the sudden silence. I jumped off the chair and joined him, staring at the melted hulk of the CPU. "I guess that's what you call a physical construct."

"Yeah."

"At least we got the word figured out." He turned to look at me, and I wondered if my expression mirrored his dazed look. I felt numb. "My mom is going to blow a gasket."

He slid a comforting arm around my shoulder. "It could have been worse."

I nodded, and rested my head against him. The desk was scorched, but otherwise the fire hadn't gone farther than the computer. Of course, the peripherals were all shot: the printer, the scanner, and . . . A bone-deep chill seized me, followed by a rush of liquid-hot fury through my veins.

"My English paper was on that computer! Ten thousand words, up in flames! That bastard!"

"Didn't you back it up?"

I blistered my fingers pulling a misshapen lump of plastic from the USB port. I held up the ex–flash drive and Justin's dark brown eyes softened with exquisite sympathy as he echoed, "That bastard."

25

I woke facedown on the kitchen table, with Dad's hand gently shaking my shoulder. "Hey, kiddo. Did you get your paper done?"

My thoughts struggled upstream against the current of exhaustion. Rewrites. Dad's laptop. Parental freak-out over the fire. My paper going up in smoke. Oh yeah. I remembered that.

"Yeah." I creaked upright and tried to straighten my neck. "Just need to print it out."

"What time did you fall asleep?"

"More like passed out, I think." I rubbed a desert's worth of grit from my eyes. "Maybe four?"

"Go take a shower. I'll print your paper and you can do another proofread before school."

I dragged myself up the stairs and turned on the shower, then went to get clean clothes while the water heated up. When I came back, I was so sleepy, it took me a moment to be surprised by my name written in the fog on the mirror.

Hello, Magdalena was what it said.

I've got to remember to turn on the vent fan was the first thing that came to my mind.

And then my brain caught up, and dread crawled over my skin. The thing knew my name. That couldn't be good.

Maybe I was dreaming, still lying facedown in a puddle of my own drool, having a nightmare. I closed my eyes, but it was much worse *not* seeing what I knew was there.

The rivulets of condensation that dripped from the letters reminded me of too many horror movies. Steeling myself, I wiped away the fog. Acid yellow eyes stared at me, and I flinched back, but didn't scream.

The black smoke drifted in the mirror like a negative reflection of the steam in the bathroom. I cast no reflection, but the sulfur-colored orbs floated where my head would be. Fear skittered over my nerve endings, but I was also pissed at the whole Peeping Tom routine, not to mention the destruction of my Senior Theme.

"How do you know my name, you smoky bastard?" I growled at it without expecting an answer, like you growl at the car when it won't start. So my heart lurched against my ribs when a reply appeared in the quickly refogging mirror: *Summoner knows.*

The summoner knew my name. Super.

"Then what the"—I edited myself under the circumstances—"heck are you doing here? What do you want?"

See you.

"Great. Just what I always wanted. A stalker." A semiliterate one at that.

You see me. The words appeared above the first ones. I saw the demon, so Old Smokey wanted to see me. I got it. It was scary how I got it.

"Well, I don't want to see you, so bug off."

In a new patch of fog appeared: *Soon you'll fear.*

"Why not now?" Stupid question. I was pretty darned scared, at the moment.

Not allowed.

Everything has rules, Dr. Smyth had said. You just have to know what they are.

Soon, it wrote. *Magdalena.*

There was a huge power in a name. I wasn't simply scared that it knew mine. I was sickened. I wanted to curl into a ball and just give up. Soon, it said. The taunting and toying would end, and I would be dead or wish I was.

Soon, but not yet. The mirror was like the dream, I realized. A spiritual construct. I took a deep breath of the steamy air and let the panic run out of me, leaving space for rational thought.

What came instead was an irrational idea. I put my own finger to the fog and wrote: "Azmael." The eyes recoiled. "Get out of my bathroom, you stinky son of a bitch."

The blackness in the mirror twisted and contorted in fury, and then turned in on itself and disappeared, leaving the word *Soon* superimposed on my pallid reflection.

* * *

I called Justin from the car on the way to school, waking him up. "It's the name."

"What?" he asked groggily.

"It's the thing's name. I think I may have banished it." I explained what had happened with the mirror. By the time I was finished, he sounded completely awake.

"I don't think you banished it completely," he said. "But you found a way to control its spiritual presence."

"What do you think it means that it can't get at me now, but soon it will?"

"I think it's what you said. The demon is getting stronger with each victim. The last one might not only make him solid, but also free him from constraint."

"Yikes," I said.

"That would be bad," he agreed.

"How do we know the magic number?"

"We don't know. When he finishes the list maybe. Or perhaps there's a numerology thing. I'll read up on it."

"I'm having Lisa over to my house this afternoon since she couldn't come yesterday. Can you be there?"

"Sure. No point in studying for finals on Monday when the town might be invaded by a demon before then."

"I like your sense of perspective." I pulled into the parking lot. "See you then." I grabbed my backpack and made it inside with little time to spare. It was amazing how bandying words with the Hell-spawn could eat into your morning.

✻ ✻ ✻

I told Ms. Vincent about the fire, and asked her if I could have until the afternoon to proofread the paper one more time. She replied coldly, "You shouldn't have waited to the last minute, then."

A thousand arguments sprang to my tongue, but I'd already dealt with one demon today, so I simply laid the paper on her desk and took my seat.

Lisa watched me drop into the seat beside her. "You look like crap."

"Thanks. Battling the forces of darkness will do that to you."

"If you mean Vincent, I agree."

We settled in. I wondered if Vincent was going to actually teach for once. I could use a nap.

"Hey, Lisa," I said. "Are you going to the prom?"

"Yeah. Tessa and Katie and I are going stag. We didn't ask you to join us, because we knew you'd rather die."

"I wonder if Stanley ever got a date."

"He's going with Suzie Miller. You know from the play?"

"Really?" I was stunned. Suzie was so cute, and riding her five minutes of fame. She was going to the prom with *Stanley*?

When the bell rang, Vincent rose and came to the front of the room, straightening her cardigan—apple red with school buses for the pockets. No lie. "Today," she said, "we start your last novel of the year. Fittingly, as you end one segment of your life and begin a new one, we will read *Brave New World*."

She paused, as if for applause. At the smattering of murmurs and groans, she set her mouth in a thin line and went to the shelves to hand out books.

"Have you read *Brave New World*?" Lisa asked me.

"Doesn't the future world kind of . . . suck?"

"I think that sums it up pretty well."

＊ ＊ ＊

At lunch, I had a table to myself, which was not that unusual, but everyone kept staring at me, which . . . well, was becoming more common.

Halfway through my doughy burrito, a girl I'd never met plopped into the seat across from me. I actually did a double-take, because this—the jet-black hair with pale roots, the black nail polish—was Lisa's old look before she'd given up monochrome as a lifestyle choice.

This girl had a pentagram hanging from a leather strap around her neck. She set her elbows on the table and asked avidly, "Is it true you're a witch?"

"*Excuse* me?"

"They're saying you cursed the Jocks and Jessicas. Is it true?" I stared at her stupidly. "If it is, you can tell me. I won't hold it against you. I mean, those stuck-up posers . . ."

"You should be careful." Another girl stood beside me. Unlike her dark counterpart, she was dressed in a flowing pastel blouse over jeans and flip-flops. She looked like a hippie and smelled of incense. "You know the Wicca Rede."

"The what now?" My fork full of burrito hung midair. From my hand, I mean. Not levitating. Considering the company, maybe I should make that clear.

"The first rule of the White Path: 'An' it harm none . . .'"

"What's that in English?"

"Do what you want, as long as it harms no one." Flowers-and-Light Girl sat down beside me, but not before shooting Pentagram Poser a glare. "Whenever you cast a spell to do harm to someone, it will come back on you, three times as bad."

"Yeah, well." I dropped my fork onto my tray. "That sucks for someone, but not for me. I didn't do anything to anyone."

Wicca girl put her hand on my arm. "I sense a terrible darkness around you."

That shook me slightly, but then I realized . . . duh. "Yeah, they call it high school."

Her mouth detoured into a sulking frown before she rerouted it into a smile. "When you are ready to admit your wrongdoing, my friends and I can help you. We can cleanse your aura and help you remove the negative energy . . ."

"Well," said Goth girl across the table, "if you're ready to rock and roll, *my* friends and I are down with that."

"Thank you both." I climbed over the bench and grabbed my tray. "I'll look for you where the freaks come out at night."

"Blessed be!" Hippie chick called after me.

I started to say something rude but then figured, what the heck. I needed all the blessings I could get.

Heading out of the cafeteria and into the courtyard, I ran into Stanley. Only as I stumbled back and muttered automatic apologies, it took me a moment to recognize him.

I'd been thinking a lot about Stanley over the last few days but I hadn't actually *seen* him since Friday. I stared, trying to figure out what he'd changed. And then I realized, nothing much. He'd gotten some clothes that fit—that was the biggest difference. Other than that: skinny, pale, insanely tall, drab, colorless hair. Check. No briefcase, but otherwise, that was Dozer.

But looking at him was like watching a DVD when you've been used to VHS. He looked sharper, more alive. I couldn't explain it better than that. His shoulders were back, his head was up. And he was *smirking* at me.

"Meet some new friends, Maggie?"

"Don't even go there. I had to rewrite my entire English paper last night because of you."

He looked genuinely surprised. "Because of me?"

"Yeah." I forgot I wasn't supposed to antagonize him. "You look good, Stanley. Walking around with five less bullies on your case must agree with you."

His eyes narrowed. "It would agree with anyone. Maybe I should thank you for casting that magic spell everyone is talking about."

"That's bunk and you know it."

"Do I?" He smiled. It was an expression I'd never seen on Stanley's face. He looked like a cat with a mouthful of canary feathers and whiskers coated in cream. "Unless you mean that the idea of magic is bunk, and then I agree. I mean, you'd have a real hard time proving something like that."

"You have no idea what you're dealing with, Dozer."

"Right now, I'm dealing with a runtish busybody and, according to some people, a jealous witch." He waggled his fingers and took off. "Buh-bye, Maggie."

At least I didn't have to wonder anymore. He did it. The power had given him a burst of confidence equal to any magic spell. The old Stanley could never have gotten the last word with me.

I hoped he enjoyed it while it lasted. Because I had a feeling that when the demon got loose, it wasn't going to be too happy with the guy holding the leash.

26

"It was the eyes that got me." Lisa and Justin and I sat in my study. I'd lit some candles—I was trying to clear the smell, not my aura—and the aroma of fresh baked cookies reminded me of Gran's house, and feeling safe. It made it easier, slightly, to talk about things like demons and curses.

Lisa's body language made it more difficult, though. She sat on the sofa with both her arms and her legs crossed, a scowl of rejection on her face. "The smell of brimstone, Mags? Doesn't that seem a little cliché?"

"Clichés have to come from somewhere, don't they?"

"But a demon." She glanced at Justin, and then back at

me. "You two realize we live in the squarest town on the planet, right? And you think this thing is a *demon*?"

Justin, sitting in my desk chair, read from the e-mail he'd received from his friend. He'd brought his laptop since my computer had undergone a meltdown.

"According to Henry, Azmael was a minor Babylonian demon. He mentions that the concept of 'demon' wasn't necessarily bad. It basically meant it was a spirit. Like those personal gods we talked about, Maggie."

Lisa stopped jiggling her crossed legs and relaxed her tightly folded arms. "So this thing might not even be evil. It might just be doling out justice."

"Karen Foley wasn't doing anybody any harm," I said.

"Maybe she was just an accident?"

"It's connected. But I'm not sure how." I picked up the sheet with the symbols. "There are six letters in its name. There were six in the clique, three Jocks, three Jessicas. I thought maybe when it reached six, it would be real, or free, or whatever. But judging by this morning, no."

"Maybe it's one plus," Justin suggested.

"Or two plus, or three." Lisa returned to foot jiggling. "Maybe it's like . . . roulette, or something."

Justin met my eye and shrugged. "It could be that as easily as anything else."

I rubbed my forehead, as if I could massage out the answer. "Maybe it's not just the number of victims, but how much juice it gets off each one."

Lisa rose from the couch and paced restlessly. "This just keeps getting grosser and grosser."

I half regretted bringing her in. She was the smartest

person I knew, but she was having a lot more trouble accepting this than I expected from someone called D&D Lisa.

Justin turned my thoughts back to business. "What do you mean, juice?"

"Why tailor everyone's tragedy to bring the most fear and loss? There must be a purpose to all that angst. Maybe that's what the thing is feeding on, what's making it stronger."

"Pretty sophisticated for an ancient Babylonian evil spirit." Justin cast an eye toward the sheet-covered mirror in the bathroom.

"It's pretty sophisticated for Stanley," I said. "I wouldn't think him capable of crafting something like Jessica Prime's breakdown. But if the demon knows what the summoner knows, maybe it picked up enough to make its own choices."

Justin leaned forward, elbows on his knees. "So, when will it be? What does your gut tell you?"

"That it is very close. That one more victim will hit the jackpot."

"I see . . ." Lisa put a hand over her eyes and held the other out straight-armed, with stage magician drama. ". . . a trip to Las Vegas in our future."

"Very funny." The doorbell rang, and I jumped like a cat.

Justin smiled crookedly. "If the demon is solid enough to ring the doorbell, we're in real trouble."

I gave him a that's-not-funny look, and rose to answer the door. Neither of my parents were home yet.

Brian stood on the doorstep, on his own two feet. I exclaimed in delight and gave him an impulsive hug. "You're standing up! I was so worried."

He kept me close longer than I had intended, but not so long that I minded. Only when I stepped back did I notice the cane he carried. "It's not all bad, but it's not all good," he told me. "I need help as the day goes on. But the good news is, it may remit."

My relief faded a little. "What may remit?"

"My medically impossible MS." He said it with a lot more humor than I would have.

"Come in." I backed out of the doorway. "Lisa and Justin are here. We were just talking about what's going on."

"Have you figured it out yet?" He followed me down the hall, toward the living room. I used the travel time to hedge my answer, not knowing quite how much to tell him.

"It's strange and bizarre. Twilight Zone stuff."

"I guessed that much." He stopped beside me, met my eye. "Brandon is next, isn't he?"

"Looks that way." I held his gaze steadily, gauging his fortitude, letting him see mine. "We're going to stop it, somehow. Not because of Brandon, but because of what might be set free if it builds up enough freedom points."

Brian stared at me, not really understanding, but getting the gist. He squared his shoulders, an unconsciously heroic gesture. "Right. We're the good guys. We stop the bad thing, so it doesn't take over the world. Simple enough."

"Man, I wish Lisa were so easy to convince." I gestured to a chair. "Sit. I'll call them down."

He caught my arm before I moved away. "Wait a sec. I want to ask you something."

I paused, curious at the break in his usual confidence.

He'd taken the news about big bad evil with ease. What had him looking so shook up?

"This is embarrassing, because it makes it sound like you're my second choice." He smiled at me, a little sheepish, a little roguish. "And you're not. But I was stuck going with Jess Michaels to the prom, and now she's dumped me, thank God, so I can ask you."

My jaw didn't quite drop, just dipped a little. "You're asking me to the prom? A Jock—"

"Ex-jock," he said, waggling his cane. "Jess didn't want to go with someone who'd had to drop off the baseball team."

"I don't know, Brian. I hadn't planned to go." I wondered if he knew this, or if he'd just assumed I wouldn't have a date.

"Why not?" His surprise answered my question and made me answer *his* more sharply than I meant to.

"It's just so overwrought. All the angst beforehand, about the date and about the dress. All the expectations: How much money will he spend? Will she put out?" I shrugged. "So much wasted emotion on—"

I broke off as a thought struck me, like an Acme Anvil of Inspiration. I stood there, mouth hanging, while the logic rabbits chased each other through my brain. *So much wasted emotion.*

"Maggie?" Brian sounded worried. I held up a wait-a-minute finger and ran to the staircase.

"Hey, guys! Come down, quick!" I shouted up, ignoring for the moment Brian's baffled stare. "Come on!"

Justin and Lisa rushed down the stairs, both of them

stumbling to a halt when they saw Brian. They exchanged awkward "Heys" all around, but I overrode them.

"I know when it's going to happen."

"When what's going to happen?" Brian, confused.

"How can you know that?" Lisa, disbelieving.

"When?" Justin, succinct and to the point.

"The thing feeds on emotion, right? On grief and terror and angst and woe. Where can it find all that in one place?"

They stared at me, varying degrees of comprehension in their faces. "So," began Justin tentatively, "your plan is . . . ?"

"God help me, I'm going to the prom."

27

by suppertime we'd worked out a plan. It maybe wasn't the best plan, but it was the best we could do, considering that by "we" I mostly meant Justin and his theoretical knowledge and me and my freaky intuition. Possibly this meant we were doomed, but that was certainly true if we did nothing, so this was better odds.

Or so I told myself.

Lame as it sounds, my first step in the plan? Buy a dress. As the saying goes, I had nothing to wear.

Lisa came with me to the department store; she had an uncanny gift in the clearance racks. I'd seen her reach into a bargain bin full of polyester seventies-revival rejects and come up with a beautiful silk chemise that everyone had overlooked because it wasn't the current fashion. Which of course didn't matter to Lisa, as long as it looked good on her.

I was counting on this talent as we hit the mall, because this late in the prom season, everything was on sale, and usually for good reason. She sent me to the dressing room with orders to strip, while she went through the racks like Attila the Hun. By the time I was out of my clothes, she had amassed two armloads of gowns for me to try on.

"What's with that?" she asked. I'd draped my clothes over the cubicle's mirror, unsure I'd ever be comfortable in front of a looking glass again. I wondered if Alice spent the rest of her life leery of the Red Queen's reappearance.

"I have issues," I explained succinctly, and took the dress on the top of the pile. "White? I'll look like the bride of Dracula if I wear this."

"Then don't try it on." She whisked the gown out of my hands and replaced it with a purple one. "Maybe you should have come up with an ingenious scheme that didn't involve formal wear."

Lisa did not suffer a witch to whine. I stopped complaining and obediently slithered into the slinky purple monstrosity.

"You don't have to help, you know."

She zipped up the dress before she answered. Just as quickly, she made a face and unzipped it. "It's a crazy plan. But if you're going through with it, I'd better be around to pull your fat out of the fire."

"Please don't say 'fat' while I'm standing here in my underwear."

Ignoring that, she turned to rifle through the sartorial candidates. "Say you're right and this . . . thing is really waiting for the prom to attack Brandon. He's not exactly going to stand still to be the bait."

"He's not bait, exactly." Except he sort of was. "He's just the only known element in a lot of speculation."

"See, that's what I mean. Speculation." She handed over a deep blue dress, ferreted from the bottom of the pile. "Are you sure the salt is effective against it?"

"Yes. I'm certain about that." I'm not sure my muffled voice sounded very convincing as I struggled to extract my head from the smothering folds of satin. I knew I could fight the demon. Whether I could kill it was another thing.

"But salt. That seems so simple."

"There's a folklore precedent." I wrestled the dress into submission. "Justin could explain it."

"That's another thing," she said, tugging the strapless bodice into place with more force than necessary. "If I had a smart, cute guy like Justin at my beck and call, I sure wouldn't be dangling after Brian the Jock."

I turned on her, indignant. "Okay, back up. Dangling after? And what do you mean, my beck and call?"

She put her hands on my shoulders and spun me back around, going to work on the zipper. "Suck it in. I liked this, but they didn't have it in your exact size."

I sucked. "Explain 'beck and call.'"

"I mean that every time you pick up the phone, he comes running."

"He's helping me with this problem. It's an academic exercise—Ow!" She'd pinched my skin in the zipper.

"Sorry. But the thing is, Mags, guys don't do that for an academic exercise. They don't come running when something goes 'bump.' They don't climb on your roof and check for boogeymen. They don't stay up all night researching ancient Mesopotamia, just so they can impress you."

She finished zipping; I couldn't breathe, but I was more concerned about her point. Justin had, in a very short time, made himself invaluable to me. Not just for his intellect, but for his friendship. If he walked out of my life tomorrow, I'd be the worse for it. But I hadn't let myself think—well, not seriously—that he might view me as more than a friend.

"But I'm *not* dangling after Brian."

Lisa rolled her eyes. "All I'm saying is, don't blow the opportunity you have with Justin just because a hot guy totally out of your league suddenly pays attention to you."

"Give me a little credit, Lisa. Brian's backbone is still in the embryonic stages. But he's not like the others."

Her jaw tightened stubbornly, and I knew there was no point in continuing. "They are all made of the same stuff. He's just figured out the way to work you is to let you develop his conscience." She collected the rejected dresses and flung them over the partition. "He's probably got a bet with Brandon that he can get into your pants."

Embarrassment scorched my face. "Trust me. He'd have a better chance getting into the space program than my pants."

She went on as if I hadn't spoken. "Especially now that he's got that cane. He's got to prove something to regain his place in the pack."

The blind edge to her jock-hate distressed me. Not to mention her lack of faith in *my* common sense.

"You think I'm that easy to manipulate?" Hurt and anger threaded through my voice.

"No. But I don't trust any of that crowd not to just take what he wants."

Something in her tone made me look at her, hard and questioning, but I found her gaze turned inward. Though she spoke with an odd conviction, I couldn't include Brian in that. Not that my judgment was so infallible. I just couldn't picture Mr. Don't-Make-Waves taking unwanted liberties, as Gran would say.

But there wasn't any point in arguing with Lisa when she made up her mind about something. As I learned when she announced that the blue satin dress was the one.

"But it's too tight and too long."

"Yes, but it makes your boobs look great and I'll get one of my minions to hem it up tomorrow."

"I can't pay very much."

"If the world doesn't end this weekend, give her one of your Gran's cookie recipes."

✳ ✳ ✳

School flew by on Friday. Half the senior class was absent, mostly the female contingent. Apparently, the prom takes hours of preparation—hair, makeup, nails, etc. What did I know? When I'd asked my mother to explain the use of cuticle cream to me, I thought she would cry in joy. If I'd realized it would take so little to make her so happy—just one day of shared girly-ness and the opportunity to buy me shoes and proper undergarments—I would have mugged some guy and made him take me on a date a long time ago.

Too bad I was doing it now solely in the cause of fighting Evil. But Mom didn't have to know that.

When I arrived at school Brian was in the crowded courtyard, sitting at one of the tables. He stood when he saw me. "Hey!" I said. "You're not using your cane."

"I don't really need it first thing in the morning." His smile grew forced and I was sorry I'd mentioned it. "Are you all set for tonight?"

"Yeah. I think so." As ready as I could be to face one of my worst nightmares. Not to mention an ancient Babylonian demon.

"I didn't know what color your dress is, so I just got white flowers. Is that all right?"

I stared at him blankly. "Is there some secret code for flowers?"

"No. But Jess— I was told it was important that they match your dress."

"Oh. My dress is blue, so that would be a trick." I ducked automatically to avoid a football, lobbed across the court-yard. "But you didn't have to get me—"

And then I saw his face. Yeah, he *did* have to get me flowers, because secret mission or not, he thought I was going as his date. Call me clueless—Lisa would—but I'd been thinking of my allies as individually wrapped Ding-Dongs, and he'd been thinking two-packs of Twinkies.

Boy, for a smart girl, I could be an idiot sometimes.

"I love flowers," I assured him as the football flew by us in the other direction. I saw the big body hurtling after it, right before Brandon bumped heavily into Brian, knocking him over. I wrapped my arms around him, sort of propping us both up and doing nothing to dispel the Twinkie notion.

Brandon ran by us with a grin. "Sorry, crip. Maybe you should use your cane."

It was getting harder and harder not to just give that guy up for demon chow.

✳ ✳ ✳

Upstairs in my room that evening, I risked a peek in the mirror to see if I was remotely prom-worthy, and was pleasantly surprised to find I'd turned out passably well. I rather liked the dress. Hemmed to lower-calf, the indigo satin stood out in a full, Dior-esque bell. The tighter-than-it-ought-to-be bodice cinched my waist and gave me actual cleavage. Mom had found a deep rose shrug and a crocheted bag that matched. My shoes were pointy and uncomfortable, but looked great with the dress. Even my hair was cooperating. It lay in a smooth, seal-brown bob, and I'd pinned two blue sparkly clips on one side. Besides the matching earrings, my only other jewelry was Gran's cross. Better safe, as they say.

My camera would explain my presence at the dance, since I'd been vocal about not going. If Old Smokey sensed a trap and stayed away, I didn't know if we'd ever be able to anticipate it this well again. Assuming I was correct, which, as Lisa pointed out, wasn't exactly a certainty.

It also gave me an excuse to carry my camera bag, which was packed with canisters of salt. I'd be well armed and prepared, but nothing really stopped the nervous churning in my stomach.

The doorbell rang. No more time to fret about my appearance, or the possibility of my imminent demise.

Justin stood in the living room, chatting with my mom

and dad. I froze on the stairs, a funny sort of stab in the middle of my gut. He looked amazing in black trousers and a white dinner jacket, with his hair brushed tidily back from the rugged lines of his face. He reminded me of Indiana Jones at the beginning of the (vastly inferior) second movie. Not so much in looks, but in the easy way he wore the formal clothes, and his crooked smile when he saw me.

Oof. Stabbity stab.

"Magpie, you look beautiful." My father beamed. So did my mother. I blushed awkwardly, especially when Justin's grin widened; he knew me well enough to read my discomfort.

Mom hugged me when I reached the bottom of the stairs. "I'm glad you decided to go. You see? I doesn't kill you to act like a normal girl once in a while."

Boy, I really hoped those weren't famous last words.

"Take a picture, Michael," she told my dad.

"Oh," I rushed to correct any misunderstandings while Dad went to get his camera. "Justin isn't . . . I mean, we're not . . . I'm going . . ." I'd gone incoherent. I blamed the dinner jacket.

"Maggie is trying to say that we're sort of a foursome." Justin came to my verbal rescue. "We're not really a couple."

"So you can't take a picture?" asked Mom. "You two look great together."

Dad came back with the camera. "Put your arm around her, Justin." He obliged, his hand warm against my waist. Let's just pretend my sudden breathing trouble was due to the corset-like constriction of my dress, and leave it at that.

The shutter clicked, preserving my flustered expression for posterity.

The doorbell rang again. Did I imagine that Justin was slow to drop his arm? The cool spot his touch left behind was real enough. I avoided his eye, quipping poorly, "That'll be the next member of the Scooby Gang."

It turned out to be both of them. Brian looked spectacular in his tux, the tailored jacket smoothed across his broad shoulders, the formal black emphasizing his blue eyes and his wavy blond hair. Next to him stood Lisa, echoing her Goth heritage in a dark-green-and-black silk dress with a corset-type bodice and flowing sleeves. Her coppery brown hair was twisted up in a knot of trigonomic complexity and she looked beautiful, except for the icicles forming around her at having to share air with Brian.

It was a good thing we would have demon hunting to distract us, because otherwise it was going to be a very awkward night.

28

fortunately, I hadn't gone to the prom to have a good time, because I definitely wasn't. Nerves stretched tight as violin strings, I watched for Brandon, jumped at every shadow, and sniffed the air so often that Brian finally asked if his deodorant had stopped working.

"No," groused Lisa, her elbows on the table. "Maggie's brain has."

The hotel staff had cleared away our plates of rubbery chicken, leaving the vaguely coral-and-seaweed-shaped centerpieces and a littering of fish-shaped foil confetti on the table. The theme of the evening? *Under the Sea.* One of the many items on which I'd declined to exercise my voting rights. We'd entered the Marriott's ballroom through a thick curtain of aqua crepe streamers, most of which were now on the floor. A painted paper mural covered the walls, full of sand, seaweed, cartoon fish, and even a diver getting eaten by a shark. Lovely.

"Where's Brandon?" I had lost sight of him for the fourth time since the DJ started blasting "Louie Louie" so loudly that the silverware bounced on the tables.

"On the dance floor." Brian nodded to the large parquet area laid out for our terpsichorean pleasure. Or, more accurately, for wiggling around like a trout on a line. At least that fit the evening's theme.

Brandon and his second-string friends had arrived so late that I'd become certain I'd misread the signs, and Biff lay in an alley somewhere while the freed Shadow went to town. But Stanley towered over the crowd, looking a lot like Lurch from the *Addams Family* in his tux. I was betting heavily that he would want the satisfaction of seeing the big dog taken down.

The Jocks and Jessicas, version 2.0, arrived staggering drunk. Jess Minor hadn't let any grass grow under her feet. With Jessica Prime exiled to the nut farm, she had latched onto the BMOC. Literally. His arm was probably the only thing keeping her upright.

"She looks like she thinks she's won the big prize." Brian wore a concerned knot of pity between his brows.

"The booby prize," Lisa added, as Brandon and his new entourage wove through the crowd.

"Nah." I watched Jess and Thespica giggling tipsily,

trying to stay upright on their high heels. "That's what they give to the first girl to fall out of her dress."

Justin choked back a laugh. Lisa had almost started to smile, too, then caught herself and went back to scowling.

Presently, we sat with our chairs turned toward the dance floor, wincing as the DJ turned on the mike with a squeal of feedback that made the whole room groan. "Amateur!" shouted someone over the last blast of music.

"Whoooooooooo!" shouted DJ Cliché. "Hello, senior class of Avalon High School! Are you ready to paaaaaa-aaarrrrrrty?"

"Geez," I said. "Did this guy time warp out of *Animal House*? Why couldn't we have a band?"

"I think the class voted on it," said Brian, as Jessica Simpson started singing some song I hadn't liked back when it was actually popular. That would teach me to neglect my role in the democratic system.

I craned my neck, searching the dance floor. The flashing lights and brain numbing volume made it impossible to keep track of anyone. "Do you see Brandon?"

Beside me, Lisa pressed her fists to her eyes. "Jeez, Maggie. Would you just chill? If you're right, the . . . thing will show up. If you're not, there's nothing you can do about it."

I glanced from Brian to Justin, who admitted, "She's right."

"Of course I'm right." She dropped her hands to the table with a thud. "But this waiting is making me nuts. I need to take a break."

She pushed her chair back and strode off before I could

stop her, even if I wanted to. Justin turned to me, bemused. "I thought you said she was pretty much unflappable."

"She is. Normally." I stared at her retreating back as she headed toward the door. "Should I go after her, do you think?"

Brian shook his head. "Let her go. It's not like this is a normal situation, and trying to protect Brandon can't sit well with her."

I frowned. "She has a serious hate for all of you. Brandon especially. What's that about?"

"I have no idea." This was clearly a lie, but I didn't have a chance to challenge him, because he glanced over my shoulder and said, "I see him. I think he's headed to the john."

Justin rose to his feet, looking resigned. "You get the next pit stop. There's bound to be a few, from the way he's staggering."

When he was gone, I twisted in my chair to face Brian. "You don't think I'm crazy, do you?"

He returned my gaze soberly. "Last week I had two base-ball scholarships to chose from. Now I'm walking with a cane because I have advanced MS."

My fingers covered his on the table. "I'm so sorry, Brian."

He turned over his hand so that he could grasp mine. "Geez, Maggie. I'm not dead, crumpled like a tin can in Jeff's car. I owe you for that. So no, I don't think you're crazy."

Sighing, I looked at the corsage around my wrist, white roses. Very classy. "I'm sorry for ruining your prom. I know this isn't what you had in mind when you asked me."

"Life is full of surprises." He levered himself up with the

help of the table and then tugged on my hand. "Come on. Let's dance."

One bubblegum pop song finished and something else started, equally brainless and rhythmic. "You sure?" I conspicuously avoided looking at his cane.

"I can probably manage to stand in one place and swing my arms around." He led the way toward the booming music and flashing lights.

I wondered if he'd been a good dancer when he was steady on his feet, and didn't have to worry about his legs giving out under him. Because now . . . not so much. But when one of his baseball teammates noticed him out on the floor, and flashed a thumbs-up, Brian grinned gamely. Then the boys around him started a sort of synchronized head bob. Pretty soon there was a cluster of guys dancing like Brian: feet in one place, kind of bobbing to the beat while the girls gyrated around them. Mostly around Brian, actually.

Some people are popular because they're the stars of the team, and some people are popular because they're not afraid to dance like a complete dweeb.

Despite all the slinky girls around him, when the music ended he pulled unslinky me into a tight, laughing hug. It felt just as nice as you might imagine being squeezed against the chest of a butterfly-swimming, home run–hitting jock would be. Which is to say, very.

"Hey, Crip-patrick. Hard to keep you down, huh." Brandon's voice carried in the silence between songs. Brian loosened his grip on me, but not completely. I felt one arm heavy on my shoulders, and stayed pressed against his side so as he turned, he could lean on me.

"Hey, Brandon." The kids around us swung their heads back and forth like tennis spectators. Behind the looming footballer I could see Justin, lifting his hands in an apology, though I didn't see how he could have warned us.

"Jess told me you were here with the snitch. I couldn't believe it until I saw for myself." Biff's eyes lingered on my constriction enhanced cleavage and I resisted the urge to tug at my dress. "That must be some secret talent you've got, Quinn."

Like I needed a reminder of our last meeting. "Not everyone can get by on muscle alone, Brandon."

Jess Minor wrapped both arms around her date's meaty bicep. "It's not like you can get by on looks," she said, in a pointed sort of way. And I don't mean the obviously insufficient support of her clingy pink bodice.

I smiled sweetly. "Nice outfit, Jess. Find a good sale?"

Her claws dug into Brandon's black sleeve as she looked from me to Brian. "I'm not the one here with castoffs."

Brian's arm tightened around me. I had bruises from underestimating her once. Maybe I would have gotten more if one of the teacher chaperones hadn't appeared before I could voice my next smartass retort.

It was Professor Blackthorne, who took in the situation with a glance, and a Monty Python quote.

"What's all this then?" He cast an eye around the cluster of students.

"Nothing, Teach." Brandon turned on the smarm.

The chemistry teacher was unmoved. "Do I detect the characteristic aroma of ethanol on your breath, Mr. Rogers?"

"Uh . . ."

"The correct answer would be no and a prudent retreat," Blackthorne said, confirming my love for him.

"Er, no, Professor Blackthorne," said Brandon, smart for once. With a last glare at me, he went to another part of the dance floor, taking Jess with him.

"Thanks, Professor Blackthorne," I said.

"Think nothing of it, Miss Quinn. I take my duties of chaperonage very seriously." The gleam in his eye made me doubt the total truth of that. "And now I must be about them," he said as he left.

A girl from my gym class, Amber Somebody, slid up to us in the lull between songs. "Hey, Brian. I asked the DJ to play a slow dance next." She ran her hand down his lapel. "Dance with me?"

Brian hesitated. "Well, Amber, I'm here with someone."

"It's just a dance. Maggie won't mind." She barely glanced my way. "Do you, Maggie? D and D Lisa said you wouldn't."

"How helpful of her," I said. Brian was standing on his own feet again, if tentatively. "But she's right. I don't mind."

Amber leaned in and said more softly. "Come on, Brian. Show Jess you're no castoff."

"Well." He gave me another glance, then looked back at Amber and gave in with a sheepish sort of grin. "But only to show Jess what's what."

Call it a hunch, but I had a feeling Amber wasn't asking just to tweak Jess Minor. Likewise, except for his reluctance to leave me on my own, Brian didn't seem unhappy, either. It was nice to see something work out tonight.

Justin waited for me at the edge of the dance floor. "You lost your partner."

"S'okay." The mirror ball started up and the slow strains of a ballad flooded the ballroom. "I think he'll be all right."

Hands in his pockets, Justin nodded to the floor. "You wanna dance?" I didn't answer immediately, but cast a searching gaze over the room. He assured me, "I've got my eye on Brandon."

"I was worried about Lisa, actually."

"She's over there." A tilt of his head indicated a group of girls ensconced at a table far from the blasting speakers. When Lisa caught my gaze on her, she scowled, pointed to Justin and mimed us dancing. Or something. Looking quickly back to Justin, I smiled tentatively. "Dancing sounds good."

He smiled and reached for my hand. I stepped closer, my legs suddenly stiff and awkward, feeling my face heat, my heart flutter. Then he slid his arm around my waist, drawing me in, and we were swaying to Sarah McLachlan, and I thought maybe the DJ had redeemed himself. Justin turned my hand in his, tucking it close against his chest, like a prized item. I sighed a little, feeling the knot between my shoulder blades ease for the first time all night.

"We shouldn't let our guard down." I said it to myself more than to him.

"Lisa will watch."

Would she? I wasn't so sure. "I knew that Lisa hated Brandon and his friends, but I thought it was because they were basically assholes," I mused aloud as we danced.

I'd gotten used to doing that around Justin. "But something Brian said makes me think there may be more to it than that."

He sighed. His breath smelled very slightly of peppermint, and stirred the wisps of hair by my ear, tickling my neck. All thoughts raced out of my head, as quickly as that. One breath. "Maggie?"

"Yeah?"

"Before we talk about Lisa or Brian or anyone else, can I ask you a question?"

How could I answer, when all I could think about was the way the fabric of his jacket rubbed the bare skin of my arm. Ah, friction. Finally I knew what the big deal was about.

"Brian who?"

He made a sound that might have been a laugh or a sigh. His arm tightened imperceptibly on my waist, pulling me closer still. It was the most natural thing in the world to lay my head on his shoulder and let the too loud music drum out awareness of the world.

"Justin?"

"Hmmm?" His cheek rested against the top of my head. For the first time in my life, I was glad to be short.

"Were you going to ask me a question?"

"Hell if I know."

I smiled as we swayed in a slow circle. I saw Amber with her arms around Brian's neck. She raised her eyebrows at my partner, and gave me a covert thumbs-up.

I closed my eyes again, and when I opened them, we'd gone almost full circle. I saw the klatch of wallflowers, and Lisa's empty chair.

An icy chill crawled over my skin, leaving a clammy feeling of wrongness in its wake, the sudden certainty that something *bad* was happening.

I jerked up my head, hitting Justin in the jaw. "Lisa's gone." I clapped a hand to my skull and ignored the watering of my eyes.

He held his chin and squinted toward the table in the corner. "Maybe she went to the ladies room."

"No. Something's wrong." I searched the crowd.

"Where's Biff?"

"Who?"

"Brandon! Where's Brandon?" I saw Jess hanging drunkenly from the arms of a guy definitely not her date. "Where's Stanley?" He, at least, should be impossible to miss.

Justin scanned the crowd, summing up the futility of his search with a brief but eloquent word.

"Come on." I grabbed his hand and wove through the intertwined couples until we reached Brian and his partner. "Did you see where Brandon went?"

His head turned with aching slowness. "What?"

Amber looked down at me with annoyance. "What the Hell, Maggie?"

"Exactly." I pried Brian out of her grip. "Sorry, Amber. You can have him back later. I hope."

Hurriedly, I explained my worry as we left the dance floor, summing up with, "Brandon, Stanley, Lisa ... they're all missing." Stopping at our table, I felt underneath it for my camera case. My fingers met only carpet and crumbs. I lifted the tablecloth to look, then straightened, feeling my stomach sink impossibly lower. "And so is my bag with our stuff in it."

This was definitely not how the plan was supposed to go. We'd lost track of our bait, our quarry—the human part, anyway—our ammunition, and our ally.

"Okay." Justin used a let's-not-panic voice. "Maybe Lisa saw Brandon leaving the ballroom and followed."

"By herself? She doesn't even really believe what we're dealing with."

"Exactly. She might think she can handle it on her own."

There was still something not right about that, but I couldn't think clearly with the alarm bells going off in my head. I snatched the saltshaker off the table and turned for the door. "We have to find them."

We exited the ballroom by the double doors and paused in the hallway to get our bearings. The lobby lay in one direction, the bathrooms in the other, and straight ahead were glass doors leading to the terrace.

"Check the restroom," Justin said, "just to be sure. I'll check the lobby." Brian's breath had grown labored just from the walk from the dance floor. "Stay here in case they come back."

I hiked up my skirts and dashed for the bathroom in a noisy rustle of satin. I don't know how those girls in the action movies do it. After I'd scouted, I had to slip off my heels and jog back in my stocking feet.

Justin returned as I did. "They didn't go that way."

"I know where they went." It wasn't entirely the process of elimination. Maybe I was getting the hang of this psychic stuff. I straight-armed the glass door leading to the terrace that circled the conference level of the Marriott, overlooking the golf course.

Brian followed us out, then had to stop and lean a trembling hand against the wall. His face looked ashen in the dim light. "You guys hurry. I'll catch up." When I hesitated in concern, he waved me on.

"He'll be all right." Justin grabbed my hand; heart pounding, ribs heaving against my too-tight dress, I ran behind him, down the moonlit path.

29

the plan had been simple. Stick to Brandon. Follow him if he left, especially if Stanley left, too. Use the salt to protect him from the Shadow, since it was the only thing we knew worked. See? Simple.

The stench hit me the moment we rounded the corner. Oh yeah, the demon was here, all right. My gorge rose in my throat and I fell against the terrace wall, losing my struggle to keep down my dinner.

"Jesus Christ, Quinn!" Brandon's voice rattled my skull. "You're here, too? What is this, the whole goddamn circus?"

I blinked stupidly, trying to fit the puzzle together.

Brandon stood in the center of the patio, his tux jacket thrown over a wrought-iron chair, a smoldering joint pinched in his fingers. Oddly enough, this was the only part that made sense. What I had to wrap my head around was Lisa with my camera case at her feet, empty now of easy-pour canisters of salt, and Stanley, wild-eyed and belligerent, clasping the now-familiar brazier in his arms.

Justin came to my side, looking green, so possibly he could smell the demon, too, though the other three seemed oblivious.

"Lisa?" She hadn't even glanced at me. "What's going on?"

"Yeah, Lisa," said Brandon. "I'm just out here getting some fresh air, and this one"—he pointed at Stanley—"shows up talking crazier than a shit-house rat. And this one"—meaning Lisa—"starts playing Betty-effing-Crocker."

I looked at the ground and saw a salt circle on the pavement, white in the moonlight. It looked as though most of the pattern had been put in place earlier and closed just now, where the line was cleaner. Raising my eyes to Lisa's grim face, I realized she'd been holding out on me, and protesting entirely too much, perhaps from the very beginning.

"Lisa?" I repeated her name.

"I'm fixing this, Maggie." She still didn't look at me. "Just let me handle it."

"Why are you interfering?" Stanley's drab hair stood up in wispy spikes as he confronted her. "You hate these ass-holes as much as I do."

"Shut up, Dozer," she snapped. "You don't even know what you're dealing with."

"Yes I do." He held the brazier in both hands. It looked smaller in real life, but somehow . . . more. As if the evil contained in it were distilled down, latent in the beaten brass. "I'm the one who found the key. I'm the one who realized what it could do. I'm the one who can control it."

"That thing doesn't control it, idiot."

"Lisa," I cautioned, seeing Stanley's face flush blood-dark. "Maybe you shouldn't piss him off too much." Just in case he could let the leash go early, better not antagonize the crazy guy.

Brian arrived then, leaning heavily on his cane. He stared in obvious confusion and Brandon, seeing him, made a disgusted sound. "You, too, Crip-patrick? This is a real loser convention. I'm out of here."

"Stop!" At least three of us shouted at him. Justin because he was about to step across the salt barrier, Stanley because he was in full raving lunatic swing, and me, because I could sense the demon waiting, its anticipation invading my brain the way its stink invaded my lungs.

The footballer paused at our outburst, and Justin stepped into his path. He raised his hands in a gesture both calming and emphatic. "You really don't want to head back right now."

"Look, dickhead. I don't even know who you are, but you'd better move before I kick your ass."

Justin's eyes narrowed and his face hardened. "You could try." He may have been bluffing, but he convinced me.

The tension seemed to thicken the air, growing dense

with every harsh word. I didn't know whether to warn them or not. If we drew the Shadow out of hiding, we could fight it, with Brandon safe in the protective circle. The uncooperative bait, however, was one wild card. The other pushed his way past Lisa to get in my face.

"Do you think you can stop me? No one can stop this now."

"Geez, Stanley. Did you get your dialogue from an old James Bond movie? Listen to yourself."

"No, you listen, Margaret Quinn."

Margaret?

He pushed my shoulder with the hand not holding the brass artifact. Brian stepped forward with a protective "Hey!" but Stanley ignored him. "You are an interfering little bitch and I don't know why you're not lying at the bottom of that swimming pool right now."

I remembered the list of names in my dream, offered to the demon in parchment and blue flame. "You put my name on the hit list?" I don't know where I found the room for indignation. "What did I ever do to you?"

"You *pitied* me," said Stanley, pushing at my shoulder again. "And you *meddle*. So I put you on the list. I don't know why it missed you, but . . ."

I shoved him back, remarkably restrained in confronting someone who'd tried to kill me. "Maybe because my name isn't Margaret, jerkwad."

Stanley stumbled backward; his heels scuffed the line of white crystals, but didn't break it.

"Maggie!" Justin shouted a warning and a remonstration. I saw immediately why. In the shadows by the terrace wall a nightmare coiled in on itself, writhed into being.

Lisa grabbed Dozer by the arm and yanked him away from the circle and away from me, trying to reestablish control of the situation. "Stop it. Now."

I looked at her, tried to sort out her involvement in all this. The demon knew my real name, but Stanley didn't. If Azmael knew what its summoner knew . . .

Still inside the circle, Brandon took one last hit off his joint and pinched it out, letting the smoke escape slowly on a lazy laugh. "Are you the loser queen, Lisa? These your court jesters?"

. . . then Stanley didn't actually summon the demon.

"Or maybe you got it bad for one of them." Brandon continued his languid taunt, while Lisa stared at him, loathing in her eyes. "Is it Quinn? Did I put you off guys for good?"

"Shut. Up." Her voice bit frozen chunks from the night air.

I stared at her. We all did. Nothing moved but darkness and shadow, growing in the corner of my vision.

Stanley didn't know my full name. But Lisa did.

"I was drunk." Bone-deep hatred twisted her words.

Brandon met it with indifference. "Duh. It was a college party. Everyone was drunk."

A vague memory flitted through my head: spring break, leaving for Colorado with Mom and Dad, and Lisa telling me that she and Katie and Tess were going to get a feel for campus life while I was gone.

Her fists clenched at her side, gathered more air and clenched again. "I was too drunk to say no."

Brandon's careless shrug was another assault. "Not my fault you changed your mind."

I took a furious step toward him, trembling with the temptation to do violence on him, to wipe that indifference off his face. "You unconscionable bastard." Justin put out a hand, kept me from crossing the line. I glared at him, then turned my anger on Brian next. "You knew about this?"

He avoided my gaze, swaying on his feet. "I drove her home that night. I offered to take her to the police, but she didn't want to."

"Why not?" I looked at Lisa. Her whole countenance, her entire being rejected sympathy. "Why didn't you tell me?"

"I didn't want anyone to know." Her gaze flicked to Brian, and I glimpsed part of her unreasonable hatred of him. He'd witnessed her weakness.

I grabbed for Lisa's hand, didn't let her push me away. "He did wrong, not you." Brandon snorted, and I ignored him.

Her chest heaved with the effort to control her emotion. "No, I was just stupid and naïve." Two fates worse than death in Lisa's book. She turned to Brandon. "All I wanted to do was punish you."

Two burning yellow sparks flickered in the solidifying darkness. "Lisa," I cautioned. "Don't do anything stupid."

"Something more stupid than summoning a demon, you mean?"

"No!" Stanley wrapped his arms around the brazier. "It was my idea. Mine. You just helped me, threw some ingredients in the pot." He stared, transfixed, at the agglomeration of shadow. "And now it's here, and you'll see who is in charge."

"You are *all* bat-shit crazy," said Brandon with almost as

much horror as contempt. The only time I would ever agree with him. "I'm done listening to this crap."

The darkness broke free from the corner and spread across the patio in a dank, hell-born fog. "Don't move," Justin ordered.

"You are not in charge here!" shrieked Stanley.

The Shadow chortled, less a sound of laughter and more the noise of bugs scuttling across rock.

"Christ on a crutch!" Brandon frantically searched the dark. "What was that?"

Lisa's face shone white in the moonlight. "I came up with the formula to evoke it. I can control it."

"I found the brazier." Stanley backed away from the fog, pressing his back to the wall. "I gave it the list of names."

"Shut up, Stanley."

Brian collapsed without warning. Justin turned instinctively to break his fall, and Brandon took his chance. He stepped out of the circle. As soon as his foot broke the line, it happened, more quickly than my mind could completely process.

The haze wound together, spinning into a noxious cyclone that amassed into a malformed approximation of legs and arms and trunk, sulfurous orbs where eyes should be.

Stanley dropped the brazier, three millennia of burnished brass hitting the concrete with a clang that echoed all the way back to its forging. Brandon's arm jerked suddenly up and back, like a police control hold, and kept going until I heard a crack and a wet pop and a tearing sound, then it fell to his side like a dead thing.

The pain reached his brain and he began to scream. His

other shoulder cracked, the joint splintering. Then the rib cage . . . Oh God, the sounds it made.

Do not pass out, Maggie. Think! I still clutched the shaker I'd taken from the table. My fingers lost precious time fumbling to unscrew the top. The metal cap bounced on the ground, and I poured the fine white crystals into my hand, until they ran through my fingers.

The screaming stopped.

Lisa fell to her knees, doubled over with horrified sobs. Stanley pressed himself to the wall as if he could crawl through it. Brian lay lax and still, but I could hear his breathing in the grisly silence.

Justin stood slowly. We watched as the Shadow dropped Brandon's broken body over the terrace wall, like so much rubbish, then turned to face us. It looked almost the same, a mostly human shape with a miasma of smoke clinging to it, trailing as it moved.

"Now we meet in the real world, Magdalena," said the demon Azmael. "At last face to face."

30

It knew my name because Lisa did. I hadn't quite wrapped my head around that, but I didn't take the time to analyze it now.

I flung the handful of salt. It hissed and fizzled against the creature's cloaking outer layer, and the acrid smell redoubled until I choked on the burning fumes, my eyes streaming until I couldn't see to defend myself. That was some deflector shield.

"Don't be rude," he —it?—chided. "I've waited so long to meet you."

"Sorry," I wheezed. "I left my book of demon etiquette

at home." I don't know how I found the courage to quip. But I figured collapsing in a gibbering puddle of terror wouldn't do anyone any good. Least of all me.

Justin's hand slid into his pocket. I knew he was armed, too, and I drew the demon's attention to me with another lame verbal sortie. "I gotta tell you, buddy"—Behind it, Justin silently opened his Ziploc bag—"now that you've got armpits, I suggest some deodorant. Because . . . damn."

"This century is full of wonders." A tendril of its smoky layer snaked toward me, winding as it came, twisting into a thin rope of shadow. I forced myself not to retreat. "The human capacity for false courage is just one of them."

The cord snapped around like a bullwhip, and I flinched as it struck Justin's hand, sending an arc of fine white crystals flying harmlessly across the paving stones. The tentacle lashed again and wrapped around Justin's throat.

His fingers tore at the blackness without effect. The demon didn't even look at him, but cocked its head at me. "Was that sporting, Magdalena? No. I think not." It lifted Justin higher, until he was hanging from the smoky extension, his back bowed as he tried to find purchase. He couldn't even draw enough breath to choke.

"Let him go!"

"Drop your weapon." I tossed my carton to the ground, next to Lisa whose fingers twitched, just barely. Justin made tiny, gasping half-coughs, and his grip on the demon noose began to slide away. "Now ask *nicely*."

Slowly, as if forcing my stubborn knees to bend, I took a supplicant's position. I couldn't read the creature's expression—I could only see its eyes through the concealing black miasma—but I sensed its surprised pleasure.

Arrogant son of a bitch. "Please," I said, my fingers creeping across the stone until they met cold brass. Lisa's hand inched to the carton of salt. "Let . . . him . . . Go!"

On my word, Lisa and I moved together. She snapped the canister up, throwing the contents across Justin and the demon-tentacle that held him. I lurched to my feet with the brazier, and slammed the metal with all my might and momentum into the monster's amorphous head.

Solid was a relative thing. The weapon clanged, I felt the impact up my arm. Acid yellow eyes dripped like the yokes of two rotten eggs, then congealed and rolled back up to where they belonged. Where the salt struck, its smoky extension sizzled and evaporated; Justin fell to the ground as the creature reeled back, making an animal squeal of pain.

"Close the circle," I shouted at Lisa. The demon had stumbled backward into the broken ring. "Close it!"

Lisa jumped forward and poured salt over the gaps. I felt a strange subliminal buzz as the line became complete again, a scant instant before the demon collected itself.

I hurried to Justin, who pushed himself up, wheezing painfully. Pulling loose his tie and opening his collar, I saw his skin was blistered and bruised, but his breathing eased quickly. "You all right?"

"Yeah. Help me up." He staggered to his feet, squaring his shoulders as we turned to face the trapped demon.

"Oh Lisa," it said, disappointment in its tone. "You had such potential. That one"—it gestured to the unconscious Stanley—"was just a clown. I had high hopes for you."

"That's enough, Azmael." I stepped forward, speaking the creature's name aloud for the first time, bringing it into the open and reducing its psychological power.

It hissed at me, eyes burning brighter for a moment. "Your bravado annoys me. You will be very afraid before I'm done with you, Magdalena."

The demon knew the power of a name, too. "You're trapped, Ass-my-el. And I'm going to punch your return ticket."

A tendril of its cloaking layer gestured carelessly to Lisa and Justin. "I will kill these two first, to give you great pain."

I raised the brazier like a shield. "It would give you a lot of pain, too. I know you're solid now."

"Not that solid." Its voice skittered with amusement, like dry, multilegged things in the dark.

The creature gave a heat-mirage shimmer. A layer of its swathing haze pulled away, like a wet peel of sunburned skin, and fell to the ground in a congealed lump. The blob twitched and writhed, as the demon shed another layer to plop beside the first. Clump after clump became semisolid until the imprisoning circle was filled with contorting masses of ectoplasm, heaving and struggling to be born into something vile.

I stepped instinctively back; beside me, Justin went taut with the same revulsion that held me transfixed. Stripped of his outer coating, Azmael looked as though someone with no real understanding of human form had tried to sculpt it out of dry and filthy earth. Eyes sat in sockets without lids and the nose recalled the vestige holes on a mummified corpse. And when the misshapen mouth moved to speak, my skin crawled at the *wrongness* of it.

"Do you not like my inner form, Maggie Quinn?" the demon taunted me. "Perhaps you liked me better as a shadow?"

280

"I certainly liked you better before you could talk."

The pseudo-face showed little more emotion than the veiling layers of smoky ectoplasm, but it managed anger pretty well. "And I prefer you quivering with fear."

The first Hell-blob leapt up. It wasn't done cooking, but it had too many legs, too many eyes, and its gaping maw seemed impossibly large, impossibly full of ragged, sharklike rows of teeth. The jaws snapped; I stumbled back, even as the thing hit an invisible barrier at the circle's limit.

"What are those things?" Lisa stood at one shoulder, Justin at the other.

"Trapped," I said, relieved, but not entirely. The beasts pawed the ground, a distorted hunting pack, growling with foul, sooty breath.

Azmael stood in the center of its minions. "It has been a pleasure doing business with you, Lisa." The beasts at its stubby feet snarled and sniffed the air. "I'm grateful to you for opening the door for me. The tasks you and the boy set before me allowed me to gain a liberty I haven't had for centuries."

"I never wanted—" Lisa began.

"I knew what you wanted better than you knew yourself." It made a tsking noise, almost droll. "Yet you give me no thanks."

I picked up one of the discarded cartons of salt. "I hope you enjoyed your leave, Smokey, because your pass is about to be revoked."

A derisive, dismissive snort. "I think not." The sulfurous eyes turned to me, anticipation making them swell. "You were right about this much, Maggie Quinn. I am hungry after so long without a solid form. And your kind is a wealth of rampant emotion."

With a certain drama, it crouched and brushed clear a section of the white line. Its hand smoked and blistered and stank, but remained intact. "Oh, that does sting."

The pack of demon-spawn slipped their invisible leash, poured out of the gap. They scrabbled on phantom claws past our horrified eyes, buffeting us as they rounded the corner and headed for the smorgasbord of teenagers dancing in short-lived blissful ignorance.

"Oops!" said Lisa. At least, the voice was hers, but the tone was Azmael's taunting humor. She turned, and I recoiled from the otherness in her eyes. "You'd better get going, Supergirl." She reached out and took the salt that I cupped, forgotten, in my hand, and let it run out of her fingers. "I think you know where to find us, if you survive."

Her body turned, walked away, stiff-jointed like a puppet. I took a step after her, but Justin caught my arm.

"Leave her."

"But Lisa . . ."

"Is one person." He pulled me insistently toward the front of the hotel. "We have to stop those things, or they'll kill everyone inside."

Stanley hadn't roused from his faint, and Brian was still unconscious. I didn't know if Brandon was even alive. But those demon-dogs were going to cut a swath through the senior class unless we stopped them.

I gave up arguing and ran, still clutching the brazier, leaving behind the fallen, and racing to save those I could.

31

I wondered how the beasts would get inside, since they didn't have arms to open the doors. As we rounded the corner, though, we saw the last two creatures squeezing through the crack between the doors.

"They're not solid," I said in relief. "They can't really—"

The last Hell-dog launched itself at me with a cougar-like scream. Pure reflex jerked the brazier up as the quite solid weight of the monster sent me sprawling to the ground. I screamed, too, as razor teeth hammered at the brass, trying to get through to my throat.

Justin kicked the beast aside. It immediately flung itself back at us, but I whacked the snarling thing with the brazier and it exploded in a cloud of infinitesimally small dropules of the primordial goo. Almost instantly they began to gloam together and rebuild themselves.

"Semisolid, I'd say." Justin pulled me up from the ground and away from the quickly growing Hell-blob. "Keep that weapon handy."

We each yanked open one of the glass doors. Terrified screams poured from the ballroom. By my quick and dirty reckoning, the monster-per-kid ratio lay in our favor; only it wasn't how many people they killed, but how much terror and pain they inflicted, feeding Azmael's hunger.

There was nothing to do but wade into the carnage. I swung my big brass bowl of kick-ass at a demon-dog that had pinned a boy from my chemistry class. The monster burst into a satisfying, if temporary, wet mist. Grabbing a napkin from the nearest table I handed it to the guy. "Keep pressure on the bleeding."

Justin grabbed a chair and smashed a creature savaging a girl's leg. She burst into hysterical tears, and he had to pry her loose before moving on to the next fight.

Three monsters down. Seventeen left. Eighteen, I amended, as the first re-formed beast leapt on a fleeing band geek. I quickly un-formed it again. At the end of the room, one of the light stands crashed to the floor in a shower of sparks. A speaker went next, conveniently squishing an eight-legged monster beneath it. Anything heavy, applied with enough force, could smash the things, but I noticed my brazier, perhaps because of its link to their master, made the smallest bits.

A few students tried to fight back. But the more the kids

screamed, the more blood that soaked the ugly carpet, the stronger the monsters became and the more quickly they remade themselves. Despite the numerical advantage, we were fighting uphill.

The demon-hounds herded and pushed with flashing teeth until the crowd stampeded like Irish fans at a soccer match; tables, chairs, and fallen students were only temporary impediments while the beasts picked off the stragglers. Feeding time at the watering hole, and survival of the fittest.

A heavy student, side-blocked by an even heavier dog-beast, crashed into the table in front of me. I jumped back as empty dishes and silverware catapulted into the air. I brought the brazier up like a shield; something clanged against it, and dropped at my feet.

I looked down. The salt shaker lay on the carpet, spraying my stocking-clad toes with white.

Something important lay in the memory of Azmael casually brushing aside the salt circle, something besides his new invulnerability to sodium chloride. It had cleared a path for the pack of minions, given them a clean way out.

So . . . what the Hell, to use a fitting phrase. I picked up the shaker, unscrewed the lid and climbed over the table to get to the student, who screamed as the beast teethed on his arm. "Close your eyes!" I shouted over the din, and dumped the entire shaker over them both.

The Hell-dog disappeared in a puff of black smoke. No tiny droplets, no wet mist. Just a dry, clean 'fffft!' and then nothing. Even the smell vanished.

"Dude!" I turned my head to see Backstage Guy, the one

I'd met at play practice, his tux spattered with blood and black demon-goo, a mike stand in his hand, heavy-side up. "Yo, Glowing-ass-girl! What did you do?"

"Salt," I said, clambering down from the table. In the wreckage of another setting I found two more shakers, handing both to Dude. "Unscrew and dump."

I ran through the tables, gathering as many shakers as I could. Professor Blackthorne was holding his own with one of the beasts, standing over it with a chair leg and splattering it apart every time it re-formed.

"You will not"—splat—"defy"—squish—"the laws"—scrunch—"of nature."

I dumped one of my saltshakers over the monster between squishings. The droplets fizzled out of existence, and Blackthorne looked at me, eyebrows shooting all the way up to his wildly askew hair.

"Supernatural creatures follow supernatural laws," I explained, grabbing ammunition off the nearest table.

"Of course they do," he said, smoothing white wisps out of his red face and regaining his sangfroid.

"Unscrew and dump." I dropped two shakers in his hand and left him to it. I saw other students getting the idea, and felt the tide turning with every *poof!* Just like magic.

Jessica Minor was perched on a table, defending the high ground from a snapping beast by whacking at it with a paper-seaweed centerpiece. It was tempting to let a Hell-dog take down the Hell-bitch, but a blast of white from behind me ended my moral dilemma and obliterated the demonette so quickly that its mad snarl hung in the empty air.

"Viva Maggie!" called the guerrilla of the Spanish Club. Don de Chiclet raised a fist full of salt. "Viva la revolucíon!"

The stampede had ended. Jocks, band geeks and brains, preps, ropers and stoners stanched each other's wounds and helped one another up. Thespica was sucking Backstage Dude's lungs out—in a good, nondemonic way—with a pile of salt at their feet. Good for you, Backstage Dude.

I saw Justin and hurried toward him, limping barefoot through the carnage. He was bleeding from some teeth marks on his arm, and his face was streaked with sooty demon residue. "I'm okay," he assured me, as the sound of sirens reached us.

"Come on." I pulled him toward the back door. "They won't let us leave once the authorities get here."

"Hang on, Maggie . . ."

Seeing Professor Blackthorne directing the first aid efforts, I stopped. "Professor, there are three more students out back. One of them is . . . he fell over the terrace wall."

The teacher gave me a level look. "That's what I'm supposed to tell the police?"

"I . . . I don't know." I was out of lies. "I have to go stop the . . . the thing that started all this."

Another stare, an instant's examination that seemed eternal. Finally, he said, "Go. I'll think of something. But your final grade is going to depend on your explaining the supernatural chemistry at work here."

"I will, I promise."

And if I live that long, I'll make good . . . somehow.

32

The Jeep raced along Beltline. I hoped all the cops were at the Marriott, because I was way past the speed limit.

"How do you know where they are?" Justin asked me, one hand clinging, white-knuckled, to the roll bar. The wind whipped my hair around my face and I had to drive with the skirt of my dress tucked tightly under my thighs. I never found my shoes.

"I just know. It's the way the quest always ends. Luke goes all over the galaxy, but he still has to come back to the Death Star to meet Darth Vader."

"You know this isn't a movie, right?"

"Yes. That ugly bastard has my best friend, and I have no idea how to fight it." I zipped through a yellow light. "Now think. Why did the salt work before, but not tonight?"

"It might have to do with its solid form." He shook his head. "All the supernatural traditions say it should have worked. Jewish folklore uses salt to bless a baby and keep the demons away. Chinese women take salt baths for the same reason . . ."

"So what do we use instead? Crosses? Holy water?"

"Azmael predates the birth of Christ. I don't think either of those would affect him."

I whipped onto the street that ran behind the school, my mind racing through the problem. If Azmael predated Christ, then he, it, also came way before Morton.

With a squeal of the tires I turned the Jeep in a tight U, changing directions as quickly as my thoughts. "We're using the wrong salt."

"What?"

"Azmael isn't going to be afraid of easy-pour, iodized, table salt. We need the real unprocessed thing."

"Where are you going to find sea-salt at this hour?"

I pulled up in front of a corrugated aluminum building and pulled the brake. "Landscaping shed. They keep fifty-pound bags for deicing the sidewalks in winter. Grab the bolt cutters in the back, will you?"

Justin stared at me, wasting precious moments on bewilderment and perhaps a little awe. "You were a Girl Scout, weren't you?"

"Nope. But Nancy Drew was *always* prepared."

✳   ✳   ✳

My bare feet met the cold tile of the natatorium with a quiet slap-slap; the diving board loomed above, and I saw the man-shaped darkness waiting there.

It was all about knowing the rules. Quests were circular; Azmael held to tradition, obviously. The accident at the pool had been the first time I'd glimpsed the Shadow. Even if the accident had misfired because Stanley wrote my name down wrong, it was still where the demon had come for me.

And of course, the deep water terrified me. Lisa knew, so Azmael knew; there was simply no other place they could be.

The smell confirmed this, faint but distinct. Chlorine and brimstone and rotting flesh. It was a good thing I had nothing but dread churning in my stomach.

Outside the gym, Justin had helped me shoulder my backpack and balance the weight. "Can you carry all this?" His paladin's face pinched with worry.

I grinned. "I've been in training for twelve grades." Then sobering, I went over our hastily constructed plan. "I have to go in by myself, but once I have him distracted—"

"I'll be there." His hands rested on my bare shoulders as he looked down at me, a riot of emotions in his eyes. If this were a movie, he might kiss me now, or tell me to stay alive, no matter what, or vow to rescue me. And I might be wearing shoes and have less mascara running down my face.

Though come to think of it, "I'll be there" had been the perfect thing to hear just then.

"Are you alone, Magdalena Quinn?" The demon's reedy voice echoed in the big, empty gym. The water in the pool beside me shivered, then returned to placid lapping.

"Yes, I am, oh great and powerful Az."

"You took your time. One would think you were leaving your friend to reap her own wickedness."

Judge not, lest you be judged. I remembered that much from Sunday school. Lisa would have to answer for her ancillary role in the events of the past two weeks, not to mention tonight's carnage. But not to me.

"Lisa is my friend. And I don't let jumped-up, minor demon jackasses take my friends."

The smell intensified with said jackass's anger. "Then come up and try to rescue her, mighty demon-hunter. I'm waiting."

I guess that was netherworld speak for "Nyah nyah nyah, I'd like to see you try it."

Ahead, the diving pool glimmered darkly; diffuse light reflected on the surface, but did not penetrate the inky blackness at all.

"Leave the backpack on the ground," Azmael said. "Do you think I'm a fool?"

An ominous growl rumbled out of the shadows. I saw the gleam of teeth. Great. Another doggie. We'd destroyed the ones at the prom, so the demon must have regained enough ... power, mojo, whatever ... to create more. Not the best news I'd had all evening.

"I'm leaving it," I shouted up at him. "Call off your dog."

"When you obey me, stubborn child."

I had to get my burden to the pool, so I walked forward, the beast shadowing me, its claws clicking on the tile. The growl deepened as I reached the base of the diving platform, the claws sped, leapt. In a practiced move, I slipped one shoulder from its strap, let the weight of the pack swing down, around, to meet the dog's attack. The monster sank its teeth through the nylon and *pffft!* disappeared without time to whimper.

Whoa. It had barely touched the salt inside, hadn't taken a dousing at all. I wish that had worked as well on the Jacobson's dog when it had chased me to school every morning of fifth grade. I began to think this insane plan might actually work.

I heard another growl, and figured a second minion had come to ensure my compliance. But hell-dog number one had done me a favor, ripping a large hole in the fabric. In the blind spot beneath the platform I set the pack on the edge of the pool and let the big crystals of the unprocessed rock salt pour into the water.

"Okay. I'm coming up. No backpack."

I hiked up my dress and began to climb the ladder to the high dive, another thing easily accomplished by heroines in movies, but a major pain in real life. In my next battle with a creature from Hell, I would definitely forgo the formal wear.

An eternity later, I crawled onto the wide platform, winded and trembling from fatigue and nerves. Turns out I like heights only slightly more than I like the depths. There's irony for you. I stayed on all fours as I fought off the vertigo and tried to catch my breath. I was one scary demon-fighter, all right.

Azmael stood in the center of the dais. Lisa lay unconscious near me. If we survived this, she was going to be pissed that she'd been cast in the helpless female stereotype, getting kidnapped and fainting.

"No quip, Maggie Quinn? No witty repartee?"

I stared at the creature's feet, as not-quite-right as the rest of its mistake of a body. "Just wondering if you shouldn't have cloven hooves."

"I am exactly as I should be!" Its voice rang against the steel beams and concrete. "Exactly as I have been for ten thousand years."

Slowly, I got my legs under me. Movie heroines never have to hitch up their tops, either, but I'd be darned if I'd give Azmael a thrill by falling out of my dress. "Ten thousand years, huh? No wonder you go around with the veil-o'-stench. You must be pretty sorry to lose it."

The demon lurched toward me, angrily. I sidestepped, letting it drive me farther from the ladder. Live and die by the wisecrack. Sir Justin had a gift for prophecy.

"No matter." Old Smokey recovered its aplomb. "I'll rebuild my form quickly." Lidless yellow eyes burned more deeply with hunger. "How I love every neurotic, apprehensive, irrational member of your generation. I will feed on your kind until I have power to build an army of shadow hounds." It looked down at me with an eerily human expression of distain. "Then we will see who is the *minor* demon."

"Don't feel you have to prove yourself on my account."

"Insolent insect!"

Our dance of quip, lunge, and dodge drove me toward the pool. I thought I saw movement below, knew I heard a growl. But I couldn't warn Justin about the hell-dogs without drawing their master's attention to him.

"I feel your terror, Magdalena." It moved again, herding me. "It boils below the façade of your bravery."

"That's my acid indigestion." Prickles of sweat broke out on my skin as I reached the edge of the platform. I guess this is what they mean when they say "Between the devil and the deep blue sea."

"I can smell your fear." It drew a noisy breath through the two elongated ovals of its nose, and smacked its misshapen lips. "Your stubbornness hides a bounty of dread."

The balance tipped with my final step; the effect was tangible, an inevitable teeter-totter slide into the depths. Azmael's horrible mouth curved into something like a smile.

An updraft caught at the bell of my skirt. The familiar, irrational terror of the deep—of sinking into the abyss—crawled around in my brain like a parasite, and I gave it rein. I hung my heels over empty space, and opened my mind to my ravaging phobia.

The demon couldn't resist. It sprang at me with a voracious scream, like an animal, a feral, starving thing. I fell back, into the void, and the creature jumped after me.

Dear God, let this work.

I hit the water with that prayer, and then wished that I'd listened to Coach Milner's instructions on how not to die a horrible death coming off the high dive. She might not have covered the part with the Hell-born psychic vampire, but at least I might have known that surface tension was not my friend.

The impact felt like hitting a wall at five or ten miles an hour. As the water closed over my head my entire being, down to my cells, screamed in protest. Then I heard the demon splash down beside me. It sank, grabbed on to me with long, sinuous arms and pulled me deeper, drinking in my terror and my despair.

Part of the plan. I chanted it in my head as my skirt billowed up around me like a shroud. Part of the plan, a salt bath, a cleansing, a solution. But the Maggie that curled up in my brain, catatonic with fear, only knew the tentacles of a monster dragged me down.

Part of the plan. The creature's limbs had gone amorphous and pliable. The demon was losing substance, and its elongating fingers entwined my arms and legs like slimy, rotten vines. With a spark of hope, I started to kick.

My legs churned the water, sped the process as each molecule of NaCl bound to a demonic atom, making it inert. The snaky fingers that gripped me broke apart. I reached blindly out, stretched my arms into the water and grabbed double handfuls of the protoplasmic mess that remained of Azmael. Now that it was shadow-substance again, I could hear it in my head, flailing mentally in fury.

And then it disintegrated completely. My hands held nothing, and my mind was empty.

Numbing panic rushed to fill the void. I swirled my arms and legs through demon-free water, but I had no idea which way was up. The burning in my chest grew intolerable, and little dots of light jumped at the edges of vision.

A hand grabbed my arm, a solid, human hand, pulling at me insistently. I tried to kick, tried to move my arms, but it was like moving through Jell-O. My skirts wrapped around my legs, trapping them. I was so tired, and the dancing sparkles flooded the whole of my sight.

33

My head broke the surface of the water and I sucked in a greedy lungful of air. Something constricted my middle—Justin's arm, holding me afloat while I coughed and sputtered and reminded my body what oxygen felt like.

"Good to see you," I managed between gasps.

"Told you I'd be here." He swam to the ladder, pulling me along. "Can you climb up?"

"Maybe," I lied. My limbs were spaghetti.

He wrapped my arms around the railing. "Just hold on."

That, I might manage.

He climbed from the pool, then hooked his arms under

mine and hauled me out. I think I was heavier than he expected. I hoped he assumed it was my waterlogged dress. He fell back, and I sprawled on top of him like a big, soggy fish.

For a long time neither of us moved. I didn't think I could. Not one muscle in my body wanted to obey my commands. Truthfully, though, it felt good to rest there, Justin's chest rising and falling under my cheek as he caught his breath. There was another issue as well, but I hadn't figured out what to do about it.

"When I saw you dive from that board"—his hand stroked my back, almost absently—"and I use the word *dive* very loosely—I thought my heart would stop."

"You, too?" Mine still beat kind of erratically.

He looked at the pool, which rippled innocently against its concrete borders. "Is it—the demon—gone?"

"Yeah." It *felt* gone. The way it had disappeared from my head with a little pffft, just like its Hell-dog offspring, made me certain. Well, as certain as I could be, with my vast experience in matters mystical.

"Do you think you can get up?" he asked.

"No."

"Why not?"

"Because my dress slid down when you pulled me out of the water. I'm not decent."

"Oh." His cheeks flushed visibly in the dim light, which I thought was kind of cute, until I noticed a tinge of guilt in his blush, and it occurred to me he might not have been completely unaware of that fact.

Call me clueless. And slightly flattered.

He covered his eyes while I sat up and quickly tucked things back where they belonged. Collecting the dinner jacket crumpled on the tile nearby, he handed it to me, his head still turned.

"Thanks." I wrapped the fabric around my bare, wet shoulders, grateful for the warmth. "You can turn around now."

He offered a hand and pulled me to my feet. My knees buckled—no, really, they did—and Justin caught me tight against him.

"Thanks." I rested my hands on his shoulders, not quite able to meet his eyes. "For helping me save the world and all."

"Anytime." His crooked smile never looked better. If this were a movie . . .

The kiss couldn't possibly have felt so good. He bent his head and fit his lips to mine, as naturally as, well, breathing. But I'd never again take oxygen for granted. I slid my arms around his neck and kissed him like I might never kiss anyone again, ever. He kissed me as though I'd scared him to death, and he needed to tell me something important before I did something else foolhardy. I think I got the message.

A few blissful centuries later, he broke away and wrapped me tightly—tighter still—in his arms. "Maggie Quinn, when you take a leap of faith . . ."

"I knew it would work." I rested my cheek on his shoulder, very warm beneath his sodden shirt. "I just thought: water. The universal solvent."

He laughed. Even with the incredulous shake of his head, it was a wonderful sound.

"Hey!" I startled guiltily at the voice, calling from above. "Maggie? Is that you?"

"Lisa? Are you okay?" I saw her pale face at the edge of the diving platform.

"What the Hell am I doing way up here?"

"It's a long story," I said. "Can you make it down?"

"Yeah. If I made it up in this dress, I guess I can make it down." Her head disappeared.

Justin let his arms fall away from me, obviously reluctant. "I'll give her a hand." I wrapped his jacket close and watched Lisa's shaky descent; once on the ground, she stood for a moment, grasping the ladder and brushing off his assistance.

Then she looked at me, confusion knotting her forehead. "Why are you wet?"

Justin spoke, not coldly but not kindly, either. "She vanquished the demon with a trap in the water."

Her eyes widened. "The dive pool?" A dizzying jumble of emotions chased each other across her face. Shock, awe, relief . . . shame, grief, and regret. Finally she raised a shaking hand to her face. "I didn't understand what it was. A vengeance spirit, Stanley said. I didn't think it would . . ." She trailed off as we all remembered what it had done.

"Why did he come to you?" I asked.

She gave a bitter laugh. "I'm D and D Lisa. He thought I knew about sorcery and things."

"But you came up with the spell." Justin's tone clipped the damp air.

Lisa walked to a bench and sat, as if her legs wouldn't hold her any longer. "Research and improvisation. An academic exercise. I didn't really expect it to *work*."

I moved to her slowly, my arms folded. "Did you send the demon after me?"

"Of course not." That sounded more like Lisa, impatient with me for even thinking it. "Stanley made the list. It had to be written in the same ancient script as on the artifact, and he had his mother's books. I couldn't even read it. Fortunately, he thought your name was Margaret."

"Not so fortunate for Karen," I pointed out. "Was it just coincidence, that she was your closest competition for valedictorian?"

"I hoped so." She sank her face into her hands. "But it was like the thing was taking thoughts out of my head. I knew what would hurt the Jocks and the Jessicas, but I never wanted to *act* on those ideas, not seriously. Except maybe Brandon. And I would only want to beat Karen fairly."

I could sense the guilt that wracked her; I'm not sure how. Still as stone, she didn't ask for forgiveness. I suspected from the starkness of her voice, she didn't think she deserved it.

"We should go." Justin touched my arm. "I'm going to check the hall. Meet me at the door."

I nodded, understanding he was giving us privacy. I sat on the bench and took my friend's hand. "You forged the weapon, Lisa. You didn't wield it."

She raised her bleak gaze to mine. "But I didn't stop it, either."

"I'm not sure you could have, once it started." I looked away, at the rippling blackness of the pool. Curiosity, anger, arrogance, denial. I couldn't judge Lisa, because I'd been guilty of all those things at one time or another. Sometimes all at once.

And we would need each other. Azmael knew us. He was gone from this plane, but had he ceased to exist? Vanquished was not the same as destroyed.

I stood, decisively, and pulled her with me. "Come on. It's time to go."

34

"Hallucinogenic Drugs Suspected in Wild Dog Attack on Senior Prom"—that was the headline Saturday morning.

"Wild dogs?" I posed the incredulous question in our living room, full of family. "Who's going to believe that wild dogs attacked the Marriott?"

Dad settled on the couch, a fresh cup of coffee in his hand. "More people than will believe demon-spawn did it."

"I would rather believe in wild dogs," said my mom, warming her hands on a mug of tea. "I'm not sure I can handle the truth."

She might not believe it at all if I hadn't brought Justin

home to tend to his bite marks. The circumference was more like a shark than a dog, but fortunately it hadn't gone very deep. I couldn't say the same for Mom's denial.

Justin was still there—Mom had insisted he stay in the guest room. Lisa had stayed upstairs with me, but she was gone by the time I woke up.

Gran had arrived with doughnuts, just as the coffee was finished perking, of course. She stole a moment to tell me how proud she was, then pinched my ear, hard, for not keeping her in the loop. She couldn't have been too angry, though, because she brought blueberry-filled doughnuts, and no one likes those but me.

I stuffed the rest of a doughnut in my mouth and read the article. "Listen to this: 'When asked about strange reports of ghost dogs that couldn't be killed, Dr. Silas Blackthorne said, "Ridiculous. That would run counter to all natural laws of physics. Clearly someone must have spiked the punch with some kind of perception-altering drug. You would be amazed the effect that certain combinations of chemicals can have on the brain."'"

Maybe Silas Blackthorne had a career in fiction after all.

"Well," said Justin, sounding very amused as he read the paper over my shoulder, "he did say he would make something up."

I looked up at him from the floor in front of his chair. "Do you think people are really going to buy that?"

"Your mom is right. No one wants to believe in demon-dogs. Even eyewitnesses search for a logical explanation, no matter how big a stretch."

A valid point. And really, there were few who knew the

whole truth. He, Lisa, Brian, and I. Brandon and Stanley weren't talking.

The doorbell rang. "I'll get it," I said, levering myself up from the floor. "Maybe it's Lisa."

I had seen no reason to go into details of either Lisa or Stanley's involvement. Stanley's parents were going to have enough to deal with. The EMTs had found him wandering the golf course, babbling about the snapping jaws of Hell. His condition backed up the "experimental mind-altering drug" theory, and he was undergoing psychiatric observation. Maybe he would recover, maybe not. My gut told me, though, that he'd been a victim of Azmael, too.

As for Lisa, she stood on my doorstep, the purple shadows under her eyes speaking to a sleepless night. "Hey, Mags."

"Hey. Where'd you go this morning?" I floated the question, not wanting to make it an accusation.

"The hospital." Running a tired hand over her face, she seemed to unravel a little as I watched. "He's not dead."

I knew she meant Brandon. His critical injuries were mentioned in the paper, but no death.

"He doesn't remember anything at all. And he's going to have months, maybe years of orthopedic therapy ahead of him. But he's not dead."

I pulled the front door closed, leaving us in privacy on the porch. "You talked to him?"

"Yeah. Sort of. I snuck in. He was on serious drugs."

"How . . ." I tried to think of a way to ask if she was all right, when she obviously wasn't. "How are you feeling?"

"I don't know." She shook her head. "I used to think I would do anything to get back at him for making me feel that way, so powerless." She looked up at the gabled roof, blinking hard. "But when the demon was tearing him up, I lost track of which one of us was the monster. It was an ugly place to find myself, Mags."

"I know." Except that I didn't, really.

"Nothing justifies that."

Possibly I could say something placating, like she didn't really know what she was letting loose, or he deserved it. Both those things were true but both were also too easy.

"I think you should talk to a counselor," I said.

She looked at me strangely. "About summoning a demon?"

"No. About what happened over Spring Break. You need to deal with that. Atonement can come after." I put my hand on the doorknob. "But first, you need to come inside and have a doughnut."

Somewhere behind her weariness, maybe there was a spark of hope, but she was still Lisa. "That's not going to fix things."

"No, but with a cup of coffee, it's a start."

We went in. The folks greeted her warmly, Justin with a reserve that made Gran glance at him curiously. Mom, oblivious, fussed and asked where she'd run off to.

"I went to see Brian in the hospital," Lisa said, surprising me. She'd mentioned only Brandon.

"How is he?"

"Good. Apparently having a remission as abrupt as his onset. And his room was already filling up with female visitors when I left." She snuck a look at me, which I ignored, because I wasn't anything but happy for him. I thought maybe Justin was looking my way, too, but I didn't turn to see.

"I'm going to Karen's house later," I said, not quite changing the subject. Brian's recovery made me hopeful for her own return to normal. "She called at the crack of eight a.m. to ask for the scoop."

Hesitancy seemed such a foreign expression on Lisa's face. "Maybe I could go with you?"

"I think that would be nice."

I understood what Lisa was doing. When you almost lose something, you have to touch it often to reassure yourself it's still there. None of these people had been that dear to her, but they stood for what she'd put in jeopardy by helping Stanley. They represented her soul, nearly sacrificed to vengeance.

Then I *knew* Justin's eyes were on me, sending a strong "I've got something to say about this" vibe. Not subtly at all, I looked down at my empty cup and said, "I need more coffee. Back in a sec."

I left them discussing whether wild dogs might really roam the thickly forested State Park near Avalon. Their voices hummed from the other room as I emptied the last of the coffee into my industrial-sized mug, and grabbed the milk from the fridge.

When I closed the door, Justin had joined me. "So everything's okay now? Everyone is chummy again?"

I gave him a tart look, because sarcasm didn't suit him at all. "No one was that chummy before. And it's not all okay. But it might be, someday."

He studied me a little longer, then unwound with a sigh. I liked that about him, that he could pick his battles and let other things go, at least for the moment. I'm not so good at that. But then lately, my battles seemed to pick me.

"What about you?" he asked. "Are you all right?"

"Why wouldn't I be all right?"

He leaned on the counter. "I don't know. You faced down the dark forces of the universe. And went to the prom."

"Don't ask me which was more traumatic." I stirred my coffee thoughtfully. "I feel . . . different."

"A lot has happened."

"I'm never going to be able to ignore my dreams again. I'm always going to wonder what is a hunch and what is, you know . . . the freakitude."

"Maybe it'll get easier with practice. You could talk to your gran about it."

I watched the whirlpool in my cup. "You know what the weirdest thing is? I have to go to school on Monday. Shouldn't I get special dispensation for saving the world?"

"From wild dogs?" He grinned. "Probably not."

"Gee, thanks." Mug in hand, I started to breeze past him. He caught the back of my T-shirt.

"Listen. What do you say we go on a date that doesn't involve ghostbusting or demon hunting?"

A shy sort of smile crept to the corner of my mouth. "Just you, me, and a basket of chicken fingers?"

"Maybe even a movie."

I pretended to think about it. "Okay. But not a horror one."

"No? I was thinking about *Prom Night*."

"Very funny."

"What about *Carrie*?"

"Don't make me hurt you. I'm a demon slayer now, you know."

"Look out, Buffy."

And that was how I survived the senior prom. I had faced down a demon, saved the senior class, and even managed to snag a date in the bargain. Now all I had to do was survive the three weeks to graduation.

But that's a story for another day.

ACKNOWLEDGMENTS

There's an axiom among authors that you have to write a million words of crap before you can produce publishable prose. Here's to everyone who suffered through mine.

But especially I'd like to thank . . .

My agent, Lucienne Diver, who answers my newbie questions with good humor, and Krista Marino, who has spoiled me for all other editors. What a great way to start.

Candace Havens, Britta Coleman, Shannon Cannard, and all the Divas. But especially Candy and Britta, for recognizing greatness underneath the stark terror.

The Dallas–Fort Worth Writers' Workshop and the after-hours IHOP Irregulars, especially Shawn and Dan. Rachel Caine, the LJ crew, and the Old Guard: Carole, Jennifer, et al. You may not even realize the little things you said that kept me coming back to the keyboard.

The young thespians of Victoria Community Theatre. There's something of each of you in this book. Hopefully you'll never figure out which parts.

Haley M. Schmidt, who wanted a manuscript for her graduation present.

My husband, Tim, because you've seen "better" and you've seen "worse" and you love me anyway.

And all my family, Mom, Peter, and Cheryl Smyth, sister of my heart. You all believed in me, even during the times when I didn't believe in myself.

Hell Week

In memory of Trini—
May heaven be full of Frisbees
and unguarded dinner plates.

I

Bright teeth flashed; I fought the instinct to recoil. Perfectly white, perfectly even, possibly once human. Coral pink lips pulled back all the way to the gums, giving the smile an unfortunate equine quality. "Soooo . . . ?" The owner of the teeth and lips drew out the word and flipped it up at the end in a question. "What's your major?"

"English." An untruth. I don't tell them, as a rule, but I'd been asked this question five times in the last hour, and the lie rolled off my tongue now with ease.

"Gosh, you must have to read a lot, huh?" Another blinding smile; I hoped my squint passed for an answer.

"So, Maggie. What made you decide to go through Rush?"

She pronounced it with a capital *R*. Five rounds of the cattle call officially known as Sorority Formal Recruitment had run together in my banality-numbed brain, and I couldn't remember where I was. I glanced around the crowded room for a clue. The noise was formidable, the chatter of a hundred or more coiffed and groomed girls like purebred dogs at a show, their yelping echoing from the walls.

Just like every other sorority house I'd been to in this first series of parties. Here, though, the décor was Cotton Candy Pink and Tampax Box Blue. Verily, I had reached the lair of the Delta Delta Gammas.

"Well, Ashley . . ." My slightly breathless drawl mimicked hers. "I thought Rush would be fun. Get to know people, you know."

She laughed, her eyes squinched up in two half-moons of insincerity. "Soooo? Which dorm are you in, Maggie?"

She kept checking my name tag. At every house, the girls had used my name exhaustively, making me feel as though I'd wandered onto a used car lot.

"I'm living at home." This much was certainly true. "I grew up here in Avalon."

"Oh." Her smile, and I use the word loosely, was forced. "Well, at least you know your way around. You probably have a car, too. What kind is it?"

Her segues could really use a little polish. "It's vintage."

"Oh, really?" She raised her brows with renewed interest.

"Yeah. A Ford Pinto."

"Really." Beneath her carefully applied self-tanner, the

corners of her mouth were white with strain. "Your parents live here in Avalon?"

It would be hard to live at home and go to school here if they didn't. But smart-ass wasn't my persona here at the International House of Snobcakes, so I merely answered enthusiastically, "My dad works here at Bedivere University. He's an engineer."

"Is he really? Mechanical or civil?"

"Custodial."

"O-kay." She glanced at her watch, then searched the room for rescue, or maybe just an avenue of escape. "Well, it's been real nice meeting you, Maggie. I need to go . . . um . . . talk to these girls over here."

She took off; I knew from my research that leaving a rushee standing alone was a big fat no-no. Unless, of course, you'd rather invite a chimpanzee to join your sisterhood. And no one in the Delta Delta Gamma house looked like Jane Goodall to me.

But since I'd been deserted, I reached into my purse and turned off my microrecorder. No sense in wasting megabytes.

✳ ✳ ✳

The *Avalon Sentinel* is an independent small-town paper, which is almost an anachronism in itself. The historic Main Street offices smelled of ancient cigarettes, even though the place had been smoke-free for twenty years.

I sat in a hard wooden chair that had been squeaking beneath anxious backsides for decades. My colleagues—or rather, the guys I'd stepped and fetched for all summer during my internship—kept making excuses to walk past the office, peering into the windows as the editor-in-chief read my submission.

Ethan Douglas was probably thirty, but he had pale skin, freckles, and flaming red hair, all of which made him look more like Opie than Spencer Tracy. Like me, he had journalistic aspirations beyond the *Avalon Sentinel,* but—also like me—he had to start somewhere.

He lifted his eyes from the paper and gave me a dubious look. "You made this stuff up."

"I swear." I raised a Boy Scout salute. "The only stuff I made up was the lies about my dad being a janitor. Oh, and I don't drive a Ford Pinto."

In a skeptical voice, he read what I'd written: " 'I'm an English major,' I said for the umpteenth time. 'I wish I was an English major,' said Sorority Sue. 'I mean, I speak it already, and everything.' "

Laughter from the doorway behind me. Ethan glared in that direction, not terribly menacing with his freckled choirboy face. The guys from the newsroom went back to work, and I got down to business, too.

"You said if I brought you a story that no one else here could, you would give me a shot."

I was uniquely qualified to infiltrate Rush, being that I was a girl and an actual college freshman. I might as well use it to my advantage.

Anyone who drove by the frat houses on a Friday night could tell that fraternities evaluated their future pledges based on their ability to chug beer and score with the coeds. But the closed-door secrecy on the distaff side of Greek Row lent a certain mystery to what was, in essence, about as exciting as six successive tea parties with your grandmother and her septuagenarian friends.

Not *my* grandmother, of course. When the mood struck her, Granny Quinn could put on the doily better than anyone. But tea with Gran might mean anything from an authentic Japanese ceremony to a formal reading of your tea leaves. Gran had "the Sight," as she called it. So do I, though for most of my eighteen years I didn't consciously acknowledge the fact.

But then I had to rescue my senior prom from a ravenous horde of demon spawn. I learned the hard way there's nothing like a supernatural smackdown to make you wake up and smell the brimstone.

Ethan Douglas rubbed his chin, which was slightly red and shiny from his morning shave. "I'll give it to Janey and see if she has a place for it on Friday."

"Lifestyles?" I tried to tone down my unprofessional indignation. "With the pumpkin recipes and 4-H announcements?" Not to mention that Janey Cotton still displayed pictures of her college chums in a Delta Zeta picture frame. My story would run between the obituaries and the funeral home ads, if at all.

"Where else would it go?" Ethan said, annoying me with the truth. "It's more social commentary than scathing exposé."

"But . . . ," I sputtered, with no real argument. "The pretension and the elitism . . ."

"Maggie, females of all ages have been throwing hoity-toity parties and shunning the inferior for centuries. I shouldn't have to tell *you* that."

I wasn't sure if I'd just been insulted or commiserated with. But he was right about one thing: He didn't have to tell me about the rabidity of the alpha bitch in defending the social hierarchy. I had the bite marks to prove it.

"Okay, what about the perpetuation of an outdated system of stratification and false superiority ...?"

Ethan handed the copy across the desk. "If that's your point, the story isn't done. You've only been to one round of parties."

I stared at him in dawning horror. "You mean ... I have to go *back*?"

"Bring me the story that I don't know." He spun his chair to face his computer screen. "That is, if Professor Quinn lets you live when he finds out you made him a janitor."

I'd been dismissed. Folding the rejected story into thirds, I stuffed it into my satchel and headed out of the office, then down the stairs. Out in the bright September morning, I paused on the Main Street sidewalk, lifted my face to the sunshine, and breathed deeply. The too-warm breeze stirred my short, dark hair across my eyes, hiding their childish watering.

Stupid to be so stung, when Ethan had only told me the truth. The rejection smacked me, deservedly, in the pride. Ace reporter for the high school paper was about as real-world applicable as presidency of the local *Star Trek* club. My first taste of Small Fish and Big Pond went down badly.

The clock in the square struck the hour, and I blinked away self-pity, mentally squaring my shoulders. *Never give up, never surrender.* That was my new motto.

Besides, what else was I going to do? I lived at home and

all my friends had gone away to school, including my best friend, Lisa, who was halfway across the country. The guy I was nuts about hadn't called me since he spent the entire summer doing an internship in Ireland, and none of my freaky intuition could tell me why not. Because *that* would be useful.

My wicked psychic powers didn't give me winning lottery numbers or insight into pork futures. No, what I got was the inspired idea to strap on a push-up bra and infiltrate the Delta Delta Gammas.

Let's face it. The saddest thing about this whole undercover sorority thing was that I really didn't have to *pretend* to be that much of a loser.

2

"Maggie Quinn," said my grandmother, her Irish accent deepening in familiar exasperation. "Saying that you are just a little bit psychic is like saying you're just a little bit pregnant."

"Gran!" I glanced around the coffee shop. The overstuffed couches and scratch-and-dent-sale chairs of Froth and Java were full of Bedivere University students, but hopefully we sat far enough from the midmorning caffeine zombies that her comment had gone unheard. The last thing I needed was word getting around campus that I was psychic. Or pregnant, for that matter.

"You either are, or you aren't," she continued, lifting her mug of tea. "The only question is how noticeable it is."

Gran had called me right after I'd left the *Sentinel*'s offices, before I'd even reached the Jeep; fifteen minutes later she met me in F and J, where she listened to me whine, then told me to get over myself.

Besides being psychic, my grandmother was trim and trendy, and busy with her volunteer activities, which included the altar guild at St. Stephen's Catholic Church and teaching yoga to senior citizens at the Spiritual Enlightenment Center. (Avalon was small but eclectic, rather like Gran.) It must have been New Age day, because she wore a sage green cotton jacket and pants, her bright red hair all perky.

I slouched across from her, cradling a paper cup of caffeinated goodness between my hands, dressed in my least ragged jeans and a fitted oxford, shirttails out. I'd ironed both my shirt and my hair in an attempt to look more polished. The pale yellow cotton had held its press longer than my sable bob; I could feel the latter reverting to its usual cappuccino froth by the moment.

The wavy brown hair I got from my mother; the rest of me was all Quinn. In addition to the Sight, I'd inherited my grandmother's green eyes, pixie-shaped face, and pointed chin, as well as a certain broadness in the beam I could live without.

"I thought you'd be happy that I've accepted my freaki-tude."

She rolled her eyes. "Somehow I'm still sensing a lack of true commitment."

"I wonder why that could be. Maybe because last time, following my instincts almost got my friends and me killed?"

Pained guilt deepened the soft lines of her face. Gran still hadn't forgiven herself for not sensing the depth of trouble I'd been in last spring. I wished she'd cut herself some slack. The things under your nose are the hardest to see, in any sense of the word. Plus, I'd gone to some pains to keep the whole truth from her, and I suspected other forces might have been doing the same. No proof, of course. Just a hunch.

But that was the thing about my . . . whatever you wanted to call it. Most of the time, it didn't *feel* any different from simple—if eerily strong and accurate—intuition. I kept hoping for an instruction manual, but the best I'd been able to do was a copy of *ESP for Dummies* that I found on the bargain table at Barnes & Noble.

I hunched over my coffee cup, breath running out in a sigh. Just the smell of Froth and Java usually made me feel better, and I was trying hard to follow through on my resolution to drop the drama. "I just wish I didn't feel so stupid. When I had that dream about the Greek letters, I thought there would be a story there." That was how my psychicness had first shown up, in the nighttime, when logic couldn't override the subconscious. "I thought, just once, my intuition was picking up on something useful."

Gran clicked her tongue and cast her gaze heavenward. "What did you think you would discover in one night? Don't they arrange these things to get more in-depth as the week goes on?"

"Yes." Nice of my gran to join the Maggie-is-an-idiot refrain. "It's a good thing I didn't burn all my bridges."

"See." She smiled over her paper cup. "Your intuition did tell you something useful. So where will you go?"

I fished in my satchel for the e-mail I'd printed that morning. Mom had been appalled. Apparently, when she went through Rush—my own mother; I'm so ashamed—their invitations to the next round of parties were delivered to their dorm rooms. On silver platters, for all I knew.

During the past Friday's orientation—excruciating in length and level of enthusiasm—I learned about "recs" and "bids" and "legacies." All the talk of leadership and sisterhood was, considering we'd all shelled out registration fees, sort of like trying to sell us a car after we'd already made a down payment.

Rush—Recruitment, I should say—worked by double elimination. In the first round, which took two days, you went to all ten houses for the short torture sessions I'd described in my article. Then six tonight, four tomorrow, and two the last night. At each round, the sorority could choose to invite you back—or not, in which case you were "cut"— while simultaneously you had to narrow your choices. Theoretically, I could have had to choose six out of ten houses to visit for tonight's second round. Needless to say, I faced no such quandary.

"Maggie Quinn?"

The speaker had a rounded, evening-news sort of voice. I turned, looked up, and up again. A tall, thin blonde stood beside our table, the light from the window behind her. I answered warily, "Yes?"

Her hair was pulled back in a tight ponytail, which bobbed as she looked me up and down. "*Where* is your name tag?"

"Uh . . ." I recognized her now, and the other young woman with her, carrying a tray of drinks. Both were Recruitment guides, or Rho Gammas, as the Panhellenic Council—the organizational body of sororities on campus—called them. Which said something about the pretentiousness involved, if "Panhellenic Council" wasn't your first clue.

There were fifteen Rho Gammas, representing all the different houses, and though it was supposed to be a secret, some of them were easily identifiable. The blonde was Hillary, and I had her pegged for a Delta Zeta—aggressive perfectionists. Their party had been orchestrated to the millisecond with robotic efficiency. The girl with the drinks was Jenna, who wasn't so easily pigeonholed.

"Potential New Members are supposed to wear their name tags at all times," said Hillary, with a gravitas that implied I'd left the space station without my helmet. I'd also noticed that the tendency to speak in capital letters seemed to be a Greek trait.

"Sorry. I'm having coffee with my grandmother, and she already knows my name."

Her instructions were brisk and sober. "The selection process goes on twenty-four-seven, Maggie. The houses will be watching to see how the Potential New Members comport themselves on campus, in class, in the cafeteria, and even off campus."

"Like Big Sister?"

"Exactly!" she chirruped, pleased I'd seen her point. I thought I heard Jenna snort back a laugh, but I couldn't be sure. I know I heard Gran chuckle. "Is that your schedule for the next round?" Hillary asked.

"Yes, ma'am."

She took it from my hand, her eyes flicking over the e-mail. "Only four invites, I see. At least you don't have to make any choices tonight."

"Yes. Considerate of so many houses to cut me."

She scanned the list. "Epsilon Zeta. Yes, that figures. Theta Nu. Zeta Theta Pi and . . ." Her brows made an eloquent arch of surprise. "And Sigma Alpha Xi. How . . . interesting."

She said "interesting" like she meant "unfathomable."

"Maybe they're filling a dork quota."

"Of course not," Hillary demurred, in a tone that said, *That explains it.* "You must have impressed them with your wit and charm." Behind me Gran chortled again as Rho Gamma Blonda handed me back the schedule. "Put on your name badge as soon as possible. And you know the dress for tonight?"

"Black tie?"

"A simple sundress will be fine." She turned toward the door, beckoning the other young woman after her. "Come on, Jenna, before the mochas get cold."

The other Rho Gamma didn't follow right away. She was more subtle all around. Her brown hair had expert highlights, like strands of gold woven through chocolate-colored satin, and if she had on any makeup, I could see no sign of it on her flawless skin. With a secret little smile, she sized me up. "That's funny. I didn't see any Ford Pintos parked outside."

I cleared my throat. "Well . . ."

"Also odd—I had Professor Quinn for history last year."

Gran looked from her to me and back again. "Maggie, just what were you telling them?"

"Um."

Jenna intervened with a friendly grin. "Nothing too bad." She offered her hand. "I'm Jenna Nichols. You must be Maggie's tea leaf–reading grandmother." Her amused glance slanted my way. "Or was that a lie, too?"

"An embellishment, really." I avoided Gran's glare; she disapproved of lying. "I thought you Rho Gammas weren't supposed to talk to the sororities about the rushees."

"We're not. But rumors get around." She grinned and lifted her cardboard tray of drinks. "I've got to go. You're all right with your schedule? No conflicts with classes?"

"No, I'm good." The parties would all be in the evening, and I had no night sections. "Thank you for asking."

"That's what I'm here for." She smiled at Gran. "Nice to meet you, Mrs. Quinn. See you later, Maggie." Then she made her retreat to the September sunshine.

I heaved my satchel over my shoulder, stuffed the printed e-mail into the front pocket, and, grabbing my half-full cup, I turned back to Gran. "I gotta run. I'm meeting the school newspaper adviser to ask about joining the staff."

Her annoyance evaporated quickly. There are advantages to being the only granddaughter. "Take care of yourself, Maggie. Tell your mother I hope she's feeling better."

"I will, Gran." I leaned forward and kissed her soft cheek. "See you later. Thanks for the coffee."

I turned to go, but Gran's lilting voice stuttered my step. "Oh, and tell Justin I say hello."

Slowly, I pivoted to face her, and I could feel my cheeks beginning to heat. "Justin?"

"Yes. He's back from Ireland, isn't he?"

My brain slogged through a morass of mixed emotions that had churned throughout the summer—hope and affection tamped down by a growing weight of worry, and thickened into a soup of romantic uncertainty. "I suppose he must be, since classes started last Thursday."

"Well, don't worry, dear. You'll see him soon. And then you'll get everything straightened out."

Vision, hunch, or wishful thinking? I wove through the tables and shouldered open the door. Matchmaking grandmothers were one thing; matchmaking *psychic* grandmothers were a whole other level of irksome, even when you loved one as much as I did mine.

Part two of *Maggie Quinn, You're Not Special* featured Dr. Hardcastle, possibly the most boring journalism professor ever. I'm not saying that Media and Communication is the most fascinating thing to begin with, but it takes a new level of tedious to make me struggle to stay awake in a journalism class.

He was also the adviser for the *Ranger Report,* Bedivere University's newspaper. I had made an appointment with him during his posted office hours and brought along my sample articles and photographs. A wasted effort since as soon as I told him why I was there, he said, without looking up from his computer: "I don't take freshmen on the *Report* staff."

I stood stupidly in front of his desk, the portfolio hanging from my hand. I didn't know how he could see anything; the room was dim and cluttered and smelled as though he had his lunch there a little too often. Or maybe that stale smell was the professor himself. He had a Grizzly Adams thing going for him.

"Never?" I asked.

"As close to never as makes no difference."

Never give up, never surrender. "Here are some samples of my work." I opened the binder to an eye-catching photograph of the Avalon High star forward making a spectacular jump shot. "And in addition to working on the AHS paper for three years, I was an intern at the *Sentinel* this summer."

Dr. Hardcastle glanced at the picture and flipped dismissively through a few pages. "Not bad."

"I can write captions, do layout, proofread, whatever you need."

But Professor Hard-ass had gone back to Web surfing. "Come back after you have six hours of prerequisites."

"I'm already enrolled in six hours of journalism—"

"Then come back after you finish them."

He wasn't going to budge. I didn't need to read minds to see that.

"Okay," I said, because there was no point in pissing him off. "Thanks for your time."

I slumped out of his tiny office and leaned against the wall, weighed down, for a moment, by self-pity. It was right next to the journalism lab, where they put together the paper. I could hear the familiar click of multiple keyboards, smell the printer toner and film developer.

Dismissed again. Would the suck never end?

Someone touched my shoulder, and I spun around with a stifled squeak.

"Sorry." The speaker was a young man with intelligent eyes and a Byronic shock of thick, dark blond hair falling across his forehead. He had a friendly smile, and as my brain transitioned from grouchy, grizzled professor to cute young guy, he took the binder out of my limp hand.

"I overheard your conversation with Hardcastle. By which I mean I shamelessly eavesdropped. Let's see what you've got."

"The journalistic clap, apparently." I cracked wise to calm my nerves as he leafed through the pages. "No one wants to touch me this morning."

He raised one brow. "You tell me that after I'm already holding your portfolio?" Then he smiled and gave it back. "I'm Cole Bauer, editor of the *Report*. Anytime you want to submit something to me, go ahead."

"Really?" My roller-coaster day took an upswing.

"Sure."

Belatedly I remembered my manners, and held out my hand. "I'm Maggie Quinn."

"I know." He nodded at my name tag, which I'd dutifully put on when I returned to campus. "How's Rush going?"

I touched the plastic-covered card self-consciously. "Actually, if you'd really like to know . . ." On impulse, I slipped my hand into my satchel and pulled out the folded article.

Both his brows went up at that. "You don't waste time, do you?"

My cheeks heated. "Not when I have a feeling about

something. I think I may have written that for you without realizing it. Er, for the *Report,* I mean."

He nodded. "I know what you mean." Unfolding the pages, he gave them a cursory glance. "I'll read it and let you know."

"Thanks." I felt a quick shot of relief. I'd offered it; he hadn't laughed. Now I just had to let things shake out. I took a step backward, making my exit. "I'll be in touch."

Waving the pages, he moved to do the same. "Or I will. See you."

He turned and disappeared into the newspaper lab, and I headed for my next class in that fog of abrupt reversal, when things take a quick turn and you're not sure you're responsible for it. I don't know if it's the instinct talking, or fate or whatever. But I never know where that left turn is going to take me.

✳ ✳ ✳

Case in point. For eighteen years I'd planned to go away to school, much to my parents' frustration. Bedivere University is a small old liberal arts school with stiff admission criteria and an excellent reputation, which attracted students and teachers from all over and kept Avalon from being more small-town backward than it could be. In fact, the whole place—college and town—felt connected with the rest of the world but slightly out of step with it, making the name seem more than coincidence. It's a great school, I could walk from home if I wanted, and my professor dad got a tuition discount.

That said, the reason I am not, in fact, attending the University of Anywhere-but-Here, despite having been admitted and financially aided, lay with my parents, who could not behave like respectable, decently middle-aged people.

I knew my mother was pregnant before she did. In the pharmacy one day, with one of those half-aware impulses I get, I had picked up a plus-or-minus test and put it in the cart. Mom was surprised, to say the least. "Something you want to tell me, Maggie?"

"It's not for me," I said.

"Do tell." Her calm was admirable, under the circumstances.

"Really. Unless the Angel of Annunciation dropped by to leave a message while I was out, it's for you." As soon as the words left my lips, the feeling went from hunch to certainty. Not even the fall of Mom's face, the paling of her cheeks, could dim it.

She firmed her mouth and put the test back on the shelf. "Don't be ridiculous. That's just not possible."

I returned the pink and blue box to the cart. "Humor me."

My only-child status had not been my parents' choice. Memories of those stressful years of roller-coaster disappointment are fuzzy, and I don't know when, exactly, they gave up hope. But now I was about to have a sibling, even if Mom didn't believe me until she'd started the daily puke.

As for my staying at home, I don't remember making a conscious decision; one morning I woke up knowing that Avalon and Bedivere was the right choice. Gran says that sometimes people like us are led where they need to be, if we just listen to our inner voices.

I tend to think inner voices are only good for getting a person locked in a padded room or burned at the stake. And

I'll tell you right now, I am no saint, because I'm not sure I would have listened to my mental Jiminy Cricket if Justin weren't returning in the fall.

Justin, who still hadn't called me, even though I knew he'd been back in town for a week.

3

I arrived at the Epsilon Zeta house breathless and wind-blown, my cheeks hot with exertion. I'd had to rush—no pun intended—home to change after class. I'd brushed my hair and powdered my nose, too, though the effort was wasted by the time I drove the Jeep to Greek Row, found a parking spot, and hightailed it to where my group had assembled, cool and composed despite the warm September afternoon.

"Sorry I'm late!" I gave an exaggerated roll of my eyes. "But you would not believe my professor, wanting us all to stay until the end of his lecture. Can you imagine?"

The buxom brunette beside me shook her head. "I

know! We have all semester to go to class, but Rush only lasts one week, and affects our Entire Lives!"

Sadly, she spoke without irony. Up on the steps Jenna rapped on the door, telling the Epsilon Zetas that the next round was assembled, and beside her, Hillary looked at me with no small disapproval. I reached up and smoothed my hair with my hands, an involuntary reaction.

Such was the power of the Rho Gamma stare. In addition to shepherding our group from house to house, they ran herd on the rushees throughout the day, enforcing the rules. Besides the mandatory wearing of name tags, we weren't allowed to talk to "actives"—that is, sorority members—outside of the parties.

My name tag was dutifully pinned to the bodice of my sundress, where it scratched the pale skin of my bare arm, and the only sorority girls I'd talked to today had been Jenna and Hillary, which was, obviously, allowed. But I was pretty sure writing pithy articles skewering Rush traditions was against the Rho Gamma rules.

$$* \quad * \quad *$$

Two houses later, my brain and my butt were both numb.

Every round had a theme, and tonight was the philanthropy round. Every sorority chooses, at the national level, a pet cause or organization, and each chapter is required to do an annual fund-raiser to justify the other fifty weeks of purely self-indulgent social activities. And for the past eternity, the rushees had been required to hear about it, mostly through video montages and PowerPoint presentations.

The propaganda also showed the house's personality.

The Theta Nus had managed to work their GPA ranking into their presentation. The Epsilon Zetas had lots of guys in their pictures, always with arms thrown around the girls. I'm not saying the Epsilon Zetas were a sure thing, in any sense of the phrase, but . . . well, when your house is called the EZs maybe it's just inevitable.

Dusk was sitting heavy and humid in the sky as Jenna and Hillary escorted us to the next house on our agenda, the Zeta Theta Pis. The curvy brunette from before—Miss Entire Life—drew up alongside me. "I like your outfit," she said as we walked. "It's kind of sixties retro."

It was. Gran never got rid of anything. Yellow and red, with splashes of orange, the frock had useless little spaghetti straps and a full, pleated skirt. I wore ballet flats and a Band-Aid on my ankle where I'd cut myself shaving. "I raided my grandmother's closet for something to wear."

"Grandmother's Closet?" she echoed. "I've never heard of that store."

"It's, uh, very exclusive." There was another girl, a red-head, stuck with us behind the rushee bottleneck on the sidewalk. I caught Red stifling a smile, but the brunette was oblivious.

"Anyway. Great dress. I'm Tricia, by the way."

"Thanks. I'm Maggie."

We reached the Zeta house slightly ahead of schedule, earning a restorative break. Lip gloss tubes and compacts appeared for synchronized primping. Only Red-haired Girl and I abstained, and lounged against the stair rail to wait.

She reminded me of an Irish setter, in a good way. Her dark red hair fell, slightly feathered, to her shoulders, and she had a rangy, athletic grace. She looked as if she would be more at home on a ball field than a sorority house.

"What houses are you interested in, Maggie?" Tricia asked. She had whipped out a little battery-operated fan and was using it to blow her long brown hair from her flushed face.

I mimicked Hillary's ultraserious tone. "How can I possibly decide when I've yet to hear all the philanthropies?"

Irish Setter Girl smirked. Tricia looked suspiciously between us. "What's so funny?"

"Nothing. Except that 'Recruitment' "—I made little quotes in the air—"is like comparing the gas mileage of a Mustang and a Corvette. You say you're being practical, but all you really care about is which one looks best for picking up guys."

Hillary strode past us; along with her black T-shirt with its green *RG*, she wore pressed khaki shorts and sneakers that had never seen a workout. She glanced at me on her way up the steps. "I see you managed to find your name tag." Then she stopped, her blond ponytail swinging as she stared with narrowing eyes at my chest. "*What* did you do to it?"

I glanced down at the tag, which now said: *Maggie Quinn. English major. Lives at home.* "I thought this was more efficient."

Tsks and titters from the rushees. Irish Setter Girl snorted, in a laughing-with-me kind of way.

"Prospective New Members," said the scandalized Rho Gamma, "are *not* supposed to alter their name badges!"

"Oh. I didn't know."

Jenna climbed the porch steps past us. "Don't worry about it, Maggie. We'll get you a new one tomorrow."

Hillary bit back her opinion on that, and followed her up. "We'll see if they're ready for you."

As soon as Hillary and Jenna turned to the door, the red-haired girl hissed at me. "Hey. Have you still got the pen?"

"Sure." I reached into my little handbag and fished it out. She pulled the paper from her plastic holder. Under her name—Holly Russell—she wrote "ΣΑΞ Legacy" while I peered shamelessly over her shoulder.

"What's that?" I asked.

"Efficient." She grinned at me and folded the card back into its sleeve.

"Why efficient?" I asked. I knew from the interminable orientation that a legacy was someone whose close relative was a member of a certain sorority.

"Spares everyone the trouble of making nice when it's a done deal."

A legacy wasn't supposed to be an automatic in, but that didn't mean it wasn't. "I guess that explains why Zeta Theta Pi asked me back."

"You're a Zeta leg?" She handed me the pen. "Write it down. It'll impress the other houses. Everyone loves the Zetas."

"Really?" I glanced at the double front doors, embla-zoned with ΖΘΠ. I'd been there yesterday, of course, but those parties had been short and the houses pretty much blurred together. "Why?"

"Because they're cool, why else?"

I tried to picture my mother in a cool sorority and failed

utterly. My mother is an accountant. "What about the Sigma Alpha Xis?" I pointed to Holly's name badge. "Did you write that to impress people?"

She sighed. "No. I wrote it so they won't feel they have to bother being nice to me. No SAXi leg goes anywhere but SAXi."

"What are they, like the mafia?"

She barked an Irish setter laugh. "No. Not exactly."

The Zeta doors opened before I could ask her anything else, and we flowed in, carried by the inexorable tide of Sisterhood with a capital *S*.

✻ ✻ ✻

Our merry band left the Zeta house as the sun dropped low in the west.

"Didn't I say?" Holly shortened her strides and we hung at the back of the pack along with Tricia, making our way toward the SAXi house near the center of the block.

"You did." The Zeta Theta Pis exemplified cool: effortless, amiable, seemingly unconcerned with status or social hierarchy. That unforced confidence reminded me of my friend Lisa. She'd gotten tagged with the nickname D&D Lisa during the role-playing phase of her youth, but by the time she graduated summa cum laude, it had become more of a title. Uniquely beautiful (once she emerged from her Goth cocoon), smart, and sarcastic, she wasn't part of any group at Avalon High, but she had an impressive network of minions and a small fiefdom of friends.

She'd be pissed to think she had anything in common with a sorority. Maybe I just missed her because there was so much on Greek Row worthy of mockery, and I had no one to share it with. I hated that she was so far away, and hated even more that we'd argued before she left.

"I would totally pledge the Zetas if they gave me a bid." Tricia bounced with excitement, which was a brave thing for a girl with her generous bosoms in a strapless dress.

"I thought your heart was set on Delta Delta Gamma."

"Well, all my friends from home, who have already finished Rush at other schools, they went Delta." She laughed, but there was a brittle edge to it. "I'd be the only one from the old squad who didn't, and what fun would that be?"

"A lot more fun than doing something just because your old friends are doing it." I'd gotten a fix on Tricia pretty quickly. Sweet and eager to be liked; girls like the Deltas would smell her insecurity the way sharks smell blood in the water.

Holly spoke from her other side, sounding very reasonable. "You should pledge where you have the most in common with the members here at this school." I found myself liking her, and Tricia's naïve good nature kind of grew on me, too. If we had met under different circumstances, or if I was who I said I was, I might be thinking of them as new friends, or at least potential ones.

"Maggie?"

I recognized that baritone voice instantly, though I'd last heard it distorted by a transatlantic phone connection.

Darn Gran and her stupid Sight.

Slowly I turned, conscious that Holly and Tricia had stopped, too, and were staring curiously at the tallish young man across the tree-shaded lane.

He wore running clothes, was flushed and sweaty. His

brown hair stood up in spikes and his T-shirt clung in dark blotches, which looked nicer than it sounds. Despite the utter lack of traffic, he looked both ways before he crossed the street, which was so very Justin that I felt a painful, twisty flip in the region of my heart.

I waited, feeling strangely tentative considering how much I'd missed him. A zillion questions hopped around in my brain, but something knotted my tongue. Maybe it was the way he smiled and moved as if to embrace me, but then stopped when he saw our audience.

Holly seemed to have some intuition of her own, because she grabbed Tricia's arm, spun her around, and double-timed to catch up with the group. But the moment had passed, and Justin and I shuffled in that awkward way you do when you really want to touch a person but a hug might be too much and a handshake is definitely absurd. A kiss, which was how we had parted, seemed out of the question.

"I haven't heard from you," I blurted out, because a moment like that can always use more awkward.

He looked sheepish, apologetic. "I know. Jet lag, then getting my stuff out of storage, then I had to meet with my adviser about my thesis. The days got away from me."

"Okay." I didn't point out that he'd found time for a run. I didn't point out a lot of things because I didn't want to be snide, and sarcasm is pretty much all I have when I feel this out of my depth.

His gaze took in my uncharacteristic dress, then narrowed on my name tag. "Are you going through *Rush*?"

I smoothed the folds of my skirt. The evening air was cooling quickly as the sun disappeared. "I'm undercover."

He had a crooked smile that always hit me in the gut. It turned his clean-cut, Boy Scout face into something subversively rakish. "Can I buy you a cup of coffee and hear about it?"

"I'd like that." I said it in shamelessly eager haste. "But I have to finish this first. Why don't we meet at F and J? About nine o'clock?"

He nodded, decisive. "Froth and Java, nine o'clock."

"Maggie!" Jenna called back from the group, sounding impatient and a little annoyed.

"I've got to run." I edged up the hill, reluctant to leave and break the tentative reconnection.

"See you then." He smiled and gave me a little wave.

"Yeah. See you." I lifted my fingers, too, and watched him return to his workout already in progress, wishing my psychic mojo extended to reading minds.

✳ ✳ ✳

The Sigma Alpha Xi house was in the colonial revival style, popular when the university and its nearby neighborhoods were built in the late nineteenth, early-twentieth century. The lawn sloped down from the house and the rushee herd ranged there when Jenna and I arrived; the Rho Gamma climbed the steps to the columned portico, where she rapped on the door. Holly and Tricia waited for me at the back of the group, near the sidewalk. Night had fallen in earnest, but didn't hide their avidly curious faces.

"*Who* was that?" Holly asked.

"A friend." At her disbelieving look, I sighed and tucked a lock of hair behind my ear. "It's complicated."

She made an "I'm waiting" gesture. Tricia helpfully added, "I want to know, too. He's adorable."

Holly turned to her, her brows climbing. "Adorable does

not begin to describe a guy with thighs like that." Then, swiveling her attention back to me: "So what gives?"

I looked toward the house, hoping for a reprieve. No dice. "We went out in the spring, a couple of times." An oversimplification, but—taking all the world-saving and monster-hunting out of it—true enough. "Then he went to Ireland for a three-month internship."

"So what's so complicated?" Holly asked. "He's back and obviously happy to see you—" Tricia snickered and Holly smacked her arm. "Not like that, pervert."

I shrugged, looked away, needlessly smoothed my hair again. "We e-mailed over the summer. Great, chatty letters about nothing and everything."

"That's so sweet." Tricia grinned. "Kind of like *You've Got Mail.*"

"Yeah. Only in reverse, because his letters started getting shorter, less personal, slower." I lifted my hands helplessly. "It sounds lame, I guess. Hard to explain."

They nodded, synchronized head bobs of sympathy. Holly summed it up nicely. "So now you have no idea where you stand."

"He probably got really busy with his internship." Tricia, clearly the eternal optimist. "You'll see."

"Maybe." I studied the toes of my shoes, flecked with grass and bits of pine needle. There was no point in pretending that my heart wasn't hanging in the balance; at least after meeting up tonight, I would—

Then the door to the sorority house opened, spilling light into the dusky shadows and bringing me back to the task at hand.

The Sigma Alpha Xi chapter room was nothing short of elegant. Hardwood floors shone beneath an oriental rug, and dark blue and deep red echoed through the décor. No one thing screamed money; it was the way everything fit together. If the Zetas had been intrinsically cool, then the Sigmas were fundamentally classy.

I had the dance down by now. The doors open and we rushees enter like cattle into a chute. One of the sorority members steps forward in a well-orchestrated move, takes a girl by the elbow, and leads her to a designated area of the room. It took me a few rounds to catch on to the architecture of the "random" party groupings and the carefully choreographed mingling.

The smiling girl who met me this time managed to make it look natural. "Hey!" she said, guiding me to an empty spot in the crowded sitting area. Like all the other SAXis, she wore a khaki skirt and a button-down blue oxford, very preppy but cute. She had short blond hair that flipped up at the ends, and freckles danced over her nose.

"I'm Devon. And you're . . ." She read my name tag and laughed. "Yeah. You'd think that we could come up with better questions than that. But your brain goes kind of numb after a while."

Her candor connected with me, and I found my cynicism—not slipping, exactly, but bending enough to concede, "I can totally see where that would happen."

Her nose crinkled with her grin. "Right. Now I'm left with nothing to ask but if you're enjoying Rush."

"Don't you mean Formal Recruitment?" I replied.

"Right. And are you?"

I hedged my answer. "It's been very interesting."

Another laugh. "How tactful of you."

"How do you stand it?" I looked around the room at the blue and khaki members, the rushees in their sundresses and sandals. "Smiling and asking dumb questions all night?"

"Wait until tomorrow. It's Skit Night."

"Oh God." The groan slipped out before I could catch it. I hadn't meant to be that honest. This Devon was either genuinely disarming or very sneaky.

"*We* all had to go through it," she said. "Think of it as a rite of passage."

I could be sneaky, too, I guess. "What do you remember most from your Rush experience?"

She smiled. "The friends I made. How overwhelming everything seemed, when you go through that door and girls are swooping down at you. Those dumb songs all the houses sing."

"Is it easier on the other side? Except for the lame songs, I mean."

"It can be stressful at some places. This is serious business. Most houses have to make a quota."

"The SAXis don't?"

"We keep a smaller membership. We're very selective, so our pressure is on finding the right girls, not just the right number."

I must have looked surprised at her frankness because Devon laughed again. "It's not money or class or GPA. It's not easy to define at all. Our members just know when a girl

346

is right, usually early on. And usually our pledges know when SAXi is right for them."

Something about the way she said that: "just know." How many times had I described my intuition that way? I *just knew* things.

"Did you 'just know' that SAXi was for you?"

I expected a flippant, canned answer. Instead she gazed at me for a moment, an odd sort of half smile on her lips. "Yeah." Her tone was uninterpretable. "SAXi sort of chooses us, Maggie. You'll know, too."

I couldn't tell if she meant that as a good thing.

"Hi, Devon." A new girl joined us—a young woman, really, with maturity and an air of command. "Are you going to introduce me to your friend? You've been speaking together for almost ten minutes."

Devon's freckles disappeared into her flush, confirming that the reprimand hadn't been my imagination. I wondered if it was really the ten-minute monopoly, or if the other girl could read the exchange of information from across the room.

"Of course," she said. "Maggie, this is Kirby, our chapter president. Kirby, this is Maggie. She's an English major, and lives at home."

I glanced at her, expecting a smile or a wink, some hint at the shared joke. But with a smile that didn't reach her eyes, Devon took her leave, moving on in the rotation.

"How are you enjoying Rush?" Kirby asked.

"Well enough, thank you." I caught myself speaking to her like an authority figure, which was crazy and disturbing. She wasn't *my* president. "I was enjoying talking to Devon," I said pointedly.

As a member came by with a silver tray full of glasses of lemonade, she snagged one and offered it with a napkin. "Have a drink?"

I eyed the beverage as if the decorative twist of lemon might jump out and bite me. "This is my fourth party of the night. My back teeth are already singing 'Anchors Aweigh.' "

She smiled. "It's a little party trick. Gives you something to do with your hands."

"In that case." I took the glass, mostly to get her to leave me alone about it. No wonder Devon had scuttled obediently on her way.

"Now that we've been through the niceties . . ." Kirby gestured toward the wooden folding chairs set artfully around a cleared space. "Maybe you'd like to take a seat. We're about to have a short presentation on our philanthropy."

"How thrilling." If President Kirby noticed my irony, she didn't let it show. Hers was the gently imperturbable smile of a political hostess.

I slouched into a spot next to Holly. The space contained a piano and a Chinese screen, behind which I could just detect movement. "Please God, don't let it be a skit."

Holly glanced at me, saw the drink in my hand, and lifted her own. "I thought you said you were already sloshing on the way over here."

Raising a toast, I clinked our glasses. "Why are we here, if not to drink the Kool-Aid."

"Cheers, then," she said.

"Sláinte," I answered, and we drank.

A cherub-faced girl came out from behind the screen,

and I groaned softly. Worse than a skit—a skit by precocious children. She went to the piano. A lanky boy emerged, and to my surprise and bemusement, slipped the strap of an electric guitar over his head. A couple of SAXis moved the screen aside to reveal, along with the amp for the guitar, a small drum set with a pigtailed preteen seated behind it, sticks in her hands and a smile on her face.

A woman—older than us, but not elderly by any measure—walked to a small podium. She wore a smart, charcoal gray pantsuit, a silk scarf at the collar. Her strawberry blond hair was neatly coiffed and her smile warmly practiced.

"Good evening," she said. "I'm Victoria Abbott, one of the chapter advisers."

"She says that like it's supposed to mean something," Holly whispered in my ear.

"She's the wife of our congressman," I hissed back. Holly wouldn't know since she wasn't from here. "Nice suit."

"Well, yeah. It's Armani."

I processed this—the distinction of a three-thousand-dollar suit, and the fact that Holly recognized one. Casting my eye over her, I paid closer attention to the excellent cut of the black and white dress she was wearing.

"I'd like to briefly tell you about the Roll Over Beethoven Foundation—Sigma Alpha Xi's chosen philanthropy, not least because it was started by SAXi alum Susie Braddock."

An awed ripple moved through the group. Even a loser like me had heard that name. Ms. Abbott continued. "The Roll Over Beethoven Foundation promotes music education in schools, and funds free after-school music programs. But why don't I let the program speak for itself."

I tensed as the kids began to play. The opening bars were instantly identifiable. They were covering one of my favorite songs by—I kid you not—the Talking Heads. And they did not suck.

If I *was* looking for a sorority, for sisterhood or networking, or for mixers with the frat boys across the way, I would have totally taken it as a sign.

4

I arrived at Froth and Java for the second time in the same day, which was actually not that unusual for me. What had me a little off balance was a message from Cole Bauer that had been waiting on my cell phone, asking me to call him. I did, but ended up leaving him a voicemail in return. So much had changed since that morning, and I felt slightly disconnected as I smoothed my windblown hair and checked my reflection in the front window of the coffee shop, wondering if I should put on lip gloss.

Justin was already inside, staking out a pair of deep chairs good for conversation. He stood when he saw me, and we did another one of those unsure dances of greeting. Finally he took my shoulders, leaned down, and kissed my cheek. And I blushed. I could feel it spread over my skin, from the top of my dress to the roots of my hair.

"Hey," I said, brilliantly.

He stepped back and grinned as he looked at me. I still wore my sundress, though I'd taken off the despised name tag. He'd showered and changed into jeans and a green and white rugby shirt. Close up, I could smell him, clean and sort of spicy, beneath the overwhelming scent of coffee. While there might be some uncertainty to our relationship, there was no ambiguity about the way I felt when I was near him.

"You look great, Maggie."

A short lock of hair fell against the heat of my cheek, and I brushed it back. "Thanks. I've been working out."

Justin laughed, because he knew how ridiculous that was. He gestured to the chair perpendicular to his and I sat, setting my cell phone and car keys beside his on the side table.

"So, what's this about going undercover?"

"With the Future Stepfords of America, you mean?" The chair was too soft and deep. I had to balance on the edge to keep from sinking into it like quicksand. "Newspaper story."

"So how is it?"

"Interesting." I solved the quicksand problem by tucking my legs up under me and leaning on the poufy upholstered arm. "It's more of a social commentary sort of thing than hard-hitting investigative journalism."

"So nothing . . ." He gestured vaguely. "Weird?"

"Sorority girls from Hell, you mean?" I laughed. "That's so seventies B movie."

His smile turned rueful. "It does sound cliché when you put it that way. How's your mom?"

"Aside from the morning pukeathon, she's doing great."

"And your gran?"

"Good." I anticipated his next question. "And Dad, too."

He smiled that crooked smile. "And Lisa?"

"Fine, I guess. She left for Georgetown last week."

"Is she still . . . ?" He faltered, maybe because of the busy coffee shop, maybe because of the baggage it brought up.

"Studying the dark arts?" I tried to hit a droll tone, but missed the mark and landed closer to sour and dejected. "It should make her fit in well in Washington, D.C., I guess. If I wasn't worried about her moral compass before, living that close to the Capitol would do it."

"I don't know." Justin had better aim, and he struck the perfect note of comforting humor. "Georgetown University is affiliated with the Jesuits. Maybe it will be good for her."

That made me smile. Not because of any renewed hope for Lisa's ethical education, but because Justin was such a font of eccentric information.

I left the uncomfortable subject of Lisa for a happier one. "Was the internship everything you'd hoped it would be?"

"It was great." His face lit with warmth for his subject. "Hearing their folktales in Gaelic, looking into the weather-beaten faces of those living so close to the land and the legends, and seeing the belief that's woven into the tales. And the pictures we took of the haunts of the fair folk and the giants . . . I have enough for a whole book, let alone a thesis."

"That's fantastic." I had to grin; his enthusiasm was contagious. Justin's graduate studies were in anthropology, specifically the folklore of magic and the occult. Or as I called it when we met, an advanced degree in "Do You Want Fries with That." Dad said Justin was hard to classify academically, but they let him hang out with the history folks anyway.

"After what happened this spring," I ventured, curious, "how will you write about all this in a scholarly paper? Don't you question everything now, wonder what's myth and what's real?"

He fiddled with his cell phone on the table. "I still have to record it empirically as folklore and fairy tales. We don't know which is which, do we?"

I paused, a little surprised at that noncommittal answer from Justin, the true believer. And there was that ambiguous "we." I knew he wasn't talking about me. I had the theoretical advantage of my Spidey Sense to tell me when the boogeyman was real. "No. I guess not."

He rose to his feet, dusted his hands on his jeans. "Can I get you something to drink? Vanilla latte, extra shot, right?"

"Yeah." I smiled, feeling a melty warmth inside at the fact that he remembered.

Our friendship had been a brief, intense proving ground, but romance-wise, he'd left before we'd gone out more than twice. We'd kissed—which was a little like saying Mount St. Helens had exploded once. But I suppose I could understand the "just friends" uncertainty of our relationship when he boarded that plane, and why we were starting over now.

I even understood if he'd gotten too busy, too involved with his work to e-mail me the way he did at first. Three months was a long time. He was across the ocean, building his career, and . . .

His phone rang. I glanced toward the counter, where Justin waited for the drinks. Clearly he couldn't hear his ringtone over the chatter and music. I swam out of the chair and picked up the phone, intending to flag him.

It was playing that Irish song, the one they use in every movie with a bar fight or a leprechaun. Everyone knows it's the Irish song, and Justin's phone was playing it and flashing the name *Deirdre* on the caller ID.

A vision popped in my brain—in the space of a held breath, a series of images flickered in front of my mind's eye like those old film reels where you see the blink between frames: A black-haired, green-eyed, creamy-complexioned woman trekking through a boggy field, sitting with Justin over a couple of pints in a pub with a smoky peat fire. The two of them, heads together in intimate conversation, him inclining to say something, her leaning forward to meet him and . . .

The phone clattered to the floor, falling from my nerveless fingers. Maybe I broke it, but I couldn't care. Head whirling, I tried to bring the room back into focus. My heart slammed against my ribs. What the hell had just happened?

"Maggie?" Justin had returned, drinks in hand.

"I dropped your phone." My own voice sounded flat and cold. I stared stupidly at the phone on the floor, not about to touch it again. Something was *wrong* with me.

He set down the drinks. "Are you all right? You look sick."

I *felt* sick. I was seeing things while I was awake. My freakitude had just reached a whole new level.

"Deirdre called." The words blurted out, the way the images had blurted into my brain. "I wasn't spying on you."

"What?" He blinked in confusion, brow knit in concern. "Spying? Of course not."

"I just picked it up and . . ."

"And what, Maggie?" Bending slightly, he searched my face, trying to trap my gaze. "What happened?"

But I couldn't tell him. Too many emotions had seized my brain and nailed my tongue to the roof of my mouth. I couldn't make my lips form the questions that would clear everything up. Who was Deirdre? Was she why you stopped writing? All valid questions, but I couldn't get past the part where, oh my God, I was even more of a freak than I thought.

"I need to go." I grabbed my keys from the table and he snatched them neatly from my shaking fingers.

"Maggie, what the hell is wrong with you?"

I pressed my hands to my pounding head. "I have a headache all of a sudden."

"Then let me drive you. You look awful."

"No." My latte, all three shots of it, stood on the table. I grabbed it, took a scalding drink, gasped, but felt better. The burn, like a slap in the face, calmed my hysteria. One more deep breath and I squared my shoulders. "I'm fine."

"You are *not* fine." His voice had a taut edge, from trying to keep it below the general hum of conversation and the music playing in the background.

"All right. I'm not fine." Another sip of espresso and I could lift my eyes to his and hold out a steady hand. "But I can drive. Give me my keys."

His gaze searched mine, and I wondered what he saw

there. I had no clue to his thoughts, though his confusion and worry were clear. Finally he relented. "Will you call me when you get home so I know you made it okay?"

"Fine." Anything to get him to give me the keys. He hesitated a moment longer, then dropped them into my palm. I didn't wait, but fled the coffee shop like the coward I was.

5

Parked in my own driveway, I called Justin and told him succinctly that I was safe at home, answering his concern. Yes, I was all right. I'd just had a long, stressful day, and my psyche was wrung out like a dishrag.

By the time I'd driven home, the warm September wind whipping through the open Jeep and clearing my head, the panic had abated, and these didn't even feel like lies. My *ESP for Dummies* book had said emotional state can affect your Sight. Of course, it talked about blocking reception, not suddenly getting an imaginary slide show, but still.

I'd justified away my intuition for almost eighteen years. I have a talent for denial that puts even my mother to shame.

When I went inside, the living room was dark, but there was light from both my parents' bedroom and Dad's study. I called a greeting, got goodnights in return, and climbed the stairs to what we jokingly call my suite. There's a study area on one side, and French doors, which I almost never close, mark the bedroom.

My phone rang as I was dropping my satchel by my desk; warily, I dug it out of my pocket. The caller ID flashed a number with the university's prefix, and I flipped open the phone and tried to inject some perky into my "Hi. This is Maggie."

"Hi, Maggie. This is Cole Bauer."

"Hi, Cole." I sat on the edge of the desk chair. "Sorry about the phone tag."

"It's all right, as long as you're working on round two."

The words went in, but my spent neurons failed to process them. "What?"

"I want a report for each round. We'll carry it through the week, with a blacked-out photo. You don't mind a pseudonym, do you? You need to preserve your anonymity."

Slowly, my brain translated. "I guess you liked the piece?"

"The way the Greeks dominate this campus, they deserve to be skewered a bit. Plus, it'll sell papers. Well, the *Report* is free, but you know what I mean."

"Yeah." Beyond my agreement, comment was unnecessary. With contagious excitement, Cole outlined a scheme of James Bond complexity for keeping my identity a secret.

"So what's my code name?" I asked, when he gave me the chance. "Can I be Secret Squirrel?"

I'd been joking, but he answered, "Morocco Mole would be more appropriate."

"But too obvious." I used the same serious tone. We agreed on the details of the rest of the week, and said good-bye.

I hung up the phone, numb and fatigued, as if the ping-pong bounce of my emotions all day had burnt out my circuits. But I wasn't quite done yet. As I dug in my dresser for a pair of pajamas, the cell rang again.

I flipped it open without checking the caller ID. "Hello?"

"Maggie?" Lisa. I must have at least one emotional circuit left, because my throat closed up at hearing her voice precisely when I needed her.

"Hey," I managed.

"What's wrong?" Her tone, always brusque, was tinged tonight with concern. "You sound weird."

I flung myself onto the ancient love seat in the corner of my study. "I've had a very weird day."

"Uh-huh." She didn't sound particularly surprised.

"How did you know?" I asked, unable to keep the wariness from my voice.

"I looked in my crystal ball, what do you think?"

That was the thing with Lisa. She joked about things like taking over the world or raising an army of zombie minions to do her bidding. Things that, in retrospect of the last year, weren't funny at all.

"Seriously, Lisa. You didn't do a spell or something, did you? Because you know I'm ethically opposed . . ."

"Look, I didn't call for a lecture, all right?"

Silence, while I weighed how much I desperately wanted to talk to her versus my conviction that her dabbling in—jeez, "sorcery" sounded so melodramatic. Let's say, my fear that her arcane studies would do nothing to obliterate the enormous blot already on her karmic account book.

Lisa broke the silence first. "I just called to chat. I didn't know you were upset until I heard your voice."

"Oh."

"I'm an evil genius, Maggie Quinn. I can add two and two without the benefit of a magic wand."

I sighed and slumped deeper into the cushions. "You're not evil, Lisa. Just . . . goal oriented."

She gave a bitter laugh, and redirected the conversation. "So what's up?"

"First I had a piece rejected by the city paper and my journalism professor is kind of a dick. Then the editor of the school paper liked my story, but it means I have to keep going through this Rush business, which is wearing on my nerves. And I finally saw Justin, but I think he might have an Irish girlfriend."

"Did you *ask* him if he had an Irish girlfriend?"

"No."

"Maggie, you idiot." She'd said that so many times over the years, I could picture the roll of her eyes, the shake of her head. "You know those books, where the only thing keeping the moronic heroine apart from the hero is the fact that they don't talk to each other? How you always want to smack the girl?"

I knew exactly what she meant, but I had new sympathy for those morons. "You don't even like Justin."

"That's not the point. You do."

"And then there's the *way* I found out." Time to turn the subject from what an idiot I was. "I had a vision."

"Like one of your dreams?"

"No. Well, sort of, but different, on fast forward or something. And awake." I explained picking up Justin's phone, and the psychic slide show. "Images and impressions, really fast. It was weird." And scary, but I didn't tell her that.

She paused, and like a lot of Lisa's pauses, it was uninterpretable. "This is a new thing?"

"Yeah. Maybe it was a fluke."

"Maybe some jealous Irish witch zapped you through the phone."

"Gee, I'm *so* glad you called to cheer me up, Lisa."

"Don't mention it." I heard a squeak, like bedsprings or a chair, the sound of settling in. "How are classes?"

"All right so far. Mostly jaunting back and forth across campus, collecting syllabuses. Syllabi? How about you?"

"Georgetown is pretty cool, but expensive. Good thing I didn't blow through my savings account after I got the scholarship. I'll need it to keep me in Diet Coke and eye of newt."

"Oh, really," I said, in the same matter-of-fact tone. "Do they have one-stop occult shopping over there?"

"No, but you wouldn't believe what you can get on the Internet."

"Don't scare me more than I already am." I meant it as a joke, but it fell flat, the way things do when they're too true.

A pause. I pictured her in a dorm room, a cramped, drab place transformed with posters and throw pillows and thrift store finds. She'd be sitting cross-legged, her chestnut hair falling around her elegant face. The only thing I couldn't imagine was her expression. Regretful? Wistful? Stubborn?

All three laced her voice when she finally spoke. "I wish you'd understand. Studying this stuff . . . it's something I have to do."

"Why?" I challenged her, not for the first time. "Because

it's there, like Mount Everest? An intellectual challenge you can't resist?"

"It isn't just idle curiosity."

"Oh, well, that's a relief. I'd hate to think you were jeopardizing your soul to satisfy a mental itch."

"Jeez, Mags. You make it sound like I'm sacrificing kittens or something. I'm making a scientific and theoretical study of occult folklore. It's not any different from what Justin is doing."

"Justin is studying brownies and green men. You're practicing spells and potions."

"Your point?" She was 100% stubborn now.

I pressed my hand over my eyes. "It's harnessing a power that isn't your own and making things *happen*. It's exactly what got us into so much trouble this spring."

"Maggie, there are things out there. Real things. Scary things."

"Things we shouldn't be messing with!" I said.

"Don't you think it's better to understand them? How the supernatural works and how to fight it?"

"No." I was adamant, but *ESP for Dummies* mocked me from the floor by the couch. "I think we were lucky the last time, and we should leave that stuff alone."

"Says the girl with the Psychic Friends Network in her head."

"*I* can't help it." Which seemed truer by the day. "*You* have a choice."

"No." Her voice was taut with sadness. "No, I really don't."

I wanted desperately to understand why she thought that, when this path could only be dangerous for her, when she knew what awful bloody things that kind of power could lead to.

"We always have choices, Lisa."

"That's what this boils down to, isn't it? You don't trust me."

Now it was my turn to pause, condemning her with my reluctance to answer.

"Right." She charged on when the silence stretched too long. "Well, you have no reason to, I guess. Except maybe that we've been friends since the seventh grade."

"I trust your *intentions,* Lisa, but—"

She cut me off. "But we all know where those lead. I'm sure Azmael is keeping my seat warm for me."

"That is not funny." I felt sick, furious at her, terrified for her, and completely freaked by her saying the demon's name aloud. "Do *not* joke about that."

"Evil genius sorcerers never joke about Hell, Maggie." Self-loathing clipped her words. "Later."

She hung up. I called her back immediately, but she didn't answer, had turned the phone off or simply ignored it. For all I knew, she'd blown it up with her magic wand.

Nothing had been the same between Lisa and me after that night at the prom. Though arguably, neither of us was the same person that we were going in. Facing demons will do that to you. We emerged intrinsically bound by the experience, but in a way, strangers to each other.

We'd tried to ignore it. But then I'd dreamed about her on Midsummer Night. I'd seen her in a circle of girls I didn't know, some kind of New Agey ceremony that seemed innocuous. I got a feeling of renewing energy, something like the smell of green spring grass or the heavy, lush scent of ripe berries. No alarm there. But from my mental perspective I could see Lisa's face, could sense her whip-smart intellect crackling behind a carefully neutral expression. And I knew that was trouble.

Our confrontation afterward was pretty well recapped in tonight's argument. I told her what I thought about her playing with fire; she insisted I didn't understand what she was trying to do. I thought I understood very well. Lisa was trying to control the uncontrollable.

I picked up the ESP book and it fell open automatically to the pages of exercises, worn and gray on the edges, the spine creased where I'd held the book open while I practiced meditations for clarity, protection, and strength. Hokey, yes. I'd felt ridiculous sitting cross-legged and still on the floor. But I did them anyway, all summer long. Clearly, I was no stranger to the need for control.

✳ ✳ ✳

Eventually, I made it to my desk chair and contemplated the blank screen of my laptop. I needed to get my Rush thoughts down while they were still fresh, but my brain churned restlessly. Opening my playlist, I looked for something soothing.

Nothing in the library appeased my frayed nerves. Barenaked Ladies—too flippant. Kelly—too power pop. Joss—too blond. Fiona, Sheryl, Sarah—all too Lilith Fair. Where was the "you've pissed off all your friends and now you're all alone" music?

Susie Braddock's name leapt out at me. I'd forgotten I had one of her songs.

In a new browser window I typed her name into Google. The search engine helpfully supplied the first ten of a gazillion entries. I clicked on the official fan page of the Grammy-winning artist, free-associated through Susie Braddock's bio, then on to the Roll Over Beethoven Foundation, and other notable SAXis. Finally I felt calm enough to do some work on my newspaper assignment and started closing windows.

The bottom page was a pop-up window; a lousy ad, though, because I couldn't tell what it was selling. It consisted of an animated GIF that took up the entire window, some kind of diagram, like a black and white test pattern made up of circles and linking lines. They pulsed slightly as I stared, so subtly that I couldn't tell if the motion came from the symbols or an optical illusion.

I went to click on the window, to make it active. But as soon as I touched the trackpad, the whole image disappeared, and a new box appeared to tell me that MS Extorter had unexpectedly quit.

Crap. The only thing I hate more than pop-up ads are ones that crash my browser. One Java applet too many, I guess, telling me how I could get bigger boobs, which I might be interested in, or see nude girls on ice, which I definitely was not.

6

My article appeared below the fold on the front page of Tuesday's *Ranger Report*. The Greeks were aghast, the rushees were titillated, and the Rho Gammas were on the warpath.

This was *so* much better than buried with the obituaries (no pun intended) in the "real" paper.

"Who do you think it is?"

My ears perked up while I stood at the Starbucks kiosk in the student union, watching like a vulture as the barista steamed the milk for my latte. Somehow I'd made it through my eight o'clock class on only one cup of coffee, but now I needed a high-octane infusion ASAP.

A second girl answered the first. "I think it's that skinny

girl from Sutter Hall. You know, the one with the Lisa Loeb glasses. She looks like that snobby intellectual type."

"She can't *look* like the type. That would defeat the purpose of being incognito."

"Is that what you're wearing?"

Since I'd been shamelessly eavesdropping, it took a moment to realize the question was directed at me. Turning, I saw Hillary with her hands on her hips, the *RG* on her chest standing out like a blazon. It's a bird, it's a plane, it's . . . Rho Gamma Girl.

I pointed to my new name tag. "Look. No graffiti."

Her blond ponytail whipped back and forth as she shook her head. "You look like you just rolled out of bed."

As a matter of fact, I *had* just rolled out of bed and into a clean pair of jeans, a T-shirt, and a worn Bedivere U. hoodie, then on to my eight o'clock calculus lecture. There had to be something unhealthy about math that early in the morning.

"Sorry. I guess I should have dressed up for class. Like that." I pointed to a pair of Kappa Phis walking by wearing the exact same thing I was, except their hoodies said KΦ and they had standard Greek-issue ponytails instead of unruly dark brown bobs.

Hillary huffed in annoyance, then waved the subject aside, back to serious Panhellenic business. "Forget it. I'm asking everyone"—she addressed the girls at the table, too, unfurling the newspaper that had been rolled up in her hand—"if you have any idea who this is."

No question who she meant, but in the interest of clarity she pointed to the anonymous silhouette beside the byline—not Secret Squirrel, to my great disappointment, but the Phantom Rushee.

"We were just discussing that," said one of the gossiping girls. They all had name tags pinned to their T-shirts. The speaker was Lindsey. "Brianna thinks she knows someone."

Brianna didn't look happy to be put on the spot. "I said I knew someone who looked like the *type*."

"And I still say she won't be a *type*," argued a third girl.

"There's no way she can completely hide it," volleyed Brianna. "Surely it will show."

"What will show?" I asked, figuring it would be suspicious to remain silent.

"That she's not one of us, of course."

Maybe that was the purpose of the ubiquitous ponytail— to show there were no sixes on the back of any necks.

Hillary saved me from saying this aloud and wasting good material for my next article. "Since you girls know each other best, Panhellenic is asking for your help. Just keep your ears open, and if you have any ideas who this Phantom Rushee might be, you'll tell one of the Rho Gammas."

The rushees nodded, and I did, too, projecting innocence and cooperation as hard as I could. Maybe a little too hard, since Hillary's glance lingered on me, a little too long and a little too narrow-eyed. Possibly she suspected me, possibly just disliked me, but clearly I'd better tone down the smart-ass a bit if I wanted to avoid the scrutiny of the Panhellenic Council, which was starting to scare me just by reputation.

"Where are you going tonight?" she asked me, meaning, of course, which houses had invited me back.

"The same as last night." Meaning all of them had, since I'd been on my best behavior. The only one that surprised me was the Sigma Alpha Xis, since the girl there—Devon—had said outright that they were fairly exclusive. But maybe she'd put in a good word for me.

"Don't be late this time," Hillary chided. "Recruitment is serious business, and the houses need to know if you are committed."

I nodded obediently, and she left to continue her witch hunt. No falsehood there. I certainly agreed that we should all be committed.

✳ ✳ ✳

My favorite class was History of Civilization (Part I). An honors class, it was engaging, participatory, and challenging. Also, my dad taught it, and it was the first time I'd seen him in days, even though we lived in the same house.

"Hey, Magpie." He greeted me as I came down the steps to the front of the lecture hall.

"Hi, Dad."

A copy of the *Ranger Report* lay on the podium, and he tapped the anonymous picture. "I don't suppose you know who this prankster is, do you?"

"Not a clue," I said, perusing the page.

"Too bad." There was a mischievous twinkle in his eye. "I think she's rather droll."

"I think she's rather frivolous. There are serious issues in the Greek system, and she's cracking jokes."

"Can't please everyone, I guess." Zipping his computer case, he gathered his binder of lecture notes. "Are we going to see you for dinner tonight?"

"Can't. Third-round parties." I smiled too brightly. "It's Skit Night! Oh boy!"

Dad's mouth set in an unhappy line. I'd overheard a

couple of girls saying he was good-looking in a Robert Redford kind of way. I bet they wouldn't say that if they'd ever gotten the Frown of Paternal Disapproval. The one I was getting now.

"Every year I see these girls burning themselves to a cinder before the semester is half done, trying to keep up with their classwork and this sorority business. That's not going to be you, is it?"

"Come on, Dad. You know me."

"Exactly." He glanced over my shoulder, directing a question to someone near the door. "Did you need me?"

"No, sir." Justin's voice. "I wanted to talk to Maggie a sec."

"Sure thing," said Dad, deserting me with a cheery wave.

I thought about just following my father out, and my expression must have shown it. Justin raised his hands as if to show he was unarmed. "I only wanted to make sure you're okay."

"I think so." I'd justified and compartmentalized the weirdness. My distrust and confusion, however, was unresolved.

He closed the distance so that he could lower his voice. Out in the hall a river of students went by, no strangeness in their lives. "You want to tell me what happened?"

My lips pursed as I considered it. Really, how does one say: I had some kind of psychic power spike and saw what looked an awful lot like some girl making a pass at you.

"Who's Deirdre?" I said it like that, a non sequitur bomb.

His brow knit in confusion. "How did you know her name?"

"I'm Psychic Girl, remember?" The most I was going

to admit until I knew he was still on my side. "Also, the caller ID."

"Oh." He smiled sheepishly, laughing at himself. "She was one of the other interns on the oral history project. We—all of us—worked pretty closely and got to be friends."

"Uh-huh."

He held up a hand. His eyes, warm and brown and without guile, met mine. "Honestly, Maggie."

Here's the thing about people like Justin, people that Lisa—in D&D parlance—called "lawful good." They can't lie worth a damn, and when they try, it shows, even to normal folks, not just weirdos like me.

The truth of his statement resonated. The deepest part of me knew that if he had something going on with another girl, his honor would require him to tell me about it. And I guess if I hadn't been so insecure, the shallow part of me would have realized it, too.

"Okay." My gaze wandered over the empty lecture hall and I wished we were having this conversation someplace that felt less like being onstage. "I'm sorry I freaked out the other night. I wasn't really jealous." He didn't speak, but gave me an even look that forced me to admit, "Well, not *just* jealous. It's complicated."

"Then tell me," he said, reasonably.

My eyes went to the ceiling, as if maybe my feelings would be outlined there, and I could manage to articulate them. "I just wish I knew what to think. About us. I mean, I don't know if I'm . . . If we're . . . I mean, obviously not yet, but could we be . . . ? Do not laugh at me."

"I'm not laughing." And he wasn't. He reached out and caught my hand, met my eye. "I really like you, Maggie."

Oh God, here it comes.

"But—"

I groaned, loudly, and tried to pull my hand away.

"Would you just listen?" He held fast to my fingers while I looked anywhere but at him. "I'm working so hard right now. My whole focus is getting this degree, and I've got this teaching assistant job, and the thesis, which may turn into a dissertation. I'm not going to have a life outside of school for a while."

Great. My first boyfriend was breaking up with me before he'd ever really been my boyfriend. With an audience of 150 empty seats to witness my "it's not you, it's me" humiliation.

"I know your studies are important to you," I said.

"Not just to me." He dropped his voice. "Occult folklore needs serious study and documentation by someone who understands and . . ."

"Believes in it, I know." I made his argument for him. "Preaching to the choir here, Justin. Been there, vanquished that. Trust me, I am *very* sympathetic to the time you spend doing research."

Pulling my trick, he lifted his gaze to the ceiling, looking for answers. I wondered if he even realized he was still holding my hand. "But you're also a freshman," he said, "and you should be doing all those freshman things."

"You are *not* going to turn this into a conversation about you knowing better than me what I want."

He sighed—resigned, determined—looking me in the eye as he dashed my hopes. "No. I'm telling you what I want, which is to concentrate on work without feeling like I'm taking you for granted. I want to be your friend right now."

If only he was lying, had suddenly discovered a talent for it. But he wasn't. His feelings might not be as simple as friendship, but he wasn't lying about his wishes.

"Okay," I said.

"Okay?" Finally, he let my fingers slip from his, and my skin felt colder. *I* felt colder. "What does that mean?"

"It means I like you. A lot." Gathering my books from the lecturer's table, I clutched them tightly to hide the shaking of my hands. "And I need you when things go wonky in my life. I would rather be your friend than lose you completely, so if those are my options, then fine, okay, we can be just friends."

I didn't force a smile, didn't even say good-bye. I left without meeting his eye again, but I felt his gaze follow me out of the hall. The whole thing would have been a lot easier if he'd been a jerk, or if the romantic cliché was his way of letting me down easy. But it wasn't, and I was going to have to wrap my heart around the reality of right guy, bad timing.

7

"If I ruled the world," I told Holly and Tricia as we walked between houses that evening, "I would ban all skits."

"I like the skits," Tricia said. Of course she would.

"You like everything." I looked up at the stars as we walked. "The skits, the stupid songs, the watery lemonade..."

The night was warm and still. Was it my imagination, or were even the heavens full of Greek letters? Lately I saw them everywhere—campus and store windows, and still in my dreams.

Holly walked backward, facing us, hands tucked in the pockets of her corduroy blazer. "You know, Maggie, someone *might* think you weren't having a wonderful time."

"Did *you* enjoy watching 'Mary Potter and the Half-Greek Princess' as performed by the Adam Sandler School of Dramatic Arts?"

"Well, no," she admitted. "But all of Rush is kind of hokey, you know."

"I know now." I kept more laughter in my voice than cynicism. We'd formed a kind of foxhole camaraderie, especially Holly and I, but I still had to remember my camouflage.

"What made you decide to do it?"

I shrugged, sensing nothing behind the question, but hedging anyway. "Same reason as you."

The trees that lined the sidewalk shaded her face from the moonlight, and hid her expression. "I'm going because my mother made me."

"Your mom the Sigma Alpha Xi?" asked Tricia.

"Yep." She turned forward, closing the subject. I sensed—and it didn't really take my crazy Jedi mind tricks—a bit of a raw nerve there.

I waited until Tricia turned off toward the Kappa Phi house, then caught up with Holly, stretching my legs to match her longer stride.

"So what's the deal with the SAXis?" I asked. "I mean, every chapter has a kind of personality. The Kappa Phis take their cute pills every morning, and the Deltas cut me because they think my dad's a janitor. The Theta Nus are the brain trust and the Zetas are the cool club. The EZs are . . . well, you know."

"Right."

"But I can't get a handle on the SAXis. The only thing I've been able to pin down is they've got really great hair."

Holly folded her arms as if she were cold, despite the balmy evening. Her gaze stayed on the sidewalk, on the places where tree roots had pushed up the pavement into treacherous fault-line ridges.

"The SAXis," she said finally, "get what they want."

I wanted to ask her what she meant, but she lengthened her stride, and short of breaking into a run, I couldn't keep up.

✳ ✳ ✳

The Sigma Alpha Xis had transformed their chapter room into a Parisian sidewalk café. Little round tables covered with checked tablecloths—each with a tiny vase of delicate flowers—filled the room, and on the wall was a mural of the Eiffel Tower. A street artist painted at an easel, and a mime wandered through the crowd. Accordion music played softly, and I swear I smelled baking bread. The transformation was so complete that it must have been accomplished with a lot of money, if not by magic.

I admit, the idea occurred to me. But really, if you had the ability to do magic, would you squander it to impress a bunch of college freshmen?

"Welcome back, Maggie." I turned to see the president of Sigma Alpha Xi smiling at me. My brain supplied the name Kirby, which I remembered because it was like Furby, which was amusing only because she looked nothing like a gremlin toy. Except, maybe, that her smile didn't reach her eyes, which were all business. I'd seen that a lot at these parties.

Kirby gestured to the woman with her. "You remember Victoria Abbott, one of our chapter advisers."

"Good evening, Mrs. Abbott." She wore another classy suit tonight, a hunter green that looked amazing with her complexion.

"Please, call me Victoria." She smiled, and it did reach her eyes, just barely crinkling the corners. Her husband was quite young for a U.S. congressman—early forties—so his wife was probably about the same. She must moisturize like crazy, because she looked nowhere near that.

"Impressive, isn't it?"

"Excuse me?" I didn't think she meant her skincare routine or her designer suit.

She gestured to the room. "One of our alums is in graduate school for set design. She helped with the backdrops."

"Very nice," I said inadequately.

"And I believe you met Devon yesterday." A wave of a slim hand indicated the painter with the beret. "She's a fine art major."

"Cool." I was just full of brilliance tonight, but my brain was processing her knowledge of my social activities.

"I understand that you are an artist, too." I looked at her, my expression blank, and she gazed back expectantly. Finally she prompted, "You're a photographer?"

"Oh! Yeah." That was the problem with lying; you had to actually remember what you told people. "I was on the yearbook staff in high school."

Mrs. Abbott nodded. "I saw that on your Rush application. Are you thinking about continuing in photojournalism?"

Ah. Now I understood. She was feeling me out to see if I was the Phantom Rushee. At the other houses there had been a lot of questions about hobbies, but no one else had made the leap from yearbook photog to newspapers.

"I haven't decided yet," I told her, lying with the truth. My guard was up, but it was hard not to *look* as though I'd raised my defenses. "I'd like to take some pictures for the *Report*, see if I like it, but they don't let freshmen on the newspaper staff. My major is English right now."

"Oh? Are you a writer?"

The woman was like a terrier on a rat. My hole was getting deeper and she was digging in behind me. "I love literature. I've thought about being a professor, like my father."

"Ah, yes. Dr. Quinn. He was a TA when my husband was in college here."

I jumped on the opportunity to turn the subject away from me. "Did you meet at Bedivere?"

"Yes. We're both active alumni. Your sorority will be a vital part of your lives during college, and for the Sigmas, it remains so well after graduation. We're a special group."

Her hand touched my sleeve, and I felt a tingle, not on my arm, but in my brain. I stiffened, and I thought about my psychic exercises for dummies, about putting up a shield between us. Whether it worked or not, I wasn't sure, but there was no repeat of last night's voyeur-vision.

"Sigmas form a close bond, Maggie," Victoria continued seamlessly, as if she'd noticed nothing odd in my reaction. "You'll see what I mean, if you decide to join us."

Fortunately, she excused herself to introduce the skit, saving me from the most obvious response to that.

* * *

" 'Resistance is futile.' " A fraternity guy, slumped in his desk in the back of the classroom, read aloud from the latest Phantom Rushee report while we waited for Dr. Hardcastle to arrive. " 'All will be assimilated. Come into the light,

379

where all have shiny, shiny hair and many, many boy-friends.' " His buddies, all wearing some part of the Greek alphabet, laughed heartily. I wondered if they'd be so amused if the Phantom had been a guy rushing a fraternity.

He continued his recitation: " 'Unfortunately for the Sigma Alpha Xis, my mother always told me that if it looks too good to be true, it probably is.' "

The guy one seat down snatched the paper away. "She ragged on the SAXis? Man. This girl has balls."

Frat Man grabbed his newspaper back. "She's got to rag on them all, dipwad. It's like, equal time in the media or something."

"That's political campaigns, asshole."

Our class, by the way? Media and Communication. This is your brain on testosterone.

"I wonder if she's hot."

"She's probably some militant feminist lesbian."

"Lesbians are hot, dude."

Behold, the future broadcast executives of America.

✳ ✳ ✳

My days had begun to bleed together. The last night of Rush was Preference Night, when the sororities invited only the girls they were prepared to give a bid. There were only two parties, so we—the rushees, I mean—had to narrow the choices, too.

Leaving Hardcastle's class, I'd glimpsed Cole as I passed the journalism lab, but as per our secret agent code, we did not make eye contact or acknowledge each other. I headed to the library to do some work and check my e-mail, and found a message waiting.

From: cbauer@bedivereu.edu
To: mightyquinn@mailbox.net
Re: Secret Squirrel Retirement
I know we only made plans through Rush
Week, but are you sure you don't want
to keep going and pledge? Think of the
book you could write. Look at this:
www.newsnet.com/articles/greeksgowild

The link was to a news article about the seedy underbelly
of Greek life—drinking, drugs, hazing, promiscuity—and
the media blackout on the whole Greek system. How, unless
an event got onto the police blotter, no one really knew
about day-to-day life on Greek Row. This was what Ethan
Douglas at the *Avalon Sentinel* had been talking about when
he said my article lacked anything newsworthy.

The thing was, the longer the Phantom's opinions appeared in the *Report,* the greater the chance that I would be
discovered. If I actually *pledged* a sorority—

My phone started vibrating across the table. I picked it up
and leaned forward into the study carrel to whisper, "Hello?"

"It's Holly. Can you come to my room? We need to do an
intervention."

"What?"

"The Deltas cut Tricia."

"I'll be right there." I'd jotted down her dorm and room
number and closed my laptop before I realized that I was
treating this like a real emergency—which was the other
danger of continuing my undercover work. Perspective could
be a slippery thing. How easy would it be to lose it?

"I don't understand!" Tricia sobbed as she sat between us on Holly's bed in Sutter Hall. Her hands were full of soggy Kleenex, and her eyes puffy and red. "I did everything right. I studied the house and I got my hair done and I bought new clothes and the right kind of purse."

"You did great," said Holly, rubbing her back in a soothing rhythm. I looked at Tricia's handbag, wondering what was so special. She'd dumped it onto the floor, along with her books, by the room's built-in double desk. "They're idiots. You're beautiful and sweet."

"Much too sweet for the Delta Delta Gammas," I told her.

"I should have dyed my hair." Miserably, she fingered one of her glossy brown curls. "That's what the consultant said, if I wanted to go DDG."

I had to speak up, because even undercover, there was only so long I could keep repressing my opinion. "If you ask me, you should be thanking your lucky stars that you aren't stuck for the next four years with a bunch of skinny clones, making yourself sick and miserable to be someone you're not."

"But what am I going to do?" She lifted her tissue-filled hands helplessly. "How will I get to know people? How will I get anywhere in life? When I called my mom, she said now I'll never find a husband!"

"Oh, for God's sake." My sympathy went a lot farther than my patience. Holly swiftly intervened before I could say something really unfortunate.

"Here." She went to her bureau drawer and brought back an airline-sized bottle of vodka, handing it to Tricia. "Drink this. Then you can lie down for a few minutes, and pull your-self together in time for the parties tonight. Those aren't the only Greeks in the sea."

Tricia made a brave face and unscrewed the cap. "You're right," she said, throwing back her shoulders and then throwing back the liquor, downing all three ounces in two deep swallows.

"Wow," I said.

She gave a coughing wheeze, a relaxed smile on her face. "I feel much better now."

Luckily, we were standing there to catch her when she slid off the bed and into careless oblivion.

✳ ✳ ✳

Holly and I managed to get Tricia back to her own dorm room; the major obstacle, once we got her upright, was to keep her from calling out "Screw the Delta Delta Gammas" to everyone we passed, especially after that one frat boy called back, "Been there, done that."

We put her to bed, made sure she was still breathing—snoring, actually—then grabbed a couple of hamburgers from the cafeteria before heading back to Holly's room in Sutter Hall.

I sat cross-legged on the extra bed, the Styrofoam to-go box in my lap. I'd assumed Holly had a roommate, but it turned out she was just schizophrenic. The decorating scheme was half Posh Spice, half David Beckham—designer sheets on the bed, soccer trophies on the shelf, all wrapped in a subtle scent of Prada perfume mixed with eau de athletic shoe.

"I don't get it," I said around a french fry. "My mom was

in a sorority, but she never made *me* feel like I had to join one to be a success."

"Was *her* mom Greek?"

"No, they were German." Holly rolled her eyes at the feeble joke. "But really. Come on. It's such a cliché, the carbon-copy girls and the MRS degree."

"Where do you think clichés come from?" She flipped her hair over her shoulder and took a bite of burger. For a lanky girl, she could pack away the cals. "You're going to pledge with me, right?"

"What?"

"SAXi." She swallowed her mouthful and looked at me levelly. "You're not going to make me go in alone, are you?"

There was nothing helpless about Holly—competent, confident, down to earth. But something about the way she said that . . . She munched on her burger as if we were discussing a trip to the mall, but something underneath that thrummed with the tension of checked emotion.

"What makes you think they're going to invite me?" I asked, resisting the pull of my crusader instincts.

"Only Sigmas know Sigma criteria." She turned her careful attention to tucking a tomato slice back into her burger. "But I've got a feeling."

I understood about feelings. My thoughts turned to Tricia, who was a little silly but not at all atypical of the girls going through Rush, hanging not just four years of hopes on the outcome of this week, but certain that their foreseeable futures hinged on what letters they pinned on their lapels. Bad enough that the Greeks considered themselves better than the rest of us. Normal, likable people seemed to think so, too. It seemed to me there was a pertinent, immediate need to puncture these pretensions.

"Okay," I said, decisively. "If they give me a bid, I'll pledge."

"I knew it." She grinned and wiped the mustard off her fingers. "We're going to be pledge sisters!"

She stuck out her hand and I clasped it, my guard completely down. Sight and taste and touch exploded like paparazzi flashbulbs in my brain: Holly in a private-school blazer and scratchy plaid skirt; on the soccer field, with no one in the stands to watch her; arguing with an elegant auburn-haired woman; then sneaking drinks in her room, amber in the glass, smooth and smoky on her tongue, the one oasis of color and warmth in her cold marble house.

It lasted the space of one caught breath. This time, my stomach stayed down; only my heart leapt, beat against my breastbone as I tried to get my bearings. Back in the dorm room, dizzy and befuddled.

Holly stared at me strangely. My hand still rested in hers. "Are you all right?"

"Yeah." I had to try again, with more confidence. "Yeah. I'm fine."

Only I wasn't. I was slipping a psychic gear, and no book could help this dummy now.

8

Gran took the teapot out of its cozy, poured a cup, and pushed the sugar bowl across the table to me. "Now, drink that and tell me again. Slowly this time."

The tea was almost the color of coffee. I like it strong and sweet when I'm in a panic. The first sip burned the roof of my mouth, but the pain was psychologically grounding.

"I don't know what else to say." The china cup barely rattled as I set it in the saucer. "I've never had vision things like that before. Not all flashy and . . . visiony." There were cookies, too, but even the rich chocolate smell wasn't enough to tempt my stomach out of its knot. "Maybe I've got a tumor."

Gran gave a dismissive snort and stirred her tea, the spoon clinking against china. "You don't have a tumor."

"All I know is that when this started happening to Cordelia on that show *Angel,* she went into a coma and died."

"Honestly, Maggie. Do you get all your psychic instruction from TV and movies?"

"No. I have a book, too."

She set her cup on the table. We were in the breakfast nook of her kitchen, as bright and cheery a place as I knew. Gran's house was all about tea and cookies and comfort. Though not always comfort in the way I envisioned. She had a limited tolerance for self-pity.

Folding her hands in her lap, she asked in a pointedly prim tone, "You consider a Dummies book the exhaustive source?"

I picked up my cup, but it was still too hot to drink. "It isn't like they have classes at the Y, Gran. You said I have to work it out my own way, and I'm trying."

"That's true." She softened, reached to cover my hand with hers. I tensed, waiting for the psychic shock treatment.

I did feel something. Love, which smelled just like Gran's face cream, the one she'd used when I was a kid; security, which tasted like Earl Grey tea.

My eyes sought hers. "Did you do that on purpose?"

"What do you think I did?" she asked, withdrawing her hand, her expression that of a patient teacher.

"Kept your baggage, I guess, from hitting me in the head."

She rose from her chair. "Come to the study."

I followed her through the living room into the second

bedroom, which had been in use as a study for as long as I could remember. When I stayed with Gran as a kid, she would put a soft pallet on the floor, and I would sleep among the books. When I got older, I stuffed my blanket into the crack beneath the door so that the light wouldn't show, and I could read all night.

Today, the blinds were drawn and the lamp that Gran switched on was golden and warm. She went to a corner and ran her fingers over the spines of a hodgepodge of new and old volumes.

"Does your book talk about using imagery to build up defenses?"

"I guess." There was a section about protecting yourself from negative energy. Naturally, I'd been pretty interested in that. "The guy talks about surrounding yourself with a halo of love and pixie dust and unicorns. Like that would last a second against some Hell-spawned demigod."

Gran paused to look over her shoulder, amused. "Well, pixie dust is sufficient for most people. What do *you* imagine?"

I fiddled with an incense burner, collapsing a spent cone of ash and releasing the scent of rosemary into the air. What was Gran trying to remember, I wondered. Maybe my grand-dad. I hadn't even known him, but I got a sense of him in this room, a big, ruddy-cheeked man who loved to sit in the arm-chair with a glass of scotch and a mystery novel.

Maybe this vision thing didn't have to be horrible scary.

Pulling a book from the shelf, Gran faced me, expec-tantly. What had she asked? What did I imagine when I thought about psychic protection.

"The *Millennium Falcon*," I said. She laughed immediately, and then again as I explained. "You know when the TIE fighters are swarming in, and Han Solo is telling Chewbacca to raise the deflector shields?"

"Whatever works, I suppose." She laid a book in my hands. It was glossy but well used, a *Practical Guide to Meditation*. "Maybe you can add some of those to your exercises. I used that to"—she debated the right word—"insulate my 'baggage' from you. You could use the same thing to insulate yourself from things you brush up against."

"Thanks, Gran." I flipped through the pages of the book. It had big pictures and examples and step-by-step instructions. I liked it already. "So you don't think this is weird that I've suddenly got a new superpower?"

"No, because I don't think it's new." She straightened a picture, one of me and my parents at Disneyland. "You repressed your Sight for seventeen years. I think now it has to catch up with you. Naturally, you're going to have some growing pains."

She switched off the lamp and I followed her out into the living room. "Why was it so easy for you to accept *your* gift?"

"I suppose because I grew up in the old country." The lilt of her accent deepened when she talked about Ireland. "It was a simpler age. We didn't have a television, and I didn't even learn to drive until I came to America."

"Really?"

"You're very worldly and cynical here, and the need for *proof* blinds people to what may only be taken on faith."

I thought about that while I sat at the kitchen table, where my tea was now cool enough to drink. What she had said was true. My never-was-boyfriend studied the occult and my best friend was a witch. I'd had a demon stalker and lived to tell about it. But my first thought with the visions was that I must be going crazy.

It made me wonder how many things there were in the world that people just dismissed as coincidence or fluke, never realizing the extra layer of weird that overlay our mundanity, like a high-frequency radio station that most people's tuners never reached.

9

Rush, I wrote, sitting cross-legged on my bed, wearing my rattiest pajamas and stripped of the makeup and jewelry that Mom had insisted were compulsory for the final round of parties, *is like courting. First round is like speed dating. You rotate at the ding of a silent bell, learning more about someone from their dress and manner than from any rote list of banal questions. (What's your major, for example.)*

The second round is the movie date. Can you agree on explosions vs. romance? Maybe a thriller for compromise. How will you spend your future time together?

Third round: dinner date. Your beau puts on the Ritz, shows off a little, and you learn if he makes an annoying smacking sound when he chews.

And finally, Preference Night: meet the parents. Not a proposal just yet, but a test run. A peek into the fold.

I downed the last swig of my latte. It was stone cold, picked up on my way home from Greek Row, since I knew Cole would be waiting to slip my column into place, just in time to get Friday's edition of the *Report* to the printer. The school paper had a narrow window on the press—in between the *Sentinel* and the direct mail going out to advertise the weekend's sales.

Like my psychic education, my dating experience mostly came from the movies, too. But it wasn't hard to extrapolate. The two preference parties I'd gone to that night—the Zetas and the SAXis—had been intimate, one-on-one conversations. At each sorority a girl met me at the door and showed me around the house, including her own room. At the Zeta house, they'd found my mother's picture on the wall, and I laughed to see her hair teased up like a brunette Madonna, circa "Material Girl."

Kirby had met me at the SAXi house. I'd been hoping it would be Devon. Maybe I should have been flattered that the president escorted me room to room, but there was a probing intensity to her that put me on edge, and made me think about raising my deflector shields. She was full of questions. What were my ambitions, my goals? I wasn't sad when she pawned me off on a pre-med student named Alexa, and went to circulate among the tiny number of girls that were there.

It wasn't too late to back out, to renege on my word to

Holly. She didn't need me, and I wasn't going to change the world with my little commentary. The elite had always ruled and always would.

If I did bow out, my last article could be about taking the high ground, turning my back on the shallow inanity of sororities. But tonight, I was finishing this article for Tricia.

And Rush can break your heart, just like dating. You can pin your hopes on a guy, change yourself for him, pretend to be something you're not, and if he doesn't love you back, you think it's the end of the world.

How much better would it be if women stopped judging their self-worth by somebody else's arbitrary standards. My mother always said, if he's worthy of you, he'll take you as is. This campus is full of organizations where the power of membership lies with the joiner.

And the world is full of guys who don't read Greek.

I saved what I'd written and checked my watch. Just enough time to print it out and try to catch the most egregious typos. Unfolding myself from the bed, I carried the laptop to my desk and plugged it into the printer. Then I proofread, fiddled with the hook at the end, sent it to Cole via our supersecret system, and finally fell into bed.

✳ ✳ ✳

"Maggie!"

Dad's voice dragged me from the well of slumber. The dregs of a dream had come up with me, twisting my thoughts into dizzying patterns. I had to climb the shreds of reason and try to make sense of my room, which seemed fractured and reassembled in parts, like a cubist painting.

"Maggie! I know you have class this morning."

Downstairs. Dad was shouting up at me. I oriented on the familiar sound—it was far from the first time I'd been shouted awake—and the room came into familiar focus.

Unfortunately, the first thing I saw with any clarity was the clock on my bedside table.

"Crap." I rolled out of bed and went to the stairs to yell, "I'm up! I'm up!" Immediately I regretted it, and squeezed my pounding head between my hands.

Okay. Not a normal nightmare, then. I get these sometimes. Psychic hangovers, the aftermath of one of my real dreams, as opposed to the random firing of neurons that happens to nonfreaky people in their sleep.

Fortunately, I'd showered the night before, so I just had to find clean clothes and grab my homework and my laptop. When I woke up the screen with a tap on a key, I saw that I'd left a browser window open when I went to sleep. In it was the pop-up ad from the other night, the one with the strange, hypnotic pattern.

Without moving the cursor, I hit Control-P to print the screen. The window closed—and the browser crashed—as soon as I moved the cursor, but this time, I'd captured a hard copy. A spark of recognition gave me an idea. Wherever else I had seen that pattern, its most recent appearance had been on the back of my eyelids. And that, if anything, rated investigation.

✳ ✳ ✳

Dad handed me my travel mug of coffee when I reached the bottom of the stairs. "This isn't going to be a pattern, is it?"

"What?" I was still thinking about the pattern in my dream, which had somehow transferred into the waking world. Or vice versa.

He was in no mood for a sidebar. "If this sorority thing is going to interfere with your grades . . ."

Mom answered for me. "It won't." She was dressed for work, but she still looked green beneath her carefully applied makeup. The doctor had assured her that as she was out of her first trimester, the puking would stop any day now. He'd been saying that for two months.

"You won't let it get the best of you, will you, Magpie?" She kissed my cheek, her breath smelling of mint toothpaste and ginger ale. "I'm so proud of you. And if you want to continue in a sorority . . ."

"Really, Mom," I assured them both, "I'm not setting out to become a Stepford Greek. I have my reasons."

This earned me two sighs—one of dismay, and one of relief. "Oh, Maggie," said my mother. "Can't you, just once, do things like a normal girl?"

"Of course not, Laura." Dad grinned, his humor restored. "She's a Quinn."

I headed for the door, mug in hand. "Sorry, Mom. We can't all choose a destiny in accounting."

"You could choose a destiny outside of *The Twilight Zone,*" I heard her grumble as I hurried on my way.

* * *

Since I have biology lab only on Tuesdays, I used the open space in my schedule to visit Dr. Smyth in the chemistry department.

The earth science building was bustling, and redolent of an experiment gone wrong. Or so I assumed. Chemistry could be stinky, even when it goes right.

I tapped on the door to the professor's office, which was just off the lab. Because of the ventilation fans, the smell of burning tires was less pungent than in the hall. I loved the anachronism of the computers and modern equipment in the hundred-year-old space. It reminded me of *A Wrinkle in Time,* and how Dr. Murry had her electron microscope set up in the stillroom of their farmhouse.

"Dr. Smyth?" She looked up from her work, a frown of displacement on her face as she reoriented herself. "I'm Maggie Quinn. You helped me out with a chemistry question last spring."

"Oh yes!" Recognition swept away her confusion, and she waved me to a chair by her desk. "You were working on some kind of fantasy story the last time we talked. How did that turn out?"

I perched on the seat and set my satchel beside me. "Better than I thought it would." In that I was still alive.

"Why aren't you taking chemistry with me?" she chided.

"All the sections were closed. I'm in biology instead."

With an impatient wave, she dismissed the principles of our biological existence. "You should have called me. I would have opened one of the sections for you."

"I still have another science credit to earn. I'll be sure and take it with you." I wouldn't dare do anything different. Dr. Smyth was a force of nature, with flaming red hair and a vibrant personality to match. "I have another question for you."

"Excellent." She leaned her elbows on the desk. "What can I do for you?"

I pulled out the printout of the browser window. "This seems familiar to me. Maybe some kind of crystal-line structure?"

She took the picture and immediately identified it. "This is a fractal design."

"A fractal! I couldn't place it." My moment of clarity was short. "But that's math, not chemistry."

"Well, it's both," she said. "You can create fractals by putting a solution of copper sulfate between two glass plates and applying voltage . . ."

I know my eyes must have glazed over. "And in non-geek?"

She started again. "Basically—and I'm really oversimplifying here—a fractal is a system of illustrating things that cannot be described with normal geometry. Tree branches and snowflakes and the stock market. Things that seem random, but if looked at in a mathematical way, aren't really."

"Like chaos theory."

"Right."

All I knew about chaos theory came from watching *Jurassic Park,* but I didn't mention that.

Dr. Smyth laid her hand on the printout. "Most people see fractals in computer graphics. Pretty pictures made out of irrational numbers."

"Irrational numbers," I echoed. "Like pi."

"And phi." She was into it now, like a kid showing off a favorite toy. "Phi—1.618—called the Golden Mean or sometimes the Divine Proportion. Grossly oversimplified, it means that the sum of a plus b is to a as a is to b."

"Um. I left my math brain in calculus. Can you translate?"

"All that's important is the proportion." She drew two equal squares touching, and then on top of it drew one rectangle that was equal in size to the two squares. Then she drew another rectangle that was equal in size to the first three put together. Then another, et cetera, until she had a diagram that looked like a stack of blocks.

"These rectangles are all in the 'divine' proportion," she said. "The Parthenon and the Great Pyramid at Giza were both built incorporating this ratio. It's been shown to be universally pleasing to the eye."

"Okay." I took her word for it, not least because it resonated in my memory.

"But watch this." She drew a curved line connecting all the corners of the progressively larger rectangles, until she had a spiral that looked familiar.

"That's a nautilus shell."

"And a cochlea." She tapped her ear, and I remembered that little shell thingy responsible for hearing from high school biology. "And even . . ." She drew a parallel spiral and connected the two with hastily drawn lines, like a ladder.

"DNA?"

"Subtly, but yes." She turned the paper back over and tapped the design from the computer. "Fractals. A pattern that repeats with self-symmetry to an infinitely small, or infinitely large scale."

I stared at her, a little helplessly. "You realize I have no idea what this means."

Dr. Smyth sat back in her chair. "It means that if you look at things from a certain perspective—in this case mathematically—there is nothing truly random in the universe."

"You couldn't have just said that?"

She grinned and handed me the paper. "What kind of educator would I be?"

I thanked her, promised she'd see me, eventually, for a class, and left. I wasn't sure I had any answers, but I definitely had more questions.

The first was why had this design popped up, twice, on my Internet browser.

And theoretically, if seemingly random events were mathematically not really random, then didn't it follow that if you changed the math of things, you could change the outcome?

I suddenly had a new appreciation for arithmetic. I guess I was going to have to start paying attention in calculus.

10

The campus of Bedivere U. is tree-shaded and quaint, full of redbrick colonial revival buildings on an unregimented layout. The buildings went up gradually over the last century, wherever was convenient or empty. It lent the campus a lot of charm, but made learning your way around, especially when you had back-to-back classes on opposite sides of the campus, a little challenging.

I'd grown up here, more or less. The two places I could find with my eyes closed were the library and Webster Hall, which housed the history department and archives. My father's office was on the third floor, and I headed there after my chat with Dr. Smyth. Dad was out of the office, and that suited me fine. I didn't need him, just a little privacy.

I cleared a space on his desk, made myself at home, and took out my laptop. It was new, acquired this summer after my old computer had gone up in a hail of brimstone. But what the heck. I needed one for college anyway.

Going into the application folder, I clicked on the SpyZilla icon. No red flags had popped up since I first saw that fractal screen, but that only meant that the software didn't find any cooties it recognized.

So I ran a manual search and found, without much effort, a suspicious script that the program didn't know how to identify. It wasn't known spyware or adware. It was just . . . spookyware.

Destroy unknown script? I clicked. "Hell yes."

"Dr. Quinn, did you see this—" Justin entered with a token knock on the open door, then drew up short when he saw me behind the desk. "Oh. Hey, Maggie."

"Hey." We stayed frozen for an awkward tick of the clock. I was trying to remind myself we were just friends. Whatever he was thinking, his brows were drawn into something approaching a scowl. I looked at what he had in his hands. "Something interesting in the paper?"

He held up the page with the Phantom Rushee article. "You're not really going through with this, are you?"

I glared, gesturing to the traffic in the hall. "I don't know what you're talking about."

"Oh, come on."

Closing my laptop—after making sure SpyZilla was done de-fractalfying my hard drive—I stood. "I'm working on something."

"In a sorority." Not a question. Just incredulous.

"Don't think I can pull it off?" I asked, slinging my satchel over my shoulder.

"I know you can. That's what worries me." He tapped the page. "It says right here: 'Resistance is futile.' These things—historically, sociologically—they suck people in."

"It's a sorority, not a cult, Justin. I'll be fine."

I swung out the door, already regretting the words. When would I learn not to tempt fate?

* * *

Bid Day. The drama and angst of the whole week came down to this: The sororities submitted their choices—the list of girls to whom they would extend a bid. Meanwhile, the rushees listed their top three houses, in order of preference. There was a certain strategy in what you listed. You didn't have to list three, and some had only one pick, preferring to try again as sophomores rather than take a second choice. Others made sure they had at least one house on their list that they were assured of getting into. EZ, for example.

Then we all assembled in the Student Center ballroom to learn if we'd "matched." The doors were closed and no one was allowed in or out until we'd all received our envelopes.

Holly and I stayed together in line—Quinn and Russell are reasonably close alphabetically—an island of dispassion in a sea of drama. There were many tears—of disappointment, joy, or simple relief. Mostly there was hugging and squealing. Lots and lots of squealing. It bounced from the wainscoted walls and the parquet floor. The chandelier tinkled an echo. But the noise was nothing compared to the way the stratospheric emotion was scouring every psychic nerve in my body to a bloody, raw thread.

No story was worth a whole semester of this.

I had to do something; it figured it was desperation that made me put Gran's imagery book to practical use. Closing my eyes, I pictured deflector shields, like on the *Millennium Falcon*. I visualized the laser beams of angst bouncing off my defenses, ricocheting harmlessly back into the throng.

Holy cow. It actually worked. The muscles of my shoulders began to unclench and the knot in my stomach . . .

"Maggie! Holly!" Tricia threw herself at me, wrapping an arm around my neck and drawing Holly into the embrace. "It worked!"

"That's great, Trish!" Holly hugged her back.

Something had worked, until I'd completely lost concentration. The noise and emotion surged past my fallen defenses.

"Beta Pi totally wants me!" Holly had talked her into putting down her next highest choices after the Deltas. The Betas were brunette and bubbly, so we'd figured she'd be a fit.

Tricia bounced off to find other Betas; Holly bent down to frown critically at my face. "Are you feeling all right?"

Clearly, I looked as bad as I felt. "It's really hot in here." Someone squealed nearby and my eye twitched in reaction.

"We're almost done." This was relative. There was still a lot of alphabet in line behind us. Darn those *S*s. The tradition was to release the rushees—now called pledges—all at once out into the quad, where our new sisterhood waited to greet us and escort us back to Greek Row.

I reached the front of the line; at least once I got my bid— I'd put down SAXi first, as I promised Holly, and the Zetas second, because I was assured of an invite, since I was a legacy—the matter would be settled, and I could find a seat in one of the chairs that ringed the room and observe from a small distance.

"Quinn," I told the Rho Gamma behind the table full of stationery boxes. "Maggie."

"Here you are." She held out a cream-colored envelope with a smile. "Good luck."

If I'd been thinking clearly, maybe I would have expected it. But my brain thrummed in my skull, as if I'd had about fifty espresso shots. As soon as my fingers closed on the invitation, a gray-white light blossomed on my retinas, like when you press on your closed eyelids and make a ghostly impression in the black. Only the brightness kept streaming in on my optic nerve, carrying impressions and images too rapid and bewildering to interpret, a moiré pattern splitting and repeating; infinite variety of waking dreams, pushed into my brain like water through a fire hose.

Consciousness tripped like a fuse, and everything went black.

* * *

I woke up on the floor, with Jenna patting my hand and Holly leaning over me anxiously. "What happened?"

"You fainted," Holly said as I struggled to sit up.

Surely not. How . . . girly. "Really?"

"Don't worry about it," the Rho Gamma said, correctly interpreting my reddening face. "Too much emotion, girls forget to eat. Happens all the time."

"I never forget to eat." They helped me to my feet; my thighs trembled, but it was better than lying there with the Ss stepping over me to get their bids.

As if anyone would notice one more Drama Girl.

They walked with me to the chairs by the wall, and as I sat, Jenna turned to Holly. "There's some bottled water in the coolers behind the tables. Would you grab one for Maggie?"

"Really, I'm fine—" But Holly was already headed over to where the other Rho Gammas were handing out the bids.

Jenna sat beside me and put a comforting hand on my shoulder. "I know it's overwhelming."

I sunk my head into my hands, rubbing my pounding temples. "Tell me about it."

I didn't expect her to take me literally. "We Sigmas have a hard time in the middle of all this excitement, though some of us are more sensitive than others."

Her face conveyed nothing, and everything. She might have just been talking about a mundane sensitivity to emotional stress. But she met my gaze evenly, significantly. "I could tell you're one of the more sensitive ones."

"So . . ." I formed my next question carefully. "I'm not the only one?"

Jenna smiled, as if my ready acceptance pleased her. "Well, no one has ever fainted before."

"Oh." I had to wrap my head around that. Of all the things I thought I might hear today, that hadn't been it.

She laid her hand on my knee, pressing lightly to weight her words. "I think you're used to keeping your specialness a secret, Maggie, so I don't have to tell you that we Sigmas don't talk about this outside the house. You probably shouldn't talk about it much with your pledge class. Most of them have no idea of the latent potential inside them."

"I don't understand." I felt the way I had when Dr. Smyth explained fractal theory, as though there was some basic, fundamental thing here that my mental fingertips could brush, but not quite grasp.

"You don't need to understand it right now. That's what pledge class is for. To get you ready for initiation, when everything will be clear."

Holly returned and handed me a bottle, still dripping icy water from the cooler. I pressed it to the back of my neck, hoping the chill would shock my brain into motion. It also gave me an excuse to duck my head and let Holly and Jenna talk while I tried to align my scattered thoughts.

All this week, I'd taken secret pride in being what the sorority girls termed "Not One of Us." Now I had found out that actually, I *was* one of them. Or they were a lot of me. Or . . . something.

I sat with my head resting in one hand, shielding my face. A cold prickle of worry spread through me, and I didn't think it was just the icy water bottle, or the cracking of my illusion that I was special or unique.

The bid envelope lay in my lap. Opening it was a formality now, but I did it anyway:

SIGMA ALPHA XI
INVITES
MAGDALENA LORRAINE QUINN
TO JOIN OUR SACRED SISTERHOOD.

In the words of Han Solo, right before the *Millennium Falcon* got sucked into the Death Star: I had a *bad* feeling about this.

II

I stood in the foyer of the Sigma Alpha Xi house with seven other girls. Other houses had thirty or forty new members—pledges, in the Greek vernacular. We had eight. No wonder SAXis had a reputation for being in a class of their own.

By their nature, the members of a house run together. They chose for type, and Sigma Alpha Xi did, too, if Jenna was to be believed—and I had no reason not to. Their criteria was definitely not physical similarity. At one end was lanky Holly, with her hair the color of autumn mums. At the other was me: short, too curvy on the bottom and not curvy enough on the top, with disobedient short dark hair. The other girls fell in the middle and had yet to differentiate themselves.

We, the pledge class, waited as a collective. Nervous, giggling, or silent, according to nature. The gigglers were Ashley, Kaylee, and Nikki. On the quiet, sober side were Holly, Alyssa, and Erica. A girl named Brittany had appointed herself pledge wrangler, and kept admonishing the gigglers to shut up and be serious.

The chapter room doors swung partially open and one of the Sigmas greeted us, wearing some kind of stole or wrap over her street clothes. We all shut up.

"Sigma Alpha Xi invites Ashley Adams to join our circle."

Ashley, a blond girl with a California tan, looked suddenly intimidated, and I wondered if she didn't have some Spidey Sense after all. She wiped her palms on her jeans, took the older girl's offered hand, and followed her into the room as another active member appeared in the doorway.

"Sigma Alpha Xi invites Kaylee Carson to join our circle." A dark-haired girl with a ballerina's build went in eagerly.

They continued alphabetically, until only Holly and I were left. Then Jenna appeared, a crimson stole hanging, Roman senator–fashion, over her elbows. "Sigma Alpha Xi invites Magdalena Quinn to join our circle."

My full name was on my school records, though I'd made it clear I preferred Maggie. We were too careless with names in modern culture, and I wasn't just talking about identity theft. Names have power, and calling things by their proper names can evoke it, or diminish it. Why else don't we call private body parts by their anatomical terms?

I followed Jenna into the chapter room, which had been transformed once again. The lights were dim; the air was cool, almost clammy on my bare arms. The rug had been rolled back, and inlaid on the hardwood floor was a spiral, like a nautilus shell or a galaxy.

Nothing in the universe is truly random.

Jenna led me inward along the loop, and I joined the ring of pledges in the center. Holly completed our group, and the doors closed.

At the north end of the room stood Victoria Abbott. Was it normal for an alumnae adviser to always be around? Something about her presence struck a wrong note with me.

In front of her was a cloth-covered table with several items on it: an oil lamp—think Aladdin and the genie—and an enormous book. Gutenberg Bible enormous, and possibly that old. A spiral of fragrant smoke rose from a small silver bowl—incense, exotic and spicy, making my head feel stuffy and strange.

Victoria spoke, in a soft but carrying voice. "We move through life in a series of patterns: family, friends, school classes and clubs."

One Sigma handed each pledge an unlit white candle as the alumna continued. "Today you will form the first of the new patterns in your life in Sigma Alpha Xi: your pledge class, a circle of sisterhood.

"Later you'll make new patterns as you get a big sister, find roommates, take offices. All of these will mean new roles, new positions in the design."

The actives moved into place along the spiral as Victoria lit a candle from the lamp. She handed it to Kirby, who stood beside her, a sober acolyte. "Like lightning, we branch out into the world, but no matter how far we get from the beginning, here is where the flame is begun."

The chapter president passed on the flame. Each girl in turn touched tapers with those next to her, and flickering lights spread inward along the spiral, toward the pledges in the center. Someone beside me sniffled, and I fought the urge to squirm at the seriousness of it all.

Then the flames reached us, and we passed them among our candles. The circle closed like a circuit, and I felt a rush of electricity along my skin. It flowed—a tangible energy potential—outward along the spiral, humming like a magnetic field in the room.

Whoa.

Eight of the girls handed off their candles and moved toward the center, making eddies and currents in the energy field, like turbulence in water. Jenna stopped in front of me with a small smile of encouragement.

"Our pledge emblem is the North Star," said Victoria. "The guide of adventurers and explorers."

Jenna held up a small, lacquered gold pin, like a tiny brooch. "This is mine," she whispered, opening the clasp. "And my big sister's, and her big sister's. So I hope you keep better track of it than you did your name tag."

She held the point to the flame of my candle, only for a few seconds. Around the circle, others did the same. Jenna reached for my hand and, stupid me, I thought she was going to place the pin in my palm. Instead she pricked my finger, and I hissed in pain and some alarm. A tingle raced up my arm, settled at the base of my skull, then dissipated.

A small drop of blood glimmered garnet on the sharp tip. After Jenna carefully fastened it on my shirt, I reached up and touched the warm gold. Images, quick and fast: Jenna, on the Panhellenic Council; a woman in her early twenties, rising star of real estate in Houston; an assistant DA in Chicago, on the board of governors of the school. All of them had worn this pin.

No fuzziness followed the vision this time. As quickly as the images came, I was able to mentally catch them, instead of feeling assaulted by each. The song the Sigmas had been singing—I hadn't heard them start—ended, hanging resonant in the room, like a chant in a cathedral.

Into the charged air, Victoria spoke. "The compass marks the path to our destination."

From directly opposite her, Kirby said, "The flame is knowledge and power shared."

A quarter of the way around the circle from the president, Jenna spoke. "Indigo for depth of feeling and depth of passion."

And across from her, Devon, the girl from the second night of Rush. "Crimson for blood, for inspiration, and creation of things special and rare."

And one ring to rule them all.

It occurred to me that I might be in *way* over my head.

12

The SAXis' powder room, like everything else in the house, was decorated in dark red and blue. Excuse me—crimson and indigo. That hadn't seemed ominous during Rush, but now I was seeing patterns everywhere.

I had Justin's number dialed almost before I locked the door, and turned on the water to hide the sound of my voice. No answer. I hung up without leaving a message and paced in the tiny space, irrationally angry with him. Forget my petty, girly worries over the status of our relationship. How could he be in class when I needed him?

A pledge had to go through a learning period before being initiated as an active member of the chapter. I had never intended to go through with initiation. Even if they were only quasi-faux-sacred sorority vows, I wasn't comfortable taking them under false pretenses. Since the pledge period was sort of probationary anyway, I'd been able to justify a little finger crossing.

But I hadn't expected this. Ritual with a capital *R*. Jenna's little sensitivity bomb was nothing compared to this.

A knock on the door made me jump. "Just a minute!" I called, then splashed my flushed face and wiped the smudged mascara with my fingers before I opened the door.

Jenna stood in the hall. "Hey. There's food in the dining room. We had barbecue catered in."

"Great," I said.

She looked at me closely. "You okay? You're not freaking out because of what I said earlier?"

"No." What I needed here was not so much deflector shields as a cloaking device, because she didn't look convinced. "Okay," I admitted. "I've never met anyone else like me. I'm a little freaked."

Taking my arm, she said, "Don't think about it too much. It just connects us more closely."

We had to go through the front hall to get to the dining room. I didn't expect to see Cole Bauer standing there.

He didn't expect to see me, either, and his face went slack in surprise. Then he looked past me, and turned the expression into one of pleasure. I glanced over my shoulder and saw Devon, the art major with the flippy hair, whom I'd talked to the second night, coming down the stairs.

She looked from Cole to me to Jenna as she walked over to us. "Hi," she said, a slight strain in her voice.

"Going out?" asked Jenna.

"Yes." She looked a little nervous and slightly defiant, which might have had something to do with her next statement. "Victoria knows I'm going, now that the official stuff is done."

Jenna held up her hands. "I didn't say anything."

Devon joined her date—because it was obvious he was—and said, "Hey, Cole. This is one of our new pledges, Maggie Quinn."

"We've met, actually." I was thinking fast, covering his slip of recognition. "In the journalism lab, when Hardcastle crushed my dreams of being the first freshman staff photographer."

"Oh yeah." He nodded. "That's too bad. Are you taking photography with Goldsmith?"

"Yeah."

Devon slipped her hand through his arm. "Well, we'll see you guys. Later, Jenna."

They left, and I became aware of someone standing on the stairs, looking down at the casual little scene. "Is she still with him?" It was Kirby, coming down the steps. She didn't look happy.

"She hasn't seen him all summer," Jenna said, clearly making an excuse. Then she grabbed my arm again. "Let's go eat."

✳ ✳ ✳

They were talking about me when I reached the dining room. Well, not about Maggie Quinn, überpledge, but the Phantom Rushee, undercover reporter.

One of the actives said, "Is it wrong that I thought she was kind of funny? She did have the chapters all pegged. The EZs and the Theta Moos." I choked on my Coke at that.

"And what were we supposed to be? Some kind of fembots with shiny hair?"

"That would have to be the Kappa Phis," said another.

Nikki, one of the pledges, asked, "Is it true they make all their members get boob jobs if they're not a C-cup?"

Another pledge, Brittany, directed a loud question to President Kirby and Jenna, the ex-RG. "So *nobody* knows who she is? Not Panhellenic, or the Rho Gammas or *anyone*?"

"Not a clue." Jenna munched on a chip. "But I think the Delta Delta Gammas have a hit out on her."

"Couldn't Devon make Cole tell her?" asked Melissa (I think). I was already regretting the absence of name tags.

"She wouldn't." All the actives looked at the speaker, in a beat filled with surprise, and a tension I didn't understand. The girl lifted her hands in a shrug. "That's what her big sis told me."

The curious eyes turned to Kirby, but her attention was on her plate. I knew I was missing something significant, and wondered if it was as simple as disapproval of Devon's relationship—her choosing a boy over her sisters—or something else.

* * *

By the time I pulled into my driveway it was late, and I felt as if someone had stirred my brain with a spoon. The stairs to my room seemed steeper than usual; I practically had to drag myself up by the banister.

The upstairs loft is arranged so that the stairway opens into the sitting/study area, and a pair of French doors close off my bedroom. Hanging on the left side was what, in the dark, looked like a Christmas wreath.

September had flown by fast, but this was ridiculous.

I flipped on the light; the wreath was made of crimson and blue fabric, thickly braided. Stuck on, quite artistically, were several ornaments: a lamp, a star, a compass, and what looked like an octopus. Oh yes, and the letters ΣΑΞ.

On the right side was a whiteboard framed in SAXi colors, also with the letters, with a dry-erase marker hanging from a string. Someone had written a note: "Maggie—Welcome to the Sigmas! This door decoration is to help you study for your pledge exam! You'll learn what all of these things mean soon. ΣΑΞ ♥ U!"

Underneath was another note, in handwriting I knew. "Congrats, Magpie! Your new friends seem so nice! Love, Mom." Thankfully, she wrote out love instead of drawing a little heart.

I wondered if I would feel less creeped out if this were hanging on a dorm-room door rather than actually inside my home. It seemed like something I maybe should be worried about under the circumstances, but I was so tired. I parked the thought in a corner of my brain to examine in the morning.

Stripping off my clothes, I fell into bed, relieved that the next day was the weekend, and I didn't have to speak Greek again until Monday.

✳ ✳ ✳

I woke late, even for a Saturday. My head felt furry on the inside, and the sunlight that streamed through the sheer curtains hammered against my eyes. All the signs of a psychic hangover.

With a groan, I sat on the edge of my bed and rubbed my hands through my hair. I hadn't dreamed, so it must have been the residual from yesterday's drama queen rally. A lot had happened, so much that my brain felt full, unable to process it all. I had pledged a sorority last night, yet there were no accompanying signs of imminent apocalypse.

I padded downstairs in an ancient Bedivere T-shirt, sweatpants, and socks. The living room was deserted, but Dad sat at the kitchen table with his laptop, papers spread around him.

"Good morning, sleepyhead."

With a grunt of reply, I headed to the coffee, which was tepid in the pot. Desperate, I filled a mug and put it in the microwave.

"How did it go last night?" he asked.

"Okay." I stood with my hand on the microwave and thought about that. The details were fuzzy, as if I was viewing them through a dirty window. Interesting. High emotion could make an unreliable witness. But I wondered if there was some kind of protection inherent in the pledging ceremony.

Or maybe I just needed caffeine. The microwave beeped and I took out the mug, stirred in sugar and a lot of milk. "I found out my editor is dating one of the sisters. I wonder if he'll still want me to continue the articles."

Dad rose to get some orange juice out of the fridge. "I wouldn't be sorry if he didn't. You might get home before midnight once in a while."

"It'll be better now that Rush is over."

"Hardly. Now it will be meetings and parties. . . ."

"God, what a chore. How I suffer."

Glass in hand, he looked at me in that knowing way

parents have. "So, how long are you going to keep up this Phantom Rushee business?"

"Cole and I agreed on an article a week up until initiation. Then I'm out."

"Not going to write your name in blood, huh?"

"Uh, no." Not when it might be literal. I rubbed my punctured finger and thought about symbolism. Blood brothers, candle-lighting, colors and ciphers. "Hey, Dad. Put on your historian hat for a sec. What's the evolution of fraternities and sororities? Despite all the Greek letters and stuff, they don't have roots that far back, do they?"

He considered the question, rubbing the Saturday stubble on his jaw. "Well, secret societies do. Think about the Templars, the Masons. But the first fraternity was Phi Beta Kappa in 1776, and it was more of a literary organization. Social fraternities didn't come along until the nineteenth century."

"The way they carry on about ritual and tradition, you'd think they'd been around since the dawn of time."

"They took Greek letters as their names to give that air of tradition and ritual. It's human nature. Being in on a secret makes a group feel superior to the ignorant masses."

That made sense; there was certainly no lack of superiority complexes on Greek Row. "But you don't think it really makes a difference in future success, do you?"

"Networking is a powerful tool." He shrugged. "All other things being equal, it could be an advantage later on."

"But does any one chapter strike you as more successful? At least on our campus?"

He shook his head. "I'm afraid I've never given much

thought to the Greeks on campus, unless a student's grades slip. Even then, the individual house doesn't mean much to me."

"Okay. What do you know about Congressman Abbott?"

"Just what I read in the papers." He looked at me curiously. "What does he have to do with the Sigma Alpha Xis?"

"Well, his wife is one. She's the chapter adviser."

What *could* it have to do with the SAXis? Probably nothing. But it was a place to start, when I didn't have much to go on.

It was time for a little old-fashioned, completely mundane detective work. Mumbling an excuse to my father, I rose and headed for the stairs.

"You forgot your coffee," he called.

The stale smell of nuked coffee was too much, even for me. "I'll get some on the way to the paper."

"Maggie?" I turned at the concerned note in his voice. "What are you up to?"

"Just getting my Nancy Drew on, Dad."

He met my innocent look with one of narrow-eyed doubt. "There isn't any . . ." He glanced to check that Mom wasn't in the living room. ". . . you know. Any weird stuff going on, is there?"

"Don't tell Mom," I whispered. "But all Greek stuff is weird to me."

He let out a pent-up breath. "I can't tell you how relieved I am to hear that."

I hated to lie to my dad, even by omission. But really. There just wasn't a way to introduce the subject of sorcerous sororities without getting into a much more involved discussion than I could handle before lunchtime.

Upstairs I found a message from Justin on my voicemail. "Hi, Maggie. Saw that you called last night. The reception in the old library is awful. Since you didn't leave a message, I figured you were okay. Call me if you want."

Of course I wanted. Didn't I make that clear?

But *should* I? In the security of my room, I felt a little silly for freaking out yesterday. And I knew I shouldn't always rely on Justin. The fact that I wanted to run to him, to play the damsel-in-distress card and get his attention, made me that much more determined to do this without him.

Resolved, I deleted the message.

13

A couple of decades ago, the town had passed a bond to restore downtown Avalon to its original redbrick streets and Victorian faux-gaslight glory. The courthouse was in the center of the town square; the surrounding blocks were dotted with long-standing businesses, like the *Sentinel*, interspersed with new stores, mostly antique and quilt shops. Froth and Java was on the corner, and I left the Jeep parked in the lot there rather than trying to find street parking.

Latte in hand, right on the threshold of the newspaper office, I suddenly remembered what else was on Main Street: the offices of Congressman Peter Abbott.

The skin on the back of my neck tingled, like a cold wind had blown across my nape, and I knew I'd been spotted. Frozen with my hand on the door, I raised my deflector shields, but of course they did nothing against a perfectly good pair of eyes and the ability to put two and two together.

"Maggie Quinn, isn't it?" Victoria Abbott's voice came as no surprise, but I flinched anyway.

Caught. How *stupid* could I be?

I turned, brushed my hair from my face. The buildings made a wind tunnel and turned the mild day brisk in their shade. "Hello, Mrs. Abbott."

She was dressed casually today, like a Ralph Lauren ad instead of a *Vogue* spread. If not for the dread curdling the cream in my coffee, I would have really coveted the leather bag she had slung over her shoulder. Her eyes looked me up and down, canted over to the words *Avalon Sentinel* on the office window, and came back to my face.

"Perhaps we should talk."

"Um. Sure." Perhaps I wouldn't just die on the spot. Victoria Abbott was intimidating on a mundane level—even without the memories of last night's ritual flooding back to me when I saw her. How could I have forgotten?

I expected her to lead me back to the congressman's office, but maybe she didn't want my body discovered there. Instead, she headed toward Froth and Java; gesturing to an outside table, she asked, "Would you like a refill?"

"No." I remembered my manners. "No, thank you."

She sat, crossed her legs, and waited.

Cops use that technique: Keep quiet and let the suspect hang himself. There's a need to fill silence, and when you're guilty, it becomes a compulsion. I had to bite the inside of my lip to keep from blurting out . . . everything.

She was strong, but I was stubborn. I looked at the puffy clouds blowing across the sky, the Saturday antique shoppers, the clock on the courthouse—anything but Victoria.

Finally, she said, "I know what you're up to."

I powered up my psychic force field. "All I'm up to is research. I need the *Sentinel*'s archives for a school paper."

All technically truthful.

She lifted a perfectly sculpted brow. "Then you're not the Phantom?"

I started to speak, but no sound came out. No lie, no truth. Nothing. Victoria leaned forward and said under the cover of traffic noise, "There's no point in lying. I'm good at seeing through things. Just like you, I think."

She held my gaze, watching while I considered and rejected excuses and lies, one after another. Finally, I decided to be direct. "Are you going to kick me out?"

She rolled her eyes, and the atmosphere became almost normal. "You really think I care about a pissant school paper?"

Well . . . *I* cared.

"I see great things for you, Maggie Quinn." She tapped the table with manicured fingernails. "But let's establish some ground rules. The Phantom can mock the Greek system as she pleases. The hypocrisy, pretension . . . I don't care."

That not only sounded as though she wasn't going to kick me out; maybe she wouldn't turn me into a frog, either.

"But not one word," Queen Victoria continued, "about

specific Sigma members, business, or rituals. Everything that happens in that house is off the record."

Relief turned to suspicion. "But . . . why?"

"You are a Sigma, and Sigmas excel in their careers. This is the start of yours, so why should I hold you back?"

"I . . ." Words failed me.

She set her folded arms on the table. "I don't believe in coincidence. However you came to join us, I think you're meant to be a Sigma."

"Look, it's not that I don't appreciate the second chance. But I'm not—"

"Maggie, don't be coy." She gave me a cut-the-crap stare. "Jenna told me she talked to you about the special qualities we seek in Sigmas. I need you to be a leader."

"But I'm not." The argument was pointless, but I made it anyway. I wasn't a follower, either.

Victoria's mouth turned up in an enigmatic smile. "You have ability and ambition. You could go far, Maggie, if you open yourself to the possibilities that Sigma can offer. I can put in a word for you at a real paper. A big newspaper."

Moments like this rock my world, shake my faith in my own freakitude. Was that all there was to the SAXi success ratio? Was it really just networking?

While I sat reeling, she gathered her bag from the back of her chair. "I'll let you think about it. If you come to your pledge meeting on Monday, I'll know we have an understanding."

"That might be awkward," I said. "The other houses—heck, the other Sigmas—want my guts for garters."

Rising, she smoothed any wrinkles from her khaki

trousers. "Kirby and the other officers do not know you're the Phantom, and we'll keep it that way. Our little secret."

She laid her hand on my shoulder. I'd been visualizing my psychic force field the whole time—which was one reason I hadn't managed many multisyllable answers. I *so* did not want to see into this woman's psyche, almost as much as I didn't want her to see into mine.

I got nothing but an impression of locked and barred doors. Of course. *Her* deflector shields.

She left, and I sat on the café patio for a long moment, getting my mental feet back under me after being knocked on my metaphorical ass. Victoria had a lot of confidence, not only that I'd stay with the Sigmas, but also that I wouldn't report this whole conversation.

Like anyone would believe me.

✳ ✳ ✳

The city newspaper offices were technically closed, but of course there were people working. Fact-checking had been one of my intern duties, so I knew my way to the archives. They called it the tomb—a basement room, musty and dimly lit. You didn't need a lot of light to stare into the microfiche reader.

What, specifically, I was looking for, I had no idea, but the conversation with Mrs. Congressman Abbott had given me a starting point, out of perversity if nothing else.

I started with Peter Abbott's official bio. His first office had been that of president of Gamma Phi Epsilon, here at Bedivere. He'd left for law school, but returned to Avalon to practice. Went to Congress by special appointment when the seat opened by the death of its occupant. Two years later, he won it in his own right. The guy had been flagged as a wunderkind who spoke eloquently to promote his innovative ideas.

Victoria had a marketing degree, and ran Abbott's campaign. Funny career choice, being a politician's wife, after what she'd told me about Sigmas excelling in their fields.

I'd been there awhile—judging by the crick in my neck—when a tap at the door heralded Ethan Douglas, editor-in-chief of the *Sentinel*.

"Heard there was a phantom in the basement." He grinned as he leaned against the doorframe.

"Hardy-har-har."

"Working on something new?" He nodded to the microfiche.

I turned the chair to face him, stretching my arms over my head to de-kink my back. Forties office furniture wasn't exactly ergonomic. "I'm sort of following a thread. Still on this Greek thing." Clearly he'd guessed my Secret Squirrel project. "How about you? Were you in a fraternity?"

"Yeah. Pi Kappa Iota back at Plains State University."

"Do you think it made a difference in your career?"

His freckled, boyish face twisted ruefully. "You mean, did it help me get the job as editor-in-chief of a small-town newspaper a hundred miles from any major metropolis?"

"Er . . ." I would never win awards for my tact.

He let me off the hook. "Don't go cross-eyed at that machine. What are you looking for that you can't find in the online archives?"

"Old stuff." I didn't want to go into why I was avoiding the Internet. Fractal spyware was a little hard to explain.

He turned to go, then paused, catching a hand on the doorframe. "Hey, Maggie. Your Phantom column is good stuff. Not news, but good. Can I call you if I need something covered at the university?"

I blinked, since I'd figured that ship had sailed. "Sure. Of course."

"Great." Flashing a grin, he took off, leaving me in the tomb all alone.

Okay, I had to wonder if Victoria had been busy. But, no offense to Ethan, she'd said a *big* paper.

I rewound the film and went to put it back in its box. Then I flipped through the index, free-associating a bit, the way I do when I want my logical brain to stop trying to out-shout my subconscious. Bedivere University. My fingers trailed through the subheadings until I saw Fraternities and Sororities. I found the oldest dated articles and pulled the film.

The Greeks came to BU in the 1940s, about fifty years after the university was founded. Despite some opposition, the first three fraternities and two sororities formed chapters without incident. They moved into houses at the north end of campus, converted to living spaces for the boys and girls.

Sigma Alpha Xi showed up in the fifties, followed shortly by their "brother" fraternity, Gamma Phi Epsilon. Their arrival firmly established the current Greek Row, and a line drawing from a 1957 article showed the area, labeling each house.

I printed the page and carried it to a desk lamp. Greek Row was actually two streets which dead-ended in the park that bordered campus. Some ground had been lost to parking lots, but essentially the layout was unchanged. It had a certain proportion that resonated. Grabbing a pencil, I traced a curved line through the houses—sorority and fraternity both.

What I had on the page when I was done bore an undeniable similarity to the phi diagram that Dr. Smyth had drawn, the same logarithmic spiral inlaid in the floor of the Sigma Alpha Xi house—which lay directly in the center of the coil, like a spider sitting in the middle of her web.

14

Professor Hardcastle had the personality of a piece of dry Wonder Bread—capable of holding the contents of an information sandwich, but completely without flavor or texture. Media and Communication was an entry-level class, so it wasn't a very interesting sandwich on any level. On a Monday morning, it was hell.

At the end of the hour, I roused myself from my stupor and gathered my books. Hardcastle stopped me as I walked down the steps of the lecture hall. "Miss Quinn."

I stopped, warily. "Yes, sir?" There were enough Greeks in the class to make me nervous at being singled out.

"Were you serious about working on the newspaper?"

"Yes, sir." Honestly. Was I serious about breathing?

"Bauer needs some help with layout, and I thought about you, since you seemed so fired up to work."

"Sure." I contained my glee, which of course had *nothing* to do with Hardcastle having to eat his "No freshmen" words. "When should I come in?"

"Bauer asked me to send you to the journalism lab now, unless you've got another class."

"Not for a couple hours. I'll go on down."

I assumed that this was a ruse because Cole wanted to discuss something. I'd written the week's Phantom Pledge column over the weekend, covering the trauma of Bid Day, and I'd justified leaving out all details of the Sigmas' ritual in several ways. One: the most interesting thing, i.e., the hoodoo I'd felt, was so unbelievable that I was beginning to doubt it myself. Two: most of the stuff—candles, recitation, circles—was common to at least one other house. I knew this because I called Tricia, who, per usual, was happy to tell me anything that went through her head.

And three: I kind of liked being the Phantom Pledge. And I really liked having a weekly column in the pissant school paper.

I followed my nose—ink and toner and film developer— to the journalism lab, a large room where rows of computers lined one wall and filled the middle desks. Several of them were occupied, but I didn't see Cole, so I wandered to a big whiteboard showing the progress of the current issue. There was a Linotype machine, too, one of the old ones that used heated lead to print type on long rolls, which were then cut and pasted onto the layout. How medieval.

"Maggie?" I turned to see Cole Bauer in a second doorway. He looked like five miles of bad road—worn and rough.

"Hi, Cole." I peered closer. I didn't think it was just the fluorescent lights. "Are you feeling all right?"

"Great. I'm feeling great." I had to admit that, despite his haggard appearance, he seemed very . . . bright, somehow, like a headlamp set on high beam. My eyes and my Sight were getting two different messages.

"You wanted to see me?" I asked.

He waved me over. "Come in here."

The office might have once been a closet, but it was on par with most grad student digs. He closed the door and gestured for me to take the desk chair. "I read through the clippings you gave Hardcastle with your application. Your pictures are good, too. And you've had editing experience, right?"

"Yeah. I edited the AHS paper for a semester." I had a weird feeling about this conversation; my skin prickled with unease. "But it was just a weekly, not a daily." Or almost daily, in this case. The *Ranger Report* came out Tuesday through Friday.

"Great." He laid his hand on a stack of articles beside the computer. "These all need fact-checking and copyediting. We'll start there."

"All of these?" It was a pretty big pile. "For which edition?"

"I put them in order. There are only three or so for tomorrow."

"Um. Okay." Good thing I had a long break until my afternoon classes. "Should I give them to you when I'm done?"

"The first couple. I'll be around, but I'm working on a project of my own. I appreciate your help."

"Sure." There was definitely something off about Cole today. "Are you really okay?"

Cole smiled. "I'm fine. Just . . ." He weighed his words, then shrugged. "I don't know. Maybe you'd understand. I'm writing a book."

"Oh, really." I tried to sound impressed, but honestly. I'm a communication major. Nearly everyone I'd met was writing a book.

"I've got this idea. A fully formed, like Athena from the forehead of Zeus, kind of idea." He ran his hand through his hair, which fell lankly around his thin face. "It's wonderful and terrifying both, and I just feel that if I don't write it now, quickly, the inspiration will desert me."

"Ohh-kay." His intensity was certainly terrifying—I agreed with that much. "Is that why you look like you haven't slept in days?"

"I don't want to waste writing time."

"You're not doing drugs or anything?"

He laughed in surprise. The ambush question also gave me his uncensored reaction. He was clean. In fact, he seemed to find the idea absurd. "No. I don't need drugs."

"I get it. Writing is your antidrug."

"Exactly."

I gazed at the pile of copy and sighed. "Fine. But only because you're my sorority brother-in-law."

He kissed my cheek. "I knew I liked you. I'll put you in the acknowledgments."

"Great." He left me to work on his computer. I touched my skin where his lips had brushed. No vision this time, just heat, as if he were truly burning with inspiration.

15

I don't consider myself a Faust so much as a cat—consumed by curiosity. But both meet a bad end, metaphorically, so maybe it doesn't matter, except to explain why I showed up at the Sigma Alpha Xi house for the pledge class that afternoon. I wasn't buying what Victoria Abbott had to offer; I just couldn't let the mystery lie.

The other seven pledges and I met with the active designated to teach us what we needed to know, congregating in the TV room of the SAXi house. Besides Holly and myself, there were Brittany, Ashley, Nikki, Kaylee, Alyssa, and Erica.

Tara, the pledge trainer, had a pleasantly curvy figure

and long, honey-colored hair that she wore parted in the middle, hippie-style. She handed us each a thick booklet. "These are your Sigma Alpha Xi handbooks. You will have to learn everything in here for the test, but don't worry. We'll help you."

I flipped through the pages. There were sections on the meaning of the colors, the symbols, the mascot. No chapter, however, on "How to Win Friends and Influence Fate."

"First we'll go over the rules," said Tara, settling into an armchair with a big, worn binder in her lap. The rest of us were on the sofa or the other chairs, forming a loose circle.

For an hour, Tara read out of the handbook about what Sigmas could and couldn't do. To summarize:

Sigmas keep their grades up. (Self-explanatory.)

Sigmas don't dress inappropriately. (Some ambiguity here, but the gist was that "provocative" wasn't nearly as big an issue as "tacky.")

Sigmas don't drink alcohol. (Completely ignored in practice, until someone got caught by the authorities.)

Sigmas don't have sex. (See above re: get caught, comma, don't.)

Sigmas don't talk about chapter business outside the chapter. (The first rule of Greek Club is don't talk about Greek Club.)

There was a Standards Board to enforce these rules, made up of the chapter officers, an alumnae adviser, and, if serious enough, a representative from the national office.

Next there were rules specific to pledges:

Stand up when an active enters the room.

Do everything an active tells you, unless it's hazing, but of course, hazing is against SAXi national policy.

Pledges do not have serious boyfriends.

At the general murmurs from the eight pledges, our trainer looked up from the binder. "We're serious about this one," Tara said. "Pledgeship is only ten weeks. You can hold out that long."

Brittany raised her hand, clearly appointing herself spokeswoman. "When you say hold out, you mean . . ."

Tara leveled an unequivocal stare. "No sex." The pledges giggled, maybe figuring the rule was as meaningful as the one for the actives, but she nixed that idea. "I'm totally serious this time. All your focus should be on learning about your sisters and your sorority. Sex will only get in the way of that. If you get caught, you'll be brought before Standards."

Nikki raised her hand, her face bright red. "So when you say 'no sex,' you mean, like, *nothing*?"

Tara rolled her eyes. "Do I have to draw you a diagram?"

Brittany had a prim know-it-all tone at odds with the subject. "There's a *lot* of room between the neck and the knees."

"And it doesn't seem fair," Ashley followed, "that the pledges from the other chapters will have a head start getting to know all the guys."

Tara's earth-mother patience was slipping. "You can get to know them, you just can't screw them."

"So making out is okay?" Brittany again. "I'm just trying to make sure we *all* understand the rules."

"Above the waist only? Or everything but . . . you know." In case we didn't, Nikki made a circle with two fingers and demonstrated with another one.

"Eww!" Ashley screwed up her face. "Gross, Nikki!"

"Oh, like you haven't."

"Look, people," Holly snapped. "Tab A, slot B. Don't do it. How hard is that?"

I started to laugh. What else could I do?

Tara tried to get control of the group again, and steer them back on track. "You guys are *way* overthinking this."

Brittany got huffy; with her high, clipped voice, she sounded like Minnie Mouse in a snit. "I'm just saying, we all went through Rush because we wanted to meet guys."

"You should have done fraternity Rush then," Holly said.

Tara jumped in to prevent a catfight. "I know what you mean, Brittany. But trust me. Sigmas have their pick of the guys."

"Sigmas are hard to get but worth the trouble." I didn't realize I'd spoken aloud until they all looked at me. "That's our reputation," I explained, paraphrasing what I'd read on a chat board while working on my next Phantom article. "It does seem better than 'Their pledges put out.'"

Tara gave me a studying look, and I wished I'd remained under the radar. I'd spent Sunday reading Gran's book and working on my deflector shields, but I ought to practice keeping my mouth shut.

"What's a sorority girl's mating call?" Holly asked, earning Tara's glare. " 'I'm so wasted!' "

"That's not funny!" Brittany said, outraged. If she'd been standing, I think she'd have stamped her foot. Possibly the girls laughed at her as much as Holly's awful joke. I know I did.

Tara took the opportunity to move things along, and

turned the page in her book. "We've spent so much time on this that we didn't discuss officers. Any nominations for pledge class president?"

"I nominate Brittany," said Nikki, and Ashley seconded. That seemed to be Ashley's major function, seconding things.

"Anyone else?" Tara looked around the small circle, and her gaze rested on me. "Maggie? Victoria told me you might be interested in being pledge president."

After a shocked silence, of which a lot of the shock came from me, Brittany protested. "But Maggie never contributes anything to the discussion."

"That's got my vote," Holly drawled. "I nominate Maggie."

I shook off my frozen surprise. "I can't be pledge president."

"She's right. She doesn't know anything about Greek tradition," said Brittany. I suddenly realized who she reminded me of: Tracy Flick in *Election*. She even had the Reese Witherspoon haircut.

"I second Maggie!" said Kaylee, clearly in favor of anything that didn't involve Brittany ordering us around.

"I decline." But no one was listening to me except Brittany, who echoed, "She declines!"

Tara looked at her watch. "Great. Next week we'll vote for either Maggie or Brittany as president."

"But I don't want to run."

"Line up outside the chapter room in ten minutes, girls." She dismissed us, and the group scattered. I marched toward Tara, but Holly strong-armed me out of the room.

"You can*not* stick us with Brittany for ten weeks, Maggie."

"Why don't *you* run?"

She headed downstairs. "Because my mother wants me to."

"Of course." We joined the steady trickle of girls on the central stairway that connected the three floors. "I don't know why Victoria told Tara that I wanted to do it."

Holly glanced back, the steps putting us eye to eye. "Because *she* wants you to run. You're obviously on the short track to the inner circle. Lucky you."

I would have felt a lot better about that if Holly had seemed at all jealous of my special treatment. Because the inner circle that came to my mind was the one in Dante's *Inferno,* and that wasn't anywhere I wanted to be.

16

Tuesday morning I woke up with an uneasy knot in my stomach. I sat up, rubbed my eyes, and gazed around the room. All was normal in the bedroom—morning light diffused through blue and green pastel curtains, and the disorder was minimal, at least in the bedroom half of the room. The French doors were open to the study, which looked like a tornado had hit and dropped the contents of a library. Situation normal.

I hadn't dreamed, so that couldn't be what was bugging me. Climbing out of bed, I shuffled to the bathroom, pulled the shower curtain closed, and turned on the water. Eight o'clock class today, but a hot shower always helped me think. Standing under the spray, I did an inventory. Calculus homework, check. Biology lab report, check.

I *had* dreamed. The realization hit while my hair was full of shampoo. It wasn't simply that I couldn't remember. There was an absence in my mind, a hole where the dream had been, as if it had been excised like my wisdom teeth. It didn't hurt, but I couldn't help mentally poking at it.

Weird. I rinsed off and thought about calling Gran, but as soon as I went into the bedroom and saw the clock, that impulse disappeared. I had just enough time to find some jeans that didn't make my butt look too big, and get on my way.

Downstairs, Mom was dressed for work, wolfing down a bowl of bran flakes. "It must be a good stomach day," I said, making a beeline for the coffee pot.

"So far." She swallowed the last bite and rinsed out the bowl, putting it in the dishwasher. "Lisa called last night."

I stopped, midpour. "The home phone?"

"She said she tried your cell."

"I must have turned it off for the meeting."

"Anyway," said Mom. "She wanted to make sure you were okay. Something about the last time you talked." Mom was busily gathering her purse and briefcase, making sure she had her saltines, just in case. "You didn't have a fight, did you?"

Spooning sugar into my travel mug, I tried to remember. When was the last time we'd talked? Was it the fight?

"Time to go," Mom said. "You'd better scoot, too."

I looked at the clock and said a word that made Mom protest. It was going to be a long, busy day. I'd find time to call Lisa tonight. And Gran, I reminded myself. Don't forget.

* * *

After calculus, I put in an hour at the editor's desk, hurried to the science building, dissected an earthworm, then came back to work straight through the afternoon. I didn't mind skipping lunch, because frankly the only thing grosser than the outside of an earthworm is the inside of one.

By the time I had to leave for history class, I'd entered all the corrections for the next day's edition and uploaded them to the server. Cole was hard at work at his own computer when I stopped by to tell him I was leaving.

"Thanks, Mags." He didn't look up from the screen.

"Hey, Cole." I waited until he made eye contact, and I knew I had his attention. His face had always been long and thin, but there were dusky shadows under his eyes, and furrows of fatigue around his mouth. "Don't forget to sleep occasionally, okay?"

"Sure thing." He said it absently, and went back to work. I turned to go, but stopped when he said, "Hey."

"Yeah?"

He picked up the day's edition of the *Report*. "Good job today."

I smiled and one knot of my tension slipped loose. "Thanks."

Handing me the paper, he waved me off. "Now go to class."

I dashed out the door, into the brisk September air. The leaves were starting to turn, mottling the green with yellow, and I hurried to the history building. It should be an intramural event: the cross-campus sprint.

The only thing I cared about was beating Dad there, and I managed that. I burst into the lecture hall, red-faced and puffing like a steam engine, but I'd made it five minutes before the hour.

"Maggie!"

I scanned the tiers of desks and saw Ashley pointing to an empty seat beside her. Great. As if the Sigmas weren't encroaching on my life enough already.

Unfortunately, everyone else had figured out to come early, so it was the closest empty seat. It was also surrounded by Greeks. I slid down the row and dropped into the desk, pulling out my notebook. A lot of the students took notes on their laptops, but I was a traditionalist. I also knew shorthand.

"I saved you a seat," said Ashley, unnecessarily, since I was already occupying it. "Will was just reading today's Phantom Pledge report."

"The phantom is a pledge now?" I asked, not ingenuous at all.

"Seems so," said the guy I assumed was Will. He was wearing the fraternity uniform—cargo khakis, letter jersey, beat-up athletic shoes—and slouched so far down in his chair that his butt was almost hanging off. Not that I was looking at his butt or anything.

"Listen to this: 'As I reached out to take my own envelope,'" Will quoted, "'stark fear took over, welling up from my nonconformist heart. When I took that bid I would be subsumed, assimilated. Resistance was futile, but my real terror came from knowing that part of me didn't want to resist.

"'What is more potent than the temptation of belonging? It's a Faustian lure—acceptance, superiority. All you have to do is hand over the soul of your individuality.

" 'Any sane person would end the experiment here. Yet here I go, into the social jungle, upriver to the heart of darkness. My reports from this point on may be few, carried out by pontoon boat. Wish me luck. I love the smell of beer keg in the morning.' "

Victoria might yet turn me into a frog.

I thought they might laugh, but the clump of fraternity guys was quiet, contemplative. It was Ashley who spoke first. "Well, that's a little harsh."

"Not really," said a shaggy-haired boy in a purple shirt. He sat beside the reader, Will, on the row above us. "You girls are *scary* when you get your Rush game on." The guys laughed, breaking the pensive tension. "I can totally see you going all Francis Ford Coppola."

"Come on," she protested, twisting in her seat to glare at him.

I took the paper from Will and had a surreal moment, talking about myself in the third person. "Do you think she'll go native, like Martin Sheen?"

"Whatever makes a better story," said Purple Shirt. "It's all a gimmick anyway."

"You think so?" Will looked right at me, making me nervous. "I think she got it at least a *little* right. I mean, I admit that part of the reason I pledged was to feel like a big deal on campus."

A snort from Purple Shirt. "Dude. You're Gamma Phi Epsilon. You guys are the big swinging dick on campus."

Since Will didn't hit him, I figured this was a term of respect. Guys are gross.

"Eww," said Ashley, and faced forward. Will exchanged a

grin with me before I did the same. Just in time—in walked my dad.

"Hey," whispered Ashley while Dad settled in at the front of the hall. "I think Will is totally into you."

"How can you tell?" I hissed back. "We talked for five seconds."

"That personal admission to encourage intimacy . . . he was looking straight at you." She nodded decisively. "Totally into you. You should go for him."

"Um . . ."

"And he's a Gamma Phi Ep! Perfect."

"Why's that?" The name was familiar. SAXi's brother fraternity—a redundant term.

"Because *all* Sigmas date G Phi Eps. It's tradition."

At least as far back as Victoria and Peter Abbott. I jotted a note in the margin of my paper: "Things to check out."

"Literally all, or figuratively all?" I asked, keeping an eye on Dad's progress plugging in his laptop and getting the projector going.

"Well," Ashley hedged, "everyone I've interviewed for my pledge book."

Now she had my attention. "Your what?"

She showed me the front of a binder, which was decorated with stickers and had "$\Sigma A \Xi = \heartsuit$" written on it in paint pen. "Brittany said we'd better start doing our interviews of the actives now, so we're not stuck doing all fifty right before Hell Week."

"Hell Week?"

"The week before initiation. That's when we have our pledge test, and have to turn in our pledge book with all the interviews complete. Weren't you listening in class?"

If Brittany had been talking, then chances were not.

"We're supposed to say Sisterhood Week," Ashley continued. "There's usually some fun quests and assignments and stuff to bond us all together."

"Sounds like a blast."

"I can't wait," she said, missing my irony entirely.

✳   ✳   ✳

The rest of the week progressed the same way: class, paper, class, sisterhood, homework, fall into bed exhausted. I stopped worrying about my lack of dreams; my neurons had nothing left at the end of the day. Not only were the normal brain cells getting a workout, but the freakazoid ones, too. I didn't get sick with them anymore—my deflector shields were becoming second nature to me now—but I still got flashes sometimes, still saw things in people's expressions that I wasn't sure anyone else could see. Maybe it was a trade-off—more waking weirdness for less nightmares. I couldn't say I didn't like it.

Saturday I slept and caught up on my reading for history. Dad tended to call on me whenever he asked the class a question and got nothing but cricket-filled silence, so there was no slacking off with his assignments.

Tara, the pledge trainer, had moved our class to Sunday evening so that we wouldn't have the time constraint of the chapter meeting immediately following. I picked up Holly at her dorm; on the way to the Sigma house, she grumbled that this meant Brittany could talk as much as she wanted, and then realized that "when" I was president, I could shut her up. Which I had to admit was more tempting than anything Victoria Abbott had mentioned.

We settled in the TV room, and Tara—looking more hippie than usual in a long bohemian skirt—started the meeting.

445

"From now on, the president will call the class to order. So we need to decide who that's going to be. Nominated, we have Brittany and Maggie. All those in favor of Maggie?"

Holly raised her hand. So did Kaylee and Alyssa. I did not, even when my pledge sister kicked me in the ankle. "Ow! I'm abstaining."

"You can't abstain," said Tara.

"I have a conflict of interest." My tone was as unshakable as I could make it. "So I courteously decline to vote."

Her mouth turned down. "Fine. Those for Brittany." Ashley, Erica, Nikki, and of course, the girl herself raised their hands.

"Brittany should abstain, too," Holly protested.

"She doesn't have to." Tara's voice was deep with disapproval, not of my opponent, but of me. "Brittany wins."

To halfhearted applause, Brittany beamed, put her hand on her heart, and made a face of embarrassed gratitude. "Thank you all for your support. I really appreciate the trust you've placed in me."

"Okay," said Tara, opening her binder. "Let's—"

But Brittany wasn't done. "I actually have some ideas for our class. Is it okay to do this now, Tara?"

She blinked, her earth-mother calm taking a hit. "Actually . . ."

"Thanks. It'll only take a sec." She whipped out a long, *long* checklist from the front of her own notebook. "First of all, everyone"—she glared at me—"should make a real effort to try and hang around the house more. Second, I think we should have mandatory checks of our pledge books at every meeting. We don't want *some people*"—why didn't she just say Maggie?—"waiting until the last minute."

Holly shot me the death eye, and I had to admit, I was really regretting my abstention just then.

"Are you two listening to me? This is important stuff. Now. On to Homecoming. I expect everyone to really pitch in and show the actives what we can do. . . ."

✳ ✳ ✳

On Tuesday after history, someone called my name just as I was about to duck into Dad's office. "Hey, Maggie! Wait up!"

Will, the Gamma Phi Epsilon from class, loped down the hall toward me. I'd only seen him slumped in his desk, and he was taller than I'd realized. I had to tilt my head back to look at him as the rest of the class went on by. Including Ashley, who gave me a wink of great significance.

"Maggie, right?" he asked.

"That's a good guess, since I'm the only one that stopped when you bellowed it down the hall."

He laughed. "I was just starting conversation. But I've been sitting behind you for weeks, and we haven't been properly introduced. I'm Will." He stuck out his hand. I had gotten into the habit of steeling my defenses before shaking hands. Sometimes I felt like that guy in *The Dead Zone,* and look how crappy things had turned out for him.

A slight tingle, as if I'd hit my funny bone, but no voyeur vision. I breathed in relief and surreptitiously brushed my palm on my jeans as he released it.

"Are you going to be there Friday?"

I drew a blank. "Friday?"

"You know. At the Underground. Sigmas and Gamma Phi Eps are getting together for a mixer."

"Oh yeah. They talked about that in the chapter meeting on Monday. I thought it was a type of drink."

He laughed. "You're cute."

"Uh. Thanks?" I assumed this was a compliment, but since I'd slipped into a parallel dimension where fraternity guys even talked to me, I couldn't be sure.

"Are you going to be there?"

"I don't know." The Phantom Pledge would need material, I guess. "Maybe."

"You should go." Will grinned, and it was cheeky and charming, darn it. "If you make up your mind, I'll see you there."

"Great." I smiled, a little too brightly.

"See ya then."

"Yeah. See ya."

He jogged off. I watched him go, mentally composing the opening line for next week's column: *Would this guy even notice me if I was wearing my Darth Vader T-shirt instead of Greek letters?*

I swung into Dad's office, then stopped, because Justin occupied a small desk in the corner, diligently typing notes into a laptop. He looked very industrious; maybe a little too much so. Justin couldn't lie with silence, either. Had he heard my conversation with Will? Did I care? Of course I did. No point in lying to anyone about that, least of all myself.

"Hey." He looked good; he'd gotten a haircut, neatly trimmed, short enough on the top to stand up when he ran his hand through it, something he'd apparently done recently. It suited the clean-cut lines of his face. I hadn't seen him since . . . when? My weeks were running together.

He glanced up as if I'd surprised him. "Oh. Hi, Maggie." Terrible liar. "What are you doing here?" I asked.

His attention returned to the screen and his fingers to the keys. "I'm your dad's teaching assistant. Didn't you wonder why I'm always hanging around?"

"Just figured I was lucky." I wondered if Dad had mentioned this fact. "I knew he was your academic adviser."

"Well, now he's my boss, too." He went back to typing.

"Ah." I watched, taking in the taut set of his shoulders, the clipped ends of his words. "You might as well say it."

"Say what?"

"Whatever has got you wound tighter than a Swiss watch."

"I don't know what you're talking about."

"Fine." I turned to go, but his question stopped me.

"Don't you think you're enjoying this a little too much?" He'd finally looked up, turned in his chair to give me his full attention.

"Enjoying what?"

He made a vague, encompassing gesture. "The whole Greek thing."

Casting a glance out the door to the crowded hallway, I lowered my voice. "You know why I'm doing this."

He rose, closed the distance, kept his voice at the same soft intensity. "I know why you *think* you're doing this."

"What's that supposed to mean?"

"Come on, Maggie. You were flirting. With a fraternity guy."

My mouth worked in silent indignation. So he *had* heard me. Spied on me, even. "I was not!"

"You thought a mixer was a kind of drink? Come on. The real Maggie wouldn't give a guy like him the time of day."

"What do you know about the real Maggie? You seem to think I'm so high-maintenance that a relationship with me would suck up all your study time."

His jaw clenched. "That's not what I said."

"That's what you meant."

"I think I know better than you what I meant."

"You think so?"

A cough from the doorway jolted me back to our surroundings, and I whirled toward the sound. Dad stood there, looking stern. "Should I come back later?"

"No, sir." Justin's face had turned scarlet.

"I have to get to my next class," I muttered, certain my burning cheeks matched his. Ducking past him, I escaped into the hall.

17

I'd been assigned a desk in the journalism lab. I shared it with two sophomores, but still. As I entered the last of the edits to an article about the downtown Harvest Days festival, Mike, the senior who served as the sports editor, called across the room in a harried voice.

"Hey, Quinn!"

"Yeah?"

"Bauer says you take decent sports pictures."

What was I supposed to say to that? "Well, *I* think so."

"I've got an article about how critical defense is going to be to Saturday's football game, and no current pictures of the defense. Can you run down and snap something usable?"

"Sure thing." Somehow I managed not to jump up and down and shout "Photo credit! Score!" I still had to get something he considered "usable."

I uploaded the current article to the server, grabbed my stuff, and headed to the practice field.

✳ ✳ ✳

For a girl allergic to exercise, I do know my way around a football field. Two years of photographing our high school games had at least taught me defense from offense.

"Twenty-three, thirty-two, *hike!*"

I pressed the shutter button and caught the snap. My digital camera—a graduation gift from Gran—made a vintage film sound. Click, whir, snap! Click, whir, slam! Click whir, oof!

A padded player walked into my shot; at my glare, he mumbled an unimpressed "Sorry" and continued to the bench, cup of Gatorade in hand.

Getting creative, I took some pictures of the guys lined up on the bench, shoulder to tank-sized shoulder, knees sprawled wide, forest green helmets between their feet. And then someone walked into my shot again.

This guy wore a T-shirt and track pants, which he filled out nicely without any padding. "Sorry about that."

"I'll live," I said with an exaggerated sigh.

He looked at the badge I'd clipped to my shirt. The Bedivere Rangers weren't exactly big conference football, but they didn't let just anyone wander onto the sidelines and take pictures of drills. "Are you taking over for John?"

John was the usual sports guy. I thumbed backward through the shots I'd taken so far. "Nah. Just filling in."

"Too bad."

I looked up, squinting in the afternoon light. The sun was behind him, and I couldn't see his face. Please tell me a coach hadn't just hit on a freshman. "Uh. Okay."

He took a step to the side, and I could see that he wasn't so creepy after all. "I'm one of the trainers for the offensive unit. If you need anything for an article. Or anything."

Okay, that explained it. I'd had people suck up to me when I was on the Avalon High staff, mostly to get their pictures in the yearbook or a quote in the paper.

"Just here to snap a few pics to go with John's article," I said, lifting my camera in what I hoped was a hint.

"Sure. You're a Sigma Alpha Xi pledge?"

I looked down at my shirt and feigned surprise. "Wow. I guess I am."

The guy laughed in a want-to-make-points way. "I'm AD Phi. I think we have a mixer with you guys coming up soon."

So he was sucking up because I was a SAXi? Interesting.

"So, maybe I'll see you around."

"Sure," I said, and started to turn away, my attention already back to my camera's view screen. Then I thought of something he could help me with, and glanced back over my shoulder. "Actually . . ."

Mr. Offensive Trainer snapped his eyes up to my face. "Yeah?"

Holy crap. He'd been checking out my butt.

"I, um . . ." I actually blathered, a blush heating my face. "Er . . . Can you point me to the defensive coordinator?"

453

He blinked, as if he'd expected something different. "Sure. Over there. Tall, skinny guy."

"Great." I was reluctant to leave until he did. Just in case the checking out hadn't been positive. "See you around."

"Yeah." A smile this time, and he turned away.

Okay. Maybe I did check him out just a little bit. Fair is fair, after all.

* * *

I showed off my photo in the paper at lunch on Friday. Holly and I were falling into a Monday-Wednesday-Friday habit, and often Jenna and Devon joined us. Brittany and Ashley did, too, which was less pleasant. Ashley, I'd discovered, was fine on her own, but tended to take on the other girl's most annoying characteristics when they were together.

"With your name under it and everything." Holly stopped devouring her chicken salad sandwich long enough to grin at me. "Awesome."

"I don't see what's the big deal," said Brittany, peering at the newspaper spread out on the table. "It's on the back page."

Devon came to my defense. "Anywhere on the outside of the paper is better than the inside."

Art majors often took a layout class, which overlapped with print journalism majors. I wondered if that was where she met Cole.

"Not only that," I said, "Mike said I could take pictures of the game this weekend."

"Maggie, that's huge!" Devon hugged me, nearly pulling me out of my chair. "And you're only a freshman!"

"Cool," said Brittany, finally impressed. "Football players are hot."

"No, they're not." Ashley did not defer to her on the subject of hotness. "They're all fat and stuff."

"That's the padding."

"I know the difference between padding and *padding*." She grabbed a nonexistent beer belly.

"Okay," Brittany conceded. "But the quarterback and the running guys are hot, especially in those white pants."

I stared at them in bemusement. Moments like this, I wondered if I had imagined the vibe I'd gotten from Victoria. No way were *these* girls tapped into some kind of sorcerous contract for power and world domination.

"Are you coming out with us tonight, Maggie?" Jenna had obviously decided to ignore the other pledges.

"No. I have a family thing."

"On a Friday?"

"Yeah." I didn't want to tell them that my thing involved parking my brain in neutral and watching the Sci-Fi Channel with Dad. I seriously needed some downtime. It was hard juggling homework, undercover investigating, *and* doing your editor's job for him, too.

"Come on," Holly said, with a glint of mischief. "Tell them it's a required activity."

"I'm saving that for when it actually is."

"Speaking of," said Jenna, "are you two keeping up with your pledge books and things?"

"Well, *I* am," said Brittany, even though Jenna hadn't really been talking to her. "I have to set an example, since I'm pledge president." She hadn't reminded us of that yet today.

"I'm good," Holly said between potato chips.

Jenna uncapped her Snapple. "Homecoming is in a couple

of weeks, and we've got to work on the float. You really need to make time for that, Maggie."

"Me?" I already felt like I was spending all my time with the Sigmas.

"Yes. We hardly ever see you at the house, except for pledge class and meetings."

"Blame Devon," I said breezily. "She asked Cole if there was a place for me on the *Report* staff. How's his book coming, by the way?"

I'd only meant to change the subject, but the two actives reacted as if I'd asked about the thermonuclear bomb Cole was building in the basement. Jenna gave her sorority sister a look of blistering intensity and Devon paled, the blood draining from her face, leaving her freckles standing out like raisins in a bowl of oatmeal.

"I don't know what you mean, Maggie. Cole isn't writing a book."

"Oh. My mistake." I brazened it out the best I could. "I must have misunderstood."

What was the big deal about the man's literary ambitions? He was already a journalist. How big a stretch could it be? Yet I could feel waves of sick worry coming off Devon.

I glanced at Jenna and found her watching not her sister, but me, and I wondered what I had given away.

18

"I don't know why you're so surprised, Mags." I hadn't given Jenna's roommate permission to call me Mags—only Lisa was allowed to do that—but she was driving the car, and I didn't want to correct her. "You'd be cute even if you weren't a SAXi."

"Gee, thanks." I was in the backseat, keeping my eyes on the road so that I wouldn't get carsick. Jenna had called shotgun, and Holly was beside me laughing just a little too loudly at that. Not because she was mean, but because she'd started the party early—I could smell it on her breath.

"I'm so glad you decided to come," she told me. "You can sleep when you're dead."

"Great. Something to look forward to."

Alexa found an empty spot down the street from the Underground and I tried not to flash the world as I climbed out of the BMW. When I'd shown up at the SAXi house to get a ride with the other girls, Jenna and Alexa had pronounced my jeans and cutest T-shirt unacceptable, then proceeded to go up and down the halls until they'd found an outfit that wouldn't shame the Sigma Alpha Xis' reputation for hotness.

"Stop that." Jenna slapped my hand as I tugged down the skirt. "It covers everything. Do you think we don't know the difference between hot and tacky?"

I had no doubt they did. My eye was less trained, and had widened at the amount of leg showing in the mirror.

"Here." She handed me a Maryland driver's license. "Tonight you're Mavis Bucknell. At least long enough to get in the door."

"I don't need this. It's an eighteen-and-up club, right?"

She wouldn't take the card back. "Just in case you want to have a drink."

Mavis and I looked nothing alike. At least I hoped we didn't. "This is never going to pass for me."

"Just trust me."

The music grew louder as we neared the club. When we reached the door, I could feel the bass beat against my sternum like an extra heart. An enormous guy, his bald head as shiny as an egg, sat on a stool outside. Elbowed by Jenna, I handed him Mavis's license. He stared at it, stared at me, then handed it back, along with a wristband that identified me as legal.

"It worked!" I shouted this at Jenna once we were inside,

where the lights throbbed against my retinas the way the music did against my ears.

"Of course it did!" She winked at me. "Like a charm."

Lisa and I had come here this summer, shortly after my birthday. We'd danced, guys had flirted with me to get introduced to my friend, and I'd had a good time—not everyone could dance with Lisa at the same time, so I had plenty of partners. But techno-pop wasn't my thing.

The dance floor was writhing with college kids. I didn't see anyone who looked even close to thirty—though with the strobes and dim light, it was hard to tell.

I looked around, but didn't see Jenna until she appeared in front of me and pushed a drink into my hand. "Here."

"What is this?" I took a wary sip. The drink was sweet and fruity and didn't taste like alcohol at all. The club was hot with pulsating music and sweaty bodies, and I took a deeper gulp.

"Sex on the beach." Jenna laughed at my grimace. "You're such a prude."

"It's not that." It was because even I knew it was a total sorority-girl drink. I was standing in a club, dressed in a trendy hot outfit, and drinking a sex on the beach. I had become what I most feared: a cliché.

"Hey!" someone yelled in my ear, the only way to get sufficient decibels over the music. I looked up and saw Will from history class. "You decided to come."

"Yeah!" He bent down so that he could hear me. "Jenna talked me into it."

"Excellent!" He pointed to the dance floor, his lips moving, but no sound reaching me through the din.

"Sure!" I looked around for Jenna, to get her to hold my drink, but she had disappeared again. I finished the last sip and stuck it on a passing waiter's tray.

Will grabbed my hand and we threaded through the gyrating bodies until a space opened up. The pulse of the music filled my head, drove out spare thoughts, criticism, and commentary. In the small pocket of air, we danced close together, and I didn't worry about looking like a dork, or if my legs were so pale they glowed in the blacklight. No talking, just motion and instinct.

The beat was primal, spoke to parts of me that weren't used to being included in the conversation. One song bled into another. I glimpsed the other SAXis on the dance floor. In groups and pairs, we came together for one song, then back into the mix and out the other side for the next.

I lost track of partners, until suddenly I was facing Will again. He grinned down, and I smiled up in answer. My skin was damp and hot, and when Will put his hands on my waist the temperature spiked again. Add friction and stir. His jeans brushed my bare legs, my chest brushed his shirt. He smelled of a subtle, spicy cologne and sweat; this was good. But it wasn't right.

I stepped back, bumped into the girl behind me. "I need some air."

"Sure." He blinked, seemed disoriented by the abrupt shift in mood, but let one hand fall from my waist. The other stayed there and steered me through the overheated crowd. The bouncer didn't give us a second glance as we emerged into the cold night and relative quiet.

The clean air swept through my brain and I felt immediately better. Leaning against the wall, I could feel the music pounding, muted, through my back and hips, and I closed my eyes.

"You okay?" asked Will. "You're not going to hurl or anything, are you?"

"From one drink? God, no." At least, I hoped not. My main exposure to alcohol up to this point was wine with Christmas dinner and a mostly-soda-and-not-much-whiskey Dad had let me try from his birthday bottle of Glenlivet.

"Tell me something about yourself," he said, leaning a shoulder against the wall.

I turned my head, brows knitting in confusion. "Like what?"

"I don't know." He shrugged a shoulder, looked at me with that charming smile. "Anything."

"I think the second *Aliens* movie, the James Cameron one, may be my favorite movie ever. Definite top five." Not sure why *that* was the "anything" that popped out. Maybe it was a test.

"Is that the one with the space marines?" I nodded, and he grinned. "You're a geek, but at least you like kick-ass movies."

I'm not sure if that qualified as a pass or not. While I was thinking about it, he bent his head and kissed me.

Deflector shields! I put up my mental defenses as quickly as I could. I didn't want any *Dead Zone* flashes now, while my head was fuzzy from drinking and dancing. And I didn't want him to know that, as nice a kiss as it was . . . I really, really wished he was someone else.

19

When I dragged myself home after the game on Saturday, Mom and Dad were on the couch watching a movie. "Look, dear," said my mother, elbowing Dad in the ribs and pointing at me. "Doesn't that girl look like our daughter?"

"I couldn't say, Laura. It's been so long since I've seen her."

"Very funny." I slumped in the recliner, too tired to even put up the leg rest. "And untrue. I saw you on Thursday in class."

"Was that you? I didn't recognize you, sitting in the group of Greeks."

I groaned. "Not you, too. Justin gave me grief about that already, so no need to add to it."

"Is that what you two were arguing about?" Dad asked.

"We weren't arguing. Just sort of . . . discussing in really intense voices. Why don't you guys realize, I'm just doing it for the paper."

"Ah." He used his *Father Knows Best* voice. "And it has nothing to do with Mr. Alphabet sitting behind you?"

"Wait." Mom grabbed the remote and paused the movie. "I thought you and Justin were just friends now. And what's this about a cute guy? Why don't I know about this?"

"Possibly because you have more important things to think about than my quasi-social life?"

"I'm feeling great." She laid a hand on her belly, where the bump seemed to have grown substantially all of a sudden. Just how long had it been since we'd done more than pass each other in the kitchen?

"When am I going to find out if I'm getting a brother or a sister?" I asked.

"Maybe you can read my palm and tell me."

I looked at her sharply. For Mom to even refer to my ability was huge. I guess she figured that if she didn't acknowledge it, the weirdness would somehow just go back to being science fiction. So this was Mount Rushmore big.

"Do you really want to know?" I spoke cautiously, afraid to break the fragile moment.

She seemed tentative, but intrigued. Dad, too, had picked up on the change, and he glanced between us. "You've always said you couldn't see the future."

"It's not the future. XX or XY—it's already set." Mom and

Dad exchanged a look, and I picked up the DVD rental box, pretending I didn't care what they decided. "I probably couldn't tell anything anyway."

"What the heck." Mom gave an embarrassed laugh. "Give it a try."

Grinning, I moved to the couch, nervous and excited—like a kind of stage fright. This was the first time I'd used my new superpower on purpose, but I'd been studying Gran's meditation book diligently. Mostly I'd been concerned with keeping up my defenses, but there were other chapters, too. Breathing deeply, I visualized my deflector shields powering down. After weeks of putting them up, it felt weird and naked.

Mom gave an anxious laugh, almost a giggle, and I shushed her sternly. "You are blocking the flow of positive energy."

"Really?"

"No, not really. You're just making me nervous."

I placed my hand on Mom's gently rounded stomach. A flutter, not under my fingers, but in my heart.

What a strange feeling—alone in the dark, but surrounded, buoyed, and loved. Our pulses meshed—Mom's slow, the rhythm of the universe; mine, the steady pulse of a star; the baby's quick, the turn of a day. A perfect ratio, divinely in proportion—infinitely big, and infinitely small.

Something splashed against my skin, and I opened my eyes. My parents stared at me as I wiped tears from my face, too enthralled to be embarrassed.

"Don't paint her room pink, okay? It only reinforces gender stereotypes."

Mom laughed, and pulled me into a hug. I blinked away a

strange dual vision, as if the connection between my sister and me still resonated. Dad wrapped us all up in his arms and right then, I couldn't feel worried about anything—my professional good fortune, my sudden sex appeal, the Sigma Alpha Xis, or any of it. I felt just like my sister—surrounded, buoyed, and loved.

20

On Monday morning, the chill in the air caught me off guard. Flame-colored leaves chased each other across the ground. Fall had snuck up on me somehow. Midterms and Homecoming were closing in fast. September had slipped away, and October was hurrying on its heels.

Ordinarily, I love autumn, but the obvious passage of time disturbed me; it fueled a nagging unease, as if I'd forgotten something important. The more I tried to grasp it, the more quickly it floated away, elusive as a dream.

The thought brought me to an abrupt halt on the sidewalk between the communication building and the science hall, forcing a clump of Kappa Phis to break apart and go around me.

The brisk air seemed to briefly blow a fog from my mind. How many times had I woken with the feeling that I *had* dreamed, but couldn't recall any of it? I'd been dismissing this for—God, it must be weeks now.

I pressed my fingers to my forehead. When was the last dream I could remember? It had to be over a month ago, during Rush maybe. That had to be significant. Didn't it?

A hand touched my shoulder and I whirled around with a shout. Cole stepped back, raising his hands in the universal sign for "Don't beat my head in."

"Sorry! I just wanted to see if you were okay."

"Yeah." I put a hand over my thudding heart, to make sure it wasn't actually coming out of my chest. And then I looked at him again, to make sure he wasn't wearing a Halloween costume. He looked like a zombie. The shadows under his eyes were greenish purple, as if he hadn't slept in a week.

"Are *you* all right?" I didn't mince words. "You look like crap."

He laughed and shrugged. "What can I say. The muse is a real bitch sometimes."

"Yeah, but . . ."

"Don't worry about it, Maggie." He started walking toward the communication building, and I fell in beside him. "Mike loved the pictures from the game on Saturday, by the way."

"Great. Thanks for the assignment."

"I had nothing to do with it."

I glanced up at him; he'd said it honestly. "But I'm just a

freshman. I figured you were throwing me a bone because I don't get a byline on the column."

"A column that I loved, by the way." I'd written about my suddenly elevated attraction, thanks to my Greek status. We climbed the steps to the building and Cole held the door for me. "But you shouldn't sell yourself short, Maggie. I'm a GDI and I would totally go for you, if I were any less nuts about Devon."

GDI was how non-Greeks proudly referred to themselves. I think it started as an insult, but the "God Damn Independents" had adopted it like a banner.

"Thanks," I said, not mentioning that Devon was a Sigma, too, so he hadn't exactly proven his point.

"Anyway," Cole continued as we headed for the journalism floor, "Mike thinks you're his early Christmas present. Said you always seem to have your camera pointed at the right place at exactly the right moment. That takes some serious talent. Or luck."

With a grin, he waved and turned into his classroom. For the second time that morning, I was rooted to the spot by a thought hitting me like a slap across the face.

Was I lucky? Or was something else at work, making things fall into place? Sigmas are successful, Victoria had said. Things would go my way if I took what SAXi had to offer.

I'd been slacking. Nancy Drew would never lose track of time like this. And since I had to start somewhere, I'd start with the mystery of Devon and Cole.

∗ ∗ ∗

Spying was such an ugly word. But if you want to get technical, that was what I was doing outside Devon's door. I'd brought my interview book to give me an excuse to talk to her, but she was not alone.

"We *know*, Devon," said Kirby. I'd always thought of her as Victoria Jr., but the edge in her voice was more overt. Mrs. Abbott was velvet-gloved steel. Kirby had less finesse, or wasn't bothering with it now. "Did you think you could keep it a secret?"

"No." Devon sounded as though she was crying. "I just didn't think it would matter so much."

I heard Jenna's voice next, soothing and kind, good cop to Kirby's bully. "I'm so sorry, sweetie. But you have to give him up."

Kirby spoke without pity. "We told you that Cole wasn't right for you. No, I will not shush, Jenna. We told her! There are rules to how this works, and she ignored them."

"But I met him before initiation. I didn't know," Devon sobbed. "And by then I'd already fallen in love with him."

"I know, honey." Jenna's voice, full of sympathy. "But that's why you have to let him go, now. It'll only hurt him more if you wait."

"What if you're wrong?" Devon had found some defiance. "You don't know everything."

"I know enough not to break Victoria's rules."

A tiny pause, enough for a horrified gulp. "Victoria knows?"

"Not yet." Kirby's voice was heavy with implied threat.

"And she doesn't have to," Jenna said, offering a way out.

There was a longer silence now, then Devon spoke firmly. "I'll give back my pin. I'll quit the Sigmas."

Kirby's laugh had razor edges. "Sure you will. Before or after that show in the university art gallery this December? Don't act so holy, Dev. You want that showing as much as you want Cole."

The doorknob rattled, covering any answer to that.

Maybe Devon didn't have one. With no time to retreat, I raised my hand as if I'd just arrived and was about to knock. The door swung open, and I nearly hit Kirby in the forehead.

"Oh!" I jerked my hand back. "I . . . Gosh, I'm sorry. I was looking for Devon to . . ." I held up my pledge book—an unadorned binder full of loose-leaf paper. ". . . you know. For my book."

Jenna brushed past Kirby and grabbed my arm, turning me away from the room and the president's dagger stare. "Not right now, Maggie." She sounded harried, maybe worried. "Maybe after chapter meeting."

I didn't bother to pretend I didn't know something was wrong. "What's going on?"

"Nothing. Boyfriend troubles."

"You really are serious about that no-sex thing, huh?"

"For pledges, yes." We'd reached the top of the stairs. "For actives . . . well, it depends. You have to be very selective, Maggie. That's why we don't want pledges to get too involved with anyone before they know the rules."

"Of what? Who passes the test?"

"Yeah."

"And Devon's boyfriend doesn't? Because he's not Greek?"

She gave me a gentle push toward the stairs. "It's complicated and it's none of your business. Go to the TV room. There are a bunch of actives to interview there."

I could tell I'd reached the limit, pushed as far as I could under the guise of In Everyone's Business Girl. With a last look over my shoulder, I headed down the stairs. Jenna returned to Devon's room, where Kirby stood in the doorway, watching me leave.

Holly had forgotten she was angry with me, until Brittany came into the TV room and started trying to organize the pledges for a slumber party. Then she remembered, and left me to go on to the meeting by myself.

Following the others down, I stopped on the bottom stair when I saw Victoria and Kirby talking in the lobby. The chapter president saw me first, and the alumna turned a moment later. "Maggie!" Victoria smiled and gestured me closer. "Come tell me how it's going with you."

Obediently, I closed the distance. She linked her arm with mine and drew me into the empty chapter room, which had been set up for the evening's meeting—table for the officers at one end, chairs arranged in rows facing it.

"I saw the photo you took in the *Report*. And your classes are going well? Are you finding some time to socialize?"

Everything about her said that she knew—or at least had a very good idea—that things had been going stellar for me. "Yes, ma'am. A blast."

"Good. I'm glad you're enjoying the benefits of being a Sigma Alpha Xi." Her tone was a study in ambiguity. She could have been talking about purely social benefits, but I didn't think so.

"I am a little disappointed," she continued, "that you weren't elected pledge president. It would have been yours if you hadn't abstained."

I picked my answer carefully. "I didn't feel that I could in good conscience vote either way."

She looked at me. I can't read thoughts, but I didn't have any trouble interpreting hers: *A conscience. How quaint.*

Aloud she told me, "You're already off to a great start, Maggie. Being a pledge officer could have been part of that."

I chose to misinterpret her. "Actually, at the *Report*—"

She turned to me, a layer of her mask falling away. "How do you think you got your position at the paper, Maggie? Do you think they'd keep you on for a moment if you were unable to continue that column?"

The chapter room seemed suddenly empty and isolated, the air stuffy and thick. Carpet covered the design on the floor, but I seemed to feel it pulsing with life beneath the soles of my feet, like a hibernating animal.

What the Hell?

No, wait. Let me rephrase that. Something a lot like fear gripped my chest, made it hard to breathe.

How had I forgotten this?

Victoria took a maternal tone, which seemed even scarier with the stifling power trapped inside the room with us. "We discussed this, Maggie. I see potential in you. But you must assert your position over the others early. Every class has a leader, and it is important you take that role."

"Brittany seems to have her stuff together."

Victoria dismissed her with an irritated wave of her hand. "She's not an alpha wolf, just a yapping bitch cub."

The velvet gloves were off. I could keep playing stupid; I could run away, forget about the Sigmas and whatever the Hell they had under the carpet; or I could man up. Get my Forces of Good game on.

I visualized power flowing into my deflector shields, hiding my purpose. "Here's the thing, Victoria. I'm not a front-of-the-pack sort of girl. I'd rather let Brittany be president than have her fighting me at every turn."

She considered me for a moment, then surprised me by laughing, shaking her head. The atmosphere immediately cleared, as though she'd released a spell. I'd fooled her, or she was pretending I had, and I couldn't tell which.

"I like you, Maggie." Her hand rested gently on my shoulder. "You're good for this group precisely because you have a mind of your own." Her fingers tightened, not painfully, but in firm affection. "That you are at initiation is what matters."

"I can hardly wait."

"In the meantime, you do need to be more of a presence. Spend time with your sisters, go to the mixers. Have fun."

"Yes, ma'am."

"You'll be working on the Homecoming float with the Gamma Phi Epsilons." She put her arm around me as we walked toward the door, where girls were queuing up for the meeting. "Gamma Phi Eps and SAXis make very good matches. Ask Jenna and Kirby."

"I thought we weren't supposed to have boyfriends as pledges."

"Maggie, those rules are for the girls with no understanding of what's going on here."

"That would be me, Victoria." That much was honest.

She smiled. "You know to trust me, and your officers. As long as you let us guide you, you'll have a good head start when initiation comes around."

Initiation. It all came down to that. I don't know what worried me more—that I had to play the game until then, or that the longer I played it, the easier it got.

21

I left the SAXi house immediately after the meeting, explaining that I had a midterm paper due, which was not a lie. After waking up to the chill of autumn that morning and working on Homecoming articles all day at the paper—not to mention my audience with Queen Victoria—I had a tense awareness that time was slipping away. My Spidey Sense usually kept me very goal-directed, but for some reason I'd been spinning my wheels for weeks, and now I had to make up lost ground.

The university library had two distinct halves. The west side was a century old; the shiny "new" section was built twenty years ago. They didn't match up exactly, so getting from one side to the other involved stairs and doglegs, making me sometimes feel like a hamster in a Habitrail.

I preferred the old half, which had a strong sense of continuity in the musty smell of old paper, in the cramped stacks and scarred wooden tables. I followed the bread crumbs of the Dewey decimal system to the shelves I wanted, then stood staring at the spines, waiting for something to shout "Pick me! I'll answer all your questions, even the ones you're too clueless to ask."

Regrettably, the books remained silent, so I grabbed some useful looking titles, more or less at random. Staggering out of the stacks under the weight of eight fat tomes, I had to wonder why the more abstruse the subject, the more impressively massive the book had to be.

I set them on the nearest table and paused to catch my breath. Somehow I was not surprised to see Justin emerge from between another set of shelves, carrying a large book of his own.

He stopped when he saw me, and we stood that way for a moment. I had a weird feeling in my stomach, sort of like déjà vu but not quite. His hair was messy, his jeans and sweater rumpled, and I missed him more than ever.

"Are you stalking me?" I asked.

His mouth curved in a lopsided smile and he pointed to the next table over, covered from one end to the other in paper and books. "I live here. Maybe *you're* stalking *me.*"

My inner voice hummed in a contented *See, I do know what I'm doing* kind of way. I sighed. "Nothing in the universe is entirely random."

"What's that?" he asked, bemused.

I shook my head. "Nothing."

He cast me a curious look, but let it go. I remembered that we'd argued—well, discussed intensely—the last time we spoke. It seemed as though he might say something about that, or at least something personal. Instead he set down his own book and picked up one of mine.

"The Encyclopedia of Earth Magic." He glanced at me, then warily picked up the next two. *"Sacred Geometry. Finding the Goddess Within."* Until he read them aloud, it hadn't occurred to me to wonder if we had a particularly esoteric library at Bedivere.

"Taking up some new hobbies?" he asked.

"No." I retrieved the books and neatened the pile self-consciously. "I'm working on a project."

"What kind of project?"

Crap. *Now* my skills at subterfuge chose to fail me?

When I didn't give him an answer, he laid his hand on the stack of books, as if he was going to keep them from me. "Like your friend Lisa? *That* kind of extracurricular project?"

"God, no." I tucked my hair behind my ears and explained . . . sort of. "It's an angle for the column. Origin of symbols, female power. That kind of thing."

He looked at me, hard, then relented. After all, I wasn't exactly lying. "What do you want to know? Anthropology of occult folklore is *my* deal. Why didn't you just call me?"

What a stupid question. Because I was stubborn, and he'd hurt my feelings, of course. It occurred to me that because Justin was older—definitely more knowledgeable and probably more sensible—I'd more than once put him on a pedestal. But really, guys could be so obtuse sometimes.

Instead of pointing this out, I asked, "Don't you ever think you're crazy to believe this is real? Even in the face of experience?"

"Of course," he answered quickly. "Faith isn't absence of doubt. It's belief without proof, not without question."

He spoke as if he would know, which I found interesting. Justin's character was so clearly defined: forthright, gallant, conscientious. But for such a straightforward person, he was still a mystery in some ways. He'd never given me much detail on what had formed him, or set him on this unusual course of study.

The silence lengthened, and he answered my unvoiced question. "I guess that's why I'm here, trying to bridge the gap between faith and science."

I let myself smile at that. "Not enough windmills to tilt at?"

He smiled, too, and the distance between us—from Avalon to Ireland, from Greek Row to the Bedivere library— seemed to shrink for a moment.

But only for a moment. "Hey, Maggie." Will appeared from around one of the shelves. "I thought I heard your voice."

I stifled a sigh, and greeted Will with a wave. He ambled over, a couple of books tucked under his arm, and gave Justin a friendly nod. "How's it going?" Then to me, in a teasing voice, "No fair getting help from the TA on your term paper."

Casually, I turned the stack of books to hide their titles. "If I really need help in history, I *can* get it at home."

Will shook his head sadly, but his eyes were laughing. "I just knew you were going to throw off the curve."

"Professor Quinn doesn't grade on a curve." Justin was trying to be nonchalant, and wasn't entirely successful.

If he noticed, Will amiably pretended not to. "All on me, then." He gestured to the stack of books. "You checking those out? I can carry them down for you."

"Um . . ." He wasn't a Sigma, but I didn't know how much the Gamma Phi Eps were in bed with them—metaphorically speaking—and the titles of the books were unusual to say the least.

"They're mine," said Justin. "This one is yours, Maggie." He handed me the book he'd been carrying, a history of the Knights Templar. Which, in addition to being a secret society, was also part of our history assignment. No coincidences.

"And," he added, "there's nothing wrong with calling me for help. That's my job."

Not the most flattering way to make that offer, especially given my bent pride. "I'll keep it in mind." I left it at that, since Will was rather obviously waiting to walk me out.

Would it completely have blown my cover to stay? Maybe the library wasn't the best place to talk about the weird stuff. The shelves made it too easy for someone to eavesdrop, and I knew I wasn't the only Sigma with deflector shields.

But that wasn't the real point. Would it have killed Justin to give me some hint that he wanted me to stay?

"I wasn't interrupting anything there, was I?" Will asked as we wound down the stairs to the circulation desk.

"No." That didn't sound entirely convincing, so I added, "We were talking about school."

He nodded, and we checked out our books. On the way out, he asked, "Did you eat yet?"

My stomach growled as soon as he mentioned food. "I was going to grab some McNuggets on the way home."

He held the door, and coaxed me with a smile. "I'll spring for a Happy Meal."

What the hell. I could placate Victoria, learn about fraternities for my column, and eat at the same time. It wasn't a date, it was multitasking.

✳ ✳ ✳

It was only fast food, but by the time I got home and dragged myself up the stairs to my room, the long day had crashed down on me, and I still had calculus homework. I set the Templar book on the desk and wrote myself a note on a Post-it. "What is the deal with the Sigmas and the Gamma Eps?" Further investigation would have to wait until the next day.

Later, post–math homework, I lay in bed thinking about how silent my warning system had been the last month or more. What were the odds that, as much time as I had spent with these girls, there hadn't been one eating disorder, chemical dependency, or boyfriend crisis to trip my switch?

And then there was the no-dream thing, which distressed and frustrated me. Because those were basic. That was how my freakiness had first shown up.

According to Gran's book, you could psych yourself into meaningful dreams by relaxing, inviting the dream to visit your sleep. Or you could meditate, or pray if that was your thing.

Before graduation, I hadn't been to Mass in years. But

facing Evil with a capital *E* makes a convincing argument that somewhere, in some shape or form, there was Good with a capital *G,* too, and I wanted no mistake about which side I was on.

I'm not saying Team Father, Son, and Holy Ghost is the only team in the *G* league, but it's what I defaulted to when I needed to get my spiritual ducks in a row. Even so, I'm not exactly what you call a reverent traditionalist.

"Okay, God." I stared up at the dark ceiling. "Maybe you could throw me a bone here. I'm going in circles and could really use a signpost." I paused, trying to sound at least a little supplicant. "So . . . anytime you're ready, that would be great."

I didn't really expect an immediate answer, but the silence in my head disappointed me anyway. My fingers had crept up to the small gold cross that I always wore—a confirmation present from my gran. I usually forgot I had it on, which was a fairly obvious sign that while I was committed to the capital *G,* I was a little lax on the protocol.

With a sigh, I dropped the pendant. Then I rolled over, burrowed into the covers, and closed my eyes.

God, we both know I suck at praying. But please . . . just show me what to do.

* * *

I woke in darkness, heart pounding. Fumbling for the lamp, I switched it on. My eyes darted around the room for what had awakened me, but found nothing. I *sensed* nothing.

Throwing on my robe, I padded downstairs without bothering to turn on a light. Unconcerned about the parents' privacy, I went to their bedroom and opened the door a crack, held my breath until I heard two sets of soft, even snores. They were fine, and something deep inside me unknotted.

Gran's picture was on the piano in the living room. Walking carefully in the dim glow of the hall nightlight, I picked up the framed photo. A slumbering sense of her floated into my brain, like the clean lavender soap smell of her sheets. Fine.

Why could I sense my grandmother through her photo, but from the Sigmas I got nothing? No dreams and no clear sense of their nature. That was important.

But how? Time was running out. Initiation was six weeks off, and then the window of opportunity would close.

I set the photo down and climbed the stairs, feeling like I was wrapped in wool—sweaty and hot. Why couldn't I think? I was a fast thinker, intuitively leaping tall quandaries in a single bound. What had changed?

Falling onto my sofa, I picked up my cell phone to see what time it was, whether I could get any more sleep that night. I had a text message from Justin. *Call me. Please.*

What had I said? Show me what to do.

Flipping open the phone, I dialed. He didn't pick up until the fourth ring, and sounded still asleep. "Hullo?"

Swallowed pride doesn't always go down easily. I couldn't seem to talk around mine. Alert now, he said, "Maggie?"

"I . . ." It wasn't just the stubbornness. The wet wool feeling was invading my head, seeping in through my skull, making my tongue thick and heavy. "I need help."

"Are you home?" I heard the sound of rustling fabric, as if he was getting dressed. "I'll be right there."

"No, don't. The parents—" God, my head. The more I tried to tell him there was something wrong, the more it ached. "I'll meet you somewhere."

"Not in the middle of the night you won't." Keys jingled and a door opened, then shut again. "I'll come get you. Meet me outside."

He hung up before I could protest again.

22

I think purgatory must be like an IHOP at two in the morning. The fluorescent lights ward off the dark, but give no warmth. The people who come and go look tired, like they'd rather be somewhere else but aren't. You can get food and coffee, but it's not very good.

Justin took his coffee black. He poured us both a cup from the blue plastic carafe before he even let me speak. His brown eyes were bloodshot, his hair sticking straight up. He had sleep creases on his cheek. But he was there.

"Now. Tell me about the Sigma Alpha Xis."

I did. Everything I remembered, and the things I didn't,

I told him about that, too. I told him about Victoria and the paper, and how tempted I was. I told him how I kept writing notes to myself to check things out, and then forgetting them.

He listened to all of it, then said, "That's everything?"

No, it wasn't. I was certain I was leaving something out, but I couldn't think what. The wool-headed feeling had lifted while I waited for Justin outside in the brisk air, and the headache with it. But I still had the sense I was forgetting something.

"It's everything I can recall," I said.

"So you think . . . what, exactly?"

"That's just it." Why wasn't I able to find the right thing to say to make this make some kind of twisted sense? "There's something wrong, something off. It's all feelings, no evidence." I sank my head into my hands. "I don't know."

The coffee cup scraped on the Formica as he pushed it aside, making room for his elbows. "Hey. Let's be organized. Tell me what you do know."

I looked up. He had his arms resting on the table, his head at my level, his gaze searching mine. "You'll figure it out, Maggie. What *do* you know?"

"Okay." I ordered my thoughts. They'd all poured out randomly before. "One. Victoria told me the Sigmas always succeed. Everyone else acts that way, too. Things just go right for them. Even my pictures for the paper—I always seem to have my camera pointed at the right place at the right moment."

"But you've been doing sports photography for a while, right? You might just have a knack."

"Not in *every* shot."

He conceded the point. "Okay, that's a start. What's next?"

"Two. They're freaked out about Devon dating an independent." That made Justin laugh. "I know. Not that strange, either. All sororities want status, success, and guys, not necessarily in that order. See why I doubt myself?"

"Don't start that." He poured another cup of coffee. "Your feelings are evidence enough for me. The fact that you're not remembering things . . . maybe that's because you're on the inside. It's affecting your radar somehow."

This was the first hopeful, useful thing I'd heard in weeks. "You think so?"

He shrugged slightly. "Have they given you anything? The BU bookstore is full of Greek stuff. Anything like that?"

"No." Then I frowned, trying to remember. "Maybe. A T-shirt, the pledge pin . . ."

"It would be something you might keep on you all the time, or maybe by your bed."

I shook my head, not quite in denial, but in frustration. "You see? This is what happens."

Justin leaned in again, lowering his voice and catching my gaze. "Have you considered that there may be some greater power at work here? You joke about Faustian bargains, but maybe that's not a coincidental analogy."

"Sorority girls from Hell? Isn't that like saying French people from France?"

"I'm serious, Maggie."

"I know you are, Justin." He was talking capital *E* stuff, much more than just *Mean Girls* meets *The Craft*. "But if it

485

is—and I'm not saying I think that—and I'm in a position to do something about it, I can't just run away."

He sighed. "No, you can't. I'm just worried that because you've made friends there—"

"What?" I demanded. "You think I'm enjoying myself too much? That the attention and success are going to my head?"

"No." He said it simply, taking the indignant wind out of my sails. "Because you've been wrong before."

I stared into my coffee cup. "This isn't like Lisa."

"Yes, it is." His tone was firm, but tempered with regret. "Your friendship, once you give it, is hard to lose. It's one of my favorite things about you."

I didn't want to look at him. Didn't want to hope. But, jeez, talk about mixed signals lately.

A shadow fell on the table and I looked up, thinking it was the waitress. I was surprised to see Cole standing there, hands shoved in the pockets of his jacket.

"What are you doing here?" I asked.

"Can't sleep." He indicated the laptop case slung on his shoulder. "Trying to work. Thought maybe a change of location . . ."

"You're not having writer's block, are you?"

"No," he growled, in a way that meant yes. "Don't you have an eight o'clock class in the morning?"

Justin, who had been watching this curiously, finally spoke. "You have an eight o'clock class?"

"What is this? Maggie has two dads? I'm a big girl." Cole was scowling at Justin, as if he were to blame for my being out so late. I made introductions. "Justin, this is the editor of the *Ranger Report*. Cole, this is my friend, who was helping me with a project."

"Great. I'm glad someone's getting some work done." He started to grump off, then turned back. "While you're working on that Homecoming float with the SAXis, see if you can take some pictures we can use."

"Sure." I wasn't about to disagree with him in this mood.

"And Hardcastle says you're putting in too many hours at the *Report*. So don't come in until the afternoon."

He left, taking a spot in a corner booth and dragging out his laptop. I watched him go, then turned back to Justin, who looked questioningly back at me. "He's not usually like that," I said.

"I hope not."

"Yeah." But if Cole was miserable, then I'll bet Devon was miserable, too. And miserable people like to talk about what's at the root of their problems.

Justin climbed out of the booth. "Come on. Let's see if I can get you home without your father shooting me."

"That would be a shame. To get the punishment with none of the sin."

I hadn't meant to flirt, but he looked down at me with raised eyebrows anyway. "I wouldn't know anything about that."

"Punishment or sin?" I asked as we waited to pay the cashier.

He shook his head, holding out. "I don't think I can answer that without incriminating myself."

I had out my wallet, but Justin glared until I put it back in my bag. "I'll bet you were the model student when you were in college," I said. "All studious, and home by ten when you had an early class."

"I'm still *in* college."

"I mean, when you were a normal freshman, before you decided to become a weird academic."

"Actually." His mouth turned up in rueful memory. "My friend Henry and I almost got kicked out of school."

"For what?"

He paid for our coffees with a five and waved off the change. "Nothing that I'm going to admit to you."

"Come on," I cajoled. "I know almost nothing about you before we met."

"It's safer that way."

"For who?"

"For me," he said with a grin, and held open the door.

＊　＊　＊

I used my extra time between morning classes to go over to the Sigma house. The first floor was the foyer, chapter room, dining hall, and kitchen. The floors above that were bedrooms, with two wings running out from the central hub of the staircase. The banister and balustrades were dark polished wood, the stairs creaky underfoot. The hallways were carpeted and wainscoted, like a stately home.

Devon was on the second floor. I didn't know her schedule, but her door was ajar. I tapped on it and poked my head in. She was alone, lying on her bed, a thick art history book on her chest. "Got a minute?"

She laid the book aside and sat up. "Sure."

I noticed that her eyes were puffy and her hair was less flippy than usual. "I'm working on my pledge book, and I was wondering if you had time to answer a few questions."

"Sure," she said again, and patted the end of the bed. "Have a seat."

I couldn't help staring at the walls of her tiny room. They'd been painted with a mural of the seaside, complete with sunbathing women checking out a buff lifeguard. "Nice," I said.

"Thanks. Gotta do something with all the extra energy."

Not sure what she meant by that—not sure I wanted to know—I let it go and pulled out a pen and my book. "Our pledge president has been riding us about these."

"We all thought you were going to be pledge prez." She folded her legs, Indian-style. "When Tara told us in board meeting you weren't . . . Well, I thought smoke was going to come out of Victoria's nostrils."

"That wouldn't have surprised me at all." I poised my pen. "So you're on the board?"

"Yeah. I'm the house committee liaison. I coordinate with the alumnae house board, tell them that the exterminator didn't show up or the toilets are blocked again. Real glamorous, huh?"

I grinned. "Very sexy."

"It's a thankless job. And a pain, because I have a master key to all the locks, so somehow I'm always the one that gets called whenever someone needs to get in the initiation closet."

"The initiation closet?" I chewed my pen and didn't have to work very hard at looking nervous. "They don't, um, lock pledges in there or anything, do they? I've heard stories about putting girls in coffins and stuff like that."

"Lord, no." She made a face. "The closet is just where we store all the ceremonial stuff. And the Christmas decorations.

But there's never enough storage in the rooms, so people are always wanting to stick their crap in there."

And Justin wondered why I doubt there's big bad magic here. They kept their cauldron in the broom closet.

She shifted on the bed; with her freckles and wan face, she looked young and vulnerable. "Don't tell Kirby that I blabbed anything about initiation, okay?"

"No problem." Whatever was up with her, Devon's distress had appealed to my do-gooder nature, and I was firmly on her side. I looked down at the blank page of my book, and tried to think of a decent question. "So, where are you from?"

"Alabama."

"If you were a flavor of ice cream, what would you be?"

She laughed. "Pistachio."

I made up some more questions, something to fill up the page. What I really wanted to know, though, I saved until I closed the binder and capped my pen. "Can I ask you one more thing? Off the record?"

Her gaze turned wary, but she didn't decline. "Okay."

"Why are the other sisters—Kirby and Jenna, at least—so set against Cole?"

She hung her head in her hands, elbows on her knees. "Oh, Maggie. You're just a pledge. You'll understand soon."

"Is it because he's not a Greek?"

"No."

"Because he's not a Gamma Phi Epsilon?"

"No. Not exactly." She folded her arms tightly. "I can't talk about it with you, Maggie. Please believe me."

"Then at least tell me why it was a secret that he's writing a book?"

490

Her face crumpled, tears welling and slipping down her cheeks. "Because I'm his muse." At least, that's what I thought she said. It was a little hard to tell through the sniffling.

"Why is that bad? Is the book about you? The Sigmas?"

"No." She dashed at her tears and struggled for calm.

"Okay." I let it go, waited until she got herself together, then asked, as gently as I could, "Did you break up?"

She nodded, biting her lip. Then shook her head. "We're on a break. I'm giving him some space."

"He doesn't look like he wants it."

Devon nodded and stared at her interlaced fingers. "We need it."

I didn't bother to ask her to explain. "Can I do anything to help?"

Raising her head, she gave me a miserable smile. "No. Thank you. Cole told me you were helping him at the paper. You're a good person, Maggie."

"No." I shook my head. "Not really. I'm just a sucker for star-crossed love."

23

On Thursday, Will took the seat next to me in history class. Dad raised his eyebrows when he saw the new arrangement, and called on me several times during the discussion to make sure I was paying attention, especially since Ashley, on my other side, kept giggling like we were in junior high.

After dismissal, while everyone gathered their books and tromped down the steps to the door, Will turned to me with a smile. "So, I'll see you tonight?"

"What's tonight?" No wonder I'd never had a social life; I couldn't keep track of it all.

"Working on the Homecoming float." The *Of course* was implied.

"Oh yeah. I'll be there. Mandatory for pledges."

"Great." He gestured for me to go ahead of him. I'm not sure how far he planned to accompany me, but I stopped by the front desk, making it clear I intended to linger. Dad nodded to Will, who said, "Professor" courteously back to him, then "See ya" to me before he left.

Dad did the eyebrow thing and I ignored it. Again. "Hey, Dad."

"Greetings, offspring." He closed his laptop and disconnected it from the video port on the podium.

I helped him gather the rest of his things. "Ironic that I stayed home to be with you guys while Mom experiences the miracle of childbirth, and I'm never home."

Dad gave me a fond look. "I know perfectly well why you stayed home, Magpie. So does your mother."

"Yes, well . . ." I blushed, because staying home was one of those things I knew I had to do if I wanted to be able to live with myself, but I wasn't always gracious about it. "I have to go. See you tonight."

"Will you be home for dinner?"

"When am I ever?"

"What is it tonight? Mr. Alphabet?" Meaning Will.

"Homecoming float." I rolled my eyes to show my school spirit.

"Ah." He put his hands over his heart. "Your mother would be so proud."

✳   ✳   ✳

The float construction took place by the detached garage between the Sigma Alpha Xi and Gamma Phi Epsilon houses. Convenient. The place had once been a carriage house shared by the two homes, but now it was owned by the Gamma Phi

Eps, and they stored, among things that did not bear investigating, the flatbed trailer that would serve as the base for the float.

A cold front had blown in. The guys worked on the float with their breath making clouds around their red faces. The girls stood in the shelter of the garage, wrapped in scarves, hands tucked in pockets.

The theme for the parade was "Ahead to the Future." All the clubs on campus put forward an entry, except maybe the Young Republicans, but only because they were afraid of potshots. Each sorority teamed with a fraternity, and since it was a measure of social ranking, the pairings were vitally important. Except for the Sigmas and Gamma Phi Eps, who were always first in status, and always matched with each other.

Not that they always won the school prize. That was irrelevant. The real prize was intangible—the jealousy of your peers.

This year's float, in keeping with the theme, was a spaceship. I was sure no one else would think of that.

"Well, ours will be better than everyone else's," said Brittany when I pointed this out. She was all over the place, directing the builders and chastising the observers. The rest of the Sigmas were happy to drink hot chocolate and let sexism work for them.

I had brought my pledge book, and put my time to good use. Four more pages filled before the boys had gotten the first of the framework put up.

"That's cheating," said Brittany. "You can't do two mandatory things at once."

Holly drawled, "You're just jealous you didn't think of it."

"Am not." Her hands went to her hips. "And I did think of it, I just decided it would be *cheating*."

"Here." Jenna shoved a mug of hot chocolate at her. "Have a drink."

"Please," said Holly. "Put something in her mouth to shut her up."

"I volunteer," called one of the Gamma Phi Eps. Brittany's cheeks darkened and she flounced off, finally robbed of speech.

Jenna laughed and handed the mug to me instead. The drink was steaming hot and tasted like it had peppermint mixed in. The warmth went straight to my toes.

"So," she asked, "who's the guy from the library?"

I didn't quite choke. "The who?"

She gave me a don't-be-coy look. "Will told David, who told me, that you were talking to someone in the library."

"Is it normal for fraternity guys to gossip like old women?"

Her shoulder lifted in a shrug that didn't deny the point. "Will likes you. He thinks this guy is why you've been playing hard to get."

"Hand to God," I swore with complete honesty. "Library Guy and I are just friends."

"Good." The wind pinked her cheeks; in her knit hat she looked like an impish five-year-old. "Because David also told me that Will *really* likes you."

"Gosh! Did he pass you a note in gym class?"

She laughed. "Don't you take anything seriously?"

"It's part of my charm."

Jenna glanced around, then gestured to the lowered tail-gate of someone's pickup. "Let's sit over there."

I followed her over, past where Devon was painting very realistic comets and nebulae on the panels that would go around the bottom, representing space, the final frontier. The hot chocolate—and whatever was in it—was making me mellow, so I settled beside her on the tailgate, the metal cold even through my jeans.

We watched the guys for a bit; I saw Will over by Jenna's boyfriend, David, the yenta of Gamma Phi Epsilon, horsing around with their electric screwdrivers—which sounds like a metaphor for something, but it's not. When Brittany told them to stop goofing off, they saluted her and went back to work.

"Gamma Phi Eps"—Jenna picked up where she had left off, and her tone was *significant*—"are good matches for Sigmas."

"You mean they're . . ." I tapped my forehead. I could mean psychic, or I could mean crazy. Or both, which is how I felt lately. "Like us?"

Jenna shook her head. "Not any more than any other random population of people."

Dead end on that question. "Well, that's a relief. I was worried there was a conspiracy."

She looked at me sharply. "A what?"

"To breed a master race of television psychics."

Jenna folded her arms and didn't laugh, but looked as if she wanted to. "You have no idea how special you are, do you? Even among us. That's why Kirby pushed for Brittany to be pledge prez. You could run laps around her when it comes to . . ."

"What?" I asked, when she didn't go on.

"You'll find out when the time is right."

I let my irritation show. "I hate being in the dark."

"I know." She sounded honestly sympathetic. "But you shouldn't be thinking about it so much. It'll give you a headache." Her hand squeezed mine where it rested on the tailgate, and her fingers were almost as cold as the metal. "Just wait until initiation. You'll understand everything then."

Initiation again. All roads led there, where I *so* did not want to go.

24

Two weeks slipped away in a circular blur of class, newspaper, homework, Homecoming, and Sigma Alpha Xi activities. I overheard two actives saying that since losing the election for pledge president, I really seemed to have discovered my Sigma spirit.

Whatever.

Ethan Douglas, editor of the *Avalon Sentinel,* called and asked me to do an article on the student art show in the campus gallery, and Will asked me to Homecoming. The more time I spent with the Sigmas, the more things went well.

Except, of course, that I didn't want to go with *Will* to Homecoming.

I saw Justin on Tuesdays and Thursdays, but since Will walked with me from history to the arts building, we didn't speak more than "Hey" and "How are you." Which, as I had nothing to report, was enough. Theoretically.

On Thursday before the parade, I tried my best to corral the SAXis and Gamma Phi Eps into a picture with the not-quite-finished float. I'd gone around Greek Row to interview the other houses and had the same problem; getting them all to behave long enough to get a workable photo was like herding cats.

"Come on, guys! Squish in." I framed the shot for my third attempt. "This is for the school paper, so maybe you could hide the liquor bottles this time?"

They did, *finally*, and when I was done, Devon, Holly, and Jenna crowded in to look at the camera's view screen. "Can I have a copy of that?" Jenna asked.

"Sure. I can print you one after I upload them." I checked my watch. "Which I need to do if there's a hope of this running in tomorrow's paper."

"Can you use my computer, Maggie?" Devon asked. She was looking more like her perky self, so I suspected her "break" was over. "Cole has sent stuff in from there."

"Probably. Do you mind?"

"I wouldn't have offered otherwise." She waved for me to follow her. "Come on."

Since the front door of the sorority house required a key—only Sigmas and their pledges had one—a lot of the girls didn't lock their rooms, especially if they were just going downstairs. Devon was one of them.

"Here you go." She woke the desktop computer with a jiggle of the mouse. "We're on the school network, like a dorm."

"Thanks." I pulled the USB cable out of my camera bag and started hooking up.

"Do you need me? Otherwise I'll go back outside."

"I'm good. I'll close the door when I leave."

She took off, and I uploaded the photos, first to the computer and then through the Internet to the *Report* server. While I waited for them to finish loading, I browsed the bulletin board on Devon's wall. It was full of pictures—of her and her pledge sisters, of Cole, of parties and vacations.

A set of keys hung from a hook. The fob was a woodcut cartoon octopus with indigo SAXi letters. Not the most convenient thing to tuck in your pocket on the way to class.

No way was it that easy. Keeping an eye on the open door, I plucked the ring from the hook. I got a muddled sense of a series of girls who had held them, but overwhelmingly, these belonged to the house. When I concentrated, I could distinguish each one: front door, chapter room, outside storage shed, and finally a musty, stuffy dark place. The closet.

I checked the hall: Grand Central Station. The whole chapter was here, mostly out working on the float, but also in and out of rooms to get coats and drinks, up and down the stairs. Okay, maybe not that easy.

Grabbing my own key ring from my camera bag, I flipped through it until I found one of the same standard industrial-shaped keys as the one for the closet. It was to my family's rented storage unit, so hopefully if Devon did touch the ring, she wouldn't sense anything out of the ordinary. The worry would be moot if she tried to actually *use* it, but the whole thing was a gamble in the first place.

Things work out for Sigmas. I said it over and over in my mind, like a mantra. *I'm a Sigma. I might as well put it to use.*

25

"I think I can get into the closet where they keep their supersecret stuff."

Justin stared at me, his sandwich frozen halfway to his mouth. We were eating lunch in Dad's office; he wouldn't notice any extra crumbs and—privilege of tenure—he usually left at noon on Fridays anyway.

The sandwich went back down onto the wrapper. "How are you planning to do that?"

"There's this big mandatory party tonight at the Abbotts' place for all the alums who are coming for Homecoming. I'm going to slip out, go back to the Sigma house."

"They just leave their supersecret stuff lying around?"

"Well, not exactly."

He eyed me sternly. "So you're going to break in."

"Of course not. I have a key." I took a bite of chicken salad, chewed, and swallowed, all under his inscrutable stare. "But there actually is something you can help me with."

* * *

Once again I had done my shopping at the fine establishment of Grandmother's Closet. Tonight's ensemble was very *Breakfast at Tiffany's*—black cocktail dress, pearls, and ballet flats. I'd learned my lesson on footwear: you never knew when you'd be facing down hordes of ravenous demon spawn, and kitten heels could be a real encumbrance.

The Abbotts' Victorian mansion was brightly lit, inside and out. The doors and windows opened to the veranda for guests to wander. Which they did, squealing with delight when they saw a sister, or clasping hands and slapping backs with a brother.

The Gamma Phi Epsilon alumni were there, too. Lawyers, CEOs, bestselling novelists. I knew these weren't *all* the university's notable alumni, but being in the room with them, it seemed that way.

The student members were encouraged to circulate and schmooze. There was an open bar for those old enough to drink, and the pledges took well-orchestrated shifts carrying trays of punch and canapés around. I was bringing an empty tray to the kitchen and checking my watch when Holly came up and wrapped her arm around mine.

"My mother wants to meet you."

"Your mother's here?" I set the tray on a console table in the hall, since I was obviously not going to get back to the kitchen. "You didn't say she was coming."

"I was hoping her plane would crash."

Holly had been hitting the sauce. The only thing that gave her away, though, was the brightness of her eyes and redness of the tip of her nose. Well, and the looseness of her tongue.

I knew Holly drank, but since her underwear-drawer stash consisted of little airplane bottles, I hadn't been too concerned. Now I wondered.

"Should I be worried?" I asked.

"Only if you're allergic to brimstone."

If she only knew.

Still clinging to my arm, she pulled me to a corner of the room, where a gorgeous auburn-haired woman in a three-thousand-dollar suit held court in the midst of a bunch of Gamma Phi Eps. They were, man and boy, practically tripping over their lolling tongues.

It wasn't simply that the woman was beautiful. She radiated charisma. Once you were in her sphere, it was hard to look away. The power was palpable, raising the hair on my arms. Holly had told me her mother was a lawyer; if she stood in a courtroom and told me the moon was made of green cheese, I would believe her.

"Holly!" She beckoned her daughter through the entourage. "Is this your new friend?"

"Mom, this is Maggie Quinn. Maggie, this is my mother, Juliana Baker-Russell-Hattendorf-Hughes."

Riiiight. No passive aggression there.

The multinamed lady shot Holly the briefest of glares, then extended her manicured hand to me with a smile. "A pleasure, Maggie. Holly has spoken of you often."

I braced before taking her hand, shields at full power. That battle station was fully operational. "Nice to meet you, Ms. . . ." No way could I remember all those names.

"Hughes is fine. Or Juliana, since we're sisters, after all." She released my fingers and I resisted the impulse to shake my hand the way a dog shakes off water. "I hear you're trying to decide between English and photojournalism."

"Well, the journalism seems to be out in front at the moment."

"Make sure you stay in touch, then. I have some contacts with the news services."

"Too bad Jane and Ted got divorced," Holly said. "She and Mom are like *that.*" She held up her crossed fingers.

"Great!" I grabbed my friend's arm firmly. "Nice to meet you, Ms. Hughes!" Chirruping too brightly, I dragged Holly away before her mother the Death Star could blow up Planet Freshman with her laser eye beams.

"Very nice," I drawled when we were out of earshot. "Thank you *so* much for introducing me."

"You're welcome." Once we reached the kitchen, she pulled her hand from mine and sagged against the counter, making the busy catering staff reroute around her. "God, why did I wear high heels? I'm six feet tall already. Trade shoes with me, Maggie."

"I don't think they'd fit." I glanced at my watch. I had to make up an excuse and get out of there to rendezvous with Justin.

"I hate my mother."

The caterers were eyeing us with less annoyance and more curiosity now. I patted Holly's shoulder, hoping to coax her to use, as my mother said, an inside voice. "She'll be going back home after the weekend."

"Doesn't matter." She pulled off the offending shoes and tossed them on the floor. I fetched them before they could trip an innocent food service worker; Holly grabbed an open bottle of champagne, poured a generous helping into a punch glass, and downed it before I could stop her.

"She killed my father, you know."

I stared at Holly, mouth agape, but she went on, oblivious to the dead stop in the kitchen. "He had a heart attack in the middle of fucking her. How's that for a cliché?"

"Peachy." I reached for her arm, intending to lead her to a more private place, or at least relieve her of the bottle. But she easily avoided my grasp.

"Maybe I'll just go in there and tell all those boys about *that*." She stepped in the direction of the party and yelled, "Stay away from her, boys! She's a black widow, that one!"

This was getting serious. There was a room full of alumnae witches in there, and I didn't know how far sister- *or* motherhood would protect Holly if she really made them mad.

"Come on." I tugged her insistently toward the back door. "Let's go get some fresh air."

"Why?" She looked down at me belligerently. "Because I shouldn't embarrass my darling mother?"

"Because you shouldn't piss her off!"

A flash of sobering fear entered her eyes. "No. I shouldn't. Let's go."

Ignoring the staring caterers, I led her onto the back porch, where the bracing air ruffled our dresses and, I hope, cleared her brain. She tilted her head back and stared at the bright stars whirling through the spiral arm barely discernible on the inky fabric of space.

"Sorry," she finally said.

"It's all right. Nothing like airing family laundry to make a party special."

She smiled slightly. "That's not the half of it. Steven divorced her because she was sleeping around, and this new guy doesn't even care, as long as he gets his first."

"Nice."

"She's a succubus. I don't want to be anything like her, yet here I am. At her alma mater. In her sorority."

Something struck me about that choice of word. "Succubus?"

"A demon that sleeps with men to steal their souls."

"Yeah. I know. But you mean that figuratively, right?"

She laughed. "How else would I mean it?"

Well, I'd learned not to take these things for granted. And when I say I got a feeling of power off Juliana Baker-Russell-Hattendorf-Hughes, I mean some *serious* power.

"Do you have somewhere to be?"

I looked at her, startled, probably a lot guilty. "What?"

"You keep glancing at your watch."

Some spy I am. "Oh. No." Gosh, that didn't sound guilty at all. "Well, yes. I have to—I need to—"

She raised her brows expectantly. I made one last-ditch effort at a save. "I'm meeting someone."

Her eyebrows shot up even farther. "*You* are meeting someone?"

The disbelief in her tone was a little insulting. "Yes. Why is that so incredible?"

"Because you're so . . . Gidget." She laughed at my offended expression. "Okay. Maybe not. You're too snarky."

"Aren't you going to tell me I shouldn't date an independent, or all Sigmas date Gammas, or whatever?"

"No. I'm rebelling vicariously."

I stepped off the porch, then turned back, whispering, "Aren't you going to tell me not to have sex while I'm a pledge?"

Laughter in her eyes, she asked, "Would it make you feel better if I did?"

"Yes."

"Okay. Don't do anything I wouldn't do. How's that?"

"You either. Seriously." I sobered to warn her. "Stay away from the booze and stay away from your mother."

"Deal."

26

"You're late." Justin put the car in drive and headed the few blocks to Greek Row. "I was about to go in and get you."

"Like Orpheus in the underworld?" I grabbed my jeans from the backseat and pulled them on under my dress. "That's sweet."

"You joke about those things, and I never know how serious you are. Is it any wonder I worry about you?"

"I know. I get it. I'm high-maintenance. So you've said."

"We're not having that argument again. What really bothers me is—God, Maggie! Do you have to do that?"

I had unzipped my dress and extracted my arms so that I

could pull on a black cat-burglar sweater. "What? Don't be such a prude, Justin." All the same, I yanked the turtleneck over my head and squirmed into it quickly.

He cruised past the SAXi house, which was quiet and dark, and looked for a spot to park a few doors down. "What really bothers me is that you keep picking crusades that I can't help you with. High school, now a sorority. You're going to a convent next, I know it."

"Why is my chastity such a big issue with everyone lately?"

"What?"

"Nothing." He parked the car and got out. I buttoned my jeans and wiggled the dress down my legs, stepping out of it as Justin opened my door. Grabbing my camera bag from the floorboard, I climbed out and tugged down my sweater.

"At least let me go in with you," he said.

The SAXi and Gamma Phi Ep houses were quiet, but there was plenty of activity on the street as the other chapters worked on their floats for the morning's parade.

"Then who'd keep a lookout?" I checked that I had the right keys. "Distribution of manpower."

Shaking his head in frustration, he rested a hand on the roof of the car. "I cannot believe I am so whipped," he grumbled, "and we're not even dating."

I looked up at him in irritation. One, he was blocking my way. Two, "If you're looking for sympathy, you're talking to the wrong person, *pal.*"

A rapid series of emotions moved across his face, and he opened his mouth to say something, then snapped it closed. "Later," he said, and stepped out of my way. I shouldered my bag and headed for the house, walking as though I had every right to be there.

Technically I wasn't breaking and entering since, as a Sigma, I had a key to the front door. Maybe, if I got caught, a judge would see things my way. If I ever made it to see a judge. I guess the Sigmas could decide to simply sacrifice me at the next meeting and save the court's trouble.

Justin was right. I really had to stop joking about things like that.

Still, I couldn't help feeling conspicuous as I entered the foyer, hyperaware of the chapter room to my right. Too easy to picture something lurking behind the closed door, like a monster in the closet. And the more I pictured it, the more powerful and gruesome it became, until it seethed in my mind with reason-killing ferocity.

Get a grip, Maggie. You're not five years old anymore.

But I hurried past all the same.

The stairs sighed softly under my feet as I climbed to the second floor, holding my camera bag against my side to keep it from swinging. The upstairs hallways ran north and south, with the bathrooms at one end. The storage closets were opposite, so I turned left at the top of the first flight of steps.

I crept, cat-footed, past the bedrooms, even though I'd done a mental check of all the residents while at the party. The hall seemed endless, but finally I reached the closet and contemplated the solid wood door and the deadbolt.

Not worried about fingerprints as much as I was psycheprints, I filled my mind with images of octopi and compasses and indigo auras before I inserted the key and turned the knob. I expected an atmospheric creak as I pulled open the door, but the hinges glided smoothly, without a sound.

The closet was pitch dark and a little musty, but underneath the smell of old plaster and carpet glue was something spicy, and a little earthy, with a tangy metallic thread: the incense from that first night. I'd found the right place.

I flipped the light switch with my elbow and stared at the perfectly mundane storage room, maybe ten feet by twenty. Industrial shelves against the walls. Boxes marked "Xmas Lights" and "Skit Night" and a rolled canvas backdrop on the floor. Lightbulbs and Sam's Club–sized packages of toilet paper. In the corner was a large water heater, and beside it a neat stack of luggage, stored for the semester. No sign of anything the least bit mysterious.

Poking around, I found a box of white candles like we'd used in the pledging ceremony, and the crimson stoles, folded neatly. Finally I found a few boxes labeled "Initiation," and inside were a lot of white togas, several skeins of silken cord, and more candles—indigo and crimson.

With a derisive snort, I pushed the box back onto the shelf. I'd expected something a little more exciting than inventory from the Wiccan Gift Shop.

About to give up, I made one last turn around the tiny room, this time using all my senses. Nothing leaped out and snagged my attention.

And by that I mean an actual nothingness; there was a *hole* in the back corner.

Everything, even lightbulbs and Christmas decorations, feels like something, even if it's just the psychic equivalent of white noise. The dead space reminded me of the strange blankness in my head when I woke with the aftereffects of a dream, but no memory of it.

I walked to the corner, and saw a cabinet. Plain, industrial.

Locked. I pulled a Nancy Drew: taking the barrette from my hair, I reshaped the wire clasp until I could slip it between the double doors, catch the latch, and pull it up.

The monster wasn't downstairs. It lived in this box.

A dank smell, like old, wet leaves, rolled out of the cabinet, and with it a feeling of ancient power. I'd felt something like it once before when I'd touched an artifact forged millennia ago for arcane purposes. This tangible energy was not as old, but just as icky. There was a baseness to it; death and sex and blood—the earthy, metallic smell beneath the spicy sweetness of the incense.

I saw the censer on the top shelf, the burnished metal looking warm even in the incandescent light of the bare bulb. A bowl the size of a candy dish, it had a lid with holes for the smoke to emerge. Turning on my camera, I took pictures of the censer and of the symbols etched in the brass.

The lamp sat next to it; they looked like a matched set. I took down a plastic bottle, unscrewed the top, and sniffed. Oil, with a pungent smell. I soaked one of my lens-cleaning cloths with a little of it, and tucked it in one of the pockets of my camera bag. Tucked behind the censer was a Tupperware container that held the incense, and I took a sample of that as well. Who knew all those *CSI* reruns would come in so handy?

On the bottom of the two shelves was the book, lying by itself. I wiped suddenly damp palms on my jeans. The feeling of danger and power was so strong, I would have rather put my hand in a vat of earthworms than pick up that heavy volume.

And that's about what it felt like: when my fingers made contact with the leather binding, my skin tried to crawl up my arm and away from the Evil—capital *E*—that I sensed inside.

With a deep breath, I pulled the tome from the cabinet, holding it away from my body. It was heavy: big like a coffee table book, and fat like a dictionary. The leather of the cover was pale and smooth, darker where generations of hands had touched it, and worn at the corners and edges.

No lettering or symbols marked the outside. Gingerly, I set it on top of a box of toilet paper and opened it, letting the thick pages fall where they pleased.

Calligraphy script, illuminated diagrams, and a lot of text I didn't understand and wasn't going to grasp in the short time I had. I snapped pictures of as many pages as I dared then, hoping that was good enough, I closed the book and with great relief slid it back onto its shelf.

My phone vibrated in my pocket, startling me. I fumbled it open without looking at the caller ID.

Holly's voice, tight and quiet. "Victoria and my mother just shot out of here like a pair of greyhounds after a rabbit."

"What?"

"Maggie, I don't know what you're doing, what you're *really* doing. But *they* know. And wherever you are, they're going there now."

I didn't have to be told twice. I shut the cabinet doors, using my impromptu jimmy to hook the latch back in place. The dreadful wrongness disappeared, the blankness coming back down like a curtain.

Grabbing my camera bag, I dashed out of the closet, locking it behind me, then sprinted down the hallway to Devon's room. *Please don't let this be the one day she locked her door. . . .*

It wasn't. As I fumbled the closet key onto its proper ring, my phone vibrated again: Justin, warning me they were outside. House keys returned to normal, I shoved my own into my pocket and started back out.

Too late. I heard the creak of footsteps on the stairs and ducked back into the room. What the hell was I supposed to do now? There was a fire escape, but it was on the far side of the staircase.

The women's voices came closer, becoming distinct as they neared Devon's door. I pressed myself to the wall and visualized becoming one with the house. *Deflector shields, don't fail me now.*

"You can't really think it's her."

"What I think, Victoria, is that you need that girl, so you are blind to the fact that she's playing you for a fool."

"I have the situation under control."

"Oh, you are *all* about control." Juliana's voice was derisive. "Control and playing it safe."

Victoria answered tightly. "Not everyone is about using people up and throwing them out. I'm making a long-term investment."

"So am I."

"In yourself, you mean."

"Do *not* fuck with me, Victoria." Frost rimed the woman's voice. They must have stopped directly outside. I could feel the icy power through the door, sense the dominance shifting between the women like weather patterns. "Never forget who started this. You would never have had the guts to do what I did. And if I hadn't, where would you be? Married to a city councilman with two mortgages and a minivan in the garage."

But Victoria wasn't done. "Don't threaten me, Juliana. Where would *you* be if I hadn't kept this house going the last twenty years? You need us. You need *me.*"

"Not as much as you think," she purred, clearly a threat. "But my daughter does. Now open the door and let's see if someone has put their hand in the cookie jar."

I'd been careful to put everything back, not just where it looked right, but where it *felt* right. But I worried that my fear and revulsion might be the psychic equivalent of a neon sign.

Hurrying to the window, I raised the sash and looked out. Only one floor up, but my heart pounded as if it were a dozen. Looping my bag bandolier-style, I sat on the ledge and swung out one leg, then the other, turning so that I hung out the window, then lowering myself until my dangling feet found the ledge below.

How did a girl as unathletic as me keep getting into these predicaments? And why was it *always* heights?

Clinging white-knuckled to the brick overhang, I managed to lower the window sash, which is tricky from the outside. Then I realized I was going to have to let my feet go, hang from my fingertips, and drop to the ground. Let's see—sprained or broken ankle versus the Witch Queens of Endor.

I'd take my chances on crutches.

Luckily it was autumn, and that meant rain. The ground yielded, absorbed my weight, then dumped me onto my butt, where I have the most padding. I'm telling you: Things work out for Sigmas.

27

"**D**rive," I wheezed, diving into the backseat of Justin's car after my sprint from the SAXi house. "I have to beat them back to the Abbotts'."

Justin stepped on the gas and the little Honda sped down the street while he fired questions at me. "What the hell were you doing in there? How did you get out? And what do you mean you're going back to the Abbott house?"

I pulled off my sweater, yanked the black dress over my head, struggled out of my jeans. "Holly will cover for me, say I've been there the whole time."

"How do you know that?"

"Because she hates her mother." I contorted in the backseat, wrestling with my zipper. If it were a dream instead of a nightmare, the car would be parked and Justin would be back there with me. God had a real sense of humor sometimes.

"You're determined to give me a heart attack," he grumbled, taking another turn at full speed and throwing me against the car door. "I'm going to be gray by the time I'm twenty-five."

"You know I can hear you, right?"

Letting him grouse, I pulled my phone from my jeans and called Holly to tell her I was on the way back, and what I needed from her. When I hung up, Justin asked, "Are you at least going to tell me what you found?"

"I took pictures of everything." Searching the floorboard, I came up with my right shoe. "I'll show you after I put in an appearance at Victoria's house."

"How long?"

The left shoe was harder to find. "I just have to be there when they get back."

When he stopped the car in the street beside the Abbotts' house, Holly was coming down the back steps. "You really trust this girl?" Justin asked, twisting in his seat so that he could look me in the eye.

I didn't think too hard, just went with my gut. "Right now, yes."

"More than you trusted Lisa?"

Low blow. I shot him a glare as I stuck my cell phone into my purse. "Less than I trust Lisa, if my life is at stake."

"Maggie." He caught my hand before I could climb out of the car. "You took pictures of what was there. We can figure out what is going on from outside. You don't have to go back in."

His eyes were almost black in the faint light of the dashboard, fathomless with worry for me. I wanted so much to take that away. Not that I wasn't scared; since I'd touched that book, all my flippancy, my ambivalence, was gone. This wasn't just some sorority girls with supernaturally shiny hair, tweaking the probabilities in their favor. This was the capital *E*. I'd be an idiot not to be scared.

But I'd be worse than a coward if I didn't do everything I could to stop it. And right now, everything meant going into Victoria's house and preserving my place within the Sigmas.

"If things were the other way around," I asked, "would *you* retreat to a safe distance?"

"That's not the point."

I smiled, even though there was no time for it. "I love that you're such a chauvinist."

He didn't bother to deny it. He didn't really have a chance, because the car door opened and Holly said, "Just kiss already. We've got to get going."

Justin glared at her, then at me. "If you're not at my place in thirty minutes, I'm coming back here . . . with crosses and holy water if necessary."

"Okay." I looked him in the eye as I said it, making it a promise. "Thirty minutes."

I climbed out of the car and straightened my dress. Holly grabbed my arm and we hurried to the back porch. I cast one last look back to make sure Justin was leaving. Did that make me Orpheus or Eurydice? Things didn't turn out well for either of them.

* * *

I entered the kitchen on Holly's heels. The catering staff continued packing up their stuff, casting curious glances our way, but mostly ignoring us the way Holly ignored them. "I have been hiding out back here, avoiding Mommie Dearest. We'll just say that you've been helping me while I've been . . ."

"Drunk off your ass?"

"Don't diss the drunk that saved your butt." She peered out the window as a car pulled into the drive behind the house. Justin's taillights had barely disappeared.

"Come on." She pulled me down the hall to a small bedroom with an attached bath. Holly went into the bathroom and sat on the side of the tub. I stared, bemused, until she pointed to the stack of finger towels by the sink. Catching a clue, I ran some water and soaked a cloth, ready to pretend I'd been tending to her for some time.

The back door slammed, then footsteps rang in the hall. "Holly?" I knew Juliana's voice now. Her telling Victoria to eff off had made a big impression. "The waitstaff said . . ."

She appeared in the doorway to find Holly looking wan, while I mopped her brow and her damp red hair.

"Oh, *Holly*." Her expression was a mixture of disgust and disdain. "Are you determined to humiliate me? You couldn't be drunk at one of your *own* parties?"

"What fun would that be?" Holly asked, convincingly inebriated and belligerent.

Juliana eyed me next, and I felt the full weight of it in my stomach. "And you. What have you been up to, Maggie?"

"She's been with me, Mom."

"Holly wasn't feeling very well," I said, lies on top of lies, all smoke screen. "I thought I'd better stay with her."

Victoria appeared behind the other woman and took in the scene. "Oh. Holly, really."

Juliana turned her attention to spin control. "Fortunately, Holly had the good sense to take herself out of public view."

The currents of power shifted again, and Victoria now had the upper hand. "Do you realize how serious this is? At the very least, she should be brought up before Standards."

"Oh, really. You want it to come out that a minor got drunk at your house?"

Victoria didn't blink. "She'd nevertheless be out of the sorority."

To my surprise, Juliana backed down. She might have the edge where mojo was concerned, but Victoria had boxed her in. Her eyes flashed at the knowledge, and her mouth went white at the corners, making her look much closer to her real age.

"I won't forget this, Victoria." She turned to go, calling her daughter to heel. "Come on, Holly."

"Can't I just go back to the dorm?"

"Now." In her anger, all semblance of shielding dropped away, and she stood before us, a mass of fury and frustration. Holly rose, jaw jutting but silent, to face her.

I felt a protective spark in my chest, wanting to shield the girl who, screwed up as she was, had helped me. But Victoria's tiny head shake silenced me; I would only make things worse for Holly by speaking up for her.

Instead I just offered her a hand up, and steadied her once she was on her feet. "Will you be okay?" I whispered.

"You say that like I've never done this before." She gave me a tipsy salute and trailed after her fuming mother.

When they left, the chapter sponsor folded her arms and

leaned against the doorframe, studying me, reminding me I wasn't off the hook yet.

"You two have become rather good friends, haven't you?"

"We hit it off during Rush."

"Her mother expected her to be the head of her pledge class. Holly lacks your ability and ambition, but don't let your friendship bring down your guard."

"No, ma'am."

"Even among wolves, there are alphas and there are betas."

"I understand." In the other room, I'd thrown my purse onto the bed, and it began to buzz in time to my vibrating phone. Had it been thirty minutes already?

"Go ahead." Victoria stepped aside to let me pass.

I answered as soon as I fumbled the cell free from my bag. "Hi, Mom."

"Are you on your way?" Justin's voice brooked no argument.

"Just about. Let me ask." I closed my eyes for the briefest moment, hoping my cloaking device would last just a little longer, then turned to face Victoria. "My mom's not feeling well. Wants to know if I can come home."

"Of course," she said. "You have to take care of your family."

I smiled a humble thank-you and she accepted it with a regal nod. "On my way now," I said into the phone.

"You'd better be," he said, before I closed the phone and picked up my purse.

"Thank you for hosting the party," I told Victoria, falling back on good manners to get me out the door.

"I'm happy to do it," she answered, in the same polite tone. "Now, go home and take care of your mother. She's in a delicate condition, after all."

"Thanks," I said again, and made my exit through the back door to where my Jeep was parked down the street.

It wasn't until later that I thought to wonder when I'd told her that Mom was pregnant.

28

Justin lived in an efficiency apartment, part of off-campus housing, not far from Greek Row. I'd never been to his place before. Actually, I'd never been to any guy's apartment before, so I had no idea how his compared.

Mostly, he had books. There was a futon, a milk-crate side table, a large desk with neatly organized work stacked beside a closed laptop, and some cinder-block-and-plank shelves that held CDs, a small TV, and a smaller stereo. But mostly books.

"It's not much," Justin said as he gestured me in. "But make yourself at home."

"Sure." Small, but obviously his space. Posters on the wall; a distinctive quilt covering the back of the futon. Two enormous bulletin boards over the desk were filled with notes and pictures of green, wet places and weathered Gaelic faces.

A framed picture on the bookshelf showed a formally posed couple. The man stood behind the woman, his hand on her shoulder, her fingers covering his. They smiled at the camera, but there seemed to be a connection solely between them. They could only be Justin's parents. He looked just like his dad, but he had his mother's friendly brown eyes.

Another photo showed Justin looking about fifteen or sixteen and very gangly, laughing with another boy who had him in a headlock. They wore khakis, oxford shirts, blazers with a crest on the pocket. The other boy was bigger, with shoulders like a linebacker, black hair, and startling blue eyes.

I picked up the picture. Images welled in my head, incomplete and indistinct: classrooms and chapel, roughhousing after school, fights and reconciliation.

"We look like a couple of dorks in those uniforms." I hadn't heard Justin come up behind me. "That's Henry," he said, nodding at the photo.

"The one who almost got kicked out of school with you?"

"Yeah. We'd planned to go to the same college. Man, was I mad at him when he went to seminary instead."

"You don't think he'll make a good priest?"

"It's a little hard to reconcile that with the guy who used to sneak *Playboys* into our dormitory." He set the photo back on the shelf. "Are you hungry?"

My stomach growled at the thought of food. Aside from a few canapés, I hadn't eaten. "It feels later than nine o'clock."

"I'll order a pizza while you upload the pictures."

He'd brought in my camera case, and I'd had my laptop in the trunk of the Jeep. I set up on the end of his desk and rolled the chair over, careful not to catch the skirt of my dress in the wheels.

Justin hung up with the pizza place and joined me. "Okay. Let's see what you've got."

I opened the pictures on the laptop screen. "This is the incense burner from the pledging ceremony. The lamp was there, too."

Propping one hand on the desk and the other on the back of my chair, he leaned over my shoulder. "Can you zoom in on the symbols?" I did, and he made a thinking noise.

"They look like astrological signs," I said.

"Or alchemical, which borrowed a lot from astrology. Go to the lamp." He leaned in closer to look. "Yeah. Those are definitely hermetic."

"What's that?" I asked, trying not to breathe too deeply, because he smelled so good.

Fortunately—or not—he went to the bookcase and pulled down a hefty tome. "Hermeticism is an occult tradition, based on the writings or teachings of the god Hermes Trismegistus."

"Like the Greek god Hermes?"

"Sort of. Hermes rolled up with the Egyptian god Thoth. Both were bringers of knowledge to their cultures." He set the book in front of me, pointing to a bunch of symbols that looked like the ones on the chapter's brassware.

"Except that the only thing fraternities have to do with real Greeks is their letters." I looked up at him. "So what's this got to do with the Sigma Wicca Phis?"

He flipped a few pages, to a grainy picture of a guy dressed in a strange robe holding a staff of some kind. "Hermetic occultism had a renaissance in the nineteenth century. This guy, Aleister Crowley, formed a group called the Hermetic Order of the Golden Dawn. Huge influence on twentieth-century mysticism. Their ritual drew from everybody: Kabbalah, hermeticism, Egyptian paganism, alchemy, astrology . . ." He made an "and so on" gesture. "Some people think hermeticism also inspired the Illuminati, Freemasons, groups like that."

"More secret societies," I said, half to myself.

"Right." He scanned the thumbnails of the rest of the pictures, and pointed to one of the book. "What's this?"

"That"—I tried to keep my voice even—"feels like bad news." I clicked and brought the image up front. Foreign words and strange symbols crawled across the screen, and I shuddered.

He leaned closer than before, peering over my shoulder. "Oh my God." Reaching around me, he took over the trackpad and clicked through the first few pages.

"What is it?" I asked, knowing I wouldn't like the answer.

"It's a . . . Well, it *looks* like a grimoire." I could feel the tension in him, despite his attempt to keep his tone academic.

"A grimoire is like a spell book, right?"

"More or less." He pushed away from the desk, paced a little, came back to look again. "You said this thing was old?"

"Really old. And very creepy."

"Authentic grimoires were written in medieval times as

kind of magical primers. Some contain astrological corre-
spondences, recipes for mixing medicine, instructions for
making talismans . . ."

"That doesn't sound too bad." It was a feeble attempt at
hope; I knew it couldn't be that simple.

"Others have instructions for spells and potions, information on angels and demons, and directions on how to
summon them."

The bottom dropped out of my stomach. "Oh."

"Very." He stared back at me, past traumas looming large
and dark in our shared history. The air thickened with
dreadful possibilities.

Someone pounded on the door. Justin jumped, and so
did I, with a girly squeal to make it worse. He gave a shaky
laugh, breaking the tension. "Pizza's here."

While he paid the driver, I turned back to the computer
screen. I couldn't make anything of the book pages. I recognized the Latin, but even the diagrams were esoteric and
uninterpretable.

I drummed my fingers on the desk, thinking about rituals and artifacts. I tried not to think about summoning
demons. But that was like saying "Don't think of a purple
elephant." So I thought of a purple elephant, and picked up
my phone.

Justin came out of the kitchen with a plate full of more
pizza than even I could eat. "Who are you calling?"

"Lisa. We need a witch on our side."

"No." He took the phone from me. "We don't."

I stood, followed his retreat. "Maybe she can figure out
what this stuff is supposed to do."

"I can figure it out." He held the plate in one hand, and the phone easily out of my reach.

"When?" I set my hands on my hips. "I haven't forgotten about your thesis, and class, and teaching assistant job. You think I have no consideration, but—"

"Would you stop?" He faced me, mirrored my belligerence. "I never said you asked anything that I don't *want* to give. Time, resources . . . driving your getaway car."

"You *said* you were whipped."

"Well, I'm not. I'm perfectly able to say no to you, Maggie." He held up the phone. "As in 'No, we are not calling your demon-summoning friend.' "

I folded my arms. "You know what, Justin? Even if you *were* my boyfriend, I would only take that under advisement."

He stared at me for a long moment, at the stubborn set of my chin and the fight in my stance. Then, with a sigh he handed me the cell and the plate of pizza.

"Thank you." I caught his eye, making sure he knew I meant it.

He sat on the single barstool and pulled over the pizza box. "You'd just call her when you got home, so you might as well do it where I can hear."

At the desk, I put the phone on speaker so that I could eat and type while I talked. Lisa answered on the third ring. "Maggie?"

"Hi, Lisa. I need your help with something."

"Fine, thank you," she said pointedly. "And how are you?"

"Are you busy?"

"It's ten o'clock on a Friday night. Why would I be busy?"

"Great." I saved the photos and attached them to an e-mail. "I'm sending you some pretty big picture files."

Silence. "Are we ignoring the fact that you haven't returned my phone calls for the last two months?"

I felt the blood rush out of my head and pool in my stomach. "Two months? It hasn't been that long."

"Yes. It has."

Oh my God. I had a vague memory of Mom telling me she'd called. Once. Was it like the Post-it notes—written, then forgotten?

"Lisa . . . something's been going on."

She sighed. Loudly. "Let me go to my computer." I heard the squeak of a chair and the slide and click of a mouse. I took a few bites of pizza while I waited. "What am I looking at?" she asked.

"It's a long story. There's an incense burner, a lamp, and a . . ."

"I know what this is." Another pause, another mouse click. A worried sigh. "Magdalena Quinn. How do you get into these things?"

"So, do you understand it?"

Her voice turned droll. "My Latin is a little rusty to translate on the fly."

"But you could interpret what this is supposed to do?"

This time the pause was loaded. "Why are you asking me to do this? Where's the square?"

"Um, the square is right here," I said without turning around.

A beat of realization. "I'm on speakerphone, aren't I."

Justin called from across the tiny room. "Hello, Lisa."

I did glare at him then and picked up the phone, turning off the speaker. "Now it's just you and I."

"Why, Maggie? You said I shouldn't be studying this stuff."

"And *you* said the whole reason you were doing it was to counter it." I let that rest between us a moment. "Are you going to put your money where your mouth is?"

"Is that what this is? A test?"

"No. It's strategic outsourcing."

That made her laugh, once, and softly. "Okay. It's going to take me a few days. I'm just a dilettante."

"I'm relieved to hear that."

"What are you doing with a boy in your room at ten—no, ten-thirty at night?"

"He's not in my room. I'm in his."

"God, Maggie. There's hope for you yet."

"Good-*bye*, Lisa."

Shutting the phone, I let my shoulders sag. I didn't realize how tense I'd been until I felt Justin's hands on my arms. My dress was sleeveless, and his fingers were warm on my skin as he gently turned me to face him.

I stared at the top button of his shirt, the hollow at the base of his throat, shy but expectant. Giving in to my hopes, I raised my head and closed my eyes, waiting. He let go of my shoulders, and reached for . . .

My pledge pin.

He unfastened the clasp from my dress without so much as brushing anything important. Then he went to the kitchen counter and dropped it into a glass of cloudy water—salt water, for spell-breaking. Of course.

He glanced at me curiously. "Feel anything?"

Oh, the irony. It burns us, my precious.

"No." I folded my arms over my chest. I felt plenty, but didn't think that was what he meant.

"Huh." His brows knit in disappointment. "I thought maybe that was the source of the spell."

"What spell?"

"The one where you keep forgetting that you're supposed to be investigating the Sigmas."

Now I felt something. Incredibly stupid. I dropped onto the futon, pressing my fingers to my forehead. "It isn't that I forget. It's that I keep losing focus. Losing time."

Justin fished the pin out of the glass and sat beside me. "There must be something else. You've got to search your room, Maggie. Anything Sigma-related . . ."

"I know." I held out my hand and he dropped the gold pin into my palm. "This was too obvious. That's why I didn't think of it."

"Sure," he said, leaving *If that makes you feel better* unspoken.

There are two ways to sit on a futon: perched on the edge, or half-reclining. So we reclined, side by side, half friends and half something else.

"What's next?" His baritone voice rumbled in my ear.

You realize we're meant to be together, or I accept that we're not. But I wasn't making the mistake—again—of assuming we were in the same headspace.

"I have to be with the Sigmas on the parade route at six a.m. to help put the finishing touches on the float. I don't have to ride on it, thank God, because I'm taking pictures for the *Sentinel*."

He turned his head to look at me. "The Avalon paper? Not the *Report*?"

"Yeah." I gazed at the ceiling, ignoring his gaze on my profile. "The guy who was covering the Homecoming festivities came down with strep throat. Ethan Douglas called this morning and asked if I'd do it."

"Okay." His tone was condemningly neutral.

"I *know*!" I thumped the cushion with a frustrated fist. "But how could I leave him in a jam? Curse this SAXi luck!" Justin laughed and I sat up, thinking about the problem while I could, before I lost focus again. "It's a karma engine or something. The probabilities always go in their favor. It's like they're manipulating chaos theory."

"Nothing is without a price, especially where magic is concerned. So, what's the trade-off? Something has to be powering this magic."

"That's what I'll work on." I flopped back down, turned my head to look at him. "You'll remind me when I forget, right?"

His hand covered mine. "If you promise to be careful." He looked me in the eye, weighting his words. "They're not really your friends, Maggie. Their goals are not your goals. You can't trust anyone."

That was the thing. Even knowing that this blanket of complacency was false, was laid on me somehow, it was hard to remember. Trust no one. Not even, it seemed, myself.

29

I woke slowly on Sunday morning, enjoying the warm light on my eyelids, floating on the surface of sleep like a leaf on a lake, suspended between awareness above and the knowledge below. The shreds of a dream were close this time, the closest they'd been in months, but as soon as I tried to grasp them they skittered away, blown by a wind that stank of old bones. I stretched my thoughts like fingers, but the images dissolved and sank out of reach.

"Dammit!"

"Magdalena Lorraine." Mom's voice popped my eyes open. She stood at the open French doors, her arms full of folded jeans that I must have left in the dryer. "That's a hell of a word for Sunday morning."

I groaned and sat up, pushing my hair out of my face. The only thing worse than no dream was psychic hangover with no dream. "What time is it?"

"Ten." She stayed on the study side, viewing my bedroom with extreme displeasure. "What on earth happened in here? It looks like a tornado touched down."

And it did. Shoes spilled out of the closet, drawers vomited out their contents. "I was looking for something."

"Well, clean it up before tomorrow. You don't want to start the week like this." She used the "My house, my rules" voice, and I didn't argue. "Did you have a good time at the game?"

"It was work. I took pictures for the *Report.*"

She found a place to set the jeans. "You were out late."

"The game went late. Overtime. We weren't supposed to win, but we did, with this crazy play." Even *I* knew it was awesome, and I didn't even like football.

"I noticed that Justin drove you home. And you sat talking in the car for quite some time."

"Jeez, Mom. At least it was the front seat and not the back." I wondered if I would have been so cranky if Justin and I had done anything other than talk about the Sigmas.

"Okay, okay." Raising her hands in surrender, she turned toward the stairs. "Hurry up and get dressed. Dad said he'd take us to brunch before your pledge meeting."

Pledge meeting. Speak of the devil.

✳　✳　✳

535

When I walked into the Sigma house and saw Kirby and Victoria in the foyer, I thought for sure they were on to me. I mean, on to me in a way they could prove. I froze in the doorway, ready to flee, but then I saw Holly behind them giving me the thumbs-up.

"I'm afraid we have some bad news," said Victoria, a great disparity between her sober expression and her satisfied, even gleeful, mood. I didn't know which Sight to trust.

Kirby, on the other hand, was all displeasure. "Brittany was brought before Standards this afternoon, and asked to leave Sigma Alpha Xi."

Behind them both, Holly was almost doing a happy dance. I let the front door close. "But, what happened? She was such an . . . enthusiastic pledge."

"A little too enthusiastic." The chapter president looked ready to spit nails; it wasn't aimed at me in particular, but the white-hot frustration held tightly in check made me question Brittany's safety.

"That's not important," said Victoria, taking my arm and guiding me toward the chapter room. "She broke the rules, she is out, and now you, as vice president, must take her place."

I pulled away from her grasp. "What?"

She regarded me calmly, never considering I'd refuse her. "It's time to step up, Maggie. Your sisters are relying on you."

Placing a hand on my shoulder, she urged me through the inner doors. The temperature in the chapter room was so cold, I thought someone had left the window open. But then I saw Juliana seated in the armchair, and realized the icicles were metaphorical. Maybe that was why Victoria was so smug. I wondered if she'd convinced the other alum to help her get Brittany out of the way, on the pretext that Holly would move up.

The other pledges were sitting in a loose semicircle, very straight-backed and uneasy. I didn't think it would take any superpowers to pick up on the atmosphere. Tara stood between the girls and Juliana, as if she were defending her chicks.

Jenna met me at the door with a hug. "It's all right," she whispered. "Brittany's all right, and you're going to be where you ought to be, so don't worry about Kirby or Juliana."

"Um . . . okay." I could tell she believed it, whether it was true or not. Her protective assurance seeped in through her embrace, and lulled my judicious fears.

Kirby had gone to the head table; Victoria positioned herself opposite Juliana, as if to counterbalance the weight of her anger. The carpet covered the floor, but I guessed the spiral's arm encompassed us all.

"Let's get this thing going," said Kirby, all steel, no glove. "I am very sad to announce that Brittany has decided to resign from Sigma Alpha Xi."

No murmur of surprise or outrage; no one called the chapter president on this blatant lie either.

"According to the chapter bylaws, we will now install the new pledge president. Maggie?"

Jenna placed a hand on my back, and, feeling like I was climbing to the guillotine—Juliana's glare was sharp enough—I let her lead me to join Kirby and Victoria, making four points around the circular table. Brittany had been installed like this, but with just Kirby and Tara present, and I'd felt no real sorcery then, which was why I wasn't having a complete freak out.

"With this sign," began Kirby in a pro forma tone. Jenna unclasped the pledge badge from my shirt and looped a little gavel charm through the pin.

"And with this flame"—the chapter president struck a match and lit a white candle, like at the pledge ceremony—"we install you as president of the pledge class, and charge you, by the North Star you wear as your emblem, to guide and represent your sisters, in all things and in all ways Sigma Alpha Xi."

The three of them gazed at me expectantly. Was I supposed to say Amen? So say we all? Then I realized Kirby was holding out the candle. I was supposed to accept it.

When I'd insisted to Justin that the only way for me to get to the bottom of the Sigmas' power was from the inside, this wasn't what I had in mind. Yet as I looked around the circle, at their studying expressions, I realized it was a test of faith.

Of course it was. But not between me and the Sigmas.

Here I go again—stepping off the ledge, trusting everything to turn out right. I reached out and took the candle, and accepted all things Sigma.

Amen.

✳ ✳ ✳

When the alarm pierced my sleep on Monday morning, I hit the snooze button and rolled over, pulling the covers over my head. The erased feeling was worse than ever. Instead of a neatly excised spot in my psyche, there was a raw, torn hole where a dream should have been. When I took stock of the situation, I tried to look on the bright side. At least now I *knew* I was blundering around in a fog.

The second alarm went off, and I went to the shower and soaked my head under the hottest water I could stand. After I'd come home from pledge meeting, I finished my column—Victoria was not going to be happy about my writing that our alumni mixer looked like an episode of *Desperate Housewives*—and tried to figure out why it disturbed me that Brittany had been kicked out of the sorority. She was annoying but harmless, and she really bought into the whole Greek thing.

So why get rid of her, other than to clear the way for a more favored candidate? Was it that she was bossy? Or because she was disobedient? Maybe all these inane tasks and absurd rules were really a test not of commitment or "sisterhood," but obedience.

Mulling it over, I dressed in jeans and a purple sweater, dried my hair, and put on some lip gloss. When I was done, I still had no answers, and all the good the hot shower had done in clearing my head was wasted.

Muddled and fuzzy again, I grabbed my books and my satchel and left for my first class of the day—journalism with Dr. Hardcastle. I felt the need for industrial-strength caffeine, and swung by the campus Starbucks for a latte, then hurried to the arts building through the morning chill.

As I walked, the fuzziness fell away, replaced by a vague unease. It couldn't be the three espresso shots making me jumpy—I'd only had time to drink down two of them at most.

By the time I reached the classroom, I felt wound like a

clock. And when Professor Hardcastle came in and pointed to me, I wasn't really surprised.

"You. Quinn. Go over to the journalism lab. Take your books and do whatever Mike tells you."

I didn't ask any questions, just grabbed my stuff and went, dropping the remains of my latte into the trash can by the stairs. I had adrenaline to carry me to the fourth floor and down the hall at a double-time pace.

The air seemed to thicken as I neared the lab. With a hand on the doorframe I swung into the room, where the staff worked in hushed voices. Weaving through all that anxious industry, I went to Cole's office and found Mike sorting through files.

"What's going on?"

"Cole didn't show up this morning." Mike ran his hands over his cropped black hair. "He's not answering his phone or e-mail, and none of the stuff he usually has waiting on Mondays is here."

I edged past the assistant editor and sat in the chair, logging on to the computer with Cole's pass code, which he'd given me to use after Hardcastle griped that a freshman was spending too many hours in the lab. "He last accessed this file—tomorrow's edition—on Friday. Will that help you?"

"It's better than starting from scratch. Can you put it on the public server?"

I moved the file then jotted down the pass code in case he needed it again. "Has anyone gone to Cole's place to check on him?"

"I was planning to, once I got things going here." He looked at me as if the idea were his own. "Could you do it?"

Try and stop me. "Where does he live?"

Mike gave me directions to an off-campus apartment and I headed there with dread eating at my insides. Maybe it was nothing. Maybe he and Devon had gone away again, and had car trouble getting back. Maybe they eloped. But my heart banged against my ribs the same way I banged on the apartment door.

"Cole!" I shouted through the window and rapped on the glass. Just as I'd decided to get the manager or call the police, the door swung open.

"What?" he growled, squinting at the sunlight. He was almost unrecognizable, with several days' growth of beard and cadaverous shadows under his bloodshot eyes. On Thursday he'd appeared fine, but now, only four days later, he looked as if he'd spent a month in a cave.

I swallowed my shock. "Why didn't you answer your phone?"

His gaze was feverish, glazed. "What do you want?"

"You didn't show up this morning. I was worried about you."

"I'm working." He left the door open and retreated into his apartment. When I followed, he said absently, "Don't step on any pages. They're in order."

I tiptoed through a minefield of paper, all covered with notes scrawled in a bold, assertive script that bore only a slight resemblance to Cole's neat, professional printing. Reference books towered on every flat surface; sticky notes covered the wall by the desk.

"Have you slept at all?" I tried to sound calm and not completely freaked out. "Eaten anything?"

"Don't need to." He sat down at the computer. "Can't. Have to get this out before I lose it again."

I stepped over a pile of fast-food wrappers. "Cole, I think you're sick. Ill, I mean."

"I'm fine, if you'll just go away and let me work."

"Come with me to the Health Center, and then I'll bring you back here to write."

"No!" He jumped out of the chair, shaking me off. "Haven't you ever had an idea so incredible, so glorious that it burns inside you, and you have to pour it out or be completely eaten up?"

I followed him, trying to reach any part that might still hear reason. "I know it feels that way, Cole. But the book will still be here after you rest—"

"I have to keep working." He began moving around the room, rearranging piles of paper.

"No, really. You have to stop."

"Don't you understand?" His voice was plaintive, almost pleading. I put my hand out to him, to restrain or reassure. He caught it, brought it to his chest, and laid my palm against his heart, beating as fast as a bird's. "I can't stop."

Fire raced up my nerves. *Inspiration* was too mild a word. This was the forge of creation, the blazing gift of da Vinci or Michelangelo. Of Shakespeare or Beethoven. Of all of them together, in one human body too fragile to hold the terrifying genius that had been ignited there.

My dawning realization brought a smile to his face. "I knew you'd understand, Maggie." Then his knees buckled, and he collapsed.

I leapt forward, but all I could do was keep him from

hitting his head. My fingers felt scorched where I touched him, but it wasn't figurative this time. All analogies aside, Cole was burning up. His skin felt desert-sand hot.

Laying his head down gently, I ran for the phone and dialed 911. The dispatcher was able to call up the apartment address while I told her Cole's symptoms as best I could: blistering fever, seriously altered mental state, and, finally, unconsciousness. She read off a list of instructions for me in case he started having a seizure, which I prayed—*really* prayed, as respectfully as I could—wouldn't happen.

When I hung up, I soaked a dish towel in the kitchen sink, then bathed his face until the paramedics got there. They would think he was sick, or on drugs, or maybe even crazy. But there was no mundane explanation for this.

Cole had been touched by sorcery, and the price for his fit of genius had been more than his body could pay.

30

The emergency-room resident had a brisk demeanor, very businesslike.

"We think it's meningitis." She briefed me outside Cole's curtained cubicle while I folded my arms tightly and tried not to shiver in the frigid, antiseptic air. "I've started him on broad spectrum antibiotics, and we'll do a lumbar puncture. You've called his girlfriend? What about any family?"

"Devon may be able to help you, and if she can't, his parents' number should be on his school records." She nodded and made a note. I'd found Cole's wallet and brought it with me, so they had his social security number and his insurance card—hopefully everything they'd need to help get him better.

"So . . . he hasn't regained consciousness?"

The doctor didn't look up from her clipboard. "No."

"That's not good, is it."

It wasn't a question, and she didn't answer it. "I'm going to start you and the girlfriend on prophylactic antibiotics, and possibly the students in his dorm as well."

I tucked my icy fingers more tightly under my arms. "He doesn't live in a dorm."

"What about anyone else he worked with?" she asked.

"I can get you the names of the newspaper staff, but he's been keeping to his office a lot."

"That could be part of the infection, if he kept the lights low. Light sensitivity is—"

The crash of the double doors from the waiting room interrupted her. I turned to see Devon pushing off the restraining hand of an orderly and quickstepping toward us. Her blond hair was a mess, flecked with the same multi-colored paint that spattered the oversized shirt she wore.

"Where is he, Maggie?" Her blue eyes were wide and bright with frantic worry. "Jenna just said—"

She broke off, her gaze focused on the curtain behind me. Ignoring the doctor, she shoved it aside and crossed to the bed to touch Cole's face, as if that were the only way she could believe it was him. Her countenance shattered, the pieces dissolved into helpless tears. Sinking to her knees, she pressed her face to his hand and cried as if her heart had been ripped out.

"Miss—" The doctor glanced at me, and I supplied a

name. "Devon. We're treating him now. Calm down and I'll explain what's going on."

Devon continued to sob, giving no sign she'd heard. I crouched down, putting my arm around her. "Come on. There's a chair right here. We'll pull it close, and you can listen to the doctor."

Her slight weight lay against me, her strength all turned to grief. "It doesn't matter." Her choked words were almost too muffled to hear. "It's my fault. I just love him so much."

I glanced up to see that the resident was consulting with a nurse, and took the chance to whisper in urgent secrecy. "What's going on, Devon? I can't help if I don't understand."

"It doesn't matter." Her voice had become a mournful drone. "It's done. They'll save him or they won't."

A pair of sneakers appeared in my line of sight, and I followed the scrubs up to the face of Dr. Disapproval. "If she doesn't calm down, she can't stay here."

Devon pulled herself together after that last, fatalistic whisper. She drew back from me, wiped her streaming eyes, and stood up. "I'm all right."

Her withdrawal was more than physical. I felt her defenses going up, and I knew she'd tell me nothing more now that she had her wits about her. The grip was tenuous, but unless it slipped, my time was wasted there.

*　*　*

I'd stolen Cole's keys when I stole his wallet, but I hadn't turned them over at the hospital. I planned to remember to do that after I'd checked out his apartment.

The paramedics had made a mess of his piles of paper. I

546

picked some of them up, glancing at the notes. From what I could tell with my grasp of not-entirely-current affairs, Cole was writing a thriller based on the international politics of oil. Sort of like that George Clooney movie where he grew that awful beard. What I didn't get was what Devon had meant when she said that she was his muse. I didn't see the connection between cute, artistic Devon and OPEC.

Laying that aside, I started searching for any clues to what might have happened to him. I riffled through his bedroom, under the mattress and under the bed itself, and through the medicine cabinet. I checked his desk, the kitchen, beneath couch cushions. Nothing out of the ordinary; no poppets, voodoo dolls, talismans. *Nada.*

My phone rang, the caller ID flashing the number for the journalism lab, and I answered. "Maggie? It's Mike. How's Cole?"

"Not so good. They're thinking it may be meningitis."

"That sucks. Poor guy."

"Yeah. You're going to be getting a call about a prescription for preventative antibiotics."

"Wow. I never thought I'd get that kind of call in regard to a guy."

I reminded myself that he didn't know how serious this was. "That's more than I need to know about your personal life, Mike. Did you call just to check on Cole?"

He got down to business. "Listen. I was going to finish my article on Saturday's football game with some quotes from the trainer who came up with the defensive strategy. Coach attributes the win to him. But now I'm doing Cole's job, so I need you to call this guy and ask him about it."

"I guess I—"

"Great." He gave me the name and a phone number. "Sooner the better, Maggie. Thanks."

He hung up before I could say anything else. I looked at my watch. It was midafternoon, I'd missed biology, and at this rate I wouldn't make it to my last class, either.

What the hell. I dialed the number Mike had given me and Troy, the student trainer in question, answered quickly. I explained who I was and what I wanted, and he laughed.

"I can't believe Coach is giving me props for that. I just came up with the idea, and he was like, hey, this is great. And I was like, whoa, I'm just a student trainer. I thought, they won't listen to me, but I couldn't not say it, you know."

I deciphered that into English, jotting on a legal pad from Cole's desk. As I did, something struck me. "When you say you couldn't *not* tell the coach your idea, do you mean you felt a responsibility to the team, or . . ."

"Well, yeah. Like, I want to win. But also—and this is weird, right? It was one of those ideas you know is really great, and you'll just pop if you don't say it. You know?"

Yeah. I think I did know.

"Thanks. I hope I'm not keeping you from class or anything."

"Nah. I took the day off. I was feeling kinda crappy yesterday. Probably too much partying, right?"

"But you're okay now?" He assured me he was. "Do you know a guy named Cole Bauer? Ever take a communication class?"

"You're, like, joking, right?"

"You live in a dorm?"

"Yeah. Is this going in the paper?"

"Um. No. This is just for, um, demographic research. Thank you for your time . . ." I glanced at his name. "Troy."

I hung up and tore off the page, then sat back, looking at the pieces of future bestseller littered around the room. Supernatural inspiration. There was something there, something important, but it stayed elusive. And Cole didn't have time for me to chase down dead ends.

✳ ✳ ✳

I decided that exposure to meningitis was a good enough reason to skip class, so I spent the rest of the afternoon in the journalism lab, helping Mike get up to speed on Tuesday's edition of the *Report*. Fortunately, since he asked me to prepare something on meningitis, I had an excuse to call the hospital for updates on the patient's condition. ("Unchanged," all afternoon.)

In the end, however, the doctor called *me*. Cole's lumbar puncture was positive, and I was to start taking the Cipro they'd given me as a preventative.

Meningitis, Wikipedia told me, was an infection of the membranes covering the brain, and it could cause all sorts of things, including brain damage, hearing loss, and, oh yeah, death. (That's when I paused in my research to take the antibiotics.) The disease was particularly contagious in close living quarters, like college dorms.

Lovely. I called the university Health Center and spoke with a nurse practitioner who told me that yes, they were aware of the situation, and they were working with the community hospital, outbreak prevention, blah blah blah.

I jotted down a few quotes, then asked, "Do you have any

record of the last time a BU student was diagnosed with meningitis?"

"Hang on." The tapping of a keyboard came over the line. "It was about twenty years ago. Oh dear."

"What?"

"One boy died, and another one was in the hospital for two weeks and had to drop out of school."

"Did they live in the same dorm?"

"Let's see. Not the same dorm, but the same fraternity house."

"I don't suppose it was Gamma Phi Epsilon."

"There's no note of the name."

"Great. Thank you, Ms. Stevenson. You've been a big help."

I hung up and stared at the computer screen for a long while. The date she'd given me, twenty years ago, would have been about the time that Victoria and Juliana were in school. And for the first time, it dawned on me that my mom would have been, too.

Typing like a madwoman, I entered the information from the Health Center and the quotes from the nurse practitioner into the article, called the hospital one more time ("Status unchanged"), and uploaded the draft to the server.

"Mike," I called, grabbing my jacket and book bag, "article's ready for proofing. I need to run home for a few minutes before meeting tonight."

He didn't look up from the screen, but I saw his hand appear over the monitor and wave.

On the walk to the Jeep, I tried Devon's cell again, then Justin. Neither answered. I called Lisa, too, but got her voice mail as well. I tried not to imagine anything ominous in it, but it was hard not to when I had no idea what was going on except that it was bad, and getting worse all the time.

✳ ✳ ✳

Mom was fixing a snack when I got home—a sandwich of peanut butter, sweet pickles, bacon, and mayonnaise. On toast, with a glass of milk on the side.

"It must be an obedient-stomach day," I said, going to the fridge for a Coke.

She sat on a barstool, elbows on the counter, as she took a big bite of sandwich. I didn't know who this woman was, who'd replaced my stickler-for-manners mother. "I have to eat while the eating's good."

Eyeing her plate, I said, "I'll take your word for it."

"What are you doing home?" She wiped a drip of mayo from her lip with a ladylike dab of her napkin. That was more like her. "You don't usually come home before chapter meeting."

"It's been a weird day." I leaned against the opposite cabinet. "Listen, Mom. Do you remember two Gamma Phi Eps who got meningitis while you were in school?"

She took a sip of milk, her expression thoughtful. "Yes," she said, then with more surety, "yes, I do. I was a sophomore, I think."

"I don't suppose you remember who they were dating."

"Goodness, how would I know that?"

"Well, they were Gamma Phi Eps, so . . ."

"So chances are they were dating Sigmas." She bit into her sandwich and chewed it, and the question, over. "No, wait. They *weren't* Gamma Phi Eps."

I leaned back in surprise. I was sure I'd been on the track to something.

Mom reminisced, smiling at things past. "We were all so jealous of the SAXis. Homecoming, Greek Week . . . It was always Sigma Alpha Xi and Gamma Phi Epsilon."

"And that didn't seem odd?"

"That they were so lucky? Not really. Do we have any potato chips?"

I got them out of the pantry, and she put a few in her sandwich. "There was something, though, now that you remind me, about their being jinxed."

"Jinxed?"

"Yes. I think the Deltas started the rumor, because they were always coming in second in everything." Her face lit with a click of memory. "That's right! Those guys who got sick weren't Gamma Phi Eps, but they *were* dating Sigmas. That's when the joke started. It was those guys, and a Phi Delta broke his leg, and then everyone came down with food poisoning after a SAXi party. A couple of the guys even ended up in the hospital with dehydration."

"But this jinx. It didn't stop the frat guys from wanting to date them?"

Mom shook her head. "It was a mark of status. The SAXis' boyfriends were chapter presidents, football captains, fellowship recipients . . . I guess when you think of the good things that happened to guys that dated Sigmas, it pretty much balanced out the bad. So they couldn't really have been jinxed, right?"

I didn't answer. She laid down her sandwich and looked at me closely. "Right, Maggie?"

"Sure, Mom." Funny how much concentration it can take to read a Coke can when you don't want to look at your parent.

"Oh, Maggie." The maternal unit in question sighed. "You're not in the middle of something *weird* again, are you?"

Picking up my satchel, I headed for the stairs. "Weirder than my being in a sorority in the first place? Come on, Mom."

Question evaded, I went up to my rooms, hearing her call up to me: "Did you clean up that mess?"

"Sure!" I yelled back, staring right at my self-ransacked bedroom. Dropping my bag onto the study sofa, I went to close the French doors. Out of sight—

The door swung shut and there, two inches in front of my face, was the answer. Crimson and indigo, compass and North Star. Even a stupid octopus. The door decoration had been there since the night I pledged, turned back against the wall.

Out of sight, out of mind.

31

MightyQuinn: I'm such a *moron*!!!
0v3rl0rdL15a: You're not a moron, you
    idiot.
MightyQuinn: How could I not SEE
    this?
0v3rl0rdL15a: That's the whole point
    of it. Did you soak the door thing
    in the bathtub like I told you to?
MightyQuinn: Yes. I used a whole carton
    of salt.
0v3rl0rdL15a: Table salt or sea salt?

MightyQuinn: Are you sure you don't think
  I'm a moron?
Justin578: No one is a moron. Can we get
  back to business?

I'd gotten Lisa and Justin online—despite the fact that he
hated IM for anything but brief exchanges—because they
were both in semipublic, and a phone conversation about
sorcery was bound to attract the attention of their classmates.

As soon as the door decoration—which I'd seen on
Holly's door, too, so I wasn't special—was submerged in the
salt bath, I'd felt something like when your ears pop in an
airplane, a change in the pressure around my head. And
clarity. Finally, I could think and talk about the Sigmas without the muffled, wool-headed feeling.

I considered the plethora of crimson and indigo decorations in every SAXi room I'd seen, and wondered how many
girls never questioned their good fortune, accepting it with
perfectly normal Greek elitism. But that led to more questions. If you accepted something suspicious without question, did that make you guilty, or just stupid?

Either way, it didn't change what I knew, now more than
ever, I had to do.

Justin578: Just help me out here, Lisa.
  Tell Maggie she has to get out of that
  sorority.
0v3rl0rdL15a: I don't tell Mags what to
  do. You can try if you want to.

```
MightyQuinn: Hello! I can see you guys.
Justin578: OK. Just say that she doesn't
    need to be *inside* the sorority.
```

He wasn't going to like her answer. I didn't, either, but I was prepared when Lisa typed . . .

```
Ov3rl0rdL15a: Just a little longer.
Justin578: How much?
```

A pause while we waited for her to type.

```
Ov3rl0rdL15a: I've almost got the
    components of the spell identified. Then
    I'll know if it can be broken from outside
    or if she has to stay in the circle.
Justin578: How long to initiation?
MightyQuinn: Maybe two weeks.
```

It had seemed so far in the future, like I had all the time in the world. And now the end of the semester, and of pledgeship, was almost here.

And speaking of time, I had to get to the Sigma house for the chapter meeting. I couldn't afford to be late, now that I was pledge president and all.

```
MightyQuinn: I've got to run. Can't be
    late for meeting.
Ov3rl0rdL15a: I'll call you tomorrow,
    Mags.
Justin578: Just be careful.
```

I typed a quick acknowledgment to both of them, and logged off. I didn't need Justin's reminder that I needed to keep my wits about me. Not only did I have to keep my normal façade going, now I had to make sure no one guessed that I'd neutralized their secret signal-jamming device.

* * *

I had to park a block away from the Sigma house—every chapter on Greek Row had meetings on Monday night—and arrived at the door flushed and out of breath. The girls were already lined up in the foyer, alphabetically by class. I joined the freshmen, sliding in beside Holly.

"You okay?" I asked. She'd been elated yesterday, probably at thwarting her mother. But today she seemed like a guitar string, tight enough to vibrate if you plucked her.

"Yeah. Mom's still here." That served as her explanation.

Ashley, at the front of our line, turned back to tell me, "Some of us are going to the hospital after meeting. If you want to come."

"Thanks." One of the juniors glared at us, and I lowered my voice. "But I'm not sure they'll let you in to see him, since he's in bad shape."

Ashley frowned. "Who are you talking about?"

"Cole." Her look was blank. "Devon's boyfriend. Who are *you* talking about?"

"Brittany. She was in a car accident yesterday. She'll be okay, but her leg is broken in about three places."

A clammy chill started in my gut and spread out. I looked up at Holly, and she avoided my eye.

When Sigma luck ran out, it ran out big-time.

* * *

The chapter meeting began as normal, but the girls seemed subdued, sitting stiffly, their chatter muted.

Holly's mother was indeed still there, sitting with the other alumnae advisers. Victoria had on her game face, all political smiles and gracious nods; Juliana was annoyed, but pretending to be amused by her rival's presumption of superiority. The tension between them telegraphed clearly to the assembled SAXis and put them on edge.

And then there was Devon's usual chair, sitting in empty accusation. I reminded myself that I was there to help her and Cole, but if I'd just wised up sooner . . .

Kirby started the meeting with a rap of her gavel. "Some rumor control before we start. The Standards Board met this weekend, and I'd like to thank our alumnae advisers, including our legal counsel, Ms. Juliana Hughes, for their time. In a completely unrelated event, one of our pledges has decided to resign, and Maggie Quinn is the new pledge president."

The actives murmured and Kirby's frown deepened, especially when her eyes found me among the pledges. Impatiently, she pointed to the seat beside Tara. "You're supposed to be over there, Maggie."

She held the meeting so that my first act as pledge president was to cause a delay of game while I changed chairs. I had to go around the seniors, and as I did, the doors—which are supposed to stay closed once the meeting has started— flew open. Devon, wild-eyed and pale, stood framed on the threshold.

"He's gone." She squeezed the words out of a throat broken with grief. "Cole's gone."

No one moved or spoke; in the horrible stasis of the moment, her words refused to compute. Then she swayed on her feet, and I jumped forward, wrapping my arm around her. Her sorrow snatched away my breath. How was she still standing?

"I killed him," she whispered, her eyes fluttering closed.

"What?" My brain still refused to assimilate the first shock. It flatly rejected that phrase. "What do you mean?"

"She doesn't know what she's saying." Jenna had gone to the girl's other side. "Come on, Devon. We'll take care of you."

She shook her head, violently. "No." When her eyes opened, she focused behind Jenna, where Kirby and Victoria and Juliana had come forward while the rest of the chapter watched in silent distress. "No. I'm done with you."

Kirby sheathed the steel in her voice. "You're upset, Dev. You've suffered a terrible loss. But don't say something you'll regret."

"Regret?" She stared at the older girl, a knife's edge of bitter outrage in her tone. "Re*gret*?"

"Dev, don't." Kirby reached out, laid a hand on her arm. "We tried to tell you."

Devon wrenched from our grasp. "I regret the day I met *any* of you." Her voice climbed into the rafters of hysteria as she backed as far from them as she could, pressing her back to the wall. "You did this. You *made* me what I am. Well, you can all go to Hell!"

A great sob wracked her, and she threw back her head, face contorted with anguish, tears slipping into her hair. "You will, you will," she keened. "But you'll take me with you."

She slid down the paneled wall, crouched in a heap of misery. Jenna knelt, and Devon accepted her arm around her shoulders. When Kirby took an impatient step forward, Jenna's head came up, eyes flashing a warning.

Juliana, arms folded, turned to Victoria. "I see how well you've managed things." Ignoring the other woman's death glare, she stepped forward like an auburn-haired icicle.

"Devon. Control yourself immediately."

It wasn't the voice of a mother or the voice of authority. It was the voice of *power,* and it vibrated along my nerves and settled at the top of my spine, resonating in my brain. My jaw went a little slack with it, and the command was not even aimed at me.

Devon stopped her hysterical sobbing. She raised her head and looked at Juliana, hatred and fear in her eyes, body taut with grief and useless rage. But silent.

"That's better. Now go to your room. Jenna will go with you."

I stepped forward. "I'll go, too."

"No." Juliana was implacable. "Jenna is sufficient."

"Devon is my friend." I set my chin. "And so was Cole."

Two flags of color appeared on Juliana's cheeks, the only sign of warmth I'd ever seen in her. As her anger grew, so did the ice in the air. This was the alpha. The queen bitch. And I had just disobeyed her in front of the whole chapter.

Probably not one of my smarter moments.

When she spoke, it was for my ears only. The rest of the room seemed to retreat beyond reach of voice or aid. "Do not think," Juliana began, her eyes glittering like the sun on a glacier, "that your ability grants you any special powers or protections. Not from me."

"I can see that would be a mistake."

She studied me the way an entomologist might a bug. "I have not yet figured you out. You reek of do-gooder, but yet you've accepted what Sigma Alpha Xi has to offer. You seem the model, if somewhat sarcastic, pledge, but I think you are fooling them all. Yet Victoria wants to add your power to ours. She says we need you."

"It's always nice to be needed." There was something about her eyes. Something *other* that spoke to the primal part of me, the part that recognized a predator.

She tilted her head, an animal-like expression of consideration: *Do I eat you now, or later?* "Perhaps we do. But we need you obedient. So think about the things you love, Magdalena Quinn. And do not cross me."

It was my full name that did it. Prickles of bone-deep fear marched over my skin like ants. The murmuring of the girls reached me once more, and the strange, isolated feeling of our conversation dissolved.

The triad—Kirby, Juliana, Victoria—returned to their places and rejoined a sober membership. Jenna met my gaze as she led the silently crying girl away. I watched them go, feeling in my soul that I'd failed Devon twice.

32

"What could you have done, Maggie?"

Justin watched me pace his tiny apartment. Wall to wall took me only eight steps, and my legs aren't that long.

"I don't know." Frustration choked the words. "Something. I should have just stolen the book. Maybe there would be something in there to tell me what the hell is going on."

"You did the logical thing. If the Sigmas found their grimoire missing, they would have done anything to find it."

Think of the things you love, Juliana had said. I shuddered, even in the safety of Justin's home.

"I should have known." Back and forth I paced. Arguing

about what was done and unchangeable was easier than facing my fear of failing the next task, whatever it might be.

"Not even you see the future, Maggie."

Forward and back, running my hands through my hair. "I should have found the spell sooner. I thought I had until initiation. It never occurred to me that someone would die while I was out *partying* with the Sigmas."

He blocked my path, forcing me to look at him. I raised my eyes to his, which were warm and dark, melting with compassion that I didn't deserve. "You did not cause this to happen. They did."

Tears stung and blurred my vision. His handsome, earnest face disappeared behind a watery haze of guilt and grief. "I couldn't stop it. I didn't even *see* it. What's the point of having my Sight if I couldn't save him!"

Justin wrapped me in his arms, tucked me tight against his chest, making me feel sheltered and forgiven. "Evil is deceptive. You fight it, you do the best you can. Sometimes you fall short."

He pulled back and met my gaze again, brushing the tears from my cheeks. "But you have to get over yourself. You can't get back into the fight until you do."

Think of the things you love.

I loved that he didn't deny my feelings, he just told me to get over it. I loved that he was chivalrous to a point just shy of chauvinism, but still held me accountable to fight the good fight. I loved him for being quixotic and square, holding himself to a higher standard, but not thinking less of those, like me, who made a mess of things.

He could have stopped me when I rose up on my toes and

pressed my lips to his, but he didn't. I think he considered it, because he froze for a moment, not in horror, thank God, but indecision. And then he pulled me close, and kissed me back.

Friends don't kiss like this.

There was nothing chaste or amiable about it. His hands cupped the back of my head, fingers threading through my hair. I wrapped my arms around him, kissed him with my whole body—my whole being. My nose was stopped up from crying, and I couldn't breathe and I didn't care, because if I pulled away to take in oxygen, this glorious moment might end.

It did. Justin put his hands on my waist, pushed me back just a little, his eyes dazed in what must have been a reflection of mine. "I'm still the TA for your history class."

An incredulous laugh bubbled out of my throat. "This is your big objection?"

"No." He drew me back in. "I'm just getting that off my chest."

And then he kissed me again, and it didn't seem possible that it could be better than the last one, but it was. For a lawful good square, Justin knew a lot about kissing. Granted, I didn't have a huge basis for comparison, but I didn't have to be a rocket scientist to recognize an explosion when I felt it.

I don't know how we got to the couch. I don't know how we ended up horizontal, tangled in each other, our breath loud in the silence but still drowned by the pounding of my heart. His fingers danced across my ribs, and I gasped at the tickle. He started to pull away but I caught his wrist, kept his hands where they belonged, against my skin.

I suppose that's how I lost my shirt. The more of him I touched, skin against skin, the more I could feel him in my blood, like a drug, like a shot of tequila. The denim of our jeans rasped as we wrestled closer still. He nuzzled the curve of my neck, the line of my collarbone. I kissed his shoulder, the indentation of muscle in his bicep, and he trembled. A rush of power zinged through me. I was invincible. I could have it all.

When his fingers touched the clasp of my bra, I wanted to shout *Yes. Do it.* I wanted it more than anything ever, but more than that, I *deserved* it. I'd waited all this time and I was *entitled* to this.

The very foreignness of the thought was a splash of cold water. And I heard my voice like a stranger's: "Stop."

That was *so* not what I wanted to say.

Justin stopped, of course, but his hands shook. I moved away, all the way to the other end of the couch, before I could change my mind. "I need to think."

"Yeah." He sat up . . . slowly . . . and rested his elbows on his knees and his head in his hands. "Okay."

I'd reduced him to one-word answers. Which was fair, I guess, because I was incoherent myself.

"This feels weird. I mean, I want to do this, but my head feels strange."

"I know." He sat back, looked at me with an expression of chagrin. "Too fast," he said, still monosyllabic. Still breathless.

That was only part of it. I was old enough to vote and in love with the guy, so it wasn't as if I would cry if my untested virtue died a timely death tonight. Except that I was getting a feeling—maybe it was my intuition, back in the game after two months on the bench—that I knew why the pledges had a proscription against sex. The strangeness of my thoughts, driving and hungry, made me think this wasn't solely between Justin and me.

"Let's get out of here." He rolled to his feet. Handing me my shirt, he pulled on his own. "I can't think with you sitting there."

Probably one of the nicest things he'd ever said to me.

✳ ✳ ✳

As I don't go to church much on Sunday, it seemed particularly weird to be there on a Monday night. Especially after the way I'd spent the last hour of it.

"You pick the weirdest places to take a date."

Justin looked down at me in amusement as he pulled open the heavy, carved wooden doors. "You're one to talk."

Good point. When you almost die on your first date, you shouldn't cast stones. I ducked under his arm to enter. Automatically, my hand went to the font just inside, and I dipped my fingers and crossed myself. Some things were just like riding a bicycle, I guess. Spectacles, testicles, watch and wallet. Jimmy Lopez had taught me that when we were kids. He'd thought it was the funniest thing ever, but I guess you do when you're an eight-year-old boy.

I'd grown up in this church, and the wooden pews and stained-glass windows formed my idea of what a sanctuary should look like. It was a warm, solid place, and despite my lingering feeling of trespass, I was aware of a peaceful welcome, too.

Footsteps echoing on the stone floor, I followed Justin

down the side aisle to an alcove. Under an icon of the Madonna and Child was a rack of votive candles, each in a red glass holder. A few already burned; I reached out a finger and touched the fluted glass edge of one, then another. Someone's mother, dying in hospice care. A husband, lost to cancer.

This was becoming natural, the sixth sense integrating with my others. The thought came to me that this may be a Sigma gift, too. Maybe not the Sight itself—I'd had that already, except the *Dead Zone* thing—but the skill I'd developed. Or maybe it was because I'd gotten so much practice around them. Nothing like battlefield training.

The strike of a match made me look up at Justin as he lit two candles, side by side. They flared brightly as he touched the match to the wick, then flickered in tandem. His parents. I glanced up at him, but his gaze was turned inward; not sad, exactly, but poignant. My fingers reached for his, and he squeezed my hand tightly.

"Have they been gone long?" I asked. He'd never spoken of them.

"Since I was ten."

"Does it help?"

He handed me the matchbox. "It can't hurt. Sometimes rituals have deeper power, sometimes they just give us comfort."

I thought about Cole as I shook out a match and struck it. Remembering his friendly nature and his talent and potential, I held the match and let the flame creep closer to my fingers.

I hope you're at peace, Cole. Forgive me for not seeing until it was too late. I swear, I'm going to stop these girls from harming anyone else.

It did help. But not as much as solving this mystery would.

✳ ✳ ✳

That night, it was as if the dream had been waiting for me, long past patience. It drew me down swiftly, as soon as I closed my eyes, with no time to prepare.

I stood in the empty Sigma Alpha Xi chapter room; the phi spiral on the floor, instead of being flat, inlaid wood, descended into the ground. Standing at the outside arm, I felt the cold reaching up from below, from the dark well of earth.

Okay, Maggie. You're not going to find out what's going on from up here.

I stepped onto the path, spiraling down and down; I kept to the outer edge; the other side dropped into nothingness. The cold intensified as I descended and the natural light faded, until I was seeing only by the frigid pale phosphorescence that came from the spiral itself.

Dream time was stretchable, like Silly Putty; I walked until my feet were blistered and my skin was numb with cold. How long was this going to go on?

Indefinitely. Phi was an irrational equation. Self-symmetrical, to the infinite power.

The realization brought me to a halt, and in the same instant, an icy wind roared from below, whipping my hair and tearing at my skin. I pressed myself back against the spiral wall, shielding my watering eyes. In the center of the well, a frosty vapor formed; wisps of winter breath that twisted together into something . . .

568

No. It was some *thing*. No shape of man or beast, but a *creature* nonetheless.

The wind became sleet. I squeezed my eyes closed as ice lashed at my cheeks. Just a dream. The glacial storm flayed my skin, and I clung to that thought. A thing of spirit, not of body. My muscles cramped, my limbs drew in to protect my vital organs from the cold. I tried to scream, but the howling gale snatched the sound away as I tried to force myself to . . .

✳ ✳ ✳

Wake up.

In my own bed, I lay curled in a tight, shivering ball, too painfully cold to move, too miserable not to. Reaching over, I grabbed the fallen quilt from the floor and pulled it around me, my teeth chattering in the silent room.

This was what the thing on my door had kept me from seeing, this frozen well connecting the Sigmas to an infinite power. I'd been thinking *Faust*, and Mephistopheles. I should have been thinking *Inferno*. The center of Dante's Hell was not fiery, but frozen.

Not just capital *E* then. Capital, boldface, italic *E*. And I was going to have to find a way to stop it.

33

At seven the next morning, I let myself into the Sigma Alpha Xi house. The atmosphere was heavy with slumber, and I headed for the stairs. I had to maintain my cover—until Lisa finished her translation, or until initiation—only I didn't want to lose anyone else in the meantime.

But Devon's room was empty.

Not just vacant. Unoccupied. Her bed was stripped, her walls naked. Her closet and bookshelves, bare. The seaside mural was the only evidence that she'd ever been there at all.

I stood in the doorway and cursed—mostly myself, for

not coming back last night. Then I turned to go, and found Kirby standing in the hall behind me.

"Looking for Devon?" she asked, arms folded.

"Yes." I kept my hands at my sides and my cloaking device set on harmless. "I was worried about her."

"Don't be." She reached around me and pulled the door shut. "She decided to go home."

"But there are only two weeks left in the semester."

"She's devastated, as you can imagine, and she wanted to be with her family." Kirby looked me in the eye, and I felt a Juliana-esque chill, slight but distinct. That was new.

"Was there anything else you wanted to know, Maggie?"

The way she phrased the question said I'd reached the bounds of justifiable curiosity, at least in the Kirby camp.

"No, ma'am. Thank you."

I left the house and headed for the Jeep, unsure what to do next. Journalism class was one option, but Hardcastle was hard to listen to even when I wasn't distracted by life-and-death matters.

Journalism made me think of the *Report,* which reminded me of another inspired guy I'd talked to yesterday. It was a long shot, but I felt better about those since despelling myself. Grabbing my cell phone, I scrolled through my recent calls and found the number I wanted.

He picked up on the fourth ring. "Mmph."

"Troy Davis? This is Maggie Quinn from the *Ranger Report.*"

"Wha?" A fumbling clatter. "What time is it?"

"I have one quick question. Do you know any Sigma Alpha Xis?"

"Whaaa?" Still barely coherent. "None of them would have anything to do with me."

"What about a blond girl. Short hair, pointed chin. Bossy."

"Oh, her. *Legally Blonde* Girl. Yeah." He sounded more sleepy than lascivious. "We just, like, hooked up last Thursday at a club, you know?"

"Thanks." I hung up and drummed my fingers on the steering wheel. Cole had writer's block when he and Devon were on a break. Troy the trainer had a great idea after hooking up with Brittany—who had said she liked football guys.

I was just closing my mental fingers around the next variable of that equation when the phone rang.

Justin spoke as soon as I answered. "I think I've found something." His voice rang with excitement, and my heart sank.

"Are you okay?" I asked. We'd only made out. How badly could he be affected?

He kind of laughed at the question, which was both reassuring and not. "Where are you? Do you have class?"

"Why?"

"Let's meet at your gran's place. I think she can help."

"Gran?"

"Wake up, Maggie. Let's get to work."

He hung up without once saying the word *careful.* Now I was really worried.

* * *

Gran was not only up and finished with her treadmill time, but she also had a pot of tea steeping, with three cups set out, when Justin and I arrived.

She poured as she listened to Justin's question, then sat

back and looked at us. Him. Then me. Then back to him. I could feel myself blushing all the way to the tips of my ears.

It didn't help that he looked as though he hadn't slept at all. Not scary bad—who hadn't pulled an all-nighter once or twice? But still.

Finally, Gran took the spiral notebook he'd brought and peered at the handwritten entry. "Liannan Sidhe." Then she studied us again, her eyes narrowing. "How did this come up in conversation, then?"

"Hypothetically," I assured her. "We just need to know more about it."

She made a doubtful face. "I never told you about the Liannan Sidhe?"

"No." She'd told me the Sidhe—"shee," she said, slurring the *sh*—were Irish fairies who lived under hills and danced in fairy circles that trapped the unwary. There were the Dannan Sidhe, the bright folk, and the Bain Sidhe, who, if you saw one, you were basically screwed. But I'd never heard of this variety.

She poured a mug of tea, added sugar, stirred it. Obviously trying to kill me with impatience.

"Liannan Sidhe are female fairies who inspire creativity in human men who they . . . Well, let's say love."

Granspeak for *hooking up,* I guess.

"So, it's like a muse," I said, remembering Devon's word.

"To a fearsome degree." She sipped her tea. "The inspiration of genius, but it burns the man out like a candle while the Sidhe feeds on that creative energy."

"Why couldn't you have told me about that when I was a kid?"

"Well, I didn't want to scare you out of being creative. Besides." She cleared her throat delicately and glanced at Justin. "There's the sexual component."

He blushed, and discovered something very interesting on the ceiling. I tried to keep my own mind on the line of inquiry. "So these fairies sleep with men, feed off the creative energy, and then . . ."

"The man usually dies."

"Dies?" asked Justin, not blushing now.

Gran nodded, and I narrowed my eyes at her. "Are you sure this isn't a cautionary tale? Don't go into the woods or the big bad wolf will eat you?"

"I'm only telling you what I heard as a girl."

"How come all these things that lead men to their deaths are always female? Mermaids drowning sailors, the banshee, this Liannan thing . . ."

Gran took a rather coy sip of her tea. "We are the deadlier of the species, darling."

Justin laughed, and I gave him the hairy eyeball. "More like the stories were written down by men. When you write your book, you'd better dig up some male tempter to balance things out."

"I'll do my best," he promised, still smiling as his eyes met mine.

More blushing, this time from me. Not that it mattered. If the Sigmas really had transformed me somehow, I wasn't going to be able to get near Justin. Maybe ever. The Sigmas had screwed me over big-time. So to speak.

"Why do you need to know this?" Gran had gone back to staring, now with twenty percent more suspicion.

"Research project." Justin lied without a blink. It seemed I'd contaminated him.

Gran knew whom to blame. "Magdalena Quinn . . ."

I decided it was time to get out of there. "Gotta run. Journalism class. Hardcastle would love an excuse to throw me off the paper."

Justin grabbed his notebook. "Thanks, Granny Quinn."

She caught his hand before he could go. "You, go home and sleep at least four hours. And no more fooling around with Maggie until she fixes whatever is wrong with her."

"Gran!"

"Yes, ma'am," he said without hesitation.

She let him go, and we headed out to the driveway. I couldn't look at him; I might combust with embarrassment.

"I'm sorry," I said when we reached the Jeep.

"I'm not."

"You would have been if I'd killed you."

"Maybe."

I shot a look up at him; he was smiling slightly, in a way that nearly had me blushing *again*. "It's not funny."

"No. It's really not." He opened the Jeep's door for me, but his grasp on it was tight, as if he was holding on as much for support as for courtesy.

I stared at his white knuckles, and let the thought catch up with me, the personal repercussions of all this. The Sigmas had done something to me. And I had done something to Justin.

"Hey." His voice drew my eyes up to meet his reassuring gaze. "I'm all right, Maggie. A nap between classes, and I'll be good as new."

My mouth curved in a rueful smile. "How can you always tell what I'm thinking?"

He shrugged. "I've always been good at reading people. Especially when I . . . know them pretty well."

That was interesting for two reasons: (a) "know" had more than one connotation, and (b) he definitely changed the direction of that sentence.

We exchanged good-byes and I started the car, flexing my hands on the steering wheel the same way I gripped my renewed determination. I had to figure this out. There was no other option. Forget the long-term adverse effects of a karmic imbalance on the space-time continuum. Forget that my budding romance was now on ice. If I didn't fix this, I was going to end my days a dried-up, lovelorn virgin with a houseful of cats.

✳ ✳ ✳

"It's all about sex."

I'd gone to Dad's office to confer with Lisa long-distance; it had been the only private place on campus I could think of. Dad was in class, the door was locked, but I still expected lightning to strike me for saying s-e-x while at his desk.

"It's *always* about sex, Mags." Lisa's tone was dry, and the sound of shuffling paper underscored her voice. "Are you just finding this out?"

"Um, in regard to the Sigmas? Yeah."

The rustling stopped abruptly. "Maggie Quinn. Have you been a bad girl?"

"No! Of course not." Her silence was disbelieving. "Okay, not exactly."

Lisa sighed. "You'd better tell me what's going on."

I brought her up to speed about Cole and Devon, the guy Brittany had hooked up with, and—quickly and without going into detail—about Justin. Then I told her about the legend he'd come up with in his inspired state, and Gran's confirmation of it.

"Okay," Lisa said, when I finally paused for breath. "That makes what I've got here fall into place."

"You figured out the spell?" A glimmer of hope sparked in my chest, followed by a stab of irritation. "Why didn't you warn me?"

"Like it's my fault you picked *now* to give up on eighteen years of chastity?"

"Can we get back to the magic? Am I right? Is it like the Liannan Sidhe, but stealing luck instead of life force?"

More rustling over the phone, then the slide of a computer mouse. "More or less. Are you at your laptop?"

Swiveling in the chair, I tapped the trackpad to wake up my screen. "Okay."

An IM window popped up with a link. On my click, a browser window opened, showing one of the pages I'd photographed.

"This is part of the initiation ritual. Luckily, you got the important stuff."

"Sigmas are very lucky."

"Whatever. These symbols at the top—the same as are on the lamp and censer—are for transformation. But there are also things in the spell for binding and amalgamation."

"What's that in nonwitchspeak?"

"It means that the individuals become part of the whole. What's yours is mine, basically."

"Does it go the other way, too? What's mine is yours?"

"Not so much." I got another IM link and this page showed me a diagram of a familiar looking spiral. "This is—"

"On the floor of the Sigma house." And in my dream. "A focaccia spiral thing."

"Fibonacci. It's a representation of the golden ratio, but it's not exact. It's supposed to be like fractal geometry—self-symmetrical, which means that at whatever level you look at it, it's a repeat of the smaller or bigger picture. But the Sigmas' deal isn't like that, exactly. It's weighted toward the center."

A new diagram appeared, one of the same spiral, but three-dimensional, so it looked more like a funnel . . . or the well that I had seen in my nightmare.

I ventured a guess. "So the psychic juice sort of runs to the center."

"Right. If these girls really are sexual karmic vampires, then what they take in goes toward the top. I'm guessing that's the alums. The longer you're in, the more you get."

"Like a psychic pyramid scheme."

"Essentially. The younger girls—meaning the college students—have more sex and there are more of them. While the bulk of the energy comes from them, the load is spread out, so that no one girl draws too much from one hookup."

Before I'd called her, I'd looked through my pledge book, noting which actives had boyfriends, and which of those had any particular status or accomplishments. A few seniors and juniors had steadies—guess which fraternity they were in—but the rest of the girls were . . . let's say *shopping*.

I checked my understanding. "So, as long as a Sigma just

hooks up with a guy once or twice, he's okay." Lisa confirmed this. "But if she goes too often to the same well . . ."

"Don't think water," she said. "Think electricity. The sex generates psychic energy potential; the Sigma draws it off, creating a current. If you exceed the capacity of the human design, the wiring burns out."

Talk about metaphysics.

"And the inspiration before the burnout?" I asked.

"The part of the generated potential that isn't drawn off."

My headache kept getting worse. It seemed that for every question answered, three more popped up. "So . . . that's what happened twenty years ago? The jinx, I mean?"

"I'm sure. It might have started with just a few girls who somehow found this book and did the transformation spell—either not knowing or not caring that they were screwing guys over in more ways than one. Then someone got the idea of sharing the wealth to reduce the current, and modified the arrangement to include the whole sorority."

"Victoria, I think." Eavesdropping behind Devon's door, I'd heard her talk about long-term plans. "It was probably not so much about sharing as about not attracting so much suspicion."

"True. Not to mention that whoever's at the center of that spiral gets the most bang for her buck."

"Then, how is Gamma Phi Epsilon immune?"

"It looks like Victoria pulled them into the pattern, protected them from burnout. It's the why that I don't know."

I remembered the article about Peter Abbott, president of his fraternity. "Victoria's future husband was a Gamma Phi Ep."

"Of course. A little old-fashioned, but does get rid of the black widow problem."

That explained why everyone was so freaked that Devon was going steady with Cole; it was the ultimate unprotected sex.

"So, what's the big deal about pledge celibacy?" I'd given this some thought. "If we're the youngest, and we haven't gone through the initiation spell, then we shouldn't draw much current at all, right?"

"Finally, you get around to asking me that. Or didn't you wonder why you whammied Justin just by making out?" She left a leading pause. "You *did* just make out, right?"

"Yes! You're not my mother. Why would I lie?" Except in leaving out about how easy it would have been to let that foreign hunger slip its leash. "Well?"

"First, tell me more about this pledging ceremony. You were at the center of the spiral, right?"

"Yes." I stared at the funnel diagram on the screen. "Oh my God. Where the energy is strongest."

"Right. That ceremony set in motion the transformation part of the spell. It takes a lot of power, so you're connected to the center until the change is complete. Think of it like a negative electrical potential in the middle of a highly charged dynamic—"

"Lisa, let's pretend I'm not, on a good day, almost as smart as you. Just cut the crap and tell me what that *means*."

"Sure. It means you guys suck the most." I rolled my eyes, even though she couldn't see it. "Next question?" she said sweetly.

"How do I break the spell?"

580

She sighed. "I'm still working on that."

"Can we just destroy the grimoire?" I asked. "If nothing else, it would stop the ritual. Stop them from making any more Sigmas."

"But it wouldn't put everything, or every *one*, back to normal. It would only destroy the power-sharing structure, which would make things worse, not better." I heard more fidgeting noises from her end; not industry this time, but stalling. "There's one more thing, and you're not going to like it."

"Unless you're about to tell me there's no way to reverse the transformation—"

She made a short, derisive sound. "Please. No one out-evil-geniuses me. We'll break the spell."

We, she'd said.

"No. It's about the power source. Not the karma suck, but the transformative and binding power."

She didn't continue; she didn't really have to. The weight of personal history lay heavy on the line.

I said the words for her. "It's a demon."

"Yeah." She breathed easier once it was spoken. "The pages you gave me don't show its name. That's the biggest hitch in figuring out the countermeasure."

"Lisa, all you have to do is help me work it out. You don't have to be near the thing. It's my deal this time."

She didn't even address that. "How long until initiation?"

"End of next week, I think. Sometime during dead days."

Ah, life's little ironies.

"Dad bought me a plane ticket home for Thanksgiving," she said, "so I'll see you this weekend. We'll work it out then."

"Okay." I hung up and stared at the screen, my head full of information, unsorted and chaotic. One thought, though, lay on the surface.

Victoria had been married to Peter Abbott for eighteen years. But on the flip side of that was Juliana Baker-Russell-Hattendorf-Hughes. So it seemed they hadn't gotten rid of the black widow completely.

* * *

When I got to the journalism lab for my usual Tuesday-afternoon duty on the *Report,* Mike avoided my eye and sent me to see Professor Hardcastle. Somehow, I didn't think this was going to be good news.

I hitched my satchel higher onto my shoulder and headed down the hall, my sneakers squeaking on the newly polished linoleum. Dr. Hard-ass looked up as I came into his cluttered shoe box of an office, then turned back to his computer.

"Quinn. Right. That Phantom business stops now. I don't want to deal with the complaints and letters."

"Okay." I don't know why I said that, when it wasn't okay. The column had an end date. This was like canceling a TV series right before May sweeps.

But churning with the anger and disappointment in my stomach was a sudden fear. A yellow flag had just gone up. Luck is not supposed to happen in reverse.

"You can submit photos and stories for consideration," he said, "but you're off the staff. And don't expect any more favors. You were Cole's pet project, not mine."

"Yes, sir."

"That's all." He waved me out, his eyes still glued to his screen.

I left the office and stood in the hall, not quite sure what to do next. Newspaper staff was the thing that kept me from going postal, kept me focused on something besides the waiting game with the Sigmas.

With the thought of the sorority, something clicked in my head. The Sigmas giveth, and the Sigmas taketh away.

Think about what you love, Magdalena Quinn.

I didn't even bother reaching for my phone. I just took off for the history building at a dead run.

34

I slid to a stop at Dad's office door, grabbing the frame to keep myself upright as my exhausted legs tried to buckle. My face burned with exertion and my heart pounded so hard, I thought my eardrums might blow out. Fitness hadn't gotten me there, only adrenaline.

Justin was at the computer, and on the phone. He glanced my way, doubtless alerted by my gasps for oxygen, and didn't look surprised to see me. Just carefully neutral and calm.

"She just came in, actually." He spoke into the phone, talking about me. "Don't worry, Dr. Quinn. I'm on it. You want me to call your mother?" I staggered into the office, worry ratcheted up to panic. "Okay," he told Dad, and hung up.

"What?" I demanded. It came out as more of a plea.

He stood up and came around the desk. "Catch your breath, Maggie."

"Is it Mom?" My stomach ached like I'd swallowed a handful of tacks. "The baby?"

"At your mom's checkup, her blood pressure was really high. They've admitted her overnight for observation and—"

I started for the door, all action, no thought. Justin caught me by the shoulders, made me stop and listen.

"Everything is okay, Maggie, but they're watching her closely. Here's the room number." His hand slid down my arm to capture my fingers, keeping me from running off while he grabbed a Post-it from the desk.

"I have to teach your dad's class, or I would drive you over there. Are you calm enough to manage?" He bent to hold my gaze, expression inarguable. "Maggie?"

"Yeah." That didn't sound very convincing, so I said it again more firmly. "Yeah."

The dazed, distant feeling resolved into the here and now. Justin saw that in my eyes, and released me. But not before he touched my hair and promised, "I'll be there as soon as I can."

* * *

The elevator ride to the OB floor of the hospital was the longest in my life. I hurried down the hall, checking numbers, passing carts full of flowers and rooms full of laughing, giddy people. How could they be so happy when worry was trying to claw its way out of my gut like a cat from a bag?

Finally I found the room, and tapped on the open door. "Mom?"

"Magpie!" She smiled at me from the bed. I ran and hugged her tightly until she gave a laughing protest. "I'm not dying, sweetheart. We're all okay."

"The Quinnlette, too?"

"Yes. I just have to stay in bed until tomorrow, while they poke around and see if my blood pressure goes down."

"Can I do anything?" I asked. "Get you anything?"

"No, sweetie." She squeezed my hand in reassurance. "Your dad went downstairs to get me a few magazines from the gift shop. My biggest problem is I have nothing to read."

"So you're really okay?"

"I feel fine." Which was not the same thing. She didn't look ill. In fact, with her hair in a ponytail and her face free of makeup, she could almost be one of my classmates. A slightly annoyed classmate. "Sit down and stop hovering."

I did, talking to her about inanities until Dad came in, his arms loaded with periodicals. "Why didn't you call me?" I demanded.

He gave me a stern look. "Hello, Maggie. Glad to see you, too."

I gave him a hug and a proper greeting, then asked again. "Why no phone?"

"Couldn't get through. You must have been in one of the older buildings."

Pulling my phone from my pocket, I checked. Four bars of signal and no voice mail waiting.

"Honestly, Michael," said Mom, "did you buy every magazine in the place?"

I left her in Dad's care and slipped out of the room, finding the nurses' station at the hub of three pastel-colored halls. "I want to talk to someone about Laura Quinn, room three-eleven."

A nurse with dark skin and steel gray hair sized me up; when I didn't flinch, she grabbed a chart and flipped through a few pages. "What's your name?"

"Maggie Quinn. I'm her daughter."

"Your mother's blood pressure is still quite high. We're keeping her in bed and monitoring her condition."

"What does that mean, quite high? My blood pressure goes quite high every time I watch the news."

She raised a we-are-not-amused eyebrow. "Yes, but you're not pregnant, I assume. If you were, it would be called preeclampsia, and that can be a very bad thing."

All my bravado drained away, and I clutched the counter with white-knuckled fingers. "You mean she might lose the baby? Or . . ." I couldn't say the other possibility.

The nurse's expression softened a bit as she closed the chart. "Your mom is okay for now, and so is the baby. We're keeping a close eye on them both. She'll probably be on bed rest when she goes home, maybe blood pressure medication. The numbers aren't so high right now and there's no significant protein in her urine, so that's good. But she's got a way to go to full term."

"Okay." I closed my eyes and assimilated that. "Okay," I repeated, as if that would make it true.

"The main thing is to give the fetus as much time as possible to grow and for her lungs to develop."

I nodded, understanding what she was saying. My sister was a ways from being able to survive on her own.

Thanking the nurse, I wandered farther down the hall, not ready to go back to my parents just yet.

Think about what you love, Magdalena Quinn.

It was one thing to threaten me. It was another to have my nature altered to the point where I was facing a life as the spinster cat lady. But to drag my mother and unborn sister into things? That was fighting dirty.

Next week was Hell Week, the trials of sisterhood leading up to initiation. I was scared and pissed off, but I could only go forward, so I focused on the pissed. The SAXis were going down. I was going to use what was left of my Sigma luck against them, and I was going to show them a thing or two about how to handle demons.

35

Wednesday night, I had just enough energy to sprawl on the couch with Justin and watch a mindless Thanksgiving special while we recovered from the efforts of getting the house ready for Mom's return. He and Gran had consolidated all their folklore knowledge to protect the house: doors, windows, and hearth. Justin washed the porch with a concoction that an Irish woman had sworn to him would keep witches away.

Gran had put together little bags, like sachets, and told me to put them under Mom's pillow and mattress. "What's in them?" I'd asked after an experimental sniff.

"Angelica root, mostly. My own granny swore by it." Next she handed me a jar of bath salts. "Get her to have a nice long soak with these, too."

I might be able to manage that, if I passed it off as aromatherapy. Hard enough getting her to wear the medal I'd gotten her—St. Margaret of Antioch, patron saint of pregnant women. I was covering all my bases.

"The house is as secure as we can make it," Justin assured me. "She'll be safer here. Home is a sanctuary."

I agreed. "And hospitals are nasty."

We sat side by side on the couch, our knees touching. I was aware of him in a vivid way, but too tired to do anything about it, even if I weren't worried about putting him in a coma.

"Think you can get some rest this weekend?" he asked, interlacing our fingers.

"Yes. Holly said she and Juliana are headed back to Chicago until Sunday." I gave a tired laugh. "Hell is closed for the holiday."

I would need the downtime, for rest and preparation. And turkey. Not to mention pumpkin pie. I had to keep up my strength, after all.

* * *

Lisa sniffed the air as soon as I opened the front door, and arched a brow. "Been practicing your herbology?"

"Gran," I said in explanation, and invited her in with a gesture. "I saw you stumble on the front walk. Are you okay?"

"Stepped on a loose rock." I could never hide much from her, and she slanted a wary look at me as she came in. "Why?"

I pointed to the porch before I closed the door. "Witch repellent."

She turned to stare at me, her expression carefully blank. "Does that mean it doesn't work very well, or that I'm not very much of a witch?"

I studied her for the first time in three months. She'd lost weight, and she hadn't been hefty to begin with. Tall and lean in her jeans and leather coat, her chestnut hair falling in a silky curtain around her shoulders, she looked composed and powerful. But there was a shadow on her. I could See it written on her heart, indelible and absolute.

"What do you want it to mean?" I asked, keeping my own answer out of my voice.

She looked away first, something that never would have happened with D&D Lisa. "I think we should get to work."

✳ ✳ ✳

We went upstairs, wasting little time on pleasantries—how's your mom, fine, etc.—and got down to business. Lisa had brought a black duffel bag with her, and we sat on the bed with her visual aids laid out for my instruction.

"The spell is divided into three parts," she explained. "Binding, transformation, and amalgamation. You'll have to break each one. First is the binding. It closes the circle and makes the members one unit for magical purposes."

"Do they lose free will?"

"Not exactly. It's more like a permanent version of that charm on your door."

I got that. "Complacent and unlikely to ask questions." She nodded. "So, the girls wouldn't necessarily know what's going on?"

Lisa met my eye levelly. "What sane person would think the reason they're lucky and successful is an elaborate contract with a demon? Does that excuse them for not questioning it? I'm not the one to answer that."

She flipped to a new page of her notepad, closing that door firmly. "Moving on to part two. Transformation. This is the part that empowers or transforms the girls to be able to draw energy from the guys."

"Which you said began at the pledge ceremony."

"You get a gold star for paying attention." She pointed to her drawing, where stick-figure girls were arranged at the center of the spiral. "Part two completes what was started when you pledged. It's not permanent until then."

I hadn't taken this into account. An exit. "So, if I didn't go through initiation, I'd go back to normal?"

"I think so. The problem is that there's a backlash effect. That's likely what happened to that girl who got kicked out."

"Brittany."

"Right. As long as you haven't been channeling too much energy, you would probably survive it."

Part of me wished I didn't know that, even with the worrisome word *probably,* I *could* get out of jail free. "Part two," I prompted, turning the subject back to initiation. "Transformation is finished, and the pledges become karma vampires."

"Right. Straight up, no power sharing." She turned to the next page, where her notes were completely indecipherable. "Only it doesn't stop here. Part three is amalgamation, which ties the knot tighter. That's the pyramid scheme part. All the energy—which is all magic is, at its essence—that the actives collect from the sex feeds upward through the pyramid. As below, so above. Basic alchemy."

"So do all the alums stay connected to this scheme?"

"The binding is permanent, unless broken by a counterspell. Each time they initiate more Sigmas, it refreshes all three parts of the spell. An alumna wouldn't have to be there every time, but she'd get a bigger piece of the pie if she came back every now and then."

"Okay." My brain was full. "So, do we know why Peter Abbott isn't dead after eighteen years married to Victoria?"

"This is the ingenious part." She spoke with real animation, the weight of her baggage lightening in her enjoyment of the puzzle. "Remember I said that sharing the wealth reduces the draw on an individual. Hook up with a guy once or twice, he might ace his test the next day, feel like he's got the flu, but no harm no foul."

"Well, I wouldn't say *no* foul. You're still taking something that isn't yours."

"Yeah, but it's a renewable resource. As long as there's recovery time . . ." She looked up from her notebook and saw my expression. "Okay. Maybe some foul."

"Maybe a lot of foul if you fall in love with someone and can't sleep with them." I was mostly thinking about Devon. But not entirely. "How did Victoria get around that?"

"It's so simple. She funneled some of the karma power to the Gamma Phi Ep house, protecting them from the effects of the drain. It's a current converter fueled by their own stolen energy, feeding their own stolen energy back to them."

"So, the guys have no clue?"

"It's completely passive on their part." A smile curved one corner of her mouth. "Well, not completely passive."

"Don't need a mental picture, thanks."

"Prude."

"Yes. So how do I break this down?"

Lisa went back to her notebook. "I'm reasonably confident I've got the components right."

"Reasonably confident?"

"Well, the modifications are the problem. I know all the pieces, and I know how *I* would combine them. But neither of us has been through Victoria's version."

I sighed. "We need Devon. She's got no loyalty left. I'll bet she'd tell us everything she knows."

"Do you know where home is for her?"

"Birmingham. How many Brinkerhoffs can there be in Alabama, I wonder?"

"Not a clue," said Lisa, though I could see her storing the information as she got back to business.

"Basically everything that the Sigmas do, you have to counter. They bind, you break." She began removing things from her duffel bag. "It may be as simple as this." She held up a pair of silver embroidery scissors, laid them down, and pulled out some more vials. "Salt or salt water. Lemon oil. Valerian. Black or red pepper."

"It's like cooking."

"Spells are all about combining the right ingredients plus a power source. So . . . yeah. Kind of like cooking. Only they're using hellfire in their furnace."

"I know. I've seen it in my dreams." Her busy hands stilled and she looked at me, maybe sensing I had more to say on the subject. I steeled myself, because speaking this aloud seemed to make it more real, and more frightening. "It's not the same as Azmael."

Lisa considered that, filed it away. "Worse?"

I shook my head, not really denying or agreeing. "Different. Formless, elemental. Powerful. Deep, raw power. How am I going to counter that?"

"Everything they do, you do the opposite." Reaching across the bed, she grasped my pendant, holding the tiny crucifix tightly between her fingers. "Time to put your money where your mouth is."

* * *

By one in the morning, we had concocted a plan. It was either brilliant or insane. Funny how there's so little middle ground in these things. The logical parts were all Lisa. The insane parts were mine.

Lisa threw everything back into the duffel bag, zipped it, and set it on the floor. "Keep that with you. You think the ritual will be at the end of the week?"

"Yeah." I linked my hands overhead and arched my back in a stretch. "We're not supposed to know exactly, but they've told us all not to go anywhere on the weekend."

"Okay." I could see the intricate wheels in her brain turning. "My plane leaves at about eleven tomorrow morning. I've got two papers due and finals start on Tuesday." She offered this like an apology.

"I never would have thought up this plan on my own. Even with Justin's help." Maybe we could have come up with something, but not this quick and this detailed. Lisa had said it herself. No one could out evil-genius her.

She slipped on her jacket, pulling her hair from under the collar. "He's going to help you with this, right?"

"Somehow. I'm still hoping to convince this other pledge, Holly, to help me, too."

"Okay." We walked down the stairs, through the dark house to the front door. She stood with her hands in the pockets of her coat, still *thinking*. "I'll be in touch this week. Be careful, okay?"

"I will."

"And keep Justin nearby."

I smiled slightly. "You don't even like him."

"Not the point. I trust him, which is more important." Hand on the door, she turned back again. "Maybe I can fly back after my test . . ."

"How will you afford another ticket?" I said it bluntly, because I desperately wanted her to do just that, but knew it couldn't happen. "Gandalf taught Frodo a lot, but in the end he had to go into Mount Doom alone."

"But Frodo had Sam."

I laughed, but it was fond. "Lisa, you are *so* not a hobbit."

She smiled a little, too. "Good point. Be careful, Frodo."

"See you on the other side, Gandalf."

36

Justin and Gran had hit it off before he and I had even met, so I guess it wasn't that weird to come into Froth and Java and see them sharing a table. Especially since Justin had had Thanksgiving dinner at our house. Gran waved me to the third chair, and I took the box of Lucky Charms out from under my arm and plunked it down.

Justin looked from the breakfast cereal to my face. "What's with the box?"

I tilted my head and said with a vapid sorority-girl smile, "They're magically delicious."

"If you do that in a fake leprechaun voice," said Gran, her

accent as thick as an Irish Spring commercial, "I'll see you grounded till Christmas, see if I won't."

Justin laughed, and I grinned as I took off my jacket and sat down. "Hell Week?" he asked.

"No. It's *Sisterhood* Week." I nodded at the box. "Some Sigma has a twisted sense of humor."

"So, today it's cereal." He moved it off the table. "And yesterday your clothes were inside out. That isn't too scary, as hazing goes."

"We live in a kinder, gentler, more litigious society." I stole the corner of his coffee cake. "Most of the national sorority offices and school administrations have cracked down so hard on hazing that no one wants to ask pledges to do anything. Even to stand up when an active enters the room, or do interviews for pledge books."

"That doesn't sound so bad."

"Most sororities aren't." I'd researched this for my Phantom columns, the ones that would never be finished. "On the other hand are ones that circle the fat areas on the pledges' bodies with Sharpies so they know what to 'improve.' "

Justin sat back. "You're making that up."

I shook my head. "These are things girls have reported."

"After they dropped out?"

"After they graduated. The need to belong is so strong, they'd 'voluntarily' do things like drink a fifth of vodka and then go Christmas caroling through a fraternity house."

Gran set down her cup. "Do they not read the news, about what happens to girls? How can young women do that to each other?"

"The same way that young men dare each other to drink until they end up in the hospital. They think they're invincible." Maybe I was soapboxing a little, but it was relevant to my dilemma. "The predominant feeling on Greek Row is that they are specially blessed with luck and good looks and success. Who'd suspect that the Sigmas had contracted with Hell to make it true? The devil's best trick was convincing man he didn't exist."

Justin looked at me quizzically. "Who said that? C. S. Lewis?"

I broke off another piece of coffee cake. "Kevin Spacey, in *The Usual Suspects.*"

He frowned at the decimated crumbs on his plate. "Do you want your own one of those?" I shook my head, since my mouth was full. "How about a latte?"

At my nod, he excused himself to Gran and went to the counter. "He looks tired," she said, watching him go.

He did, but honestly, you couldn't tell that from the back. I'm just saying.

"It's not me, Gran." My classes were over until exams next week, but Justin's work wasn't done. "He's got papers to write and he's grading Dad's term papers, and he's helping me . . . Okay, maybe that's my fault, but not like you mean it."

"I don't mean it any way, miss." She looked at me hard. "Unless the lady protests too much."

"No, ma'am." After a whole semester, what was a day or two more unrequited? If I didn't reverse the Sigmas' spell, and/or sever their underworld power connection, I doubted this would be my biggest problem.

"Are you ready?" asked Gran, following my thoughts easily.

"Yes." I had Lisa's duffel in the trunk of the Jeep, and I had the Plan. The only thing I could do at the moment was wait, and play the Sigmas' game.

She laid her hand on mine, and I felt a gentle tide of

warmth. "You won't fail, Maggie mine. You are strong and smart."

"So are they, and they've got twenty years of experience, a chapter full of accomplices, and a demon on their side. I'm just one girl with a half-assed plan."

"Then why not just give up? Why fight at all?"

I looked up from the coffee cake, which I'd crumbled into bits. "Because it's the right thing to do."

"And that," she said, stroking my cheek with her cool fingers, "is why you are much more than one girl with a half-assed plan."

✳ ✳ ✳

I hadn't been on a scavenger hunt since I was ten, but that was the plan for the evening. It was as if I'd joined a Mephistophelean Girl Scout troop.

My pencil sliced through the next item on my team's list. So far we'd acquired a copper colander, a Manolo Blahnik shoe box, a rabbit's foot, and a picture of a celebrity.

"Okay. We still need a hard hat, some Silly Putty, and a bottle of Tabasco." I looked at Holly and Kaylee. We'd been ordered to the Sigma house after dinner, chosen teams—two pairs and a trio—and gotten our lists. "Ideas?"

Holly looked at her watch. "None, except we've got to hurry if we're going to beat the others."

Kaylee peered over my shoulder. "Maybe we should split up. The cafeteria will have Tabasco bottles. And I think I can get Silly Putty from my roommate."

"There's that new building going up on the north end of town," I said. "You two head back to campus. I'll get the hard hat."

"You should go in pairs off campus. That's what Tara said."

Holly took the list and folded it into her pocket. "Kaylee, you head to the cafeteria. We'll meet back at the house."

We ran to the Jeep, parked up the street near campus. I checked for traffic then pulled out, heading toward Beltline, and from there north. Neither of us spoke. Ever since Devon's breakdown, Holly had been quiet and distant, especially with me. This might be the only time I'd have to talk to her about initiation.

But how to start? *You were right, your mom probably did sex your dad to death* didn't seem tactful enough to win her over to my side.

"Holly, do you know why the pledges aren't allowed to have sex?"

"Why? Have you been a naughty girl?"

"No. Well, not yet." I passed a puttering Ford in the left lane. "Do you?"

"No." She was too sullen to be convincing.

"You said something once. About a succubus. Remember?"

"That's crazy." She folded her arms and looked out the window. "Besides. If it was true, there'd be a lot more dead fraternity guys, wouldn't there."

So she'd thought about it, opened her mind at least once to the idea. "Don't you think it's weird your mom, who wants so bad for you to be a Sigma, hasn't told you anything about initiation?"

"She's not allowed to."

I glanced at her out of the corner of my eye as I drove. "Why not? If it's all just fake magic?"

Her head snapped toward me, and her expression wasn't so much disbelief as denial. "You're nuts."

"Okay." I backed off quickly, since it would do no good to force the issue. I couldn't afford to have her slam the mental door on me. "Just remember, you may think you have no option but to obey your mother. But you do have a choice."

She looked at me, perplexed, her arms loosening their tight fold. "You said you'd do this with me, Maggie. You're not backing out, are you?"

"No. I'll be there. And I hope we will be in it together. On the same side."

Did she get it? She seemed to understand so much, but so little. There was no telling, not even with my superpowers, what she was thinking as she subsided into silence.

* * *

We easily climbed the chain-link fence and dropped into the construction site. It seemed I'd acquired a knack for breaking and entering.

"I'll look that way, you go there." Holly gestured vaguely. "They've got to leave some extra hard hats around for visiting inspectors and stuff, right?"

"They do on TV." Not that I would put anything on my head that I didn't know where it had been.

I pulled my flashlight from my back pocket; like any good girl detective, I kept one in the car. The construction site was full of eerie silhouettes and dangerous obstacles. Probably why they kept a fence around it, to keep kids on dares from falling into a hole or getting squished by an I-beam.

As I wound through piles of lumber, the shaft of light fell on a sawhorse table. Score. I wondered if hard hats were expensive. I felt a lot worse about stealing than I did about trespassing.

Picking the oldest-looking one, I called into the shadowed darkness. "I got it!"

A thump echoed from the skeleton of the building. I stopped. Listened. "Holly?"

No answer but the soft clink of metal on metal.

You know those scenes where you watch the movie detective go into the spooky building, and you want to shout at them not to be an idiot, because everyone knows that something bad is going to happen? Now I knew how the other side feels. It's a compulsion to go look, a twisting in your vitals that says whatever is there can't be worse than turning your back on it.

I swept the flashlight over the concrete slab, shadows taunting me just out of the beam. Another creak, and a whisper. One sneakered foot in front of the other, I went into the belly of the beast, the light bouncing over the girders like a prison searchlight.

Movement. Edging forward, I saw a great loop of chain, each link as big as my hand. It hung from a pulley overhead, swinging slowly on an intangible breeze, the metal moaning softly.

My phone rang, and a scream escaped before I could stifle it. I fumbled the cell out of my jacket pocket and answered, still scanning the site for Holly. "Hello?"

"Maggie, I've found Devon."

"Lisa?" I whispered.

Behind her voice I heard the noise of a diner or a truck stop. "I've got her with me, and we're driving back to Avalon."

"You're in Alabama? What about your exams?"

She didn't answer either of those questions. "I've explained things to her and she's explained some things to me, and we'll be there by tomorrow afternoon."

Relief and worry bubbled together in my chest. "Just be care—"

A hideous, clacking rattle shook my bones. If Marley's ghost had been a twenty-foot giant, this was the clanking his chains would have made as he visited from Hell. I whirled and saw the real chain moving, the pulley screaming as it spun, and something massive plummeting toward me.

I flung myself away as a huge tub of rivets crashed to the ground where I had been standing. My ears rang with the concussive sound; my head pulsed with it, as if the seams of my skull might shake apart. The first time Holly called my name, I could only stare at her in numb shock.

"Maggie! Are you all right?" She'd come out of the darkness and crouched beside me. I heard an echo of my name and realized it came from the phone that I'd dropped to the concrete.

"I'm okay." I hoped my answer would carry to Lisa, too.

Holly pulled me to my feet. "Oh my God. You were standing right there!" Her hands shook and her face was so pale she seemed to glow in the moonlight. "Talk about lucky."

I'd ripped my jeans and skinned my palms when I dived for safety. But all things considered, no complaints. "Yeah. Lucky."

Only I wasn't. I'd thought losing the column last week had been about Victoria's patronage, and Mom was a warning. But I thought about Brittany now, about the backlash effect Lisa had mentioned. Had my luck been revoked, too?

37

By the next afternoon, I'd gone to the door so many times to look for any sign of Lisa and Devon's arrival, Mom threatened to tie me out on the porch like a dog. After that, I tried to discriminate the car noises, and after a false alarm for the mailman, I heard an engine turn off and two car doors slam.

I opened the door to see that it was not the cavalry arriving just in time, but Jenna and her roommate, Alexa. With a hand on the knob, I hesitated, uncertain. Then Jenna stumbled and wiped out on the front walk, and I hurried out to her side. Stupid crusader instinct.

The air was frigid—I hadn't grabbed my jacket—and I helped Jenna sit up. "Are you okay?"

"Nothing damaged but my pride." Actually, she'd skinned her elbows and palms, and as Alexa gingerly rotated her ankle, she winced, going pale beneath her cold-reddened cheeks.

"It's just twisted," she said. "Help me up."

We did, and she wasn't so bad off she couldn't laugh at herself. "Well, that's not how I meant this to go." She grinned at me, and said formally, "Maggie Quinn, we are here to escort you to initiation into the Sigma Alpha Xis."

"But it's only Thursday," I said. "I thought it would be Friday. And nighttime."

"The idea is to make it unexpected," Alexa said, helping Jenna balance with her weight off her left leg.

It wasn't as if I couldn't escape. Even I could outrun a girl with a gimp foot. But that wasn't the issue.

"Can I at least get my jacket?" And my cell phone.

"The heater's on in the car." Jenna looked behind me, toward the house, and waved. "Bye, Mrs. Quinn."

"Have fun, girls!" Mom grinned at me as she closed the door. At least she would tell Lisa where I was. That was my best hope now. What was the point of a plan if it all went to crap when the bad guys didn't do what they were supposed to?

Jenna was warmly expectant as she waited for me to join them in the car. She turned and smiled at me from the front seat. "Stop scowling. It's an act of trust, Maggie."

God, I hated those.

* * *

I sat on Jenna's bed, shivering in the sleeveless white shift she'd handed me. She indicated that the other pledges would arrive soon, too, change their clothes, and we would all wait together.

There was nothing to stop me from walking out. I could forget the Plan. While everyone was distracted bringing in the pledges, I could find the grimoire and burn it. Or maybe create a diversion or delay until Lisa and Devon could get there.

The door opened, interrupting my internal debate. I poised for fight or flight until I saw Victoria Abbott, looking smart in one of her designer pantsuits. "Are you ready?"

"Is it time?" I asked, almost not panicking.

"Just about. I was hoping you could settle an issue for me."

Warily, I edged back. "I'm supposed to wait in here."

"You have special dispensation." Smiling almost maternally, she stepped back to allow my exit into the hall. I followed her down one flight of stairs, but instead of continuing to the ground floor, Victoria pointed to the left. "This way."

My bare feet slowed as we approached the end of the hall, where Juliana Baker-Russell-Hattendorf-Hughes waited beside the yawning door of the initiation closet.

"Don't you look pretty," she purred. "Vestal-virgin chic."

"Appropriate, I guess." The temperature seemed to plummet the closer I got to Juliana. I didn't know if this was literal or if my extra senses were using this as code for *Evil ahead, get the hell out.* If so, I wished for a shorthand that didn't raise so many goose bumps.

I rubbed my bare arms, deciding to play stupid. "Why are we at the initiation closet?"

"How do you know what it is," Juliana asked, circling me like a cat, "if you haven't been here before?"

"Everyone knows it's where the chapter stores the initiation stuff. And the Christmas decorations."

Juliana shot Victoria an irritated look that would have

made me laugh if my terror level hadn't just shot from orange to thermonuclear red.

"Here is what I think, Magdalena Quinn." The glacier glint in her eye drove me back a half step, toward the open closet. "Victoria says we need you. But I think that no matter how much power you have, you are simply more trouble than you are worth.

"In fact," she said, in that voice she used when she didn't want anyone but me to hear, "some *thing* tells me you're a threat to our sisterhood. And I can't have that."

She moved inhumanly fast. Her hand flashed out and hit me hard in the chest, knocking me backward onto the bare wooden floor of the closet.

"This will keep you out of my hair for now." She stood with one hand on the jamb, the other on her hip. "And if you're very, very good, and don't make a disruptive fuss, then in all probability that water heater in the corner might *not* spring a leak in the gas line."

"Wait!" I lurched to my feet, and she swung the door closed so quickly that I ran into it, face-first. I grabbed the knob and turned it, pushing all my weight against the wood. It started to open, then slammed tight as, I suspected, Victoria added her efforts. The latch caught, and the lock clicked into place with a fatal finality.

I rattled the useless knob in disbelief. What kind of evil was this? Where was the gloating monologue on how clever she was? Where was the time I was entitled to, as the hero, to think of an escape? This was just not right.

Beating my frustration out on the door was hopeless. I would be very lucky if someone heard me, and luck, I knew, was on the Sigmas' side. But the action made me feel a little better, at least until the scrapes on my palms started to crack and bleed.

I sagged against the wood and slid down to rest. *Think, Maggie. What would Nancy Drew do?*

Nancy would work her way out of captivity with her compact and a bobby pin. I had none of my trusty supplies, and was essentially dressed in a nightgown.

Crawling to my feet, I searched for something to pry open the door, or maybe just bang louder. The most promising thing I found was a plumber's helper. Maybe I could plunge the door open.

I tossed it aside and stared at the initiation cabinet, which stood ominously empty. When Lisa and Devon got to my house, Mom would tell them where I was. But even if they *did* arrive in time, how would they find me? I was certain no one would be checking the closets.

What would the other girls think? Would Holly consider looking for me? Or would she think I'd reneged on my word?

I walked to the carton of toilet paper, and after a thoughtful moment, pulled off one of the flaps. Sitting with my back against the door, I flexed my scraped hand until the sting brought tears to my eyes and blood welled from the splits in the scab.

It might surprise you how much blood it takes to write "Help" on a piece of cardboard. I left off the exclamation mark, figuring that was implied. Then I worked the stiff paper under the door, the best distress beacon I could manage.

God, maybe luck is on the Sigmas' side, but I really hope that you are on mine.

With nothing else to do, I settled down to wait.

✳   ✳   ✳

I dreamed of the vanquished demon Azmael, and its noxious, rotten egg smell. Its miasma invaded my nostrils, my throat. Vanquished, not destroyed, it lurked and waited, and sent out putrid tendrils to choke and poison.

A cough woke me. My own. I shook off the disoriented half-doze and then realized the odor, at least, was real. Jolting upright, I scanned the dark corners of the closet, but nothing moved. No *otherness* seethed.

But the rotten-egg smell remained.

Of course. The gas water heater. Juliana raised the probability, and it happened. She was the queen, and all karma led to her. Damned Sigmas and their damned luck. Juliana was going to kill me with it.

I crawled to the heater, keeping low. Surely there was some kind of safety valve. I found a knob and twisted it, but had no idea if I'd just made things better or worse.

Again I coughed, my lungs trying to expel the poison. Retreating to the door, I lay down, pressing my nose and mouth to the gap at the bottom.

Think, Maggie, think.

Footsteps in the hall. At that moment, I didn't care if it was the Sigmas or not. I didn't care if they dragged me to their initiation, and if I could never touch another guy, at least a convent was better than being dead.

"Hey!" I shouted, then started to cough. I grabbed the edge of the cardboard distress flag, sliding it back and forth. The mud brown color wasn't eye-catching, but maybe movement . . .

The footsteps hurried closer. I heard the rattle of some tool against wood, then a splintering groan. The door popped open with a shotgun crack, and I looked up to see Lisa standing with a crowbar, and Devon behind her.

"Thank God." And I meant that. I might not be eloquent, but I was fervent.

Lisa pulled me to my feet. Her face was pale and thin, and there were dark shadows under her eyes. I wondered if she'd slept at all since she left DC. "Nice outfit," she said.

"Nice crowbar," I wheezed.

"Thanks. Your friend knows where they keep things."

Devon offered a ghost of an ironic smile. "Lucky, huh."

I closed the closet door the best I could, considering the splintered latch. "There's a gas leak. Get something to stuff under the door." Eyes widening, she dashed into one of the rooms and brought out a couple of wet towels.

"They're going to know you're in here," I said, wondering why there weren't people running already.

"Devon is still a Sigma," Lisa explained. "She doesn't register as a trespasser. She invited us in, so that gives us a little grace."

"Plus," said Devon from the floor, where she was stuffing the towels under the door, "the chapter room doors are closed. I think the insulation works both ways."

"Wait." My brain wasn't quite up to speed. "Us?"

Lisa checked her watch. "Justin is downstairs. In three minutes he causes a distraction. Then we've got to get in there and reverse this spell."

"Hel-lo! Gas leak. We have to get everyone out."

She swung the black duffel bag from her shoulder and handed it to me. "If they start the spell, you must do the counterspell. You have to return things to their normal flow. Things aren't meant to be out of balance."

"Excuse me?" I searched her face for a sign she was joking. "*Who* has to perform a counterspell?"

"You do."

"I thought you came back to do it."

She shook her head. "I'm here to help you. We all are."

"Lisa." Even my voice shook with the trembling of my confidence. "I've never done a spell before."

"Neither had I." That shut me up. So did the look in her eyes as her gaze held mine. "Maggie, you *have* to do this. The butt-kicking of a righteous woman availeth much."

I didn't feel righteous. I felt like throwing up.

"Remember," she coached me like a prizefighter about to go into the ring. "Stick to the Plan. Reverse the transformation, undo the binding, cut the power supply. Whatever they do, do the equal and opposite. Basic math. Positive and negative numbers . . ."

"Cancel each other out."

She nodded. "Just feel your way. That's what you do. I'll help you."

Devon joined us. "So will I, Maggie. I trust you."

"Great." I managed a wan smile. "Everyone trusts me but me."

"That's right." Lisa shoved the bag into my hands. "So stop whining and let's go."

Nothing like winging it against the forces of darkness.

The fire alarm split the air with a brain-melting buzz. My heart bounced around my rib cage like a Super Ball.

"Distraction!" Lisa shouted. At least, that's what I read on her lips, since my fingers were in my ears trying to keep gray matter from leaking out. "Time to go."

38

By *the pricking of my thumbs.*

We three weird sisters ran for the stairs, two sets of sneakers and my bare feet clattering down the hardwood steps. Justin met us in the empty foyer, gesturing at the closed chapter-room doors.

"Can't they hear the alarm?" he asked.

"It's started." The words fell from my lips with dead certainty. The collected consciousness behind that portal built like clouds before a storm, charging the air with an electric potential. Even through the wood, I could feel the ebb and flow of energy, stinging my skin like nettles.

Something wicked this way comes.

"Once the ceremony starts," said Devon, "no one can go in or out."

I yanked on the brushed nickel handle, which was cold to the touch but utterly unyielding. When I looked expectantly at Lisa, she frowned back. "When I said I'd help you, I didn't mean I could pull a Hermione Granger on the door."

"Right. But you could try the crowbar."

"Oh." She looked at it in surprise, and I realized that despite her show of confidence, she was scared, too.

Justin took the tool from her. "Let me be the chauvinist here." He slid the business end into the gap in the double doors and applied his weight to the lever. The wood creaked and groaned, then gave with a pop. The portal flew open, and thick, fragrant smoke poured out.

No reaction from inside. It was as though what was across the threshold existed in another plane entirely.

"What about the gas?" Devon asked with a cough. "The candles, and the incense . . ."

"Gas?" Justin shot me a look.

"Leak upstairs," I said. "We tried to contain it, and it's got to fill the third floor before it comes down here." I hoped.

"Let's do this," said Lisa, her expression grim and set.

I held my breath and plunged through the door and into the smoky darkness. My companions charged in with me like matinee heroes, then stumbled to an anticlimactic halt at the static scene, silhouetted by flickering candles and wreathed in smoke and mist.

Girls in crimson shifts and bare feet ringed the outer

arm of the spiral, crimson candles in each right hand, the left raised, palm up, as if making an offering. A red cord looped each wrist, running from one girl's left to the next one's right, and on around the circle, binding the sisters both literally and symbolically.

Their stillness was eerie. Only their mouths moved as they sang a song of unity, a melody that seemed to thicken the air.

At the heart of the coil were the pledges in their white togas, swaying with the chant, their expressions dazed and unseeing. Around them, at the four points of the compass, were Kirby and Jenna, Victoria and, across from her, Juliana, the high priestess. She wore a flowing crimson robe trimmed in gold, and in front of her was a table—no, an altar—with the lamp, the censer, and the book. She made a gesture over the incense, and it curled up and out in a widening circle toward the girls.

I had to get in there and counter the transformation, but as I started for the opening of the inlaid design, a growing resistance opposed me until I was pushing against an invisible, immovable force.

At my feet, the spiral was the most obvious pattern, but I could see another inlaid piece closing the gap, sealing the outer arm into an ellipse. Justin joined me, his cheeks red, as if windburned. The fire alarm rang in my ears, even though the Sigmas couldn't seem to hear it, and rather than shout over the sound, I nudged Justin's arm and pointed downward.

He drove the iron crowbar into the wood, gouging a fissure, severing the line on the floor. The invisible barrier tore open, and it felt like I'd flung open a door to a storm of freezing rain and wind.

I tightened my grip on the strap of the duffel bag, and stepped into the metaphysical tempest. The energy raised the hair on my arms like a static charge. The incense was thicker, too, and I could feel something icy and inhuman in the smoke that curled around the girls' bare ankles and caressed their skin.

The first Sigma I came to was Michelle, a sophomore from Denver. She gazed forward like a sleepwalker, chanting along with the others. Rummaging in the duffel, I found the tiny silver scissors and snipped the cord that linked her to the girl beside her, undoing the first step, the binding. Michelle blinked, but didn't move until I dumped some black pepper into my hand and blew it into her face.

The reaction was immediate and violent. I wasn't quite quick enough to dodge her sneeze. But then she wiped at her streaming eyes and nose and looked around in cognizant fear. "What . . . ?"

"Fire," I said. "Get out of here." She blinked in confusion, and Justin, who'd come into the circle with me, turned her toward the door and gave her a gentle push.

I let him make sure she got out, and moved to the next girl. Lisa intercepted me, took the pepper for herself, and handed the scissors to Devon. "We'll do this. Get to the middle."

She and Devon got to work; I braced myself and pushed through the remains of the protective outer ring. The full force of the inner circle lashed at me like psychic sleet; I could hear a second chant now, a long, liquid phrase that licked unpleasantly at my ears.

Jenna's voice faltered in surprise when she saw me; Kirby snapped at her, "Keep chanting." The girls were east and west on the compass that was worked into the heart of the spiral, encompassing the pledges. Victoria was south, and to the north, at the altar, was Juliana.

Victoria's eyes were closed in concentration, and Juliana ignored me completely. To interrupt her position or her rhythm would risk breaking the spell.

I tried to remember all of Lisa's contingencies and instructions. Equal and opposite. Dropping my duffel at the southern end, directly behind Victoria, I took out what I needed. Wooden bowl. Dried herbs. Lighter, which I stuck in my bra to keep handy.

The chanting didn't change; I had no warning before a high heel came down on my hand, pinning me to the floor. Only Victoria Abbott would wear pumps with a toga.

"I wanted you to join us, Maggie." Her gentle disappointment was completely at odds with the tasteful two-inch heel digging into my palm. "Why did you have to betray me?"

"Maybe it was after you let Juliana lock me in the closet to die." I spit the words through teeth clenched in pain. "That doesn't establish a whole lot of *trust.*"

I drove my shoulder against her knee, only meaning to unbalance her, but I heard something snap. She collapsed, holding her leg and shrieking in agony.

"Oh God." She writhed and howled, and I stared at her, horrified at what I'd done.

Kirby hit me from behind and my body met parquet with a bone-jarring crack, driving the air from my lungs. She seized my hair and yanked; I grabbed her wrist to stop her from tearing my scalp as she hauled me across the floor, back out through the spiral. I wheezed and squirmed and dug in my heels, desperate that she wouldn't drag me out. If I lost this battle, it would *not* be in a girl fight.

Fumbling a hand in my bra, I found the lighter. The flame sprang to life, and I hauled myself up by my grip on Kirby's wrist and held the fire to her arm. Flesh sizzled; she dropped me with a shriek of surprised pain and I hit the ground, leaving a hank of hair behind. In a blind rage she kicked at me, but I rolled away and scrabbled back to the bag.

She lunged, her mouth twisted in fury, her fingers raised like claws. I flung a handful of cayenne pepper into her face, and she stumbled back like I'd maced her, screaming and wiping at her eyes.

I rested my hands on my knees, panting for breath, getting my bearings. Devon and Lisa were working their way around the circle, snipping cord and waking the girls. While one came out calmly, another came out terrified and sobbing. Next, I searched for Justin, who was carrying a struggling girl toward the door while she beat on him in blind confusion. It was hard to see through the incense smoke, but it looked as though Justin's nose was bleeding, and Lisa might have a black eye. Devon just kept cutting the cord.

"Have you gone crazy?" I looked toward Jenna's voice and found her kneeling beside Victoria. Her mentor lay curled in a ball of pain, and Jenna pulled her head into her lap and yelled at me, as much in fear as anger. "What the hell is wrong with you?"

I resumed gathering my supplies. "Don't even go there, Jenna."

Her gaze was stricken, accusing, and honestly hurt. "I thought we were friends."

"We are." I was honest, too. "And friends don't let friends make deals with the devil."

"*What?*"

I ignored her for the moment. In all this chaos, Juliana had never stopped chanting, and the pledges stood like wax figures, transfixed, bound for the transformation.

Dropping the bundle of herbs into the wooden bowl, I flicked the lighter and set them to smoldering. Marjoram and basil, sage and clove. This was the second undoing, the retransformation.

Juliana's incense was the scent of seduction, of perfumed harems and dark, secret places. It was the perfume of power and wealth, of worldly pleasures.

My incense smelled of Thanksgiving dinner, of home, of protection and family. It was the scent of things bigger than ourselves, of intangible treasures. As the smoke wafted over the inner circle of pledges, I saw them quiver, as if stirring in their sleep.

Lemon oil, to restore and renew. I dripped some into my bowl and blew across the embers. Kaylee and Nikki raised hands to their eyes. Mugwort, smelling of clean, damp earth. The rest of the girls woke up, shaking off the dazed funk the way a dog shakes off water.

The process had reversed. And Juliana knew it. She stopped chanting, slammed the ornate brass censer down on the altar, and glared at me through the smoke. "You, *child,* are really beginning to piss me off."

"I have that effect on people." I still had to finish one thing, but I couldn't move from my position, south to Juliana's north, and my comrades were still freeing the last of the Sigmas.

"Holly!" Putting my trust in her, in the independent spirit under her mother's manicured thumb, I tossed her the vial of lemon oil. She caught it, and I pointed to my forehead. "Put it here. It will cut the last connection—"

"Holly Eleanor Russell!" Juliana snapped in a very maternal voice. "Don't you move."

Holly whipped her eyes back and forth between us, suspended on a thread of indecision. Then, squaring her jaw, she turned from her mother and went to Kaylee, dotting the girl's forehead with the oil. Immediate effect. The ballerina-sized brunette started cursing like a sailor and ran for the door.

The rest of the pledges didn't question, just fled as they were released. Jenna ducked as Nikki hurtled over her and Victoria in her haste. Finally, only Holly remained, and she, too, turned to go.

"Freeze!" Juliana's command halted her daughter as if she had rooted to the spot.

The equation, hanging in balance, tipped back to Juliana's side. The pledges were free, and the actives were safe. The pattern was scattered, and chaos was as random as it ever had been or would be. All except here, where the inner circle remained.

"Will someone please tell me what the hell is going on?" Jenna demanded.

"Did you never tell them, Juliana?" I threw it across the circle, keeping her attention on me. "You're a lawyer. Wouldn't lack of full disclosure invalidate the contract?"

"What contract?" demanded Kirby. Her eyes were red and swollen, and they widened as she saw Devon come into the circle of candlelight. Justin and Lisa followed her, rebalancing the pattern: four of them, four of us, and Holly in the middle.

I looked at the woman on the floor beside Jenna. "You didn't tell them, either, Victoria? I thought you cared about these girls."

"I do." Her makeup was streaked and her face contorted with pain, but she managed a veneer of composure. "Juliana found the book and set up the spell. But I was the one who worked it out so that no one had to die, and we could all of us benefit."

"Cole died." Devon shook with rage as she stepped toward Victoria. "Cole died because of what you Sigmas made me."

"No. Because you couldn't follow the rules. Your sisters tried to tell you, but you wouldn't listen. Did you think love would conquer all?"

Devon still had the scissors in her hand, clutched like a weapon. Victoria's mocking tone goaded her forward, but Lisa's voice stayed her. "Don't, Devon."

She looked up at her like a lost little girl. "I'm already a killer, so what does it matter?"

Gently, Lisa took the scissors from her. "It matters. Believe me."

"My God." Juliana's voice was all contempt. "Just *shut up* already. I offer you the world, and all you do is whine."

The grimoire had, through all this, squatted like a living thing on the altar. Now Juliana pulled it closer, and flipped back the sleeves of her robe. "I was tired of sharing anyway. Holly, come here."

The girl moved like an automaton. Her mother didn't

glance at her, just turned to a new page in the book. Raising her arms, she started speaking again, a chanting drone of renewed vigor. The flame on the altar lamp jumped and danced, and I felt the power surge from someplace deep and elemental, beyond human reckoning.

Justin had joined me, standing close by my shoulder. "What's going on, Maggie?"

"I don't know." This wasn't in the parameters. The air was turning colder, growing thick. Devon and the Sigmas darted their eyes warily from Juliana to me as Lisa came to my other side.

With a contemptuous disregard for all of us, Juliana lifted the censer. The smell had turned bitter and noxious, like stale ice and refrigerator coolant. Cold rolled out with the smoke, raising goose bumps on my skin. It crept into my bones, along with the realization of what she was doing: calling the thing that lay hidden at the heart of the pattern.

Equal and opposite.

My backup plan was really more of a desperate improvisation. I blew across the wooden bowl in my hands, fanning the red embers to tiny flames that fought against the clammy air. Kicking the duffel to Lisa, I said, "Time to pull a rabbit out of your hat, Gandalf. Justin, there's a piece of notebook paper in there. I need you to hold it for me."

The glass on the pictures around the room had started to frost. Devon drew her jacket closed, Jenna and Kirby rubbed their bare arms, and Victoria huddled into herself. Standing beside her mother, Holly's lips were turning blue.

Juliana's voice became harsh, rasping out the sharp, cutting words of her chant. Staring across at me, she pulled

Holly's arm to her and picked up a bronze dagger from the altar.

"Don't!" I started forward, without a clue how I could stop her. Justin's hand held me in place, kept the balance from tipping even farther.

"She's mine to use," the woman said. "They're all mine."

"You can't own people," I argued. "And Hell can't take them—her—without her consent."

I heard Jenna's indrawn breath, and felt the cold intensify in answer to my naming.

"They chose to be what they are, regardless of how they were created." Juliana paused, as if she were listening to instructions whispered through her soul on an ill wind. When she spoke again, it was with cunning. "But you can trade places with them if you like. You have real power, and I would get a lot of bonus points for you."

"Give me a break, Ice Queen," I said, "do I look like an allegorical lion to you?"

She smirked. "I didn't think so." Without warning, she put the tip of her blade to her daughter's thumb and cut until blood flowed freely. It dripped into the censer and hissed on the embers of incense. The smoke poured out like fog, flowing down the altar and across the circle. Frost spread in the wake; it rimed the tablecloth, the floor, and came toward us like a diamond-hard tide.

I held out the bowl toward Lisa and she dropped in nuggets of frankincense and myrrh. The resin caught immediately, flared ruby and amber in the rude wooden vessel. "Paper, Justin."

His eye scanned the handwritten page. "Are you out of your *mind*?"

"Look." I used enough bravado to convince both of us. "I don't even *want* to know what she's summoning over there. So excuse me if I go straight for the big gun."

Jenna dragged Victoria away from the encroaching frost; Devon—after palpable indecision—ran forward and grabbed Kirby, pulling her behind Justin, Lisa, and me—a strange sort of trinity if there ever was one.

Raising the bowl, I breathed across the smoke, sending it out carrying the first words of my own spell.

"Veni, Sancti Spiritu."

Come, Holy Spirit.

Justin crossed himself, and Lisa whispered, "Amen."

39

The frost slowed, but kept creeping toward us. Juliana gritted her teeth and growled a guttural string of words. She could have been ordering a metaphysical pizza for all I knew. I had just enough Latin to get through my own invocation. Catechism class was finally paying off.

"Veni, Creator Spiritus!"

I said it more strongly now, since the first tentative whisper hadn't called down a bolt of lightning at my audacity.

The infringing ice covered the floor, a sea of frosty white. We stood on a shrinking peninsula, and my bare feet cringed from the burning chill.

"Mentes tuorum visita."

Come Creator Spirit. In our souls take Thy rest.

The incense in my bowl glowed, as if fanned by intangible breath.

"Imple superna gratia."

Come with Thy grace and heavenly aid . . .

The frost stopped, inches from my toes.

"Quae tucreasti pectora."

And fill the hearts which Thou hast made.

Holly crumpled, like a puppet whose strings had been snipped. Just as abruptly, the ice retreated, a fast-motion thaw melting the ground for the coming spring.

It converged on Juliana, ran up her robe and over her chest to her bare arms and neck. For a moment she was encrusted, like spun-sugar candy. Then the frost sank into her skin, and what looked out of her eyes was no longer human.

"Uh, Lisa?" I held the bowl in two shaking hands. "Did she just absorb that . . . whatever . . . into herself?"

"Yeah." She sounded as poleaxed as I felt. "That's unexpected."

"Why isn't it cancelled out?"

Justin answered. "The blood. You've got to—"

"You *bitch*." Victoria had gained her feet, lurching on her wretched knee, eyes fixed on Juliana's face. "You're still hogging all the power for yourself. You were never satisfied with an equal share."

Juliana—or what was left of her in there—stared at the other woman with disdain. "Like you would know what to do with it, Vicky. You never did want to go all the way with anyone *really* powerful."

Jenna tried to pull her back, recognizing the danger—maybe even Seeing it for what it was. "Victoria, please. She's not . . ."

Victoria shook the girl off, limping forward. "We were partners when we started this. And while I've nurtured this sisterhood, built it into something lasting and strong, you do nothing but take take take . . ."

Juliana's hand came up in a dismissive gesture. "Whatever. Most people *like* instant gratification. Peter, for example."

"*What?*"

Now her expression was just catty. "You don't really think *you* inspired his meteoric political success, do you? With your prissy little pantsuits and your camera-friendly hair?"

Victoria slapped Juliana across the face. The Juliana-thing reciprocated by flinging her across the room with one hand. The congressman's wife hit the wall with a plaster-cracking thud and fell to the floor.

The thing turned her—*its*—gaze, blazing with cold, on us. Distantly, I heard fire trucks approaching. Had they taken that long, or had that little actual time passed? It seemed as if we'd been waging battle for days.

"Still have those scissors, Lisa?" I held my thumb over the bowl.

Justin pushed my hand away, put his in its place. "She didn't use her own. You shouldn't, either."

"I'm not sure I can hurt you," I said honestly.

Lisa opened the scissors and put the silver point to Justin's thumb. "Get on with it."

"What are you doing?" The transformed Sigma Prime demanded an answer, but I heard alarm thrumming through the voice.

Her agitation renewed my confidence. "Basic math, Juliana. An equal positive and an equal negative equals zero. A gift for a theft."

Lisa cut the pad of Justin's thumb and I caught three drops of blood in the bowl. They flashed as they hit the incense, and the resin heated up, red-hot, then glowing white. The bowl itself caught fire, and I dropped it.

Flame sped across the floor, encircling the witch in a fiery prison. Her clothes began to steam, then her hair, then her breath, fogging like a winter day. Juliana seemed to deflate, then collapsed to the parquet. The steam around her rose into the air and the flame followed it, entwining the trails of vapor and banishing them with angry, defeated hisses.

Hammering at the door. The firemen were trying to get in. Justin crossed the circle to Holly, lifting her limp body into his arms. "Can everyone else get out okay?"

"What about Victoria?" Jenna asked.

"Let the firemen move her," I said. "Juliana, too." Her body now a heap on the floor, she looked smaller.

They ran for the door. I ran for the grimoire, not trusting *luck* to destroy it. My hands closed on it, then I snatched them back with a yelp of pain. The thing was burning cold. Grabbing the tablecloth, I scattered the altar paraphernalia and wrapped the book enough to grasp it. Then I turned and saw Juliana—not lying where she ought to be, but standing between me and the door.

"You little bitch." She had the bronze knife in her hand. Her eyes were feverish with madness. She hadn't just looked into the abyss; she'd invited it in to set up house. And now she was hollowed out, nothing left but instinct and old patterns.

"Give me the book." She raised the knife, which suddenly seemed huge.

I lifted the heavy tome as a shield, not interested in heroics or victory, only in survival. "Let's get out of here, Juliana. The firemen are coming."

She slashed and I jumped back, staying out of reach of the blade. The fire was spreading, purifying and consuming. I tried again to reason with an unreasoning shell of a woman. "There's a gas leak, Juliana—" She hacked at me, and I skittered back to where the fallen oil lamp had spilled, and I held the book over the flames. "Put down the knife, or I'll drop—"

The blade sliced across my arm and the book tumbled from my fingers.

It didn't even hurt at first. I watched, shocked, as bright red blood welled, dripped down my skin, fell to the floor. A lot of blood. Enough to make a little pool.

I sensed more than saw her come at me again. Dodging, I slipped on the blood and crashed to the ground, hitting my head hard enough to make my vision blur. Crawling across the floor, leaving great smears of blood, I searched for something to defend myself.

My hand closed on cold iron. The crowbar. As Juliana bent and grabbed my injured arm and dug in her nails, I swung.

I swung with all my strength. I swung like a major leaguer.

I swung like someone who wanted desperately to live through the next five minutes.

The impact knocked the metal bar from my weakening fingers. It didn't matter. Juliana collapsed on top of me, pinning my legs. I couldn't tell if she was breathing or not.

Neither did I want to know. The woman—witch, demon, whatever—had tried to kill me. And as I lay in a growing puddle of my own blood, it occurred to me that maybe she had succeeded.

40

I woke up in the hospital.

On the plus side, I wasn't dead.

On the minus side, I had no idea how I got there, what day it was, or why an army of dwarves had taken pickaxes to the inside of my skull. I was also attached to an IV in one arm, which was scary, and the other was swathed in bandages and pain, which was worse.

A soft snore made me turn my head. Justin was stretched in a recliner, sleeping with a book on his chest. He was cute asleep. I hadn't thought I'd ever find that out.

"Are you awake?" a nurse in Christmas-colored scrubs whispered from the doorway.

"Yes." My mouth felt like that same army of dwarves had marched through it in their dirty socks. She must be a good nurse, because she anticipated this, and held a cup of water with a straw to my parched lips.

"Is that your boyfriend?" she asked in a teasing tone.

"Yeah. At least, I think so."

"Yes, I am," said a groggy voice from the chair. Justin sat up, rubbing sleep from his eyes. "I am," he confirmed.

That was nice. That was nicer than all the luck in the world.

He rose and came by the bed. "Your dad was here earlier, while you were getting the transfusion."

"I got a transfusion?" Alarmed, I looked at the nurse, who made a soothing noise and patted my blanket-covered knee.

"You're fine. You just lost a lot of blood." She lifted my splinted arm and looked critically at my fingernails. "Can you wiggle your fingers? It may hurt."

It hurt like the devil himself was crawling out of my wrist. But I did it.

"Excellent!"

"Do I get a cookie?"

"No, but you can have a Vicodin."

"Bring it on."

When she left Justin continued to hover, finally taking my IV hand and holding it as if I might shatter.

"I'm not going to, you know."

"What?" he asked, understandably confused.

"Break."

He let out a long, slow breath. "I thought you had. When the fireman carried you out of the house, covered in blood . . .

Dammit, Maggie, I thought you were right behind me. I never would have left you. I never should—"

"Hey." I squeezed his hand as hard as I could with a needle stuck in me. "I know you're a white knight. Now get over yourself."

He looked surprised, maybe a little offended, and finally amused. "Yeah. Okay."

We stayed that way for a while, holding hands, just . . . *being*. And then I had to ask. "Juliana. Is she . . . ?"

"She's here in the hospital."

"Alive, then?" I didn't feel relieved yet.

"Psych ward."

My heart squeezed and it got hard to breathe. "Because of the crowbar? Did I . . . ?" God. Had I broken her brain?

"No," he assured me firmly. "She woke up from that and started raving. She's under restraints and observation. Probably will be for a long time."

"And Victoria?" I asked, tentative for a different reason. I'd always suspected her, always knew she wanted to use me. But it was a twisted kind of self-interest; she thought she could make things good for everyone, no losers, as long as everyone followed the rules.

"Her neck and spine were fractured. She'll live. That's all they're saying for the moment."

I closed my eyes, a new kind of pain subsuming all the physical misery. "I feel like I failed at saving them, too."

Gently, his hand stroked my hair. "I know. But you can't save everybody."

"You saved me." Lisa spoke from the doorway, tentatively, her coat over her arm. "I'm pretty grateful for that."

"Hey! Come in here." I tried to push myself up, with no success.

She edged into the room. "Are they giving you any decent drugs?"

"Soon, I hope."

Still unsure, she glanced from Justin to me. "Should I come back later?"

"No." He grabbed his book from the chair. "Sit down if you want. I can leave you guys alone."

"Please don't," she said politely.

I figured this could go on for hours, so I interrupted, giving her a narrow-eyed stare. "Did you blow off your exams to come help me?"

"Can I get you a Coke or something? You want some water?"

"Don't dodge the question!"

She ducked her head and stared at the floor so long, I thought she wasn't going to answer. Finally, she shrugged. "A's are overrated anyway."

"Oh, Lisa."

"It's no big deal. A couple of incompletes. I can make them up."

"But your scholarship," I said, sorrow and gratitude mixed in my voice. "Your GPA."

She raised her eyes and despite her guard, I could read the raw emotion there. Something fundamental had altered in the last few days. Her soul was still wounded, but it was as if a nasty, dirty field dressing had been ripped off, exposing the injury to clean, healing air.

"It's not just that I owe you for saving my life last spring," she began. "Though I do. But after everything, you trusted me again, when I thought I'd never even be able to trust myself." She looked across the bed at Justin, who was trying to pretend he wasn't in the room. "And you did, too, Sir Galahad. Though you don't have to like it. It means . . ."

She trailed off, and after a beat, Justin supplied the answer. "Redemption."

"Atonement," she corrected, though I suspected they were both right. "A chance, anyway. Even if it takes the rest of my life." She glanced at me, deliberately shifting her mood. "Which might not be that long, if I have to keep saving your butt."

"Saving *my* butt?" I protested. "Whose idea was that invocation?"

"Who was locked in the closet when I got there?"

Justin cleared his throat. "Personally, I think pulling the fire alarm was an inspired idea. Even if the house burned down anyway."

I looked at him in surprise. "The whole house?"

He nodded. "To the ground. The prevailing theory on the news is that Juliana Hughes did a Mrs. Rochester on the place."

"Oh my God." I sat up, ignoring the ice pick between my eyes and the fire in my hand. "I need a newspaper. And my laptop. I don't believe this. I was *right there,* and I *still* got scooped for the story. *Again!*"

Justin laughed and shook his head, but he handed me a copy of the *Avalon Sentinel* all the same. No wonder I love him.

41

There's this principle in witchcraft—at least the New Agey, rainbows-and-light kind—that everything you do has the potential to come back on you three times as bad. Payback's a witch, I guess.

Kirby got caught cheating, and was expelled from the university with only nine credits left to complete her degree. Alexa, Jenna's roommate, lost her slot in medical school and her boyfriend dumped her for a plastic surgery resident.

Jenna's boyfriend also dumped her, but not before making her an STD statistic. She told me about it over coffee at

Froth and Java after everyone had gotten back from winter break. Those that were coming back, anyway.

"At least it could be cured by antibiotics," she said. "It could have been much worse."

"I'm glad it wasn't." What can I say? *G* and *E* aren't always absolute. I hope I never see them that way.

She cupped her mug between her hands. "We—the SAXis—knew we were lucky, and special. And I followed the rules. Heck, I only had two hookups until I met David, who was a Gamma Phi Ep. I figured, who was getting hurt?"

"Do I need to answer that?" Just because I don't judge doesn't mean I let people delude themselves.

"No." She shook her head. "Poor Devon. Have you heard from her? Do they think her hearing will come back?"

"No. It's permanent nerve damage from the meningitis." The doctors had thought it weird that her illness had been delayed so long after the incubation period. But they'd dismissed it as a coincidence or a fluke, which is what rational people did when confronted with the irrational.

"Poor Devon." Jenna repeated it softly, guiltily. "She was so out of her league. Over her head before she knew what was going on."

Maybe that was why she was only deaf and not dead like Cole. Though I doubt she saw that as a good thing right now.

The alums, having had more use of the Sigma power, were taking harder hits. One movie-star trip to rehab made barely a blip on the national radar, but I checked it off my list, along with a couple of CEO firings and insider trading scandals.

The wintertime bustle of Froth and Java continued, heedless of life changing events. Jenna and I said we'd get together for lunch, and we might, but I wasn't really expecting her to call. It takes a lot of history together before the investment in a friendship outweighs seeing in the other person the constant reminders of your bad decisions.

Lisa and I, for instance, would never have the same relationship that we did before. But now I had hope that *different* didn't mean *worse*. We had to stay friends. Who else could I call and say, "I think my calculus teacher might be an agent of the devil." (Not really. But his idea of homework was pretty infernal.)

After Jenna left, I sat back, looking through the window at Congressman Abbott's office across the downtown street. Victoria was in a wheelchair, with only partial use of one hand. Speculation said Abbott would finish the last year of his term and return to private law practice, ostensibly to take care of her, though possibly because his campaign contributions didn't bear scrutiny. Funny how the universe can set itself right when otherworldly forces aren't skewing the balance.

Juliana now lived in an expensive sanatorium, which is what they call a funny farm when its residents are rich and high-toned. Since Juliana had been declared non compos mentis, Holly now had control of all the Baker-Russell-Hattendorf-Hughes financial resources, which meant that not only was Juliana in a padded cell, Holly held the checkbook that kept her at the Riverview Sanatorium instead of the Illinois State Hospital.

The door to the shop opened and Justin came in, bundled against the January chill. He sat down and unwrapped; I slid my mocha across the table to him. "Mmm," he said appreciatively, warming his hands on the paper cup. "Toasty."

"How'd your meeting go?"

"Well, my thesis subject was approved. Apparently your dad told the committee I wasn't crazy."

"That was nice of him."

"It was." He grinned at me, and I grinned back. We had to stick together, those of us who saw past disbelief.

"How's Lisa?" he asked, following my train of thought with his usual accuracy. "Settled back in at Georgetown?"

"Yep." I retrieved my drink.

"Are you guys really planning a road trip for spring break?"

"Probably. Worried?"

"Not about you two. God help any evil thing in your way." He rose and grabbed my coat from the back of my chair, holding it out for me. "Ready?"

"Yep." I slipped my arms in and reached for the mocha. The pain reminded me to switch the cup to my left hand before I dropped it. Mostly I had trouble grasping things. The physical therapist said I might always have weakness in that hand. I guess there goes my promising career as a concert violinist.

Justin put his arm around me as we stepped out into the blustery day. "Excited?" he asked.

"I can't wait for you to meet her. She's not much to look at, but boy can she wail."

"No worries about her lungs, then."

"Nope. She'll probably outtalk me someday."

"I doubt that," he said as we reached his car, then kissed away my indignation.

Brigid Joanna Quinn had been born on January second

at four-fifteen in the afternoon, a few weeks early, but healthy and . . . Okay, not beautiful. But I understand they all come out looking that way.

As for me, I was pretty sure the effects of the Sigma Alpha Xis had dissipated. My dreams had returned to what passes for normal. I hadn't had any more ambush visions, but sometimes when I touched things weighted with memory or emotion, it seeped in. So I guess that's really me, and not a special Sigma gift.

The grimoire had burned; at least, I woke up in the hospital with the recollection of it dropping into the pool of lamp oil, and flames rushing up to consume it. Hopefully a real memory and not a product of blood-loss delirium or wishful thinking. But it *felt* finished, and I had to trust my instincts until there was evidence to the contrary.

Holly was the only ex-pledge not coming back to school in the spring. She'd called me after the new year to say she was going into training to try out for the U.S. Women's Soccer League, now that she had the resources to follow her own dream and no mother standing in her way. I would be following her dream, too, for a while, to make sure she wasn't extraordinarily lucky in her quest. The work of a psychic supergirl is never done.

But for the moment, I had nothing better to do than stand in the freezing wind, wrapped in my boyfriend's arms, warming up from the inside out. Sometimes, you are just in the right place at the right time, and nothing in the universe is entirely random.

ACKNOWLEDGMENTS

Sometimes I wonder if I talk to myself because I'm a writer, or if I'm a writer because I talk to myself. Here are a few of the people who keep me from being any crazier than I already am.

My agent, Lucienne Diver, and my editor, Krista Marino. How great is it that I get to work with people I genuinely like and admire? I'm also extremely lucky to have the support of so many people at Delacorte Press. You guys rock.

My BFF Cheryl A. Smyth, who knows the voices in my head almost as well as I do.

My wonderful, talented friends Candace Havens and Shannon Canard, who know I'm a dork and still let me hang out with them.

The DFW Writer's Workshop and the North Texas Romance Writers of America, two fantastic organizations. And a sundry bunch, for various encouragement, kindness, and inspiration: A. Lee Martinez, Michelle Nordahl, Delilah Peeler, Carole Millard, Ashlea Robertson, Haley M. Schmidt, Father Sherwood, Amy Frost, and the Camp Crucis Girls Cabin Circle.

My husband, Tim, and my family—especially Mom and Pete. As they say in *High School Musical:* We're all in this together.